PATRIOTS

DAVID DRAKE

BAEN

PATRIOTS

Copyright © 1996, by David Drake

A Baen Book

Baen Publishing Enterprises
P.O. Box 1403
Riverdale, NY 10471
www.baen.com

ISBN: 978-1-4391-3292-0

Cover art by Kurt Miller

First Baen paperback printing, September 2009

Distributed by Simon & Schuster
1230 Avenue of the Americas
New York, NY 10020

Printed in the United States of America

10 9 8 7 6 5 4 3 2 1

"He had his

"Let's see v

fellers?" Griggs said. He drew back a big scarred fist to swing at Mark's belly.

"Let's not," Yerby Bannock said from behind Griggs. Mark's eyes focused. Bannock grabbed the two bigger Zeniths by the neck and slammed their heads together.

The impact sounded like a maul hitting a tree trunk. The men dropped. They couldn't have been more limp if Bannock had sucked all the bones from their bodies.

One of the remaining Zeniths put his hand into his jacket pocket. Bannock caught his wrist, then reached into the pocket himself. He came out with a pistol. He dropped it on the floor as the tough punched vainly at him. Bannock transferred his grip to the scruff of the would-be gunman's neck and carried him toward the lighting sconce over the nearest door.

The fourth Zenith snatched at the fallen pistol. Mark hit him over the head with a metal bucket. It rang echoingly in the big domed room.

Bannock hung the back of his man's jacket over the sconce, then stepped away. The fellow squalled and kicked violently, seven feet in the air.

The man Mark had hit turned slowly toward him. He held the pistol, but his eyes were glazed. Mark stepped back and with all his strength swung the bucket overhead. It bonged and bounced from the fellow's skull. The Zenith's eyes rolled up. He dropped the pistol and fell over it.

"You've learned a valuable lesson, lad," Bannock said. "Don't you never hit a man with your bare hand unless your feet are nailed to the floor of an empty room." He added, "And particularly don't hit him on the jaw. You can hurt yourself bad that way."

BAEN BOOKS by DAVID DRAKE

The RCN Series
With the Lightnings
Lt. Leary, Commanding
The Far Side of the Stars
The Way to Glory
Some Golden Harbor
When the Tide Rises
In the Stormy Red Sky

Hammer's Slammers
The Tank Lords
Caught in the Crossfire
The Butcher's Bill
The Sharp End
Paying the Piper

Independent Novels and Collections
The Reaches Trilogy
Seas of Venus
Foreign Legions,
ed. by David Drake
Ranks of Bronze
Cross the Stars
The Dragon Lord
Birds of Prey
Northworld Trilogy
Redliners
Starliner
All the Way to the Gallows
Grimmer Than Hell
Other Times Than Peace
*The Undesired Princess and
The Enchanted Bunny*
(with L. Sprague de Camp)

*Lest Darkness Fall and To
Bring the Light*
(with L. Sprague de Camp)
Killer
(with Karl Edward Wagner)

The General Series
Warlord with S.M. Stirling
(omnibus)
Conqueror
with S.M. Stirling (omnibus)
The Chosen
with S.M. Stirling
The Reformer
with S.M. Stirling
The Tyrant with Eric Flint

The Belisarius Series
with Eric Flint
An Oblique Approach
In the Heart of Darkness
*Belisarius I: Thunder at
Dawn* (omnibus)
Destiny's Shield
Fortune's Stroke
*Belisarius II: Storm at
Noontide* (omnibus)
*Belisarius III:
The Flames of Sunset*
(omnibus)

Edited by David Drake
Armageddon
(with Billie Sue Mosiman)
*The World Turned
Upside Down*
(with Jim Baen & Eric Flint)

To Harriet McDougal

A wonderful editor whose suggestions
not only make my prose better, but also make it more
the way I wanted it to be in the first place.

ACKNOWLEDGEMENTS

Clyde and Carlie Howard, Gordon R. Dickson, and Tom Doherty all provided help I needed to make this a better book. They're a perfect answer to the folks who claim that "Nobody cares anymore." If you care, you'll find that other people care too.

AUTHOR'S NOTE

Truth, Heroism, and Other Confusing Subjects

Some years ago I thought that by studying history I'd learn the truth about what happened in the past. I've become perhaps wiser and certainly more cautious in my assumptions as I've grown older. I still believe in truth in an absolute sense. I just don't believe that human beings will ever run into it.

I'm not really sure about why *I* did some of the things I've done. The reasons I thought I did them were almost certainly, it now seems, not the real reasons. Do I know the real reasons? Well, maybe, but chances are that another ten or twenty-five years of distance and experience will give me a still different take on what was going on.

The above disclaimer is a prelude to me saying that as best I can tell, the action of *Patriots* is based pretty much on the way things happened in Vermont—then the New Hampshire Grants—just before the start of the American Revolution. (I modeled the climax on the capture of Fort Ticonderoga by Ethan Allen and the Green Mountain Boys.) I don't know about history classes nowadays but believe me, this isn't the way I learned about it in high school.

The cannon captured at Fort Ticonderoga were virtually the only heavy ordnance the fledgling Continental Army had. Without them the British would have continued to hold Boston and might have snuffed out the rebellion before it got properly under way. It startled me to learn that their capture was the next thing to an accident rather than the result of somebody's careful plan.

The trouble with history survey courses is that they only have space to tell you that X did Y and the result was Z. That may well be correct, but it leaves you with the impression that X did Y to achieve Z. More often than not it turns out that X didn't imagine Z, and chances are he/she didn't even intend to do Y. Remember, Columbus died convinced that he'd discovered not America but a new route to India.

I started researching the capture of Fort Ticonderoga in the belief that the Green Mountain Boys were a citizens' militia like the Minutemen in Massachusetts and that Ethan Allen was an American patriot in the mold of Paul Revere. It quickly became obvious that the Green Mountain Boys were closer in purpose and tactics to Quantrill's Raiders—or the Kansas Jayhawkers who opposed them. As for Ethan Allen himself, he was a unique individual in a time that had more than its share of them.

Vermont was really beyond America's wild frontier until the end of the French and Indian War in 1763. At that point the land which had been granted conflictingly by royal governors in both New Hampshire and New York started to be worth something. The folks who'd already settled on the land did so mostly under New Hampshire grants. New York had a better claim and the New York authorities were ready to assert that claim in their own courts, with New York sheriffs enforcing the decisions.

On the other side were investors, mostly in Connecticut, who held large undeveloped tracts under New Hampshire grants, and the settlers who were already in the area. Men and women who'd risked everything in the face of Indian raids to build homes in the wilderness weren't going to roll over and play dead when a New York process server arrived. The settlers had political and financial backing from the Connecticut investors, and for a leader they had Ethan Allen.

Ethan Allen was a smart, enormously strong man whose idea of a good time was to get drunk and smash up a tavern. He and his family had been run out of Massachusetts. He'd never committed a crime for gain, but he was too raucously violent to live in what passed for civilized society even on the edges of the American colonies.

The militia that Allen raised, the Green Mountain Boys, were local men who would lose everything (including support for their families) if the New York officials had their way. They were hard, tough fellows or they wouldn't have chosen to settle a wilderness and been able to survive. They were operating outside of any law, and they knew they'd be hanged if they fell into the hands of their enemies.

There's no evidence that the Green Mountain Boys ever used deadly force in their activities. To me this is the most remarkable tribute of all to Ethan Allen. For what the struggle could have been—almost certainly would have been—without him, look at the activities of Quantrill and the Jayhawkers of Bloody Kansas in the 1850s.

Oh, neither Allen nor the men under him would ever be mistaken for saints. The Green Mountain Boys burned houses, beat men in front of their families, and in one case hoisted an unfortunate traveler from New York onto a flagpole and left him there all day. Nonetheless they didn't kill, maim, or attempt to kill and maim their opponents.

The British government had to some degree supported the Vermont settlers against the New York authorities. Apparently the only reason the Green Mountain Boys acted suddenly and effectively against the British at the beginning of the Revolutionary War is that Ethan Allen himself decided they ought to.

Nobody knows why he did that. Nobody knew at the time it happened, and I'd venture a guess that Allen himself couldn't have told you the real reason. My guess, based on having a friend or two of a similar type, is that it seemed like an interesting thing to try at the time; and Ethan Allen never did anything with less than a hundred and ten percent enthusiasm.

Allen didn't capture Fort Ticonderoga because he was a patriot who believed in America in the sense we'd mean that now. Later during the Revolution he negotiated with the British in an attempt to make Vermont a province of Canada. When he wrote an account of the capture four years later he claimed he summoned the British commander to surrender "in the name of the Great Jehovah and the Continental Congress," but chances are he hadn't heard of the Continental Congress at the time. (There's even less chance that he said anything about Jehovah: Allen was a noted atheist and reputed to be the most profane man in America.)

I've told you that Ethan Allen and the Green Mountain Boys weren't the people I thought they were when I began to research this novel. I'm not saying that they weren't heroes and patriots.

What I am saying is that heroes and patriots are real human beings, only maybe more so. They're not perfect and they're not saints; they do things for the same sort of fuzzy reasons that you and I do. But at the end of the day, the things they've done have made the future.

And you know, maybe you and I ought sometimes to think about the future we're making.

—Dave Drake
Chatham County, NC

1. Downtown Dittersdorf

Two men entered through the caravansary's main door beside Mark. "Here, Doc," one of them said to the other. "Let me take that load for you. You're still tuckered from the ship."

Mark turned to glance at the speaker. His Quelhagen upbringing protested that it was impolite to look at strangers, but the booming voice was the first cheerful thing he'd heard on Dittersdorf.

The fellow carried on one shoulder a packing case as big as he was—which made it a large case. Rain dripped from his poncho, the broad brim of his hat, and his flaring red mustache. For all that he beamed like summer sunshine as he took the bag from his companion and tossed it expertly on top of the packing case, a minuscule addition to his previous load.

The big man noticed Mark and gave him a merry nod as he and his companion strode across the common area to their room. Mark sighed and returned to staring at the jumble of items in the caravansary's dead storage room.

1

Dittersdorf wasn't a planet of any significance for its own manufactures or agriculture, but the spaceport on Dittersdorf Major was a stopping point for ships traveling between the worlds of the Three Digits and the rest of the settled universe. The gear abandoned in the caravansary was so varied that Mark couldn't guess what most of it was, much less whether it might be useful to him on the frontier.

"Guess you'd be from Earth?" said the watchman, a fat man with a bad limp and a constant wheeze.

"From Quelhagen, sir," Mark said. He was twenty-two standard—Earth—years old, thin and brown-haired. He felt as though there were a six-inch glass wall between him and the boisterous chaos behind him.

The caravansary was a circular building with a domed roof. The doors of windowless rooms around the circumference opened onto the common court in the center. The watchman's kiosk was beside the outer door, and the first room was used to store the goods that travelers left behind, sometimes because they'd died. The caravansary staff sold the leavings for what they brought. Inevitably, the collection had been picked over many times before Mark took the watchman's invitation to look at it. Most of what remained was junk.

"Quelhagen and Zenith, they're the same as Earth, pretty much," the watchman said. He scratched himself, bored but mildly hopeful that Mark would find something worth beer money. "They're all built up just like Earth."

"Not at all," Mark said. He spoke calmly and precisely, without any emotional loading. Quelhagen's social style was quiet reserve, even among friends. Mark, so alone that he didn't even feel he was of the same species as the frontiersmen with whom he shared the caravansary, had completely shut down his emotions. "Landingplace is the largest city on Quelhagen as well as being our capital, but it would be a minor community even in the interior of the Atlantic Alliance. On the Atlantic Circuit, why, I've seen buildings more populous than Landingplace."

That was an exaggeration, but not an enormous one. Mark had seen arcologies holding a hundred thousand people, but he doubted there were any quite as big as the quarter million who by now lived in Landingplace.

He took a holoviewer from beneath a bundle of clothing barely fit to become wiping rags. The viewer was a dedicated unit, loaded and sealed instead of having a socket in which different chips could be placed.

When Mark switched the viewer on, it projected a spray of flowers and vegetables in the air of the room. SUNRISE SEEDS CATALOG FOR 2249, read a legend in fluorescent letters. YOUR BEST CHOICE FOR QUALITY, PRICE, AND VARIETY!

The watchman spit onto the floor of the courtyard. When Mark had arrived, a few hours earlier, a pair of men whose ankles were chained to their waists had been hosing the caravansary down. The bare concrete was already returning to a state of mud and squalor.

"Salesman from Hestia," the watchman explained, tapping the holoviewer with his finger. "Earth company he traveled for, but he was Hestian. Caught a bug or a bellyful of the wrong whiskey, I guess. Either way, it carried him off. Had some nice clothes, but they went right off."

He yawned and scratched himself again. "You like flowers?" he asked in vague hope.

"I don't mind them," Mark said, putting the viewer back on the pile where he'd found it.

A man in a rain-sodden poncho and muddy boots strode through the caravansary's personnel door. He shouted "Hey you! Wake up!" to the watchman and opened the double-panel vehicle door, which latched only on the inside. Three similar men and the high-wheeled cart they were pushing stood on the apron.

The downpour of an hour ago was over. The drizzle Mark saw beyond the open door was fog a trifle too heavy to remain suspended. Lights gleamed in the windows of buildings otherwise concealed by the gloom.

Mark noticed a one-cubic-foot carrying case. Its hard shell was decorated in the blue-white-gray crystalline pattern of blue john, the myrrhine that the ancient Romans had used for their most valuable cups. He tugged the case out of a jumble of chipboard containers full of obviously broken appliances.

"Ah," said the watchman approvingly. "That's a bit of a grab bag, sir. From the weight there's something inside, but you'll have to cut it apart to open it. There's no latch, you see."

The four new arrivals pushed their cart into the caravansary, slipping and swearing. The vehicle was loaded—overloaded—with a dozen large trunks of uniform design. Their ends were stenciled BIBER/ZENITH/IN CARE OF GRIGGS/N OF 12—DO NOT SEPARATE. The cargo handlers had piled individual gear—duffel bags and bedrolls—on top of the trunks. Splotches of mud indicated that several of the bags had fallen on the path from the ship to the caravansary.

"Hey, fatso!" called the man who'd opened the larger doors. "Give us a room. And don't say you haven't got one, because we'll clear one ourselves if we've got to. This baggage belongs to Mayor Heinrich Biber, it does. Mayor of New Paris on Zenith!"

The watchman, obviously nervous about leaving Mark alone in the dead storage, nonetheless turned his attention to the newcomers. "Thirty-seven's empty, sirs," he said. "Ah—will Mayor Biber be staying here himself tonight?"

"Dream on, fatso!" another of the new arrivals said. "The Honorable Heinrich Biber is returning by yacht in two stages, leaving dogs like us to carry his luggage by freighter."

"Twelve bloody stages from Kilbourn to Zenith," the original spokesman added. "And we'll be lucky if it isn't bloody thirteen! Get moving, boys."

Biber's servants braced themselves against the luggage trolley.

"You'll have to wait—" the watchman began, trotting over to the receipt pad he'd left in his kiosk.

"We don't have to do any damned thing!" the spokesman snarled. "And if *you* don't keep out of our way, you'll find wheel tracks running the length of you!"

Mark grimaced as he knelt before the stone-finished carrying case. He didn't blame the servants for being in an ill temper after shifting that heavy load through the rain, but . . . Room 37 was next to Mark's own Room 36. He'd have preferred other neighbors. Still, the caravansary was built from cast concrete, including the partition walls between individual cells. The interior of Room 36 was dark and dank, but it was certainly private.

Mark had insisted that, having completed his education on Earth, he wanted to visit the frontier for himself instead of taking articles as an attorney's clerk with his father or one of his father's Quelhagen friends. This caravansary was what visiting the frontier *meant*.

The case was of a sort introduced on Earth within the past two years. The pattern of "crystals" on two of the corners rotated. The latch could be set to a nearly infinite series of combinations, but most users just left the cases on the original setting: both latches identical, with the peak of a large white crystal bisecting each corner.

The watchman closed the large doors, then dithered a moment as he glanced between Mark and the luggage trolley squealing its way across the common area. At last he trotted after the new arrivals, waving his receipt book. Nobody yet had been able to open the case, so he probably thought it was proof against Mark's examination.

Mark twisted the patterns with his thumbs. The lid rose smoothly under its own power. Inside were two formal place settings of handblown glass. Each piece was nested in a lining of dense foam. Mark removed a soup plate and held it against the light above the kiosk to admire its peacock-tinted beauty.

"Hey, look at that, will you, Doc!" said the man Mark had seen enter with the packing case and the bright smile. "Say, have you ever seen anything so pretty in your life?"

Before Mark could rise to his feet, the man who spoke had squatted beside him. The fellow was tall and solid the way a tree is solid. He had bright red hair and a mustache that flared to either side like a hearth brush. "Yerby Bannock, lad," he said. He held out a hand to Mark. "Is this lot yours, then? Would you like to sell?"

Mark juggled the plate cautiously. The glass was so thin that it could break of its own weight if he held it wrong. There wasn't time to nestle the piece back in the case, so Mark positioned it on edge in his left hand as he shook. Bannock's fingers felt like tree roots, though he was obviously being careful not to crush Mark.

"I'm Mark Lucius—son Maxwell of Quelhagen, sir," Mark said. "Ah—"

He didn't want to insult Bannock, but this dinner service was a work of art and he owed it something.

"—these goods aren't mine, but they're amazingly delicate. Even careless pressure from fingers as weak as mine could shatter the glass."

There was nothing weak about Mark, his fingers or otherwise. He kept in shape with gymnastics, and the three weeks he'd been traveling by starship hadn't left him flabby by normal standards. Comparison with Yerby Bannock, though, was like comparison with a hydraulic jack.

"Pretty as a butterfly, ain't it, lad?" Bannock said, apparently without offense at Mark's warning. He deliberately laced his fingers in front of him as he balanced in a squat. "Doc, don't you think I ought to get these for Amy? Ain't they just the sort of things she'd love?"

The man with Bannock was of Mark's height and build, though softer for lack of exercise. Mark guessed the "doctor" was about thirty-five, some five years older than Bannock.

"Dr. Gabriel Jesilind, sir," the doctor said stiffly, extending his hand. "Of the Marques Jesilinds."

Jesilind wore "town clothes," but of various sorts. His yellow frock coat probably aped Zenith style, while his trousers were a sober gray that wouldn't have been out of place on a shopkeeper in conservative Quelhagen. The doctor's shirt had a ruffed front with pink stripes on sky blue; Mark couldn't imagine where *that* garment had originated.

For that matter, he'd never heard of Marques, either. If it was a planet rather than a district or a community, Mark wondered if it might not be a world settled by the Greater East Asia Co-Prosperity Sphere rather than from the Atlantic Alliance. Jesilind's swarthiness might as easily be South Asian as Mediterranean.

Jesilind's offer to shake created an awkward situation, since Mark had started to put the soup plate back in the case. "Very good to meet you, sir," Mark said as he concentrated on the plate, using both hands and all his care. "I'll be with you in a . . ."

The plate slid home, undamaged for the moment. Other travelers were drifting over, called by the chance of something to punctuate Dittersdorf's rain-soaked boredom. The odds were the service would be a pile of rainbow-hued fragments before the evening was out, but there wasn't much Mark could do now that he'd showed what was in the case.

Jesilind was frowning by the time Mark was able to rise and shake his hand, but if the doctor felt an unintended insult he at least didn't comment on it. His fingers were vaguely damp. He looked Mark up and down and said, "Are you a scholar, Mr. Maxwell?"

"Oh, goodness, no!" Mark blurted, amazed that anyone

would think *he* was a scholar. The three years he'd just spent taking a degree in Human Civilization at Harvard were a good two years more of academic life than he'd wanted. He'd managed to graduate partly out of his own stubbornness and partly because he could too easily imagine Lucius Maxwell's cold silence if his son admitted that he'd quit.

"Doc Jesilind here's a scholar," Bannock said proudly, putting an arm around Jesilind's shoulders. "He took the Harvard Course, he did. In General Knowledge!"

Bannock was moderately tall, at least six feet four, but Mark had met taller men. The frontiersman wasn't heavyset, and his muscles didn't bulge in sharp definition like those of a bodybuilder. Bannock stood out because the intensity he projected made him seem a force of nature rather than a human being, a very concentrated thunderstorm or avalanche.

"Perhaps you've heard of Dean Brickley, Mr. Maxwell?" Jesilind said, buffing his fingernails on the lapel of his yellow coat. "The designer of the course I completed? One of the finest scholars of the Atlantic Alliance!"

"Indeed he was, sir," Mark said, completely taken aback by Jesilind's claims. Brickley had been everything Jesilind said of him—before he died, a good fifty years in the past. There was a statue of the former dean near the entrance to the Widener Library; Mark had sat at the base of it many times.

Dr. Jesilind had obviously taken a hypnagogue course that was far older than the doctor himself. Culture is a matter of what you know, but the real value of an education was learning *how* to learn. A course like the one Jesilind took wasn't exactly valueless: it fitted the doctor to become a member of the elite culture of two generations ago. But Jesilind's boast put a whole new complexion on what the word "scholar" meant this close to the frontier, and it was too late for Mark to correct his initial answer without embarrassment to all concerned.

"Hey!" the watchman cried as he bustled back to the storage room. "Hey! What did you do? Did you break that open without paying for it?"

The watchman reached down toward the case. Mark couldn't tell whether he meant to close the lid or snatch at the plates.

"A moment, sir!" Mark said sharply. He caught the watchman's arm and held it despite the fellow's wheezing attempt to push past. "I've opened the case properly, but any clumsy groping will turn the contents into sand."

"Who the hell do you think you are, boy?" the watchman snarled, backing and shaking his arm when Mark released it.

"I think I'm not your boy, sir," Mark said with the cold fury of a Quelhagen gentleman insulted.

Yerby Bannock tapped the watchman on the chest with an index finger. "Say, friend," Bannock said. "This is yours to sell, right? Well, it's the lad's to buy if he wants it—and not for any jacked-up price either. Weren't worth a thing till Mr. Maxwell here opened it up for you."

Mark blinked. "I'm traveling with a single bag, sir," he said. "I have no use for the dishes. I only wonder how they came to be here."

"Feller with his wife, some six months back," the watchman said in a tone of grumbling politeness.

Bannock's wrists were as thick and muscular as Mark's own calves. "Their honeymoon, I wouldn't wonder. She was on the woman's side. They went out together one night and never come back. Dunno why. Had some clothes too, but they sold first thing."

Mark felt suddenly cold. This was the frontier, a place where people died of unknown diseases or simply vanished. People with cultured taste, on their honeymoon.

"All right, if the lad passes, then the box is mine to give to my sister, right?" Bannock said. "I'd say ten Zenith dollars was fair. Ten for you and ten for Mr. Maxwell."

Bannock threw back one side of his poncho of natural wool. Beneath it he wore a rough-out leather vest, fringed and studded for decoration, over a dingy checked shirt of homespun. His trousers were leather to the knee and homespun below, held up by vividly scarlet suspenders.

"Ten?" cried the watchman. "Why, that's worth a fortune! Worth a hundred, anyhow."

Bannock's belt was of nickel-steel links, supporting a rectangular purse of the same material. He pressed the thumbprint lock. "Fifteen to you and the same to the lad, then," he said. He opened the purse without losing eye contact with the watchman.

"Sir, I couldn't think of taking money for what I did," Mark said. He was shocked at the thought. "I assure you, I have no part in this negotiation."

"Thirty for me an you can have it," the watchman said. "Though it's robbery, you know."

"Twenty-five, then," Bannock said, fishing out a wad of scrip issued by at least a dozen planets, all of them Protected Worlds settled and governed by the Atlantic

Alliance. "Otherwise I'll have the lad close the box again and you'll have damn-all for your greed."

"Done," the watchman said, "but all of it Zenith money, mind you. You're not fobbing me off with no Kilbourn paper!"

Bannock snorted. "You'll take what I give you, so long as the exchange rate's fair," he said, but Mark noticed that he stripped off three bills marked PROTECTED BANK OF ZENITH, two tens and a five.

Zenith dollars, like Quelhagen francs, were through-printed on durable plastic; the back was a mirror image of the face. On the issuing planets themselves the scrip was withdrawn when it began to show age, but as Mark traveled toward the frontier he'd encountered notes worn so thin you could read a book through the center of them.

One of the tens Bannock offered the watchman was in almost that condition, but the other two were reasonably bright and clean. The five showed the first Earth ship landing at what was now New Paris, Zenith's capital; the ten was a panorama of New Paris a century ago, when it was a frontier village with a population of only a thousand.

Human settlement of planets beyond the Sol system had begun in a small way one hundred fifty years before, at the end of the twenty-first century. Colonies grew quickly as interstellar travel became easier. Getting between planets was still expensive, uncomfortable, and to a lesser degree dangerous, though nowadays diseases spreading among travelers packed for weeks like sardines were a greater risk than shipwreck. The fortunes and new lives to be won among the stars drew settlers on.

Some settlements failed, but more prospered and attracted vast ships filled with immigrants who wanted to leave Earth but who didn't have the taste for breaking ground on a virgin world. Successful colonies themselves colonized more distant stars; many of the folk who'd grown up on an empty world felt uncomfortable knowing there was a community of ten thousand within a day's travel of them.

The main brake on colonization was the Proxy Wars that festered between the two main power blocs of Earth: the Atlantic Alliance and the Greater East Asia Co-Prosperity Sphere. The Alliance and the Sphere were too cautious to risk total destruction. They fought their battles, sometimes on Earth beyond the borders of either side, but generally on colonial worlds.

The war ended in 2226, not long before Mark was born. There'd been no need to fight over land when there were a practically infinite number of human-habitable planets in the universe, but Mark hadn't needed a Harvard degree to know that the real causes of wars aren't often what the politicians claim is at stake. New Paris itself had been founded by Malays who called it Nikisastro on Palambang, eight years before an Alliance task force claimed the world and renamed it Zenith.

Peace when it came was as welcome as it would have been any time in the previous ninety years of war. Interstellar settlement increased rapidly—especially on worlds placed in regions that both combatants could threaten but neither could control. Recently both Terran power blocs had begun forcible emigration for their excess population.

"Sure I can't offer you something, lad?" Bannock said as he lifted the case he'd purchased. The lid was still up.

"Thank you, no," Mark repeated. "Ah—if you turn the white crystals so that they're pointed the way they are now and press them at the same time, the case opens. It would be safer to carry it closed, though."

Mark shut the lid firmly. He was as nervous about those blasted plates as he would have been with a kitten in the hands of a child too young to understand what "dead" meant.

"Much obliged," Bannock said with satisfaction, tucking the case under his left arm. "I'll take them over to the women's side right now when I see Amy."

His brow furrowed. "Say, lad, you'll still be around in an hour or so if there's, you know, if there's a problem with the box not opening, won't you?"

"I've booked passage on a ship lifting for Kilbourn in three days," Mark explained. "But all you need to do is press the two crystals just as they are now."

Bannock walked out of the caravansary, whistling "Lillibulero." It was raining hard again, but he didn't seem to notice it.

"Anything more out of here you'd like to see, sir?" the watchman said. Twenty-five dollars for something that minutes before had been valueless junk had made the fat man more expansive. He added hopefully, "Maybe there's something you could open or maybe fix?"

Mark glanced over the storage room again. He supposed there might be another treasure hiding there, but for the moment it looked like wreckage heaped up after a crash. From the way the watchman talked, that was more or less what it was: wrecks of lives, wrecks of hope, jumbled together in a bleak concrete room.

"No, I don't think so," Mark said. "Perhaps I'll look again before I leave, if that's all right with you."

"Any time, sir, any time," the watchman said as he closed and padlocked the door. "Ah—you might take care that you check when I'm on duty, not one of the others. I'll see that you get a better price for your help, you see."

What Mark saw was that the twenty-five-dollar windfall wasn't going to be recorded as anything like so much for division with the rest of the caravansary staff. Well, that was none of his affair.

"A larcenous oaf," Jesilind said quietly to Mark as the watchman waddled back to his kiosk. "I've half a mind to report him for dishonesty."

Mark looked at the doctor. Jesilind hadn't gone out with Bannock; the yellow coat, not in the best of shape as it was, would soak up water like a sponge. "To tell the truth," Mark said, "I don't know how much they'd have to pay me to do that man's job. More than an occasional tip, certainly."

"I tend to think educated men have a duty to direct other members of society, sir," Jesilind said. "But as you note, 'What society?' I'll let it pass."

He gestured toward the circle of benches in the middle of the common room. There was space for fifty or sixty people around the circuit. The caravansary had an eye of clear material in the center of the dome. Despite the overcast and the rainwater streaming across the outer surface, a surprising amount of light penetrated the interior.

"Will you join me for a discussion of intellectual matters,

Mr. Maxwell?" Jesilind said. "You can appreciate how rare it is to meet another man of culture on these byways of trade."

Mark had taken the watchman's invitation to look over the dead storage room because he didn't have anything better to do. Mark had thought traveling to the frontiers would be exciting. In fact, the three weeks since he left Quelhagen had been increasingly uncomfortable and boring. The spaceport on Dittersdorf Major was a new low in both respects.

Dittersdorf formed the wrist and the usual stopover for vessels traveling among the Three Digits, the strands of colonized worlds which included Kilbourn, Mark's planned destination. The gazetteer chip he'd bought on Earth said it rained at the spaceport every day, for nine hours out of ten. Thus far Mark had no reason to doubt the information, and seeing the dreary result was a lot different from planning an itinerary on a sunny day in his father's Quelhagen garden.

Dr. Jesilind was a pompous twit. Well, out of charity, Mark decided to substitute "eccentric" in his mind. On the other hand, Jesilind was a distraction in a place that was rubbing Mark's spirits to the gray hue of the concrete walls.

"I'd be pleased to sit with you," Mark said. It occurred to Mark that Quelhagen formality made *him* sound like a pompous twit in this setting.

Like all the other parts of the caravansary, the benches were concrete. More than fifty of the building's residents sat on them—talking, eating, and smoking various herbs in rolls or pipes. Some had brought over buckets or packing crates as additional seating so that members of a party could face each other as they socialized and played cards. The caravansary's windowless rooms were secure, but the jails of a civilized planet had more amenities.

Mark avoided a patch where the bench's surface had flaked away to the wire-net reinforcement. He didn't worry about dampness, because his coveralls were waterproof. Anyway, everything on this planet was wet or about to become wet.

Jesilind tutted and unrolled a cushion, which he spread without inflating. "It leaks," Jesilind admitted when he noticed Mark's surprise that he didn't blow the cushion up. "But I'm a philosopher, sir, and I believe hardship is good for the soul."

Dittersdorf's gray misery made Mark think of throwing himself off a high building, not of the soul's nobility, but no two people were the same. And some people lied, of course.

"You're a, ah, teacher, sir?" Mark asked.

"I like to say that all wisdom is my subject," Jesilind said, buffing his nails again as he smiled, "but my profession as such is medicine. I serve a varied clientele on Greenwood. I accompanied Mr. Bannock to Kilbourn in order to purchase pharmaceuticals and of course, to see what books might have penetrated to such a distance from Earth."

"You went to Kilbourn for that?" Mark said. According to his gazetteer, Kilbourn was the rawest edge of the frontier.

"Yes, I ignore inconvenience when the welfare of my patients is at stake," Jesilind said. "Besides, if I treat with local herbs, the yokels don't like to pay what my services are worth."

A look of lacquered cunning flickered across Jesilind's face. He added, "And I thought a person of my accomplishments should be present to accompany Miss Bannock from Kilbourn to Greenwood. Yerby's a fine man in his way, salt of the earth. But not, as I'm sure you appreciate, the sort of person who should be sole escort to a girl like his sister. She was delicately brought up on Kilbourn, and she's only now leaving boarding school there."

"Hey, look at the scarecrow!" called a man, one of Mayor Biber's servants. They'd apparently gotten the baggage arranged to their satisfaction in Room 37 and were reemerging with a hamper of food.

"Go stand in a field, pretty boy," the leader of the group said. He planted himself on the bench so close that his hip jostled the doctor aside. Jesilind jumped up. He bounced back down again because the stranger was sitting on the tail of his frock coat.

"Hey, Griggs," laughed the man with the hamper. "Better give him his jacket back. That color don't suit you no better than it does him."

Griggs eased his weight off the fabric and shoved Jesilind away from the bench. "Go away, boy," Griggs said, with contempt rather than anger.

Jesilind focused tightly on Mark as though Biber's chuckling servants didn't exist and said, "Mr. Maxwell, at this time I always meditate alone. Good day, sir. I trust we'll have another chance to converse before we go our separate ways."

The doctor bowed, took a step, and tripped over the

Zeniths' hamper. Jesilind scrabbled forward like a large bird lifting off. By the time he'd risen from all fours, he was halfway to the rooms and moving at a dead run. The yellow coat flapped behind him.

"Scarecrow!" Griggs cried, and spun the cushion toward its fleeing owner.

Mark stood also. "I think I'll study for a while myself, Doctor," he said for politeness' sake, not that Jesilind could hear him. "Good day."

He walked to Room 36, being careful about where he put his feet. The servants from Zenith ignored him.

2. Fun and Games

Caravansary rooms didn't have built-in locks. There was a rugged staple and strap on both the inside and the outside of each door. The occupant provided his own padlock to secure the space.

Mark's lock was Terran, sturdy and expensive. It was programmable to a variety of different styles, but he'd set it to open from the pressure of both his thumbs together. He unlocked Room 36, switched on the tiny area light he carried in a pocket, and closed the door behind him. He dropped the padlock's hasp through the staple from the other side, though he didn't bother to lock it.

The room's interior was about as inviting as a crocodile's gullet.

Rooms in the caravansary were six feet by ten, with a half loft overhead reached by a metal ladder. Occupants could use the low benches cast into the back and side walls to sit, sleep, or place their goods out of the slight pool of water in the middle of the floor.

There were no lights, no running water, and no toilet

facilities of any kind. At the rear of the caravansary were a common latrine and eight shower heads that ran constantly at full force—Dittersdorf Major had no shortage of fresh water.

The showers were, however, cold water only. Mark had learned that shortly after he arrived.

Mark had prepared for his journey to the frontier with the same degree of organization that had earned him his degree. He'd read—sleep-learned, for the most part— both official and private accounts of life on the frontier, then listed the items he would need.

Mayor Heinrich Biber's twelve large cases might have been enough to hold the proposed gear; then again, they might not. The trouble was that "the frontier" was an expanding region, not a place.

Mark's information about Kilbourn was slight and certainly out of date if the planet really had a boarding school for "delicately brought-up" girls, as Dr. Jesilind had implied. Besides, even if Mark had really been sure of the conditions at his intended destination, there were the intermediate landfalls like Dittersdorf to consider.

The second time through, Mark cut his list to what would fit in one fifty-pound pack. That was the most weight he was sure he could handle by himself in rugged conditions. Everything he carried was rugged, weatherproof, and so far as possible multifunctional. The hypnagogue, for example, could project text as holograms as well as sleep-teaching the contents of a book chip, and it functioned as a database.

Also, Mark brought money. The line of credit from his father had been long enough for him to book passage on a yacht if he needed to (and if there were any yachts around, which there certainly weren't any place Mark had seen since he left Landingplace on Quelhagen). Lucius didn't approve of Mark's choice, but he stuck to the bargain he'd made with his son: a year on the frontier, followed by either apprenticeship as an attorney on Quelhagen or a complete end to monetary support. It was hard to tell what Lucius thought about the details, but he'd never been one to stint with his backing for something he'd agreed to do.

Room 36 would sleep six merchants and their goods in as much comfort as damp concrete could offer. Several of the caravansary's rooms were now occupied by extended families of a dozen or more, squalling and quarreling in search of a new life at the lowest possible cost. Mark didn't want a companion and the room's slight cost wasn't a factor, but he sometimes wondered if a smaller space might not have oppressed him less.

Sighing, Mark took his hypnagogue from its stiffened pouch on the side of his pack. Three landfalls out from Quelhagen he'd picked up a book chip on the geography and history of the Digits. This seemed to be a good time to read it.

He slipped the book into the socket of his hypnagogue. The chip wasn't manufactured on Earth or Quelhagen, so he'd been a little surprised to learn that it fit his viewer. He'd projected the first pages of text as holograms above the viewer when he bought it in a spaceport jumble shop, but he hadn't had a chance to sleep-learn the book.

Mark lay down on his mattress, a thin pad of closed-cell foam, arranged the hypnagogue's induction pads on his temples, and cued "Greenwood" to learn something about Bannock and Jesilind. When the index beeped, he turned the unit on. The hypnagogue matched and smoothed the alpha waves of his brain, then began to transfer the book's contents directly to his cerebral cortex.

Mark wasn't really asleep, let alone unconscious. He was vaguely aware of concrete gleaming around him in his light's harsh illumination, and he could switch off the hypnagogue at any point. His intellect was disconnected unless he made a determined effort of will, however.

The hypnagogue distorted a reader's time sense, but it couldn't have been long before Mark realized there was something wrong with the way his viewer read the chip. Snatches of implanted thought reached the surface layers of Mark's mind:

The Protector of Hestia, a Satanic figure with horns and glowing eyes, scattered settlement grants among swarms of dwarfish, misshapen creatures who poured gold into his palm in return. In another part of the mental image, winged, haloed angels in shining armor from the planet Zenith were in battle with the dark legions of worlds settled by the Asian Sphere. Behind these angels, the dwarfs spread across Greenwood despite anguished looks from the hard-pressed Zeniths.

Mark dabbed his finger at the viewer's switch. The fantasy images stopped, but he couldn't sit up when he first tried to. "Wowee!" he said.

The software was close but not quite the same as Mark's hypnagogue had been designed for. The unit had filled his head with the personified moods and emotions of the book's author rather than the stated facts on which those beliefs were based. The influx was totally disorienting.

"Wowee," Mark repeated softly.

He'd thought he'd be able to pick up better information about the frontier as he got closer to it, but he'd found very few books for sale after he left Quelhagen. Part of the problem was that what book chips there were had been published in quirky local formats, so that you had to have a special viewer to read them.

Mark had shopped for information on every planet where he laid over, but he'd found only one place that had both books and viewers of the same style for sale. That was Heavenly Host, a world settled by a sect which believed rocks had souls and which published tracts explaining its faith on carbon-based chips. Using silicon would have been sacrilege.

Mark hadn't bought any of their material.

When Mark found a geography text published in standard Atlantic Alliance format that his hypnagogue could read, he'd thought it too good to be true. As usual, such apparent windfalls *were* too good to be true.

The world spun for a moment. When it stopped, Mark was no longer seeing double, though he was a little dizzy. Wowee.

He got up from the bench very carefully. Normally hypnagogue software either worked or it didn't, so this had been a real surprise. There were probably people who'd pay for the experience. A different subject matter would have more appeal, though.

Despite the book not being suitable for sleep-learning, Mark could still read about Greenwood. Not in this room, though. He picked up the viewer and went out into the domed court again. It wasn't so much that he wanted company; he just didn't want to be alone with the echoes of heaven and hell fighting in his head.

The four Zeniths had finished their meal and were passing a bottle around. Mark tried to imagine them with wings and haloes. He couldn't, but at least the effort made him smile.

Somebody had left a heavy metal bucket overturned on the other side of the circle of benches. Mark went to it, checked for other claimants, and sat down. He switched on his viewer, this time using it to project text in air-formed holograms instead of as a hypnagogue.

Nearby, two men with linked arms sang, *"From this valley they say you are going,"* lugubriously. Then they sang, *"From this valley they say you are going,"* again. Each man held an empty bottle in his free hand. Their voices weren't bad.

Mark began to read about the settlement of Greenwood. The Alliance administered newly discovered worlds through the protectors of established colonies. There was no point in sending personnel to an unoccupied planet, and it wasn't practical to govern directly from Paris a place weeks or months out in the interstellar boondocks.

Grants of extraterritorial authority to the protectors were generally fuzzy, because nobody on Earth really had a clue about what was going on at the frontier. Inevitably, some protectors exceeded their proper authority. One of the worst examples of this was the long-serving Protector Greenwood of Hestia. He'd sold settlement grants for a planet that was clearly under the jurisdiction of the

Protector of Zenith. To add insult to injury, Greenwood had named the planet after himself.

According to the book's author, Greenwood had gotten away with this arrant banditry—besides payments to the Alliance, the grantees paid fees to Protector Greenwood himself—because the protectors of Zenith during the period were lackadaisical. Furthermore, Zenith's chief citizens were wholly occupied in prosecuting the war against proxies of the Eastern Sphere.

Mark snorted and set down the viewer. That wasn't how he'd learned history on Quelhagen. The chief citizens of Zenith had always been concerned first with avoiding risk to their own skins. Their closely second desire was to make money. So long as the Proxy Wars went on, there wasn't enough money in those settlement grants to make them worth arguing about. Greenwood was wide open to Eastern attack, particularly before Alliance forces finally captured the huge Eastern base on Dittersdorf Minor. When the fighting stopped, it was time for Zenith money-grubbers to get interested.

Mark started to read again. His surroundings were a living hum, but he wasn't aware of any single aspect of them.

Somebody kicked the bucket out from under him.

Mark jumped upright, squarely on his feet. The bucket clattered from the bench between the two friends as they moaned, *"From this valley . . ."*

Mayor Biber's four baggage handlers ringed Mark. The leader, Griggs, looked disgruntled. He'd obviously figured that when he kicked Mark's seat away, Mark would fall on his ass.

That would have been Mark's guess too. It looked like instinct and his gymnastics training had paid off. The Zeniths didn't seem about to applaud, though.

"What you reading, cutie?" one of the men said. He flicked a hand at the hypnagogue. Mark jerked it clear. The Zenith behind him jolted him forward hard; Griggs pushed him back.

The caravansary watchman hunched down in his kiosk to avoid seeing what was going on in the common court. He wasn't armed, so there wasn't a lot he could have done anyway, but Mark would have appreciated even a shout just now.

The Zeniths' breath stank of the liquor they'd been drinking. Based on the smell, Mark suspected that a lab report on the booze would read: YOUR HORSE HAS GONORRHEA.

This was a bad situation, and it was likely to get worse fast. Other travelers moved quietly away from Mark and the Zeniths. Even the two singers stood up and wove across the common court toward the latrine.

"I don't like cute boys, fellows," Griggs said ironically to his companions. "Do you guys like cute boys?"

"Gentlemen, I'm very sorry if I've given you offense," Mark said. He tried to keep eye contact with Griggs while he folded the hypnagogue shut. It was a fairly rugged unit, but it could be broken if somebody tried hard enough.

So could Mark himself.

"Don't have no use a'tall," another Zenith said. He swept a big boot at Mark's ankle to knock his feet out from under him. Mark skipped over the kick. The Zenith swore and punched Mark hard on the shoulder.

There was absolutely no reason for what was happening, except that Mark had been reading. And, of course, that he was available.

Dr. Jesilind opened the door of Room 14 and peered out furtively. He caught Mark's eye for an instant, then ducked back. Jesilind's lock clacked shut audibly.

"Let's see what you got there, cutie," Griggs said. He stepped forward, reaching for the hypnagogue. Mark dodged between Griggs and another Zenith. He walked— just short of ran—toward Room 36. He wished he hadn't locked the door when he came out.

"Hey, where you think you're going?" A Zenith demanded, grabbing Mark's arm. Mark tried to shrug loose. He couldn't. Two of the luggage handlers were a bit bigger than Mark, while Griggs and the fellow holding Mark's arm outweighed him by a good hundred pounds.

"Sir, I must ask you to let go of my sleeve!" Mark said in a voice that snapped with authority. Only moral authority, though, and that wasn't what was called for at the moment.

The Zenith laughed and released Mark. They were ringing him again, tighter now so that he couldn't duck through them.

"Look, I'm going to tell you what, punk," Griggs said. "I don't like cute boys, and I'll bet you don't like real men. So I'm going to let you punch me, just as hard as you can. And then I'm going to punch you. That seem fair?"

Mark slipped the hypnagogue into a side pocket. *This isn't really happening. . . .* But of course it was.

"Sir, can't I buy you a drink?" Mark said, praying that his voice was steady.

"He had his chance, boss," a Zenith said. "Slug him."

Mark grimaced and with all his strength punched Griggs on the jaw. The shock went all the way to Mark's shoulder. His hand hurt as if he'd slammed it in a car door.

Griggs shook his head. All four Zeniths laughed uproariously.

"Your turn, Griggsie!" a rough said gleefully.

Mark stood stiff, his hands at his sides. His eyes were open, though nothing they saw was penetrating to his brain. All Mark had left was his dignity as a gentleman of Quelhagen. Griggs would take that from him at any moment, but Mark wasn't going to give it up by screaming or flailing uselessly at the Zeniths.

"Let's see what the little guy had for breakfast, hey fellers?" Griggs said. He drew back a big scarred fist to swing at Mark's belly.

"Let's not," Yerby Bannock said from behind Griggs. Mark's eyes focused. Bannock grabbed the two bigger Zeniths by the neck and slammed their heads together.

The impact sounded like a maul hitting a tree trunk. The men dropped. They couldn't have been more limp if Bannock had sucked all the bones from their bodies.

One of the remaining Zeniths put his hand into his jacket pocket. Bannock caught his wrist, then reached into the pocket himself. He came out with a shiny pistol. He dropped it on the floor while the rough punched vainly at him.

For illumination at night, the caravansary mounted light sconces above the doorways of alternate pairs of rooms. Bannock transferred his grip to the scruff of the would be gunman's neck and carried him toward the nearest sconce.

The fourth Zenith snatched at the fallen pistol. Mark hit him over the head with the metal bucket. It rang echoingly in the big domed room.

Bannock hung the back of his man's jacket over the light sconce, then stepped away. The fellow squalled and kicked violently, seven feet in the air. He could get free easily enough by slipping his arms out of the sleeves, but he'd be very lucky not to land on his head when he dropped.

The man Mark had hit turned slowly toward him. He held the pistol, but his eyes were glazed. Mark stepped back and with all his strength swung the bucket overhead. It bonged and bounced from the fellow's skull. The Zenith remained standing.

"Better hit him again, kid," Bannock suggested. "They don't give no points for neatness in a brawl."

"No," Mark gasped. He was exhausted. His right hand throbbed so fiercely from punching Griggs that he had to let go of the bucket's vibrating handle. "I can't."

I won't. The Zenith bled from a cut scalp. His face streamed blood. It made Mark sick to look at him.

"Well, it's your choice," Bannock said. He took off his poncho. Bannock didn't look particularly worked up, but he'd popped all the buttons of his leather vest.

The Zenith's eyes rolled up. He dropped the pistol and fell over beside it.

Mark set the bucket on the floor. He had to brace himself on it before he could straighten up. Rage and fear had wrung more of the strength out of him than physical effort had, though he'd swung the bucket with everything he had. The thick metal was dished in as though a vehicle had driven over it.

"Know where this lot bunks, lad?" Bannock said as he lifted Griggs and the other big man by their collars.

"They're in thirty-seven, sir," Mark said. He took a deep breath. "Beside me."

Bannock walked toward Room 37, dragging the unconscious Zeniths. "You've learned a valuable lesson, lad," he said. "Don't you never hit a man with your bare hand unless your feet are nailed to the floor of an empty room."

He looked over his shoulder, smiled, and added, "And particularly don't hit him on the jaw. You can hurt yourself bad that way."

"I think I did," Mark muttered. He could still flex his right hand, though. It hurt like blazes and had already started to swell, but he guessed he hadn't actually broken anything.

Bannock dropped the roughs in front of their door and looked at the lock. "Just the sort of trash you'd figure no-hopers from Zenith to be using," he sneered.

He gripped the padlock with one huge hand and twisted. A piece of the hasp flew off with a snap and pinged nervously on the floor.

Bannock tossed the remainder of the lock after it. Mark gaped. *A force of nature, all right.*

Bannock pulled the door open, reached down, and threw Griggs inside. He tossed the other big man after the first, then sauntered over to where Mark's victim lay. The door stood wide behind him.

"I used to be real good at this," Bannock said regretfully. He lifted the flaccid Zenith by the belt, his center of balance. "I've slowed down, though, and I don't know when the last time I cleaned out a tavern was."

Bannock lofted the unconscious man ten feet through the air. He vanished into Room 37, landing with a crash among his fellows and the Mayor's baggage.

The remaining Zenith stopped struggling. He hung rigid from the light sconce, obviously terrified of drawing further attention to himself.

"Thank you very much, Mr. Bannock," Mark said. He didn't have his voice quite under control. There were too many hormones surging through his bloodstream. "Your help was a, a godsend."

"Tsk," said Bannock, slamming the door of Room 37. "I appreciate the chance to bring dirt from Zenith to a better understanding of their place in the universe."

He looked around and murmured, "Now, what'll we— yeah, that'll do nicely."

The corner of a heavy cart had cracked the doorpost of a nearby room. Over the years, further impacts and water seeping into the weak places had flaked off most of the concrete covering a reinforcing rod. Bannock scuffed the rod with his boot heel to twist it out from the wall. He bent, gripped the end of the three-eighths-inch steel, and jerked it fiercely back and forth until a foot of it snapped off in his hand.

"Whooee!" Bannock said, juggling the rod one palm to the other. "Tell me that don't heat metal up, working that way!"

He thrust the rod over Room 37's strap and through the staple, then bent the rod into a loop. The room was sealed until somebody cut the rod. Or somebody as strong as Yerby Bannock straightened the steel out again, which seemed about as likely as a sunny day on Dittersdorf Major.

Bannock dusted his hands together. He grinned up at the man on the light sconce. The Zenith pretended to be catatonic, squeezing his eyes more tightly shut.

"Sir, you're amazingly strong!" Mark blurted.

"Ah, but you're the one who opened the dishes so I didn't have to tear the box apart, lad," Bannock said, though he was obviously pleased at the compliment. "Amy couldn't have been happier to see the plates, neither. Said she'd heard of such but never thought she'd see it for herself."

Mark saw the pistol glittering on the concrete. He picked it up and looked at it curiously. The short barrel ended in a needle spike.

Bannock shook his head. "Nerve scrambler," he said. "Not supposed to kill you, but this one likely would anyhow seeing's it's such a piss-poor piece of junk. Don't you mess with it, lad."

He took the scrambler from Mark, held it momentarily in both hands, and twisted. Bits of the weapon showered to the floor.

"How did you do that?" Mark said.

Bannock shrugged. "Well," he said, "you want to make sure you don't have your hand over the barrel because sometimes they go off. Time or two I was too drunk to remember that."

He opened his left palm toward Mark. The flesh was scarred like wax heated until bubbles rose and burst.

Dr. Jesilind emerged from his room. "Ah, Yerby, you're back," he said with a false brightness. He looked around the common area, obviously surprised not to see Mayor Biber's servants. When he noticed the man hanging from the light sconce, he said, "Yerby, you've been fighting again!"

"Well, not like you'd really call fighting, Doctor," Bannock said in some embarrassment. "Nothing undignified, like."

Mark stared at Jesilind. *He'd have thrown me to the wolves to save his own skin!* The doctor flushed as if he'd heard the unspoken words.

"I found a place we can eat all together," Bannock said. "Not Kilbourn quality, maybe, but I guess it'll do better than cold rations in this box."

He looked up at the caravansary's domed ceiling and grimaced. "Like a tomb, this place is. A big concrete tomb."

Mark suddenly relaxed. OK, Jesilind wasn't a hero, but neither was Mark Maxwell. If the doctor had come out shouting and swinging when he saw what was happening, two innocent men instead of one would have the tar whaled out of them by thugs from Zenith. It hadn't been Jesilind's fault.

"Say, you'll come along with us, won't you, Mark?" Bannock said. "It is Mark, right?"

Mark opened his mouth. He was used to being "Mr. Maxwell," to people he'd known for years. That was normal politeness on Quelhagen.

A frown as momentary as riffles on a pond crossed Dr. Jesilind's face. He didn't say anything.

Mark wasn't on Quelhagen anymore. "I'd be honored, Yerby," he said. "But you'll have to let me pay for the meal as a small recompense for you saving me a moment ago."

Bannock clapped Mark on the shoulders. The big frontiersman really did know his own strength—Mark had seen how great that strength was when it wasn't being tightly controlled—but he had an inflated notion of how strong normal people were, too. The friendly gesture almost knocked Mark down.

"You pay?" Yerby snorted. "When, besides them plates for Amy, you got me the best exercise I've had since I left Greenwood? Your money's no good when I'm around, boy! Now, let's go introduce you to my sister."

3. Dinner for Four

Mark wore a waterproof cape with a metallized layer that reflected body heat back to the wearer. Jesilind had an umbrella with clear sides hanging down nearly to the ground like diaphanous draperies. The struts kept jabbing things, including his companions if they weren't careful. Yerby whistled cheerfully, though Mark didn't think the poncho could be really waterproof even if it was woven of raw wool with the lanolin still on the strands.

The women's side of the caravansary was an identical building joined back-to-back with the men's, like two soap bubbles touching. The concrete sidewalk between the entrances was slightly raised; the constant rain washed off any mud tracked onto it.

The watchman in the barred kiosk was old, thin, female, and hard as nails. Mark didn't doubt that she had some weapon beyond her force of personality with which to control drunken men who tried to enter the women's side, but the glare she gave the three of them as they approached was icy enough to freeze him. He waited a step behind Yerby and the doctor.

Yerby swept off his leather hat, sluicing droplets from the brim. "Ma'am," he said to the watchman. "I'd appreciate you telling Miss Amy Bannock that her brother's ready to take her to dinner."

"She's expecting you," the watchman said with perhaps minutely less of a chill. She pressed a button. A lock clicked and a young woman pushed the small personnel door open to join them.

Amy Bannock was solid and red-haired, more cute than beautiful. When she noticed Jesilind, her face hardened from the smile with which she greeted her brother.

"I see you're joining us, Doctor," she said.

"And here's Mark Maxwell, the fellow I was telling you about," Bannock said enthusiastically. "I figured you'd want to thank him yourself. Anyway I like to have smart people around to talk to when I eat. You can learn a lot by listening at dinner!"

Amy's gaze fell on Mark for the first time. Her expression was speculative but only a little less cool than that she'd given Jesilind. She must think it was Jesilind's idea, that Mark join them.

"Miss Bannock," Mark said, bowing stiffly. "I'm glad to make your acquaintance—"

They *hadn't* been properly introduced by Quelhagen standards.

"—but I fear business prevents me from dining with you after all. Perhaps another—"

"Please!" Amy said warmly. "I'd be more than grateful for your presence at dinner, Mr. Maxwell."

She dropped Mark a curtsy that surprised him. *That* level of formality had gone out of style even on Quelhagen.

"His name's Mark, Amy," Yerby said with a laugh. "He's not the sort who stands on ceremony, is he, Doc?"

"But Amy, dear," Jesilind said. "You've forgotten your rain cover. You must go—"

"No, I can't use that thing, Doctor," Amy said sharply. "Don't you bump into everything when you walk around in yours? Anyway"—this to her brother—"I won't melt. You said we'd be taking a car?"

"Right here, darling," Yerby said, waving expansively to the van with big low-pressure tires which had been parked in front of the building all the time. "I told the driver to stick right here till I fetched you. Otherwise I'd find him before I left the planet and he wouldn't much like the rest of our dealings."

Amy shook her head. "Yerby, hitting people isn't the answer to everything in the universe," she said as she skipped ahead of the men.

Mark let Yerby and the doctor precede him. Amy was right, both morally and as a practical matter. Yerby's casual threat was just the sort of thing that made human history such a bloody, wasteful swamp.

But it was hard to see how the business with Biber's servants could have been ended without somebody being hit. The only question was *who* was going to be hit. Mark didn't feel he was being unreasonable in being glad matters had worked out the way they did.

The only seat in the van was the driver's. The remainder of the vehicle's interior was bare except for dirt and a box of tools. Amy gripped the back of the seat and a stiffener on one side panel.

Yerby wedged himself into the front corner of the

compartment, looking rearward toward his companions. "On to the Rainbow Tavern, buddy," he ordered the wizened driver. "Get us there in ten minutes and I'll buy you a bottle to keep you warm while you wait to run us back."

Somehow Mark had decided that if they got any distance from the caravansary, Dittersdorf would be more *cheerful*. Nothing much changed as they drove away from the spaceport. The van's tires spun through the mud, throwing up individual rooster tails. A wiper and water jet kept a patch of windshield clean enough for the driver to see where they were going, but Mark had to squat and squint to see out.

For the most part, "out" was more mud and rain. They passed a few dwellings, plastic domes gleaming with water. Houses on Dittersdorf didn't have windows, but the bright light over each front door looked surprisingly warm.

The van spun ninety degrees, then straightened. The road was unpaved but so broad that even if there'd been more than occasional traffic, it wouldn't have been dangerous. "Surely it would be preferable to fly?" Dr. Jesilind said.

The driver turned his head like an owl. "Sure, you fly," he said in a chirpy voice. "I'll watch. If this thing breaks down, we're stuck in the mud. If your aircar breaks down, you're buried in the mud—and believe me, keeping things running on Dittersdorf is no picnic."

"Nor on Greenwood," Yerby agreed, "but we fly most places anyhow. We use blimps—gas bags—for loads, and one or two people alone use flyers. Solar-powered, which ain't the ticket for here."

"There's folk have aircars," the driver admitted grudgingly. "They're no use for driving a herd, though, and that's most of what travel there is hereabouts. People bringing meat to the port and going back to their home."

"Herds of what?" asked Amy. She looked a little queasy. The combination of slithering progress and the vehicle's constant rattling vibration wasn't doing much for Mark's insides either.

"Cows, ma'am," said the driver. "Earth cows. There's plenty of plants out there—ground cover, not trees, and it's all the same color as the mud so it don't look like much. The cows like it fine, though."

Mark wondered if the cows really did like Dittersdorf or if they just endured. Though . . . the driver didn't seem morose. The constant gray skies would drive Mark screaming up the walls if he had to live here for any length of time, but there were men (and maybe cows) who didn't mind it that much. Opening the universe to settlement made it possible for every human being to find the right place.

In theory, at least. Mark wondered if he'd ever find the right place for himself.

The driver hauled hard on the steering wheel, then stopped. "Here you go," he said. "Guess you owe me a drink, mister."

They opened their doors and for the first time Mark got a good look at his surroundings. The Rainbow Tavern was a yellow plastic dome encircled by a brightly lit walkway raised on pilings. Twenty or thirty vehicles, most of them similar to the van Mark rode in, nosed up to the walkway like boats at a dock.

For the moment there was dense fog rather than rain, so even Dr. Jesilind dispensed with his complicated umbrella for the walk into the tavern. Yerby stepped into the lead to open the door, pushing aside the driver without, probably, even thinking about it.

The interior of the Rainbow was brightly lit, garishly colored, and filled with people whose happiness was a sharp contrast to the caravansary's gray gloom. Somebody'd painted the walls and ceiling with enthusiasm and considerable skill, though it took a moment to see talent through the artist's saturated reds and blues and pinks.

The color choice was dictated by the need to contrast with the world outside. It warmed Mark and raised his spirits the instant he entered the room. The caravansary was a part of Dittersdorf and perfectly functional; the Rainbow was apart from Dittersdorf and absolutely necessary for a refuge, at least occasionally.

Most of the folk wore garments of leather or synthetic fabric. The man playing "Bless Them All" on the electronic organ in a corner wasn't very good, but the three friends singing to his accompaniment seemed happy enough. So were the dozen others listening.

"We've got a table," Bannock announced to the bearded man behind the bar, "but there's four rather than the three I said when I came by earlier."

The barman waved at tables extruded from some dense plastic, each of them a bright primary color. "Pick where you want," he said. "And I guess we've got food for all of you. Nobody's gone away hungry from the Rainbow yet."

He turned and called toward the open doorway to the side, "Madge? Folks from the port are here."

In a quieter tone, with a broad smile to Amy, he added, "And one of them about as pretty as you're going to see. Pleasure to have you in the house, miss."

"Might I record the room, sir?" Amy asked. She took a camera from what Mark thought was a small purse and extended the three lenses. "Would people be offended?"

"Offended?" the barman said. "Why, not at all, miss. I know I'd take it as an honor. But why would you want to picture a place like this?"

Amy was already at work, slowly sweeping the room. The separated lenses laid their information onto a recording chip from which a projection unit could create three-dimensional holograms of the scene. Amy kept the camera level and her movements steady so that the images wouldn't jump when she played them back.

"Miss Altsheller says that women have to be the historians of human expansion," Amy said, speaking to keep her companions from getting impatient. The camera panned the room as smoothly as if it was on gimbals. "Men won't take the time, so women must if tomorrow's history isn't to be fantasy like all history before our time."

"Well," began Mark. "I don't think you can say . . ."

But you could. History was a series of decisions about what to tell and a series of accidents about what survived after telling. Not truth, but a historian could *search* for truth, and the search was as worthy as any other human activity.

What Mark realized and Miss Altsheller probably didn't is that holographic recordings were no more true and absolute than earlier attempts to record facts. But Amy's holograms were as valid as the work of the scholars of future generations who would try to piece them into the mosaic of human expansion across the galaxy.

Besides, she pleased the folk inside the Rainbow. Folk nodded, waved, and even blushed in pleasure that somebody was taking the time to record *them*.

"That should do," Amy said, closing her camera.

"About time," said her brother. "I'm starved, girl." He was obviously proud of his sister.

None of the tables was empty, but when a man seated alone saw them look around he tipped his hat to Amy and moved to the adjacent table where two men were playing chess. Yerby sat down. Mark moved to pull out Amy's chair and bumped shoulders with Jesilind.

"Thank you, Mr. Maxwell," Amy said politely as she seated herself.

"Fellow at the end of the bar," Yerby said, nodding in the direction of a man in a blue-and-orange-striped rain jacket, "he's got an aircar that I'm renting tomorrow to fly to Minor to see if I can't get some help from the army."

"You're very wise to call in the duly constituted authorities, Yerby," Jesilind said. "Alliance troops will overawe the Zenith landgrabbers and send them scurrying away."

Mark frowned, though he didn't comment. The Protector of Quelhagen was threatening to close the Landingplace spaceport with Alliance troops—Terran troops—because of a quarrel over allowable exports. Mark hadn't followed all the ins and outs of the debate: he'd been on Earth through most of it, and his father had always said an attorney had to be above causes if he was to be effective. It was hard to think of Alliance troops as friendly, though.

"Mark here had a bit of a dustup with some Zeniths today, Amy," Yerby said. "He was kind enough to let me have a piece of it."

The food arrived, heaping platters of meat, bread, and vegetables; unordered and unexpected, at least by Mark. Apparently the Rainbow had one specialty, and the staff didn't bother asking customers if that's what they wanted. If they didn't, why had they come?

"Since when has there been a brawl within shouting distance that you didn't get involved in, Yerby?" Amy said sharply.

"I would have been badly beaten had your brother not rescued me, Ms. Bannock," Mark said. "There were four of them, and . . ."

He didn't know what to say next. He'd never *seen* a man beaten unconscious, but he was quite sure the Zeniths would have gone at least that far.

"Amy, please, Mark," Amy said. "I wouldn't want you to think that Miss Altsheller's Academy had made me stuck-up."

"At the time the unfortunate events were occurring," Dr. Jesilind said, "I was considering the origin of life. I wonder, Mr. Maxwell, if you've ever considered the possibility that all life in the universe springs from a common font?"

"I can't say that I have," Mark said. He'd begun shaking when he thought about the beating he almost got. And it *wasn't* Jesilind's fault, but at the time the click of the doctor locking himself into safety had sounded like the crack of doom.

"All knowledge is my field," Jesilind repeated, beaming.

"'I have taken all knowledge to be my province,'" Mark said, correcting the quote. "That was very well for Sir Francis Bacon, but I'm not nearly so broad, and the sheer quantity of available knowledge today is greater by orders of magnitude."

Jesilind blinked.

Mark deliberately turned toward Yerby and said, "What are you going to do with Alliance soldiers, Yerby? Or if it's secret . . ."

"I've got no secrets from my friends, lad!" Yerby boomed. "Besides, I don't care if the Zeniths do hear about it."

That was true enough. Everybody in the room could hear him if they wanted to, though the Rainbow wasn't the sort of place where anyone thought quiet restraint was a virtue.

"You see," Yerby continued around a mouthful of rare beef, "all us settlers on Greenwood, we're there on proper Protectorate grants. Now, there's a bunch of folks from Zenith, they claim they've got grants too and maybe they do. But ours are older and we're *there* on Greenwood, you see?"

Mark nodded. There was the little matter of the fact that Protector Greenwood might not have jurisdiction over the planet to begin with; but in a way that didn't matter. The Protector was an Atlantic Alliance official, and he'd been acting under at least a claim of authority. His Alliance superiors might have cause to punish him for improperly making grants, but that didn't mean that the grants themselves were invalid.

"So some folks from Zenith, they come round a couple months ago, looking things over," Yerby continued. "Folks from the Zenith army, only they call it the Zenith Protective Association. And they got liquored up enough one night to talk about shipping all us Greenwoods out to a labor camp on Zenith for being trespassers."

He paused to drink. With the food, the Rainbow served pitchers of full-bodied ale. Yerby used enormous quantities of it to wash his meal down.

"I suggested to Yerby that the Alliance has a base on Dittersdorf Minor," Jesilind said. "All the commander there has to do is detach a small body of troops to Greenwood to keep the peace. That will obviate enormous future difficulties."

"I see," Mark said.

He didn't see. Rather, he saw that Bannock and Jesilind lived in a mental universe where things operated differently than they did on the Quelhagen and Earth that Mark knew. Would a base commander really send troops off to nowhere in particular because a couple of strangers asked him to?

Not in Mark's universe. But perhaps things really did happen that way on the frontier.

"Well, lad," Yerby said with a broad smile. "You want to come with me tomorrow? It's a couple days before you ship out, right? The car's a two-seater and Doc decided he didn't want to come."

You'll be lucky if you don't break your neck, flying through soupy atmosphere on a strange planet! Mark thought. Then he thought, *I was lucky that the Zeniths didn't break my neck, and all I did was sit on a bucket reading.*

"I'd be delighted," Mark said. "I'd like to see more of the planets I'm staging through, but mostly I've been stuck in spaceports." *Kept myself stuck in spaceports.*

"Done!" Yerby said, wiping his hand on his shirt before he shook with Mark. "First light in the morning, then. I want to get us back to Major before dark."

"I'll look after Miss Bannock during your absence, Yerby," Dr. Jesilind said. "Perhaps we—"

"You'll do nothing of the sort!" Amy said. "Yerby, I'm coming with you."

"Only got two seats, child," Yerby said. He chuckled. "Besides, it's too dangerous for a sweet girl like you."

"What!" Amy said. She started to get up, bumped the table—her chair didn't slide back the way she'd thought it would—and slammed back down.

"Yerby, I think perhaps you should take your sister—" Mark said.

"Are you telling me my word's no good, boy?" Yerby said. His fist curled reflexively around the handle of a full pitcher.

"No, I'm telling you I made a mistake," Mark said evenly. *Maybe it's just my day to get pounded to a pulp. You can't avoid your fate. . . .*

"Stop!" said Amy. She didn't shout, but there was no doubt from the authority in her voice that she and Yerby Bannock were kin. "Mark, you'll go with Yerby in the morning, as you agreed. I have a good deal of work to do in my room. I will be there until you return in the evening."

She resumed eating, taking refined little bites. There wasn't a lot of talk around the table for the remainder of the evening.

4. The Funny Farm

The landscape of Dittersdorf Minor rolled by a thousand feet below the aircar. Compared to Major, the terrain was hillier and some of the vegetation could be called low trees.

The biggest difference was that Mark could see more than a fog-shrouded blur.

"I don't see why the port and all the settlement's on the big island," Yerby said. "Down there looks like pretty decent land, and you can see a hand in front of your face."

He had to shout to be heard over the persistent screech of the car's power plant. The turbine ran without stuttering on any liquid-hydrocarbon fuel, but it sounded like it was about to fly apart any moment.

"The Alliance won't allow settlement because of the fort," Mark said. "All Minor's a military reservation."

Bannock snorted.

Major, Dittersdorf's larger island (or small continent), was shaped like a broad crescent whose wings flowed backward in the press of a warm ocean current. Minor was a ball in the crescent's hollow, relatively clear of the rain and fog that constantly shrouded the bigger island.

The Easterns occupied Dittersdorf for strictly military purposes. After Alliance forces captured the planet, the Paris bureaucracy permitted construction of a civil spaceport to serve traffic to the Three Digits, but only three hundred miles away on the larger island.

Minor would have been a more comfortable site for the caravansary and the civilian settlement that had sprung up to service the port, but a bureaucrat always finds it easier to forbid than allow. From what Mark had seen in the Rainbow Tavern, the silly restrictions hadn't kept the settlers from enjoying themselves.

The car lifted slightly in an updraft. Mark saw their destination sprawled ahead of them.

The military base was a vast six-pointed star with turreted energy weapons at the angles and a spaceport in the paved central courtyard. The complex covered several acres on the surface, and Mark knew that several levels of tunnels extended through the bedrock beneath.

"Say, I didn't guess it was *that* big!" Bannock said as they swept down toward their destination. "I wonder how many soldiers they've got here?"

"It held six thousand when Alliance forces captured it from the Easterns in 2223," Mark said, quoting the figure he'd checked in a data chip before he went to sleep the night before. "I don't have any recent information on the garrison, though."

"Yerby Bannock calling Alliance fort," Yerby said, speaking into the microphone pickup in the cab roof.

"We're just coming to visit you folks, so don't get your bowels in an uproar."

Mark wasn't sure the laser communicator actually worked. There was a two-hundred-foot communications tower at one point of the star, but he had no idea what format or frequency the fort used.

"Don't you think they might shoot us down?" he asked. He tried not to sound nervous.

"Piffle," Yerby said. "We don't look like an army of Easterns, do we? Besides, there's no war nowadays."

He throttled back the fans. The car dropped in a series of awkward slaloms as Yerby steered for the edge of the area marked to land three starships simultaneously. He handled the controls in a rough-and-ready fashion, giving the impression of adequacy but not skill.

But Mark knew the big frontiersman had never touched the car's controls before he climbed aboard this morning, and the chances were he'd never flown anything very similar. The fact that Yerby *was* adequate at things outside his previous experience was probably the key to his survival on the frontier.

Yerby's *assumption* that he could handle most anything he tried was likely to get him killed one day, though Mark really hoped that Yerby's refusal to believe the soldiers would shoot at unannounced intruders didn't turn out to be that fatal mistake.

As they zigzagged low to land, Mark noticed that native foliage covered most of the fort's outworks. For a moment he thought that was for camouflage, but some of the broad-leafed shrubs were growing out of the courtyard pavement. Their roots must be breaking up the structure below.

"Wonder where everybody is?" Yerby said. Mark only understood the words because he'd been wondering the same thing. Nearer to the ground, the fort's low interior walls reflected the vehicle's noise into a squadron of screaming aircars.

"There—" said Mark, pointing at what he thought was a display of flags in a line on the other side of the landing zone.

Yerby had seen the flutter also. He hopped the car off the pavement where it first touched and skidded down again near the line.

The clothesline. Twenty or thirty garments, many too small for an adult to wear, were drying in the wan sun. Some of the clothes were dresses.

Bannock shut down the aircar. "Hey, you!" shrieked a woman scarcely less shrill than the turbine. "What do you think you're doing, blowing dirt on my wash? Couldn't you find anyplace else in this bleeding place to land?"

She'd come out of an armored door nearby. Weeds rooted in pavement cracks grew around the panel. The door hadn't been closed in a long time, and maybe couldn't be closed at all. Close up, the walls' fourteen-foot height looked more impressive than it had from the air when compared to the surface the fort covered.

The woman was short, dirty, and probably even younger than Mark himself. She wore a faded Alliance military shirt and carried a sleeping infant in a cloth sling on her left side. Her feet and her legs below the shirttails were bare.

"Sorry, sister," Bannock said easily as he got out of the car. "I'll be careful when I leave. My friend and I are just trying to find the colonel."

"Colonel, that's a laugh!" the woman said. "If you're looking for Captain Easton, you won't find him in married quarters. He'd be in the next bay over, but the chances are he's out with his vegetables anyhow."

She indicated the adjacent segment of the star with her thumb. The woman's voice had dropped a couple octaves since she got a good look at the strangers. Yerby Bannock wasn't a conventionally handsome man, but power has its own attraction and nobody could doubt the big man's power.

"His vegetables?" Mark said in surprise.

"That's it," the woman said with a nod . . . and perhaps a degree of speculation about Mark as well. "Flowers too. Anything you want to know about growing stuff, the captain's the one to tell you. Anything else, you may as well ask the boy here—"

Her hand brushed just above the forehead of the sleeping infant. She didn't look down as she gestured.

"—for all the good you'll get of it. Go to the open door, then down one level, then left at the main corridor till you hit the first blue corridor. Along it and up the ladder to hatch Blue Forty-two if it's standing open, which it likely will be."

"Thank you kindly, sister," Yerby said, lifting his broad-brimmed hat as he bowed to the woman. He strode across the bay in the direction she'd indicated.

"But won't somebody mind?" Mark asked, speaking to either of the others.

"Mind what?" the woman asked. "But don't expect much of a welcome unless you've got tomato seeds. He was complaining his tomato seeds didn't arrive."

An elevator and a staircase of slotted steel plates stood on opposite sides of the anteroom within. There was no passage directly through the fortress on this level. One of the elevator doors was missing; the shaft was empty.

The frontiersman led the way down the stairs sure-footedly. The only light came from the open hatch and that, by the time they'd turned at the second landing, wasn't enough for Mark to feel comfortable. The treads were slick with condensate and the air was increasingly musty. The fort's ventilation system didn't seem to work any better than the lights did.

"Has the place been abandoned, do you think?" Mark asked. He could see some light below them, coming through another open doorway. "Is the woman just a squatter?"

"There was a ship landed in the past week or so," Yerby said. He sounded a little puzzled too. "You saw the way the plants coming up through the cracks had been squished down? Of course I don't know exactly how fast things grow here, but a week's close enough for a guess."

Mark hadn't noticed the crushed vegetation. Well, Yerby Bannock probably couldn't give a connected account of interstellar expansion over the past one hundred fifty years. People had differing skills and abilities.

But right now, Mark felt lost and completely useless in comparison with a man who was perfectly comfortable in circumstances that were new to both of them.

Nearer the doorway they could hear voices. A dozen children aged ten or younger played a ballgame in the corridor. Two of the lights in the ceiling here worked; the nearest other patches of illumination were hundreds of yards down the corridor.

A girl kicked the ball toward Yerby and Mark by accident as they stepped into the corridor. Yerby caught it. The girl screamed in surprise. A boy darting toward the kick collided with Mark instead.

"Do any of you young heroes know where Captain Easton would be?" Yerby asked, bouncing the ball back to the child who'd kicked it. "Hatch Blue Forty-two, the lady upstairs said."

"That's my mommy!" cried a child of indeterminate sex. "I'll take you!"

The child ran off down the corridor, baggy trousers flapping. He/she must have been at least six years old. Mark frowned. Either his estimate of the woman's age was wrong, or—

Or perhaps the kid was wrong about who'd given directions to the strangers. That was a comforting thought, so Mark clung to it.

A boy behind them called, "What do you want to see old Cabbage for? Are you from Earth? Is he going to be court-martialed?"

"Come on!" squealed their guide. The child's silhouette vanished down a cross-corridor, otherwise invisible in the gloom. Yerby lengthened his stride, covering an enormous amount of ground without seeming to run, but Mark had to jog to keep up.

At least half the lights worked in the blue corridor. The floor was painted, though the center was worn to bare concrete and the margins were too dingy for anyone to be absolutely certain of the color. The child stopped fifty yards from the intersection, pointing at what really was a ladder—Mark had thought the word might mean a stairway, like "companion ladder" on a starship. The three of them stared up at the oval of daylight thirty feet above.

A man stepped through the hatch and began to climb down without looking behind him. He wore a gray military uniform with patched knees and an apron over it. Tools clinked together as he moved.

"That's Cabbage," the child whispered.

When it was obvious that Easton wasn't going to notice them, Yerby said cheerfully, "Good morning, Captain!"

"Oh my goodness!" Easton said. He flung himself backward off the ladder while he was still ten feet in the air.

Mark grabbed the gaping child and dived clear of what he guessed was going to be the impact zone. Yerby caught Easton in a two-hand grip around the pudgy waist. He swung the captain first upright, then to the ground as lightly as a circus act.

A trowel dropped from an apron pocket clanged to the floor just as Mark was starting to relax. The child giggled and ran back down the corridor the way they'd come.

"What on earth are you doing here?" Easton demanded. He peered at Yerby, then Mark. His eyes were still adapted to the daylight above. "Do I know you?"

"We're from Greenwood, Captain," Bannock said, shading the truth a little for the sake of simplicity. "We'd like you to station some troops with us to keep the peace. It needn't be many. Fifty or a hundred, that'd be a right plenty."

"Oh, I couldn't do that," Easton said. He minced down the corridor at a surprisingly quick pace.

Mark and Yerby fell into step on either side. Easton looked over one shoulder, then the other. His round, bushy-bearded face took on a hunted expression. "Lieutenant Hounslow handles all that sort of thing. Yes, you'll have to talk to him. Not me."

"And you're taking us to Lieutenant Hounslow, sir?" Mark said.

They'd reached the intersection. The ballgame was still going on down the main corridor to the right. Easton turned sharply left, as if by pretending Yerby didn't exist he could make the big man vanish. Bannock skipped out of the way, holding station. He was frowning.

"Oh, all right," Easton said. "He'll be in the Command Center, I suppose. He's always in the Command Center."

Several men wearing portions of uniforms lounged in the corridor ahead. The ceiling fixtures didn't work, but a series of light-strips connected by extension cords gave off a yellow-green glow sufficient for seeing clearly.

"Hey, it's the Old Man," one of the troops said without concern.

The four doors open to the left all served a single dormitory big enough to sleep at least a hundred. Mark looked in at each doorway. There were only twenty or thirty bunks scattered across the room. Men lay on a few of them. Rows of large boxes staggered against the back walls. Some had fallen over, spilling what looked like trash.

"G'morning, sir," a couple of the men in the corridor said to Easton. One of them even touched his forehead in an attempt at a salute.

Easton grimaced and bobbed his head. He was trying to pretend the troops didn't exist either. "I don't suppose you know anything about collards, do you?" he murmured to Yerby. "Mine are getting little black spots near the edge of the leaves, and I don't know if that's a—"

"Not a thing about collards," the frontiersman said. "What're you growing collards for anyhow? Something wrong with your rations?"

"All they provide us with is processed food, processed!" Easton said with the first animation he'd shown since his shout as he fell off the ladder. "Why, if they'd give me proper support in Paris, I could turn this whole base into a garden of healthy natural delights."

The next door past the barracks was open also. The smell staggered Mark. "Wow!" he said.

"Well, the sewer system seems to be blocked," Easton explained with some embarrassment. "And we're below ground, of course. So since the pump space was two-level and the pumps didn't work anyway, we've converted it to a, ah, well, a latrine."

The holes in the floor of the room had held a pair of centrifugal pumps eight feet in diameter. The equipment had been removed—Mark wondered how—and replaced with two-by-sixes raised a foot and a half above the holes so that users could sit with their families an adequate distance out in the air beyond.

"The right hole is for officers only," Easton said. He pulled the door shut. "Now, you know, this could be a valuable source of carbon and nitrates if properly composted, but I've had difficulties explaining this to the troops."

Who are the ones who'll be cleaning and transporting the valuable fertilizer, of course . . . "I can imagine you would have difficulties convincing your men, yes," Mark said.

He guessed that the garrison's answer to any problem was "Throw it downstairs." Mark didn't want to think about what the corridors on the fort's lower levels were like.

"Look, how many men do you have all told?" Yerby asked. The furrows of his frown had been getting deeper with every additional sign of neglect.

"Oh, I don't know about that," Easton said peevishly. He waved a hand to brush the question away. "That's all Hounslow's province."

The next two doors, both closed, were labeled COMMANDANT and DEPUTY COMMANDANT with letters cast into the dense plastic of the panel. Mark noticed that the bottom of the doors had been shaved off and the top of either panel gapped a finger's breadth at the side opposite the hinges. The fort had been settling in the generations since it was built. Cracks ran across flat surfaces and doorjambs twisted out of true.

Mark remembered the latrine. Also, sewer lines broke.

The next room was labeled COMMAND CENTER, by odd purple paint stenciled onto a sheet of plastic tacked to a replacement door of wood. Below that, in straggling script hand-lettered in green, *Keep out!*

Easton tried the handle. It was locked. "Oh, dear," he said. "Maybe we shouldn't. He really doesn't like to be—"

Bannock pushed the door open with his hip and shoulder. Pieces of flimsy latch flew into the room. The frontiersman boomed, "Hello there! Hounslow, is it? I'm Yerby Bannock, and we need some of your men on Greenwood."

The man who leaped up from behind the desk was tall, black-haired and cadaverously thin. His initial expression was outraged, but it turned to horror as soon as he heard Yerby's words.

"Oh, that won't be possible," Hounslow said. His gray uniform was threadbare but immaculately ordered, down to the neat HOUNSLOW on the tape over his left jacket pocket. "Why, I've just completed the duty rosters for the next—"

He gestured at the walls. They were covered with graph paper on which lines and names were drawn in at least six different colors of ink.

"—nineteen months. Can't possibly be done. I—you aren't from Paris, are you? Are you from the Inspector General's office?"

"No, we're from Greenwood," Mark said sharply. He'd heard Captain Easton scurry off the moment Yerby burst the door open. They were here with a simple question, and there didn't seem any reason they shouldn't have a simple answer.

"No" was simple enough and acceptable so far as Mark was concerned; but it couldn't be "no" from a lunatic.

"Certainly not for Greenwood," Hounslow said, nodding vigorously. "I don't even know where Greenwood is."

From the way he talked, Mark doubted Hounslow knew where his left foot was. The data terminal built into one end of the desk was cold and very possibly as dead as the fort's sewer system. The charts on the wall were hand-drawn. The same names occurred on them over and over again, but they were written in different colors.

"Look, we just need fifty or a hundred men," Yerby said in a cajoling tone. "It'll be a nice experience for them, getting—"

"Fifty or a *hundred?*" Hounslow repeated. "Why, I've only got forty-three troops total to carry out all the necessary duties here! Fifty or a hundred? Are you mad?"

Well, I'm certainly not very friendly, Mark thought. Aloud he said, "Just what duties are these, Lieutenant?"

"Why guards, charge of quarters, commandant and deputy commandant's drivers—"

"Where do you drive?" Yerby asked.

"It's beside the point whether we have vehicles or not!" Hounslow said. "Those positions have to be filled. This is a military base!"

Could've fooled me.

"Command post runners, guards for Heavy Weapons Stockpiles One, Two, and Three—we have over a thousand tanks and heavy artillery pieces here! KP—of course that's just distributing ration packs, but the position, the *position*, is sacrosanct. And only forty-three troops!"

"Why in heaven would you have so much weaponry here?" Mark asked. The idea of a basement full of tanks sounded as dotty as everything else to do with Dittersdorf Base.

Hounslow drew himself up stiffly. "Sir, we are a pre-positioning base of crucial importance to the security of the Alliance!" he said. Deflating somewhat, he added, "And of course it would have been awfully expensive to ship all that equipment back to Earth at the end of the Proxy Wars."

Yerby scratched his head. "This whole base and . . ." he muttered.

Mark bowed formally to the anguished lieutenant. "Thank you for your time, sir," he said. "Yerby, I think we should get back to the spaceport. We don't want Amy to worry about us." *And we certainly aren't doing any good in this combination of a kindergarten and a nuthouse.*

5. Going with the Flow

With Amy at the front to steer, Yerby Bannock pushed a cart loaded to the point of overbalancing toward the ship that would take his party to Greenwood. Mark and Dr. Jesilind struggled together with the other cart holding Amy's and Jesilind's gear—less in volume and much less heavy than the machinery Yerby was bringing from Kilbourn.

"That's close enough," a crewman called from the open hatch. "We'll stow it." She scratched behind her right ear and glanced at the fellow beside her at the winch controls. "Of course, we might not have time to take care of it before liftoff . . . ."

Mark stepped away from the luggage cart, gasping to get his breath back: He'd volunteered to help get his new friends' gear to the ship. He didn't regret the offer or even the effort—but if Dr. Jesilind had been pushing with all his strength, he was even less of a baggage handler than he was a scholar.

"Twenty Zenith dollars to split between you," Yerby said cheerfully. "And let's not have any accidents. Or else maybe I'll have an accident too."

He smacked his right fist into his left palm. The threat was as lighthearted as Yerby's willingness to tip for the work, but Mark had seen enough of the frontiersman to know that both were real.

"Yerby," Mark said, "Doctor, I'm glad to have met you. Amy—"

He bowed.

"—a particular honor to have met you. I wish you well in your new home."

"Well, you have a good voyage to Kilbourn, too, lad," Yerby said. "Space ain't so big that we might not knock into each other again. I'd like that."

"I don't believe I heard just why you were traveling to Kilbourn, Mark," Amy said.

"Very likely for education, my dear," Jesilind said. "Mr. Maxwell is the sensible sort of youth who can appreciate the value of an education."

A valve on the starship let out a shriek, jetting white steam into a generally gray sky. Mark held his tongue during the release, but he kept his eyes on Jesilind. The doctor really shouldn't have smirked in that would-be superior fashion. . . .

"In a manner of speaking, that's true," Mark said deliberately in the relative silence following. "I hope to learn about real life on the frontier. But as for formal education of the sort you mean, I have a degree from Harvard."

"You took a Harvard course too?" Jesilind blurted. "I understood—"

"I took a degree *at* Harvard," Mark said. "On Earth. I didn't meet your Dean Brickley, sir, because he died before I was born. Even before you were born. But he was a scholar of great capacity, I'm sure."

Yerby slapped both his thighs, a *wham! wham!* as startling as shotgun blasts. "Don't that beat all?" he cried. "Amy, didn't I tell you right off what a smart lad Mark was? Degree on Earth, yet! Earth!"

"Certainly a visit to such a site of ancient learning is of value," Dr. Jesilind said, attempting to project a tone of icy detachment. "Though as I understand it, the instruction on Earth is by hypnagogue also."

"One side or a leg off!" the crewmember shouted as she gave Jesilind a warning push. She'd set the winch clamps on the first layer of Yerby's baggage. Five large trunks swung through the space the doctor had occupied a moment before.

"That was largely true for background materials," Mark said. "Some of the lectures were recorded as well. But I had a live seminar with Dr. Kelsing—Anitra Kelsing, perhaps you've heard of her?"

Of course Jesilind hadn't. Mark could have made up names and Jesilind wouldn't know the difference. But Mark didn't *have* to make up names.

"She takes twelve students a year, and I was fortunate enough to be accepted as one of them," Mark continued. "The seminar covered views of the political background to the settlement of Quelhagen, which of course was particularly interesting to me."

"What did I tell you?" Yerby repeated. "*Live* courses!"

Dr. Jesilind looked like he'd gulped down a bite of something he really should have avoided. That was pretty much true: he'd had to swallow the smirk he'd given Mark.

"But if you want to see the frontier," Amy said, "why are you going to Kilbourn, Mark?"

"Well, because I thought . . ." Mark said. He looked at Amy and suddenly wished that he'd been a little more careful in his phrasing. "That is, from Quelhagen, it seemed—"

"That Kilbourn was frontier!" Yerby bellowed cheerfully. "Say, that's a joke as good as the one you pulled on us, saying you weren't no scholar!"

Amy blushed and turned her head as if to watch the rest of Yerby's baggage hoisted aboard the starship. She hadn't acted vain about her education the way Jesilind did, but learning that Mark thought she was a hick from the frontier must have hurt.

He didn't think that!

"Look, lad," said Yerby, putting his arm protectively around Mark's shoulders. "Forty years ago, in my daddy's time, Kilbourn was a pretty rough place, sure. Now, hell, they've even got uniformed *policemen* and laws about how much you can drink."

He shook his head in remembered amazement. Having seen Yerby in action, Mark could imagine how the frontiersman was likely to have reacted to a bartender who told him he'd had enough to drink. "So if you want frontier, a place a fellow can make his own luck—well, you ought to come to Greenwood with us. You'll get your education and I shouldn't wonder if you got rich besides, as sharp as you are."

"Mr. Maxwell has already made his plans, Yerby," Jesilind said in a thin tone. "And besides, our ship is about to take off."

"I haven't been to Greenwood myself, yet," Amy said, her embarrassment forgotten. "I remember what Kilbourn was like when I was younger, but . . . it would be nice having someone else around who'll find things as new as they'll be to me."

"As a matter of fact," Mark said, "my time's my own for the next year. Most of a year. But—"

The winch was hauling aboard the last of the party's baggage. The cargo handler rode the load into the hatch.

"—Dr. Jesilind is right, there's no time for me to board with you. Perhaps a later vessel?"

Yerby laughed heartily. "You go bring your traps, boy," he said with a dismissive wave toward the caravansary five hundred yards away. "If you need help, the doc'll help you, won't you, Doc?"

Jesilind looked startled. "No, that won't be necessary," Mark said. "It's just the one bag."

"And me," Yerby continued, "I'll stay here and make sure the ship don't lift before you get back. Which it won't, or my name's not Yerby Bannock. You don't even need to run."

Mark ran anyway, as best he could. The combination of Amy's pleasure and Jesilind's sour expression both spurred him.

6. Home Is Where the Heart Is

"Holy Jesus Christ our Lord and Savior," Yerby Bannock murmured softly as he stumbled to the hatch from which Mark was getting his first look at Greenwood. Yerby pressed his head with both hands as though he were trying to keep the brains from leaking out through his temples. "How are you feeling, kid?"

"I'm always a little woozy after sleep travel," Mark said. "This was a longer trip than some. But I'm all right."

The ship had landed on a grid a hundred feet in diameter, big enough for a single ship but far too small to hold two at a time. The steel spiral against which ships braked themselves was buried ten feet down in the stony soil, but the ground still radiated heat from the mutually repelling magnetic fluxes. On more highly developed spaceports the surface was thick concrete or even vitrified earth. Here ships landed on dirt, and a few plants between the twists of the steel managed to survive the heat that baked their roots at every landing.

Landing-site preparation was the factor that limited interstellar trade. Ships traveling between prepared sites braked orbital velocity against the planet's magnetic field, but for actual landing they required a denser flux to cushion them down. Except for a few nickel-iron asteroids, that meant burying a huge mass of magnetic material in which the incoming ship could induce a field to repel that of the vessel itself.

The bigger the ship, the greater degree of site preparation. Even small tramp freighters like the one Mark had arrived on required hundreds of tons of metal to ease them in safely. That was a major project for a completely raw planet, but until it was accomplished all ships had to land by rocket. The weight penalty of the rocket motors and fuel was enormous, and it was a lot more dangerous than almost idiot-proof magnetic landings besides.

"Boy, I think there was something wrong with the gin I got on Dittersdorf," Yerby said. He closed his eyes, shuddered at whatever he saw inside his head, and opened them again. "The top of my skull feels like it's going to pop off."

"You drank more than two quarts of liquor immediately before we got into our sleep capsules," Mark said, trying not to scold. "I was afraid you might have poisoned yourself drinking so much."

Yerby shrugged and winced at the motion. "Oh," he said, "I always do that before transit to keep from scrambling my brains. The doc's got a machine but it never worked for me. I just get drunked up before I go under, and I come through okay."

Yerby didn't *look* okay, but Mark wasn't in perfect

shape himself. Nobody was at his best following days of electronically induced suspended animation. Mark knew how to bring his brain waves in line with the induction apparatus instead of fighting it, but sleep travel still wasn't his idea of a fun time.

The alternative was to stay awake during transit between bubble universes, where all physical laws changed and life itself was an unnatural intrusion. Starship crews had to do that, and by the time a voyage was over they were virtually psychotic.

The flight crew had disembarked before ground personnel brought the passengers out of their sleep capsules. The navigator stood near the ship, punching violently at nothing at all. Two crewmen sat catatonic at the edge of the field, their eyes focused a thousand miles away. The chief cargo handler was sobbing uncontrollably in the cargo hatch; three stevedores waited to unload the ship, but they knew that if they disturbed the crying woman she might claw them like a wounded leopard.

The captain plaited grass blades into a chain. As his fingers formed the chain from the bottom, he swallowed the other end.

There were worse things than Mark's wooziness, or even than Yerby's hangover.

The landing site was a rough plain. A dozen winch points—bollards set down to bedrock—ringed the field three hundred yards out. A ship could skid itself off the magnetic mass to allow another vessel to land. Two ships similar to the freighter Mark stood in were on the margins of the field now.

Most of the hills surrounding the field were heavily

forested. "Greenwood" wouldn't have been a bad name for the planet even if the Protector of Hestia had been a Mr. Smith. On the knoll five hundred yards to the east sprawled a complex of stone and concrete buildings. Several brightly colored dirigibles bobbed on tethers above the courtyard wall; winged flyers, seemingly too delicate to be machines, lifted toward the ship.

"There's the Spiker, lad," Yerby said. He pointed toward the buildings with the care his throbbing hangover demanded. "Blaney's Tavern to the ship crews, but all the folk on Greenwood call it . . . See the critter there at the front gate?"

Mark squinted. "I thought it was a truck," he said. "Or a tank."

"The critter" was thirty feet long, ten feet broad, and ten more feet high. It stood on six stumpy legs and appeared to have neither a neck nor a tail. The huge head was jagged with scores of spines a foot or two long; rows of similar projections ran down the backbone and the flank Mark could see from this angle.

"A spiker," Yerby said. "Ain't very many of them. Guess there couldn't be or they'd eat the place down to the rock. That one charged a bulldozer while they were building the field. Would've flipped the dozer over, too, if old Blaney hadn't finally managed to burn through the hide."

The freighter's winch hummed, tracking the first load of cargo out of the hold. Much of it was Amy's luggage. "Guess I'm ready to do some work," Yerby said. To Mark he didn't look ready for anything but embalming, but it wasn't Mark's place to judge.

Ground personnel had extended the hatch steps when

the ship arrived; in the grip of transit psychosis, the flight crew had simply jumped or fallen out of the vessel. There was no railing. Mark led Yerby gingerly down to the hot soil.

"Hope Desiree's here with a blimp," Yerby said. "My wife," he added with an apologetic grimace. "Damned if I know why I ever married her. Drunk, I suppose."

Mark's lips pursed. It wasn't his place to comment on Yerby's attitudes or domestic arrangements, either.

Amy appeared at the hatch above them, gray-faced. She moved with short, shuffling steps like a mummy whose feet were still wrapped together. She started to walk out into space.

"Amy!" Mark shouted as he bounded up the ten steps a lot faster than he'd have bet he could manage in the aftermath of suspended animation. He caught Amy by the shoulders an instant before she went off the edge of the top step.

"Something hurts," Amy said in a tiny voice. Her eyes didn't point in quite the same direction. "I think my head hurts."

"Here, lad, I got her," Yerby said. He reached past from the step below Mark. "Jump clear and I'll lift her down. Didn't the little gadget work for you neither, darling? The doc showed me the best one and I bought it."

"Do you think—" Mark said. *Do you think you're in shape to carry jour sister, Yerby?* he'd have continued, but obviously Yerby did think that and nothing anybody else said was likely to change his mind.

Mark jumped the six feet to the ground. Yerby lifted his sister and carried her as delicately as porcelain down the unrailed steps. He must still have the hangover, but Mark supposed Yerby had a lot of experience doing things hungover. And probably dead drunk, too.

"I don't know," Amy said. "If it worked, then I'm never going to travel anywhere again. Oh, Yerby, I *hurt.*"

She was still wearing a net of fine wires with a lead to the pocket of her jacket. Mark removed the net and pulled a flat, four-inch square metal box from the pocket.

"My goodness," he said in horror. "You were using this? No wonder you've got a headache. My goodness, this is worse than nothing!"

"The doc said it was the best kind," Yerby said doubtfully. "It sure cost enough, I'll tell you that."

A dirigible had lifted from the Spiker's courtyard. Three individual flyers were circling closer. The upper surfaces of the flyers' thin, rigid wings were covered with solar cells. A small electric motor drove a propeller above the central spine, and the tubular frame beneath would hold two people if they were good friends.

"Twenty years ago," Mark said, "they thought you could lock your own brain patterns over those imposed by the ship's mechanism. Some people thought that. What really happened is the two systems set up harmonics that changed every time the ship transited to another bubble universe."

He glared at the device in his hand. "Look," he said, "I can teach you both how to bring your patterns into synch with the ship instead of fighting it. When the ship changes universes, you'll stay under but you'll shift too. That's what the newer electronics try to do, but none of them are really subtle enough and you don't *need* a machine."

"Guess we don't need this one," Yerby said. He took

the device, crushed it in his right hand, and dropped the remains on the hard soil. He stroked his sister's hair very gently. "You teach Amy if you would, lad," he said. "Me, well, the booze works well enough for me."

He looked up at the hatch and called, "Hello, Doc—"

Dr. Jesilind walked into the hatch coaming. He spun counterclockwise at the impact and pitched out of the hatchway. Jesilind hit the ground flat and lay there on his back. His face bore a dazed smile.

Mark walked over to Jesilind.

"Oh, don't worry about the doc," Yerby said. "When he comes out of the capsule, it's like he's been tying one on for a week. You know a drunk never hurts himself falling."

"I didn't know that," Mark said. He didn't believe it, either. "But I can't say I was terribly worried."

Jesilind wore a wire induction net like Amy's. Mark fished into the doctor's pocket and brought out an identical control box. He looked at it, shook his head, and put the box back where he'd found it.

Yerby raised an eyebrow. "Want me to take care of that one, too?" he asked.

Mark shrugged. "I think we ought to assume that Dr. Jesilind is capable of deciding such things for himself," he said. *Like you and your two quarts of gin, Yerby.* "I just wanted to make sure that he hadn't given Amy advice that he wouldn't take himself."

"Naw, he wouldn't do that," Yerby said. "It's just that what works for the doc didn't work so good for Amy, I guess. You know how delicate women are."

Amy straightened and pushed herself out of her brother's arms. "Delicate?" she said. "Because I thought you might find some better way to relax on Kilbourn than getting stinking drunk and wrecking a bar? Does that make me delicate, Yerby? Because if it does, you could use some delicacy yourself, brother!"

"Now, Amy, I wasn't drunk," Yerby said abashed. "Now, be a good girlie—"

"Yerby!" Amy said. "You can't help being a fool, but if you'll shut up you'll be able to conceal the fact longer. In the future please remember that my name is Amy or sister or Miss Bannock. Can you manage that?"

Mark turned his head so that he could pretend not to be hearing a family quarrel. There was no doubt of the brother and sister's affection for one another, but they really did come from different worlds.

And Mark came from a world different from either of theirs. Well, they were all together now. At least for the time being.

There was almost no wind over the spaceport. Two of the flyers landed simultaneously, passing one another in opposite directions. When the little wheels touched the ground, the wings tilted into air dams and the riders put their feet down to help slow the vehicles. One of the newcomers was a man clad in leather imprinted with the pattern of scales.

A woman rode the other flyer. She was short, stocky, and looked madder than a wet hen. "Well, there you are, Bannock!" she called, still within the framework of her flyer. "Decided to come home at last, did you? How long are you going to stay? As much as a week, maybe?"

"Desiree?" Yerby said. He looked surprised. "Ah, I thought you'd bring the blimp. I've got a lot of gear for—"

"Wait for you with the blimp, should I?" the woman said. Her outfit was much like Yerby's own, a leather vest over a checked shirt, with canvas trousers and boots that looked like they'd been made by an amateur. "No, thank you. I guess you can bring it back yourself—and you can walk to the grant, too. I just came to see if there'd be news that you'd managed to get your head knocked in by something even harder."

"Mark, this here's my wife Desiree," Yerby said with a broad, false smile. "Desiree, Mr. Maxwell here's a real gentleman from Quelhagen. Wait till you see—"

"Two more mouths to feed is what I see," Desiree snapped. She was at least half a dozen years older than her husband. She couldn't ever have been strikingly pretty, but if she managed to smile and let her hair down from its tight bun, she could have come a lot closer. "Him and your sister *and* your fine Dr. Jesilind's back, more's the pity."

"Madam!" Mark said. "I assure you I have no intention of trespassing on your hospitality!"

Though Mark had planned to put up at the caravansary until he could make more permanent arrangements, Greenwood didn't have a caravansary. Such amenities were for planets with considerable transit trade, while Greenwood was the end of the line—the farthest that human settlement went in this direction. *Well, the Spiker probably has rooms.*

"Just who's talking about mouths to feed, Desiree Cartwright?" Amy said, answering Mark's unasked question of whether the two women knew one another from Kilbourn. "My share of Dad's estate was twice what you brought with you to the marriage, so I'd say if anybody was eating what another provided, it's you!"

"Come along, lad," Yerby said to Mark in a stage whisper. "I guess Miss Altsheller didn't teach Amy nothing that keeps her from holding her own."

He shook his head. "And with Desiree, too, which I could never do in a million years. Sober."

The women continued their discussion. Amy's language and tones were refined, but as her brother said, that didn't prevent her from making her point.

Mark was blushing and horrified. It wasn't just that the scene was angry: love, joy, or sorrow would have embarrassed him just as much. On Quelhagen, people just *didn't let* their emotions out in public.

A dirigible settled beside the pile of cargo discharged from the starship. The external cover that streamlined the gasbags was about a hundred feet long and painted in streaks of red, yellow, and gold.

"Hey Chuck!" Yerby bellowed to the man in the dirigible's cab. "Do me a favor, will you? Run me and my gear out to the grant. Desiree came in the flyer."

"Can it wait till tomorrow, Yerby?" the pilot said. He was a round-faced man, young-looking but so completely bald that Mark wondered if he'd lost his hair from disease or an accident. "That's sixty miles there and sixty back, and I'd really like to get these seedlings in the hothouse today yet"

"Say, you don't think I'd put my sister Amy up at the Spiker, do you?" Yerby said. "Come on, Chuck. Remember how glad you were I was around to help you run pipe when your first well failed."

"I never said I wouldn't, did I?" Chuck grumbled. "C'mon, let's get loaded and maybe I can get some work done myself anyhow."

Yerby strode toward the cargo. "Tomorrow you and me'll go off hunting, lad," he said. He nodded in his wife's direction. "That'll give Desiree a while to cool down. Or anyways, we won't have to listen to her."

Mark grabbed a trunk and began to drag it toward the dirigible's cargo sling. He didn't comment on Yerby's plan.

But since Desiree was obviously angry about the amount of time her husband spent avoiding her, it struck Mark as an extremely bad plan in the long run.

7. Free as a Bird

Dawn on Greenwood was brilliant with layers of color—purple, mauve, orange, and Mark was willing to say he'd seen a streak of green for a good fifteen seconds. 'Birds' with furry wings and spike-toothed reptilian jaws lifted onto the morning breezes. Some of them were so big that at a distance Mark had mistaken them for human flyers, but smaller versions peeping and flapping around the Bannock compound helped him correct his identification.

"Ever flown one of these, lad?" Yerby asked as he lifted a flyer onto the slide that would give it a little extra speed for takeoff. Mark had hefted the flyer. It was amazingly delicate for its strength. On the ground at least he could handle it himself, though not with Yerby's casual aplomb.

"No sir," he said. When he was nervous he got formal again, too formal for Greenwood. "Yerby, I've driven ground cars and aircars, but never one of these. Or a dirigible."

The Bannock compound was on a knoll which sloped

gently on three sides toward the river that bent about the site at a half mile's distance. The launching slide projected out over the steep-sided gully to the north. Mark guessed the updraft here was pretty much constant.

Another slide dumped into the same gully all the trash from the twenty-odd people living in the compound.

The compound consisted of about a dozen buildings, mostly sheds and barns. The house sprawled. The initial construction was stone, but wings and an upper floor of cellulose-based plastic multiplied the volume many times. When Chuck's dirigible flew them in the evening before, Mark had seen the plastics plant and a sawmill on the bank of the river.

"You know," Mark said, "you're going to fill up this gully someday, so you might as well find another way to handle your garbage right now. There's package plants you could run off the fusion power supply you've already got. You could convert most of that to something useful."

He pointed to the multicolored filth straggling up the side of the gully. Creatures flitted over and burrowed through the mass. Besides native life-forms, Terran rats and insects had arrived with the settlers. That was true on virtually every human-colonized world.

"Aw, don't worry about the trash," Yerby said. He was checking that the wing's beryllium monocrystal stiffeners were securely fastened to the central spine of the same light, immensely strong, material. "Come spring and the rains, they'll scrub the ditch clean as a rocket nozzle."

"Wash it into the river?" Mark asked.

Yerby pinged a strut with a thumbnail. "That's right," he said.

It obviously didn't occur to the frontiersman that there might be anything wrong with the concept. For that matter, with fewer than three thousand humans on Greenwood, the native biosphere *could* handle the waste casually dumped into it . . . but the population wasn't going to remain so low, any more than that of Quelhagen had.

Mark grimaced. He'd come here to learn about the reality of the frontier. It was just that he didn't *like* some of what he was learning.

"There we go," Yerby said approvingly as he stepped back from the flyer. "It's pretty simple, lad. You sit here—"

He patted one of the two saddles. The riders could carry light objects on the crossways tray of monocrystal mesh behind them.

"—and you do with the control yoke what you want the flyer to do. The throttle's in the right grip—"

He caressed it.

"—but I never been in one of these things that I didn't have the motor flat out, and that wasn't near enough power to suit me."

Yerby grinned broadly and went on, "When you want to land, you crank this back—"

"This" was a lever of one-inch tubing, as sturdy as the flyer's spine. "—and the wings tilt. But you better be on the ground when you do that, because you're sure going to be there an eyeblink later."

There were half a dozen flyers in the three-sided shed that protected them from most of the rain. One had no motor, and the wings of another lay unmounted beside the body. An aircar that seemed to have been pieced together from several very different vehicles rested on blocks at the end of the shed.

The Bannocks had two dirigibles, one of them a general-utility vehicle like Chuck's. Yerby's was still in its shed. It had a royal blue skin except for a tear near the nose that had been repaired with black fabric. The other was a heavy-lift platform, now skidding a three-hundred-foot tree trunk toward the sawmill.

Amy walked toward them from the house, wearing trousers and a jacket she'd brought from Kilbourn. The garments were sturdy, but they were more professionally cut than most of what Mark had seen on Greenwood. The Bannock compound converted cellulose into a coarse rayon that some residents used for leggings and coveralls as well as tarpaulins, but the state of tailoring was as crude as the material.

"Just showing Mark how to fly one of these," Yerby called cheerfully to his sister. "I'm going to take him out hunting and see a bit of Greenwood."

"Right," Amy said. "I thought I'd come along and fly him. The two of us are light enough that one flyer can carry us."

She smiled at Mark. "If that's all right? It's trickier than my brother probably told you. It'd be a shame to lose you down there—" She nodded to the garbage-filled gully. "—before you'd had a full day on the planet."

Yerby's lips pursed. "I don't want anything happening to you, g—Amy," he said. "These flyers, they don't have batteries like the ones you're used to on Kilbourn. If you fly under a cloud, the motor cuts out *bing*."

"Yerby, I love the dishes you bought me," Amy said. She was still smiling, but her tone was a degree or two chillier. "That doesn't mean *I'm* made of thin glass. If you think you're going to keep me wrapped in fluff, then I'll leave and book a room in the Spiker. All right?"

"Just be careful, that's all I'm saying," Yerby grumbled. "And they don't have rooms at the Spiker, they got bunks, and don't be talking about that even for a joke."

He walked over to the shed to get a second flyer. Amy stepped up so that she straddled the left saddle with her feet on the ramp. "Hop on," she directed Mark. "Push the handbar and run along to give us a little more oomph."

She switched on the electric motor. The prop spun to a whine above them. It was still feathered so it wouldn't bite. "Ready?" she called as she flicked a thumb control to coarsen the propeller pitch. "Go!"

Amy started running forward with one hand pushing on the bar and the other controlling the yoke. Mark ran and pushed too. *If Amy shoves the yoke forward as we leave the ramp, the next thing I'm going to see is a gullyful of garbage approaching very fast.*

The ramp dropped from under Mark's feet. His fanny hit the saddle, but his stomach kept right on diving. Wind rushing up the gully wall made his jacket balloon away from his torso.

Amy leaned to the right. The flyer banked and climbed, fully airborne. She kept it in a tight spiral to gain height. The feeling was glorious, absolutely glorious. The craft's nervous twitching didn't frighten Mark, as he'd expected it would. After a few moments, he deliberately raised his hands from the bar.

"We'll circle till Yerby gets up," Amy said matter-of-factly. "Besides, I want to get some altitude. Though the solar cells seem to be in better shape than I was afraid they'd be."

The slow climbing turns took them over the main house at a hundred feet of altitude. A man on the second-story deck waved to them.

Besides the folk who worked for or with Yerby, three other men were staying at the compound. Two were casual acquaintances, headed toward the Spiker but in no great hurry to get there. The third was some relative or other of Desiree's visiting the Bannocks until a starship delivered a power plant to replace the one that had failed at his own steading.

Desiree's complaint about "useless mouths" was obviously without real significance; it was just something to throw at her husband to show that she was angry. Mark didn't entirely blame the lady for objecting to Dr. Jesilind's continued presence, though.

Yerby launched his own flyer without the careful inspection he'd lavished on the machine he offered Mark. He climbed toward them, but he didn't gain altitude much faster than they had. Yerby was even heavier than he looked, because his muscular body was so dense. Besides his own weight, Yerby carried a hamper of food and a monopulse laser with a built-in solar charging system. The weapon weighed a good thirty pounds.

"This is a beautiful planet," Amy said. Despite the moan of the prop, the flyer was so quiet that she could talk in a normal voice. "Except for the settled part. That's as ugly as a picked scab."

Logging had cleared the larger trees on both sides of the valley east of the compound. The slopes were still dotted with the vivid green of new growth, however. The crews were taking the larger trees for processing as timber and cellulose base, but they weren't clear-cutting. The area would regrow.

Rather than argue—because this much of Yerby's operation seemed sustainable—Mark said, "I was surprised that Yerby wanted to bring Alliance soldiers to Greenwood. On Quelhagen, we're trying to get rid of them. And not succeeding."

"That was his friend's idea," Amy said. "Jesilind." She made the name sound like a curse. "On Kilbourn the Protector only has a few soldiers, but she's threatening to bring more in. She's claims she's taken over the planetary finances, but the elected council keeps meeting and says her decrees aren't valid without their approval."

She looked at Mark and grinned. "Which means that most people don't pay taxes to either side. That suits ordinary folk well enough, and since the council's mostly rich people it suits them even better. But the Protector doesn't have anything to pay her staff with, and it doesn't suit her at all."

"All right, let's head north!" Yerby called across the hundred yards separating his flyer from the other. "I'll show you a place prettier than anything you ever seen!"

They flew north at thirty miles an hour, the best speed the heavily laden flyers could manage in still air. Amy stayed five hundred feet up, so the flight seemed more leisurely than it would have if the trees had been closer.

"There's no need for Alliance troops anywhere in the

Digits," Amy added. "Anywhere at all, really. There'll never be another war. The Treaty of Cozumel has held for twenty years, and there's no reason it shouldn't hold forever."

"There sure aren't any troops on Dittersdorf," Mark said in what he meant to sound like agreement.

He'd had too good an education to believe that peace between the Atlantic Alliance and the Greater East Asian Co-Prosperity Sphere meant peace for all time for all men, though. Particularly with the trouble brewing between Earth and the settlers of most colonized worlds.

8. Living Toward Tomorrow

As the sun rose, the motors gained power and the flyers became noticeably more agile, though their speed didn't increase greatly. Yerby continued to lead them north.

Mark drew Amy out about Miss Altsheller's Academy. At first, Amy was embarrassed to discuss her education with a Harvard graduate. Mark did his best to convince her that she had no reason to feel ashamed. Sure, the General Knowledge curriculum was scant and dated by Earth standards, but Miss Altsheller's emphasis on deportment made her students as civilized and cultured as anyone raised on Quelhagen.

Mark had been taught to learn. Amy had been taught to believe that humans could make themselves better. Not just richer: everybody on the frontier believed that or they'd have stayed where they were born.

Mark wasn't even sure he could define "better." His education had taught him that you had to look at matters from every side, that every viewpoint was valid.

The thing was, an ivory tower attitude meant that the viewpoint of four Zenith thugs was just as valid as that of the innocent traveler they were going to beat the hell out of for fun. Mark didn't feel neutral at all about *that* concept.

The flyers sailed over a rugged crest. Before them spread a broad valley. Trees were scattered sparsely among much lower vegetation. It was the first natural open space of any extent that Mark had seen on Greenwood.

"Here we go!" Yerby called. "But watch where I land!"

He brought his flyer around low to the far side of a cliff jutting from the ridge like an axe blade. Amy followed her brother, but she was frowning and her hands tightened minusculely on the control yoke.

Mark concentrated on looking relaxed. He figured that was the most help he could give at the moment. Besides, he'd learned that sometimes when you faked an attitude, you tricked yourself into making it real.

It wasn't real this time. He was still scared.

On the other side of the cliff, a waterfall leaped a hundred feet from the top of the crag. Yerby brought his flyer in to a jittery landing on the area fringing the creek that formed at the base of the falls. The frontiersman's boots and the flyer's wheels kicked up sand as he braked to a halt, then turned in to the vegetation to give Amy a clear approach.

"Sometimes," Amy said, visibly relaxing, "Yerby shows better sense than I give him credit for."

Amy landed them easily on the sandbar, though in the moment before the whole wing lifted in a huge aileron

Mark thought they were going to do an endo on the soft sand and come to rest upside down. "Oh!" he said, amazed at how relieved he felt to be safely on the ground. Above them the propeller whirred softly to stillness.

The leaves of the nearby vegetation were broad, but they sprouted directly from the soil the way those of Terran grasses did. What looked like a smooth carpet from the air was actually a varied mixture of species, but only a few grew more than three feet high. A tree rooted in the cliff face had a trunk like wires twisted together rather than a single stem.

"Take a look to your left, both of you," Yerby said in a quiet voice. "Easy, now."

A creature the size of a large dog poked its head out of a burrow twenty feet away. Its eyes extended on short stalks. They swept the creature's immediate surroundings, then focused on the flyers. Mark held very still. The creature snapped back into its hole as if pulled by an overstretched rubber band. Its feet immediately drummed a warning underground.

"We call them pooters," Yerby said. "They do love a tree, near as much as my logging crew does, but mostly they eat this short stuff."

He plucked a clump of "grass" from the soil. The tap-root was eighteen inches long at the point it broke. "Any place the ground's soft enough they can burrow, you're likely to find them. Cute little beggars and they're pretty good eating."

Mark noticed that the frontiersman hadn't bothered to unstrap the flashgun from his flyer's rack. "Aren't there any predators on Greenwood?" he asked.

"Sure there is," Yerby said. "Nothing we need to worry about, though. They're mostly birds—that's why the pooler was scared of our flyers. Some of the really biggest ones, they run on the ground, but even they used to be birds before they got too big to fly. You'd need to go a good five hundred miles south to find any of them anyways."

"I was just curious," Mark said. It wasn't entirely a lie.

"Yerby, you're right," said Amy, looking up at the waterfall sliding through the air in rainbow splendor. "This place is beautiful. The whole planet is."

Yerby beamed as though she'd praised him personally. "Ain't it, though?" he said. "You know? I'd like to keep it like this."

"This corner?" Amy said. "This waterfall, you mean."

Yerby shook his head and grimaced. "Look, I know it don't make sense, but I'd like to keep Greenwood pretty much the way it is. You know, I just come back from Kilbourn and the way it's built up—that's too many people."

"How big is Kilbourn?" Mark asked sharply. He was trying to connect this Yerby Bannock with the man who let freshets flush his garbage into the river.

"About a million and a half," Amy said. She looked surprised also. "The population's been growing fast all through my lifetime, ever since the Treaty of Cozumel."

"And yeah, I know what you're thinking, Mark," Yerby said. "I could do a better job keeping things neat than I do. But hell, people ain't perfect, and the more of them you put together the worse they each of them gets. There's cities on Kilbourn so crowded I wouldn't board a dog there."

And how would you feel about Landingplace or Zenith's capital, New Paris? Mark thought. Aloud he said, "You know, I think a recycling plant could pay for itself in a year or two. A few years."

"Have you talked about this with Dr. Jesilind?" Amy said. "His vision for Greenwood is huge city-buildings, arcologies, like they have on Earth. Everything self-contained, everyone living in identical boxes with identical parks and artificial rain at programmed times."

Yerby shook his head glumly, looking out over the savannah. "I know," he said. "He's a smart man, the doc is, educated like I'll never be. Only . . ."

The big man leaned down and thrust his hand like a spade into the hole from which he'd plucked the grass. He crumbled the loam through his fingers. "Thing is," Yerby said softly, "there's plenty of planets. No reason to put a lot of folks on every one of them. And there's plenty already built up now, like Kilbourn. Some folks, that's how they want to live."

He scattered the last of the black dirt at his feet and straightened. "Kilbourn, it's not going to go away. Earth's not going to go away. People who want to live tight together already have plenty of places to do that. There's other folks who need to be able to stick their fingers in the dirt and look at a waterfall with just a couple friends. I'd like Greenwood to stay a place you could do that."

He laughed uncomfortably. "Well, I guess I sound pretty silly to a couple educated people like you, don't I? Don't know what came over me to talk like that."

"I didn't hear anything silly," Mark said quietly. He squatted and rubbed bare dirt between his thumb and forefinger. "You know," he added, "it could be that more people need the chance to sit with a few friends and a lot of nature than know they do."

The pooter stuck its head out of the hole again. Mark winked at it. After a moment, the creature snipped off a clump of grass and began to ingest it, bite by bite.

As they watched the creature eat, Yerby Bannock said, "Where d'ye suppose a man would find one of them recycling plants you talked about, Mark lad?"

9. Another Country Heard From

As the flyers rose above the ridgeline, their motors running strongly in the midafternoon sunlight, the tiny radio attached to the hub of Amy's control yoke crackled, "—*need help soonest. I got a gang of Zenith surveyors and their ship parked in my soybeans. Anybody who can hear me, come lend a hand. This is Dagmar Wately and I need help! Over.*"

"*This is Yerby Bannock, Dagmar,*" the speaker resumed instantly. Mark could hear Yerby's voice faintly from the flyer ahead of them a beat or two after the same words had arrived over the radio. "*I'm about ten minutes out. Anybody who can hear my signal, grab a persuader and come help Dagmar Wately talk to some Zeniths in her soybean field. That's southwest of her compound. Out!*"

Yerby banked his flyer, swinging west by northwest from the south heading he'd set to go home. He bellowed over his shoulder, "You kids get back to the compound. Send George and Elmont out to Dagmar's soybeans if they haven't already gotten the message."

Amy continued to pull her craft around to follow her brother. She looked at Mark in an unspoken question.

"I don't know what I can do to help him," Mark said, "but I wouldn't feel right not to try."

Amy smiled. "Thanks," she said. "For not telling me I'm a girl."

"You are a girl," Mark said. "But I don't see that you can be much more useless than I am."

Amy's laugh trilled merrily across the sky. She held station a little above and behind her brother's flyer, just as she had on the way north. Yerby looked back at them and glared, but he didn't waste his breath shouting further orders.

Nearly a thousand acres of soybeans filled a valley similar to the one from which Mark and his friends had just come. The Terran crop was a green with less gray in it than the native vegetation growing near rock outcrops that hadn't been plowed. The starship sat like a troll in the midst of the rolling field on four great outrigger pontoons.

Frequent heating and cooling by magnetic eddy currents colored the upper surfaces of the ship's spherical hull. The lower curves were blackened by carbon not from the rocket fuel—that was surely hydrogen and oxygen—but from the loam and vegetation that the exhaust had incinerated as it blew a crater in the field on landing.

A handful of air-cushion jeeps, each holding two people in orange coveralls, drove across the field. One of them was nearly a mile from the starship. The survey party was setting fluorescent white rods in the ground at intervals of several hundred yards.

The starship's main hatch was lowered to the ground. A flyer like the Bannocks' sat close by. A figure in Greenwood leather waved as she argued on the boarding ramp with three figures in tailored white uniforms. Several other flyers approached in the clear sky, but none of them were as close as the Bannock craft.

Yerby landed at the edge of the ramp. Amy came down a fraction of a second behind him, dropping from the sky with a verve that left Mark's stomach fifty feet behind. The flyer's frame flexed dangerously. Mark tried to take some of the shock on his own legs and managed to bury his feet ankle-deep in the soft field.

"Amy, child," Yerby said as he got out of his flyer's space-framed cockpit, "why don't you stick by the radio and relay things to the neighbors flying in. I'd like them to stay in the air just for now."

He didn't look back at the other flyer. Mark hadn't seen Yerby unstrap the heavy flashgun from his rack, but it was cradled now in the crook of his left arm. The weapon's squat barrel, a Cassegrain laser, was six inches in diameter and only a foot long.

Mark stayed a pace behind and to the left as Yerby strolled up the ramp toward the four waiting figures. "'Lo, Dagmar," Yerby said. Even standing below them on the slope, he was as tall as any of the three Zeniths, two men and a woman. "Like you to meet Mark Maxwell, a friend of mine. Gather you've got a problem here?"

Dagmar Wately was younger than Desiree but of similar build. She wore leather breeches and a jacket whose loops and pockets were full of tools. She thumbed toward the uniformed trio. "I come out when I heard them land," she said. "Thought they might be in trouble. Seems they're from Zenith and they think they got a right to be here."

"We do have a right to be here," said the younger of the two men. His epaulettes were orange, like the garments of the survey crewmen in the jeeps. "We're laying out a city of fifty thousand here. The construction crews will arrive as soon as we've completed our end. The first of the immigrant ships from Earth will be landing before the year is out."

"There's no mistake about our landfall," said the older man. "We're right in the center of the grant. You can come with me to the bridge and check the navigational data if you like."

Yerby grinned. He looked as cheerful as he had the moment before he knocked the heads of two Zeniths together in the caravansary. "You know, Dagmar," he said, "I'd always thought this was part of your grant."

"You know damned well it is, Bannock!" Dagmar said. "We fought long enough over our boundary lines that we know where each other's property lies, don't we?"

"You're talking about Hestia grants," the woman in uniform said. "We're employed by Vice-Protector Finch of Zenith under Zenith grants. If you've got a problem, take it up with him."

"Ah, but you lot are closer than Finch, ain't you?" Yerby said. "Amy, love, tell the boys to start picking up them spikes, will you? I reckon there's not much of a survey without markers."

The Zenith with orange surveyor's tabs reached into his pocket. Dagmar kicked him in the crotch. The Zenith gasped and bent forward. Mark dipped a gun out of the pocket, then stepped clear so that the overbalanced man could tumble down the ramp. Dagmar kicked him in the ribs as he fell past.

The uniformed woman took a step backward. She touched her own jacket pocket.

"Please don't do that," Mark said to her politely. "I won't hit you, but Ms. Wately will."

The flyers were dipping down across the soybean field. One buzzed an air-cushion Jeep. While a man piloted the flyer, the woman slipped from the other saddle and stood on the lower frame to snatch a surveyor's cap.

Another flyer pivoted around a survey stake—the white rods contained transponders to provide precise measurement to the satellite the ship would have dropped in orbit—and the pilot himself snatched it out of the ground. Mark wouldn't have thought that was possible.

Yerby continued to smile at the two Zeniths still standing. Mark looked at the gun he'd taken from the groaning man. It was a nerve scrambler like the one the baggage handler had carried. No way Mark could rip the weapon apart the way Yerby'd done the other one, but . . .

The upper surface of the ramp was made of plates welded to an internal framework. There was a slight gap between the edges of the two plates at Mark's feet. He stuck the needle point of the pistol's muzzle between them and snapped it off with a quick twist.

"You can't *do* this!" the older Zenith cried.

"Now," said Yerby, "there's another difference of opinion."

The jeeps were rushing back toward the ship, jouncing high at every bump and grounding jarringly as the plenum chamber spilled air. For a moment Mark wasn't sure he should have destroyed the nasty little gun, but it was pretty obvious that the surveyors were fleeing rather than coming to help their officers.

All the survey stakes were gone. Generally flyers landed nearby and took off again from the field as soon as the pilot had pulled up the trophy, but one fellow managed to blast a rod with his flashgun while his buddy flew from the other saddle.

"You have no right to do this!" the older Zenith shouted. He must be the ship's captain. "You have no right!"

Yerby stepped off the edge of the ramp so that the first of the jeeps could race aboard past the officers. Mark and Dagmar Wately jumped down beside him. A flyer banked away from the hatch as the pilot cried, "Yee-*hah!*"

"I have all law and justice on my side!" Yerby said. "And besides that—"

He pointed his flashgun at the undersurface of the starship. Mark turned and covered his eyes with his hands. The laser fired with a hiss*crack!* The target clanged like a huge bell. A little of the intense saffron pulse leaked through Mark's flesh.

"What are you doing?" screamed the female officer from the edge of the hatch where the jeep's passage had pushed her. "You're shooting at us!"

"I just blew out one of your nozzles," Yerby said calmly. He unsnapped the charging mechanism from the flashgun's butt and spread the sail to the sun. "You got seven more, that'll get you up well enough. But—"

The big frontiersman had never stopped smiling.

"—I'd suggest you take off before this fellow recharges in three minutes or so."

A second jeep drove up the ramp and collided with the first, which was blocking the entrance to the hold. The third and fourth vehicles halted by the outriggers. The surveyors scrambled aboard on foot, glancing over their shoulders in panic at Mark and the Greenwoods.

The starship's rocket nozzles were tungsten, forged hollow so that the liquid-hydrogen fuel could circulate within and chill them in operation. Yerby's laser bolt had blown a fist-sized hole in the outer jacket of the nearest nozzle. If it was used again, the uncooled metal would vaporize in a bright green flash.

The fifth and last jeep skidded to a stop. The Zenith officers were already aboard. The last pair of surveyors ran up the ramp as it lifted.

"I think," Yerby said in satisfaction, "we'd best put a little distance between us and them. They're going to tear up the landscape just as bad leaving as they did when they arrived."

Mark's knees were suddenly so weak that he thought he was going to fall down. He didn't, but he was thankful for Amy's help as he climbed onto the flyer's saddle.

10. Party Time

Where floodlights on the eaves of the Bannock house illuminated the ground, two fiddles and a locally made double bass played tunes for several dozen dancers. Only about half the couples were a man with a woman. A number of men (far in the majority at the gathering) pirouetted by themselves.

At the other end of the courtyard, vocal music wailed moodily from a recorder with over a thousand songs loaded into its memory. The selection keypad didn't work, so the unit repeated over and over a Zenith hit from twenty years before, "Apartment House Heart."

Mark sat on a shed's flat roof, watching the festivities. Eighty or a hundred people ate, danced, and drank— especially drank—in general good fellowship. Flyers and dirigibles in profusion sat on the slopes surrounding the compound.

Folk had gathered spontaneously at the Bannock compound in the aftermath of running the surveyors off. Those who'd been present in Dagmar's soybeans bragged about their heroism to neighbors come too late to take part.

"Does this happen often?" Mark said to Amy beside him. "I'd thought life on the frontier would be, well, lonely."

"There's more of a community here than there is in a Kilbourn neighborhood," Amy said. "They must have come from a hundred miles around, though. Yerby's grant is fifty miles square—that's twenty-five hundred square miles. Most of the neighbors have big tracts too."

The impromptu party would go on at least overnight. The majority of visitors had come in flyers that couldn't take off again until daybreak. Most of the dirigibles had battery backup for their solar collectors, but navigation across the nighted landscape was too chancy to attempt without need.

"I suppose that'll change when Greenwood gets settled," Mark said. "Funny that more people means less fellowship."

He couldn't help sounding sad. It wasn't that folk here were friendly, exactly. Yerby and Dagmar had obviously had their differences over boundary lines, for example. Nevertheless, the two grant holders were members of a single community. Mark was sure that Dagmar would have come equally fast to Yerby's aid in a crisis.

"Do you think that Greenwood has to be settled like Kilbourn, then?" Amy asked. "I think what Yerby's talking about is perfectly possible. There's a practically infinite number of human habitable planets, so why should any one of them have more than, say, ten thousand residents?"

"Yeah, I agree," Mark said. "But how are you going to keep people *from* settling? You heard those Zeniths today.

They were surveying for a planned community of fifty thousand. So long as somebody can make a fortune by putting up housing for immigrant drafts from Earth, that's what he's going to do. Maybe the immigrants would be happier scattered in little communities of a hundred or so like here, but that's not the way the planners in Paris arrange things."

"Maybe it's time for Paris to stop making the arrangements," Amy said.

"There's enough people on Quelhagen saying that the Protector's only in charge because she's got a couple thousand troops," Mark said. "But she *does* have the troops."

Dr. Jesilind walked by the shed, peering at the faces of the folk he passed. Mark held himself very still, hoping Jesilind would continue on. With the same thought in her mind, Amy pulled her dangling legs up onto the roof.

The motion drew Jesilind's attention. "Ah, there you are, Amy!" he said. "And, ah, Mr. Maxwell."

The shed was seven feet high in front, where Mark and Amy sat, though it slanted lower in the back. The doctor mentally measured the effort needed to mount, then decided to remain where he was. "I'd been hoping to find you," he said. "Amy, could I bring you refreshment?"

The trio began to play "Jimmie Crack Corn." The bass had a remarkably pure resonance for an instrument that looked as crude as a packing crate. The dancers formed for a reel, regardless of the sex of their pairings. More spectators joined the circle, many of them holding drinking jars of Bannock whiskey in one hand.

Amy's fingers drummed on the edge of the roof, a ridged plate of cellulose plastic rather than boards of raw wood that would need shingles to be rainproof. "No thank you," she said. She turned her face deliberately toward Mark and continued their discussion with, "If Greenwood had its own government, it could limit density of development."

"That's a fine idea, but it won't work, dear girl," Jesilind said from beneath them. The doctor's voice made it clear that he understood law and government. Amy was simply naive. "Since Mr. Maxwell and your brother failed in their mission to get troops from Dittersdorf—"

Mark stiffened. He didn't speak.

"—the only government Greenwood's going to get is some flunky from the Zenith bureaucracy. According to Yerby, the surveyors today said the investor they were working for was the Vice-Protector of Zenith. I don't imagine he's going to appoint a vicar who'll limit immigration."

"I didn't have to hear Yerby," Amy said. "I was there, Doctor. While you were no doubt at your studies."

"Amy," Mark said. He'd decided to ignore Jesilind's comments. "I agree with you, but people just don't do things the way they ought to."

"We'd better start doing things the way we ought to," Amy snapped. "Because if it's mankind versus the universe, Mark, the universe is going to win sooner or later! We can't just go on turning every planet we settle into a garbage dump."

"Well, Yerby's going to put in a package system," Mark said to soothe her. He didn't disagree with Amy, but he didn't see any point in getting worked up about what couldn't be changed.

A woman peered closely at the recorder and began

hammering at the keypad to get it to play another song. "Apartment House Heart" continued, but the singer's rich tenor voice shifted upward into a cheeping falsetto.

"Amy dear," Jesilind said, "this is a frontier. You can't expect people to be as delicate as the residents of a settled world like you're used to on Kilbourn."

"Did you look at the downwind side of the Spiker when we took off in the blimp?" Amy said bitterly. "There's a stockyard there. People drive herds to the port and slaughter them as outgoing cargo. They just let the blood and waste drain into the river."

"Yeah, I saw that," Mark agreed unhappily.

"Regrettable no doubt," said Jesilind, "but folk living so close to the edge of raw nature have no surplus for civilized amenities. Why, they can't even afford to pay a medical man properly."

"Hey, lookee there!" bellowed a man standing on the upper deck of the house. "Look east!"

He pointed. The bright lights directly above him threw the harsh shadow of his outstretched arm across the dancers in the courtyard. "There's aircars coming! Zeniths coming back, I'll bet you!"

A good score of the Greenwoods hopped the low courtyard wall and trotted—sometimes staggered; a lot of Bannock whiskey had gone down the hatch—toward the vehicles in which they'd come. Folk hadn't brought guns into a neighbor's compound, but most had come armed when they answered Dagmar's appeal. Those hunting weapons were strapped to the flyers' decks or racked in the cabins of dirigibles.

Apart from that, the crowd didn't appear to be much

concerned. People moved to where the house and other structures didn't block their view of the oncoming cars.

Mark hopped down and offered a hand to Amy. Dr. Jesilind had vanished into the house. Perhaps it would have been better to say that except for him the crowd didn't appear to be much concerned.

"Let's find Yerby," Amy said. "I saw him dancing."

The aircars approached a hundred feet in the air. Their multicolored running lights glittered like Christmas ornaments, and a great floodlight in the bow of each vehicle slanted its beam down onto the treetops.

"They're so quiet," Amy murmured as she led Mark through the milling guests.

"I guess they are," he agreed. It hadn't occurred to him that the ducted fans' muted whine was in any way unusual. The racket made by the rented car on Dittersdorf would have been unthinkable on Quelhagen or Earth. Kilbourn, for all the Bannocks' talk of the planet being built-up and civilized, obviously didn't have strict ordinances against noise pollution.

The cars hovered above the compound. Downwash from their powerful fans swirled dust and light objects. Folk moved naturally to the edges of the courtyard and let the vehicles settle.

Yerby was coming out of the house when Mark and Amy met him. He'd put on a green cloth coat with fur lapels. The fabric shimmered and sparkled in the light. Mark didn't recall ever in his life having seen an uglier garment.

"Hey Yerby!" a man called. "What do you want us to do?" Forty others muttered agreement.

"Yerby, the aircars are Quelhagen manufacture," Mark

said. He shouted to be heard. He had to push a man away to keep the press of locals from blocking him.

Yerby gestured the crowd aside and put his big arms protectively around the shoulders of his sister and Mark. "Thank you, lad," he said. "I'd have guessed they were Zeniths. Well, anybody's welcome at my house if he knows how to behave. Let's us go talk to them."

The cars were big eight-person enclosed vehicles. There were built on similar chassis, but one of them had utilitarian appointments while the other was a limousine. The latter had panels of inlaid wood and its metalwork was plated with wavy bands of gold and platinum. Metal itself hadn't been of any particular value since space travel brought asteroids within reach, but workmanship like this aircar's had never been cheap.

The plain vehicle's doors popped open first. The first three men to exit wore beige uniforms. They trotted to the limousine to open the doors. Four guards in Quelhagen business dress followed the flunkies. They held fat, two-handed weapons of some sort. Their initial intention was probably to look tough. Mark grinned to see their bravado wilt when they took in the frontiersmen—and women—surrounding them; The guards looked like boats ringed by rocky cliffs.

"'Tain't polite to carry a gun into another fellow's place unasked," Desiree Bannock said, stepping up to the nearest guard. She had a voice that would cut glass. "Where were you raised, anyhow?"

She seized the gun. The man holding it resisted. Desiree kneed him between the legs. "That's the spirit, Desiree!" another woman shouted drunkenly.

Desiree tossed the gun into the vehicle and eyed the other guards. They quickly obeyed the unspoken demand.

A fussy-looking official got out of the front of the limousine while two men and a woman of obvious wealth were handed from the back by the uniformed servants. The official said—to Yerby; when Yerby was present, he was the focus of most attention, "my principals have come to meet with Mr. Yerby Bannock. Please have the goodness to summon him."

"If your principals can't speak for themselves, they came a danged long way for nothing, didn't they?" Yerby said. The official wore a little round-brimmed hat. Yerby tweaked it down over the man's eyes and turned to the wealthy folk. "You lot are from Quelhagen, I hear. Who are you?"

The trio looked nonplussed. One of the guards started forward. A Greenwood put a hand on the guard's shoulder, swung him around, and offered him a jar with six ounces of raw whiskey.

"Madame, gentlemen," Mark said with a crisp nod, "you'll appreciate that Quelhagen caste distinctions are out of place on Greenwood." He smiled. He could hear his father in his mind, forming the words that Mark only had to speak. "Furthermore, you realize that you've intruded uninvited on a man's home and at the very least owe him a prompt explanation."

"I'm Elector Daniels," said the man who appeared to be in his late fifties. "This is Ms. Macey—"

The woman bobbed her head in formal politeness. The Macey family's various branches accounted for up to ten percent of Quelhagen's net planetary worth.

"—and Mr. Holperin." Holperin was a little older than Daniels. He had a nose like a knife blade and steel-hard eyes. "We landed two days ago at Wanker's Doodle and came to here to meet Mr. Bannock when we heard reports of today's events."

"They couldn't have come from the Doodle in no more time than that!" a Greenwood said in amazement. Wanker's Doodle was the community four hundred miles to the northwest of the Spiker. It was the only other port on Greenwood with both a full-sized magnetic mass and an automated ground-control transponder for hands-off landings.

Mark knew that aircars like these could have made the run in an hour and a bit if the drivers pushed, as they surely had. The trio must have brought the vehicles with them. The cost would be enormous, but it bought the Quelhagens a mobility unmatched by anybody else on the planet.

"Well, you met me," Yerby said. He stuck his thumbs under his waistband and stood with his arms akimbo. He wasn't exactly being hostile, but he wanted the outsiders to be very clear of his superior status.

Mark glanced at the crowd around him. He'd only been on Greenwood a few days, but he didn't feel like an outsider. To the local people he was Yerby Bannock's friend, and that was as honorable a status as any on a planet where equality was the universal religion.

These folk from Quelhagen must have thought they'd just arrived in Hell's waiting room, though. The Greenwoods were rough men mixed with a few women who could only told apart by their lack of beards. All of them had been drinking; most were drunk by Quelhagen standards, and a fair number of those closest were armed. The locals were dressed crudely (or outlandishly, which was even worse to the muted taste of Quelhagen aristocrats), and the overhead lighting threw harsh shadows across their faces.

The official whose job was to arrange protocol hadn't spoken since Yerby pulled his cap down. "Can we go somewhere private?" Ms. Macey said doubtfully. She looked as if she would have dived back into the car if she'd thought there was a chance of escaping from the compound.

"Madame, sirs," Mark said. "You're in no danger, I assure you. You're just an interesting exhibit, is all."

"Yerby," said Amy decisively, "why don't we take our guests into the house? They'd probably like something other than whiskey to drink after their journey."

"Hmpf!" Yerby snorted. "Nothing wrong with my whiskey. But sure, you folks come in the parlor with us."

He turned to the crowd in general and bellowed, "Boys, make sure the rest of our guests see what Greenwood hospitality's like. I don't want nobody sober enough to stand come dawn."

The locally hand-crafted furnishings in most rooms of the Bannock house were solid, tasteful, and to Mark's mind extremely attractive. He suspected he could export similar pieces to Quelhagen and sell them at a profit despite the transportation cost.

The parlor alone was furnished entirely with off-planet material. No two pieces were of the same style. Most of the furniture was badly copied from Terran antiques. On three of the four walls hung holoprints of fantasy castles. Yerby was so proud of the parlor's imported splendor that there was no possibility that he would bring his foreign guests anywhere else.

Yerby probably didn't notice the way the visitors blinked as they walked into the parlor, but Mark did. He cringed in embarrassment for an instant before he realized that neither he nor anybody else in the room had a right to sneer at Yerby Bannock. Yerby's taste was his own business.

Yerby opened an extruded-plastic reproduction of a Queen Anne sideboard and displayed a double row of imported liquors. "Name your poison!" he said expansively to the Quelhagens.

"Actually, we had refreshments on the flight from Wanker's Doodle," Elector Daniels said. "If you're Mr. Yerby Bannock, we have a business proposition to discuss privately."

"I'm him," Yerby said. He took a glass for himself, picked a bottle of Chartreuse—apparently for the color—and poured. "That's my sister Amy—she's part owner here, so don't just take her for a girl—"

Amy and Ms. Macey both stiffened as though they'd been goosed by broomsticks.

Yerby didn't notice. He seemed surprised at how thick the liqueur was. "And the lad's Mark Maxwell, my legal advisor. He's a Quelhagen like you are."

Dr. Jesilind opened the door from the hallway and peered at the gathering. He'd just decided the room was safe to enter when Amy deliberately slammed and locked the panel. Yerby raised an eyebrow, but he didn't comment on his sister's action.

"Would that be Mark *Lucius*-son Maxwell?" Mr. Holperin asked. "Pardon me for a personal question."

Mark bowed. "That's correct, sir," he said. "Perhaps you're acquainted with my father?"

"He was representing the other party in a contract dispute," Holperin said with a wintry smile. "A most excellent attorney, your father. He cost me a great deal of money."

He bowed to Mark in turn.

"Money's what we're here about," Daniels said, taking charge of the discussion, "We represent the investment group that owns Greenwood. The undeveloped portion of Greenwood, that is."

"You're the owners of the base grants issued by Protector Greenwood?" Mark clarified. He *wasn't* any sort of legal advisor, but he could translate Daniels's language into terms Yerby understood.

"Yes, we bought the undivided tracts over a number of years," Daniels agreed. "The value of the investment should have risen sharply now that Greenwood is ripe for large-scale immigration. Recent Zenith agitation clouds our title, however."

The investors have gotten the grants dirt cheap because of those Zenith claims. To make the profits they intended, they'd have to convince would-be settlers that Hestia grants were valid.

"I don't see what that's got to do with me," Yerby said. "You need to take it up with Zenith, right?"

"We will indeed be exercising all our legal remedies, Mr. Bannock," Holperin said. "But that won't do us a great deal of good if the situation on the ground has changed in the meanwhile."

"If there's a city of fifty thousand in the middle of a tract," Ms. Macey said bluntly, "all we can sell is a lawsuit. And that's what the matter has to do with you. As you saw today, the Zenith syndicate is regranting *all* the Hestia tracts, settled as well as open. The city could as easily be on your property as ours."

"Oh," said Yerby. His smile made Mark tighten up before his conscious mind recalled that the big frontiersman was his friend. "I don't think they'll be settling my property any time soon. Nor that of any of my neighbors."

"Exactly our point," Daniels said. "We're your neighbors too, Mr. Bannock, and like good neighbors we intend to help you. Our attorneys will defend your rights as if they were our own."

"All we're asking in return," Holperin said, bending forward slightly on a wooden captain's chair which Mark knew from experience was just less uncomfortable than a torture rack, "is that you act as our agent here. Continue what you did today, that's all. If one large-scale immigrant community is built on Greenwood, let alone a dozen of them, you and your friends will be swamped and helpless. The time to act is now."

"We think a slightly more formal basis would be useful," Macey said. "Form a planetary militia. It's important that you act in accordance with legal forms. Now—"

"Legally, Greenwood is administered by the Protector of Zenith," Mark interrupted. "Are you asking Mr. Bannock to start an armed insurrection against the Paris authorities?"

"Not at all!" Elector Daniels said. By his title, he was

one of the officials elected by the citizens of Quelhagen instead of being appointed from Earth. Given the state of relations between the Council of Electors and the Protector, the Atlantic Alliance authorities would dearly love a chance to arrest Daniels for fomenting rebellion.

"Zenith's claim is *not* certain," Holperin said. "We don't mean anyone should take arms against the Alliance, Mr. Maxwell. Zenith representatives attempting to grab land by force, however, can properly be resisted by a militia organized among the citizens of the threatened community."

"They're asking you to hold an election and have your friends proclaim you militia commander," Mark translated. He turned to Daniels and continued, "If Mr. Bannock were willing to take on that dangerous burden, there would still be the question of compensation."

"Pay?" said Yerby. "Say, don't worry about that, lad. I wonder if I'd need a uniform, do you think?"

"I had more in mind a proposal that would benefit the planet as well as you, Mr. Bannock," Mark said. He noticed how formal he sounded, but that was the part of his mind that he needed to carry on a negotiation like this.

"I don't need to be paid to do my duty, boy!" Yerby said in a near growl.

"Yerby!" Amy snapped. She stepped to her brother and shook her finger under his nose. "Be quiet and speak when Mark tells you to speak! Do you understand?"

Yerby backed a step and cleared his throat. "Sorry, Amy," he muttered toward a corner of the room.

Mark cleared his throat also. "A reasonable recompense for Mr. Bannock's best efforts on your mutual behalf," he said, "would be a plant to process stockyard waste at the Spiker. Blaney's Tavern, that is. Assuming an arrangement can be worked out with Mr. Blaney."

He cocked an eyebrow at Yerby in question.

"To do what?" Yerby asked.

"Allow us to place a ten-by-thirty-foot unit with solar collectors in the stockyard," Mark explained. "It'll take the manure as well as the slaughteryard waste and convert it into bricks of fertilizer and animal food."

"There's a market for processed organics for food on immigrant ships as well," Ms. Macey said. She frowned. "But the plants are expensive, especially since Paris has embargoed industrial production on Quelhagen."

"Sure, Blaney'd let me do that," Yerby said. "He's been complaining about the stink when the wind's the wrong way for as long as I've known him. Not that he was going to do anything about it."

They'd need a formal contract with Blaney, but that could come later. The handshake agreement Yerby visualized might not hold when Blaney realized how much profit was involved.

"A deal on those terms, then, madame and sirs?" Mark said. His palms were sweating and the hair along his arms prickled upright, but his voice was steady. He was dealing with some of the richest people on Quelhagen, and they *were* dealing!

"Wait a minute," Elector Daniels said. "You're asking us to go to considerable up-front expense against what? Whatever Mr. Bannock says now, how do we know he won't change his mind the day after we deliver the plant?"

Yerby started forward. Mark stepped sideways to put

himself between the two men. Amy shouted, "Yerby! Please!" this time in fear rather than anger. She knew even better than Mark did what her brother was likely to do to someone he decided had insulted him.

Daniels must have been able to guess, because his face went white and he babbled, "I'm most sorry, most sincerely sorry!"

Mark took a deep breath. He said, "Elector, you'll have Mr. Bannock's word, which is all you'd ever have at this distance from Quelhagen. That's why you need an agent here, remember. Also, I think your syndicate might be allowed five percent of the plant's net profits. It should be quite a little moneymaker as well as being of environmental benefit."

The investors looked at one another. Mark didn't see the signals they exchanged, but Daniels nodded to him, then to Yerby, and said, "Done on those terms."

Mark felt as though his tendons had all been cut. He was as wrung out as he'd been immediately after the fight in the caravansary.

Amy touched his shoulder to steady him. The camera was in her other hand. Mark had been so focused on the negotiation that he hadn't noticed she was recording the whole affair.

"Despite the embargo, I think it's possible to get a plant shipped from someplace cheaper than Earth," Mr. Holperin said to his colleagues. "There are ways and ways."

"Let's all have a drink!" said Yerby Bannock.

11. The Voice of
the People

The slopes on three sides of the Spiker were colorful with the patterned wings of flyers and the fabric casings of dirigibles, but the area between the tavern and the spaceport had been kept clear for people to stand. Mark sat on the courtyard wall at the base of a speakers' platform cantilevered out from it. There must be close to a thousand Greenwoods staring up at him and the platform where Yerby stood with the Quelhagen investors.

"A quarter of the whole planet's here," Amy said in her version of the same thought. "More than that, really, even though the people who've settled on Zenith grants wouldn't have come."

"Can you boys hear me?" Yerby Bannock bellowed. During the week of preparation for the assembly, the crew of the investors' ship had installed a public-address system. It wasn't really powerful enough to reach the whole murmuring crowd, but it was better than the people in the back could have expected.

Those folk could have moved forward if they wanted to hear the proceedings. They were men and women of the careful sort who were afraid not to attend an assembly called to discuss the future of Greenwood, but who were unwilling to be seen actually taking part in it. By keeping back on the fringes, they hoped to avoid all responsibility.

"The business at Dagmar's focused attention about as well as a threat of hanging would," Mark said. "And I guess most of the settlers live pretty close to here or to the Doodle, which isn't that far away. Most of Greenwood's still unclaimed."

He raised his eyes to the Quelhagens on the platform. "Except by them."

The crowd was rumbling a general agreement to Yerby's question. A dozen uniformed Quelhagen attendants stood just below the courtyard wall with handheld microphones, but most of the crowd couldn't comment except by shouting yes or no. The settlers at the base of the wall were those whose neighbors granted them status as speakers by allowing them to move to where they could reach a mike.

"Then I'm going to turn this over to Elector Daniels," Yerby said. "He'll explain what's going on and what we need to do about it."

He handed off the mike to the Quelhagen official. Daniels didn't have as powerful a voice as the frontiersman, but he was a polished speaker and better used to using a PA system to a large audience. He gestured in broad, rhetorical flourishes as he explained the history that led to Zenith surveyors arriving at Dagmar's.

"They're going to want to bring just as many people to Greenwood as the Zeniths do," Mark said to Amy in a low voice. Daniels's discussion was nothing new to the pair of them. "They won't regrant tracts already settled, but it won't make any difference to how the *planet* goes."

"Quelhagen doesn't claim to be the government of Greenwood," Amy replied. "If we get a government of our own and pass settlement restrictions, there's nothing the investors can do except obey them."

Mark started to say something. What he was going to say was "The Alliance will never let Greenwood control immigration itself. That'll be under Paris control."

Amy already knew that. Amy was talking about rebellion against the Atlantic Alliance.

Mark pretended to be watching the crowd of intent faces. The assembly was the biggest entertainment Greenwood had ever seen. Even the folk who didn't care what the Elector was saying were excited to be present at the event.

"The Alliance doesn't have any soldiers to speak of anywhere in the Digits," Amy said, making her position flatly certain She looked at Mark until he turned and met her eyes. "Even on Kilbourn and Dittersdorf."

"There's ten billion people in the Atlantic Alliance," Mark replied. He didn't want to think about rebellion. War was crazy, uncivilized.

"Most people live on Earth because that's where they want to be," Amy said. Her expression got harder, muscle by muscle, with every word. "They don't want to come to Greenwood, and they don't want to fight."

Mark shrugged. His skin felt hot. He wondered if Amy thought he was a coward.

He wondered if he *was* a coward.

Daniels had finished describing the investors' willingness to defend Hestia grants in court; he gave the mike back to Yerby. The frontiersman looked out over the assembly for a moment without speaking.

"All right," Yerby said. He wore his green jacket and a cap with a feather a foot long. Even without that he was half a head taller and twice as broad across the shoulders as the Elector, though the latter wasn't a small man. "I guess everybody here knows how we ran the surveyors off of Dagmar Wately's land last week. If we just do that by getting a gang together each time a Zenith ship lands, they're going to call us bandits. We need to organize as militia so we're legal. You all see that?"

There was a confused rumble from the crowd. A man in front took a microphone from an attendant and boomed over the PA system, "Are you telling us you figure to run this militia, Yerby Bannock?"

Half the crowd went silent, but there was a chorus of cheers scattered across the area.

Yerby stood arms akimbo till the shouting quieted. Then he raised the microphone again and said, "No, Zeb Randifer, I'm not telling you that. If you all think there's somebody who'd do a better job than I'd do, then I want you to pick him. But I'll tell you two things."

Yerby paused, grinning like a wildcat out over the assembly. "First thing's this. While Zeb there was out in his barnyard pronging one of his sheep, I was running off that ship full of Zeniths. That's the first thing."

Any reply Randifer might have made was lost in the thunderous laughter of the entire crowd. Randifer had friends in the gathering, but a joke that made Mark blink

in amazement—*it was a joke, wasn't it?*—was just the
thing to win over a thousand frontiersmen of both sexes.

Yerby let the noise settle before raising the microphone
again. "The other thing's this," he said. "If you do pick me
to lead you, you'd better be ready to obey. Because you
will obey. I won't warn you again."

The crowd dissolved into a low-pitched roar. Everyone
was talking with the two or three people nearest. Some
folks gestured violently. Mark saw a number of fights
break out, but they didn't last more than a few punches.

Mark looked at Yerby Bannock, a man he'd known less
than three weeks. All the people at this assembly were
tough and committed, or they would have stayed on their
home worlds rather than emigrate to an uninhabited
wilderness.

But Yerby had a fire in him that was as uncommon here
as it would have been on Quelhagen.

The noise muted to the point that Dagmar Wately
could be heard bellowing into a microphone, "All right, all
right. Let me say this, will you?"

Two men helped the stocky woman clamber to the top
of the wall. Mark gave her a hand.

"I guess most of you know me," Dagmar said. "Those
that do, you know I don't like worth a damn what I'm
going to say now."

She waved a hand toward the platform without looking
away from the crowd, "Bannock's the only choice we got,
people. It's him or it's fifty or so of us fighting each other
instead of Zenith. So that means it's Yerby Bannock."

The crowd shouted savage agreement. Mark, his arm
around Amy, yelled until his throat was raw.

12. Legal Process

"My name's Zebulon Randifer," the frontiersman mumbled to Mark at the table Blaney had set up in the Spiker's courtyard. "I got tract NK-twenty-five and about three hundred square miles of NL-twenty-five to the center of Blue River. I got a flashgun but the battery needs replacing. It don't hold a charge more than maybe an hour."

Mark keyed the information into his hypnagogue/viewer. The Spiker was the repository for settlement records for a large portion of the main continent, but Randifer's tract was to the north, in the Wanker's Doodle database. There was no reason the information couldn't have been combined; Mark intended to do just that as soon as he got to the Doodle and patched his unit to the repository server. For now, though, he could only note the location and add it to the map when he had one.

Randifer had a cloth cap, which he repeatedly took off, twisted in his hands, and replaced. He was stone bald. Mark didn't know if the frontiersman was embarrassed because of Yerby's joke during the assembly or if the sight of Amy recording the sign-up was making him nervous.

"And what kind of communications do you have?" Mark asked.

"Huh?" said Randifer. "Oh, I got a radio in my cabin. Tania Dolen flew over and told me about this meeting, though, because the damned thing was on the blink and I couldn't hear nothing."

Mark and Amy had come up with the checklist. In fact, it was Amy who suggested that Yerby do more than file in his head the names of those willing to "join the militia." So far as Yerby was concerned, the whole business was simply a legal fiction. He'd intended to operate exactly that way he had at Dagmar's: sound an alarm from high in the air to get the greatest coverage, then pile on. That the next attempted landing might be anywhere on the planet didn't concern him.

"Thank you, Mr. Randifer," Mark said. "Next?"

He'd processed almost a hundred and there were still two hundred people, mostly men, in line waiting to be enrolled. Others at the assembly might come to a summons also, Mark didn't have a clue as to how these frontiersmen's minds would work in a crisis, though he hadn't noticed many people on Greenwood unwilling to get into a fight.

The woman behind Randifer was looking up at the sky. The whole line snaking out the gate turned man by man to watch a dirigible crawling twenty feet in the air toward the courtyard to land.

"Hey, you danged fools!" a man shouted up. "Not here! Go out in the field!"

"Hey, that's Ardis Saunderson's blimp!" Randifer said. "He and every soul with him in Blind Cove's from Zenith on a Zenith grant!"

"Amy," Mark said as he closed his viewer, "go tell Yerby that—"

The dozen or so leading settlers were meeting in the tavern's taproom to thrash out an organization for the militia. The courtyard door flew open. Old Man Blaney was the first out, but Yerby and Dagmar Wately were next through the doorway.

The Blind Cove dirigible hovered over the center of the courtyard. Amy helped Mark move the table closer to the wall where it was out of the way.

There were five people in the gondola, three of them dressed as if they came from off-planet. One of the locals dropped a rope from the open half of the car. None of the folk in the courtyard grabbed it to haul the dirigible in as they would normally do. The pilot in the closed cabin scowled through a window and vented hydrogen, bringing the airship down with a rush and a bang on the hard ground.

The three strangers got to their feet and stepped iron-faced from the car. The woman as well as the two men wore black coats with white trousers, but the cut was flamboyant even though the garments' color was not.

They weren't armed. Mark still tried to place himself in front of Amy. She elbowed him hard and went on recording the event.

The trio faced Yerby. "Court officials," Mark whispered. "Process servers from Zenith." He'd seen their sort before in his father's office. Lucius Maxwell had a practice that involved a score of Protected Worlds and the courts on Earth as well.

"We have a summons for ejectment lodged against

persons occupying certain tracts of land in violation of the rights of ownership of Heinrich Biber and other parties," one of the men said. He spoke in a strong voice, but his face was pale and his eyes looked a mile through Yerby.

"Where you from, lad?" Yerby said mildly. "Zenith, ain't you? You're on Greenwood now."

"The summonses are signed by Magistrate Ardis Saunderson," the Zenith spokesman said. "Justice Saunderson is an official validly appointed by the Protector of Zenith. The court date is in one month in New Paris."

The woman carried a hologram projector embossed with a gold Zenith Protectorate crest. "Come on, then, honey," Yerby said to her with his usual easy chauvinism. "Let's see who it is."

The bailiffs whispered among themselves. From the corner of his eye, Mark saw the Quelhagen investors watching from the tavern doorway. They'd been in the meeting with the settlers' leaders, but they were being careful rather than rushing into whatever was about to happen in the courtyard.

The bailiff switched on the projector and handed it to Yerby, who turned it so that he could make out the shimmering orange words hanging over the unit. "Wately," Yerby read aloud. "Barnes, O'Neill, Emmreich, Koslovsky, and Chin."

He gave the bailiffs a playful scowl. "Come on, where's my name? Yerby Bannock?"

"The only tracts covered by this action are the ones owned by those individuals," the Zenith spokesman said. He'd relaxed very slightly now that he and his companions hadn't been attacked the instant they said what they were here for.

Mark stepped forward. He didn't know what he was about to do until the instant he did it. "Ms. Wately?" he said in a clear voice. "Will you please sell me an acre of your holdings? I'd like to be joined as a defendant in this lawsuit."

"Attaboy, Mark, lad!" Yerby boomed. "Dagmar, I want a piece of this one too!"

He stuck his hands on his hips and added, "By all that's holy, we'll show them what it means to mess with the free citizens of Greenwood!"

"You'll see all right," said the bailiff who hadn't spoken until that moment. "You'll see when a Zenith marshal and a dozen deputies sends you all running back into those woods!"

The other two Zeniths stiffened; the eyes of the man who'd first spoken unfocused again. Yerby Bannock laughed and patted Mark on the shoulder. "Get on with enrolling our people, lad," he said. "Wouldn't be surprised if we needed to defend ourselves one of these days."

He looked around the courtyard and added, "Woodsrunners. That's got a ring. I think we'll call ourselves the Woodsrunners!"

13. How the Other Half Lives

The spaceport at New Paris could land a dozen starships simultaneously, and there were covered storage facilities for over a hundred. Mark was too proud of Quelhagen to say that New Paris had a better port than Landingplace, but he had to admit it was impressive.

Mark held Amy's hand in a gesture of mutual support. She'd mastered the biofeedback techniques Mark taught her, but interstellar travel was still a disorienting experience. At least the ramp had handrails.

Attendants were helping the three investors to a limousine like the one in the ship's hold. Daniels and his fellows didn't intend to wait for cargo to be unloaded. Three less ornate aircars waited to take away the Greenwood defendants and the investors' servants.

"Wait a minute," Mark muttered. Four recently landed large vessels remained on the magnetic masses. One of them was still in the process of discharging cargo and passengers. The people disembarking were gray-uniformed

Atlantic Alliance troops, and a huge ground-effect tank was being lowered from the hold by a mobile derrick and the starship's own crane.

Amy opened her recorder and focused on the troopship. The self-imposed duty seemed to steady her. Mark by contrast felt distinctly queasy. The four ships together must have held well over a thousand men, even with the heavy equipment they brought with them. He wondered if the Protector of Quelhagen was getting reinforcements also.

Yerby, first of the Greenwood defendants besides Mark to drag himself out of his transit capsule, clanged into the right handrail and shook the ramp. He bounced left, bounced right with his next step, and probably would have caromed like a cue ball into Mark and Amy if they hadn't grabbed his arms and gently helped him to the ground.

"Holy Jesus Christ our Lord and Savior," Yerby muttered. "Boy, I think there was something wrong with that last batch of whiskey I got from Blaney."

He noticed the troops disembarking. They felt the effects of transit too. Soldiers shambled without any order. Individuals stumbled, hunched, and squeezed their heads to relieve the pain. Either the Alliance didn't teach effective biofeedback techniques, or they didn't teach the techniques effectively.

"Whoo-ee!" Yerby said. "Now, there's the soldiers I was looking for. Should've come to Zenith instead of Dittersdorf, huh?"

"They wouldn't come to Greenwood if you invited them, Yerby," Amy said in a hard voice. "The worst possible result would be if they *did* come, though. I'll never forgive you if you go over and talk to them."

Yerby watched the troops with an odd smile; not the broad devil-may-care grin Mark had seen often in the past. "Guess they could go through us Woodsrunners pretty quick with those tanks," he said. "Though it could be there's some tricks they don't know about being out with just himself and a couple million trees."

The frontiersman turned to Mark and Amy. "Think that's what they're here for?" he asked. "To use against us?"

"No," said Mark. "They've almost certainly been brought to strengthen the Protector's hand against the population of Zenith."

He smiled at the irony. "The same ones we're having trouble with, yes. But people who assume that they're automatically friends with the enemy of their enemy generally wind up with barbarians in their living rooms. I think Amy's right. The farther we keep from Alliance soldiers, the better off we'll be."

"Just thought it was worth checking," Yerby said. His grin spread into familiar broad cheerfulness.

"Captain Bannock?" Mr. Holperin called from beside the limousine. "Would you and your aides care to join us for the ride to the hotel? I gather most of your codefendants haven't left their capsules yet."

Every one of the Greenwoods except Yerby had trusted to an electronic device more or less like the one Amy had used on the voyage from Kilbourn. There was something about the term "high tech" that suppressed the common sense of frontiersmen who were otherwise the most pragmatic people Mark had ever met.

"Didn't drink enough before the flight," Yerby said, giving

his reading of his fellows' problem. "Well, I appreciate the offer, Holperin, but I need a little therapy myself. Seems to me the saloons around the spaceport might be more comfortable than whatever a fancy hotel's got in its lobby, so I'll wander off and join you later."

He waved the back of his hand to Amy and Mark. "You young folks," he said, "you go on. I wouldn't want you to miss riding in so pretty a rig, you know."

Amy snorted. "You think having civilized people around might cramp your style," she said. "Well, remember, Yerby, you're on Zenith for a purpose. If you spend your stay in a drunk tank, you'll be letting down a lot of people who've put their faith in you."

"Aw, Amy child," the big man said. "I never in my life been too drunk to do my job."

"Mr. Holperin," Mark said, "Ms. Bannock and I would be honored to join you if the invitation extends to us alone."

Holperin bowed. "A Quelhagen gentleman and his escort are always welcome in my presence," he said, stepping aside so that the attendants could hand Mark and Amy into the car's roomy passenger compartment.

Amy was stiffly nervous. She held her camera close to her body, but she didn't want to call attention to it by folding the lenses. The way rich folk lived on a highly developed world was as new to her as Greenwood's raw frontier had been to Mark.

The roof, sides, and floor of the passenger compartment were transparent from within. Mark was impressed, though he acted nonchalant. Amy's breath drew in when she realized that when she sat, her feet would dangle in what looked like empty air.

"It's all right," Mark whispered. "I'm with you." *I'm bragging to impress a girl I like. Well, I'm human.*

The car held eight passengers comfortably, four facing four as if over an invisible conference table. Amy tugged Mark down beside her instead of letting him put a seat between them for politeness as he'd intended to do.

The aircar lifted with only a hum as soon as the door closed. Mark pivoted his head as they rose, trying to get a notion of how many cars were in the sky with them. He guessed about a hundred, not many by Earth standards in a city of several hundred thousand. Aircars were a status symbol. He'd have been chagrined if New Paris had a higher density of them than Landingplace did.

Ms. Macey probably understood, because she said with a cool smile, "In material terms Zenith is nearly as developed as we are on Quelhagen. But their taste is execrable."

The port was set off from the community proper by a high berm. The earthen wall would protect the densely populated city in the unlikely event that a starship lost power while landing. The driver held the car steady above the four-lane highway leading out of the port. They flew about a hundred feet high, well below the roofs of many of the buildings ahead.

Two tanks and a dozen truckloads of Alliance soldiers wound slowly along the road. The tanks were so wide that each one blocked both inbound lanes.

Amy's arms were on the rests of her seat. She kept her fingers spread open so that she wouldn't embarrass herself even worse by clenching the seat furiously. Mark thought of touching her hand; he decided that might not be a good idea. For that matter, *he* wasn't used to watching through a floor as clear as the air itself as the ground flashed by at 120 miles an hour.

"Sir," said the driver on an intercom from the separate front compartment. Mark felt the car slow in the air. "There's some trouble on the ground ahead of us. Should I overfly it or go around?"

The investors looked at one another. "Overfly it if you can," Daniels ordered. "It'll give us an idea of conditions on Zenith."

"But take us higher, driver," Holperin added. In a muted voice he said to the other passengers, "We don't know what they might be throwing. Or shooting."

Mark put his hand over Amy's, for his sake as much as for hers.

Another column of Alliance troops was stalled just short of the city center. A forty-passenger bus was turned on its side, crosswise at an intersection. A mob lined both sides of the road. The local people threw things at the soldiers and shouted, though Mark couldn't hear words inside the car.

An entire desk pitched from a twentieth-floor window. It fell, spinning and flinging out the contents of drawers. When the desk hit between two of the trucks, it exploded like a wooden bomb. The mob nearby lurched back, trampling some of its number.

"My God," Amy said. "What's happening? What are they doing?"

"It's the same on Quelhagen, nowadays," Elector Daniels said. His tone held a hint of grim satisfaction that things on Zenith were no better than they were at home.

But that also meant that in the three months since

Mark left Quelhagen, things had gotten very, very much worse.

"Protector Giscard here's been implementing the Paris regulations against manufacturing on the Protected Worlds," Macey said. She nodded toward the mob below, her expression carefully emotionless. "No factories with more than six employees are permitted. Apparently the rest of the workforce is supposed to go into farming. Not all of the people who've lost their jobs feel that's a practical solution."

"Surely they can't enforce that?" Mark said. "No factories larger than six employees? That's absurd!"

"It's hit or miss," Macey said. "The Protector tries to close the factories he finds. Sometimes officials are paid off, sometimes the action is tied up in court . . . But recently the troops sent to deliver closing orders have taken to exercising their initiative. They wreck machinery instead of padlocking the plant."

Mark listened with only part of his mind. Most of his attention was on the riot. The aircar cruised slowly above the head of the Alliance column. Below, the leading tank slid forward, struck the overturned bus, and crumpled it. The tank drove the makeshift barricade slantwise across the street. Sparks showered from metal scraping the pavement. As the bus struck the far curb, it burst into smoky flames.

Mr. Holperin said, "It's rather like being struck by lightning—not a high risk, but devastating when it happens. That's why we invested in land on Greenwood."

"Sir?" said Amy in puzzlement.

"Manufacturing on civilized worlds is too risky a

proposition in the current climate," Elector Daniels explained. "If I wanted to gamble, I'd find a roulette game. Paris hasn't tried to restrict land speculations."

Alliance troops threw gas grenades at the mob. The bombs burst in gulps of opaque white that faded to dirty gray as the contents spread. Rioters collapsed vomiting or ran blindly away from the irritant gas. Despite gaps in the mob there were still thousands of people tossing rocks and cans at the soldiers.

"But—what if Zenith wins the lawsuit?" Amy said. "Isn't that a gamble too?"

The lead tank plowed into traffic that had been stalled by the mob. The tank driver was no longer making any attempt to avoid civilian vehicles. Cars flattened like foil toys as a hundred tons of armor plate ground into and over them. A few caught fire, but the flames were sluggish and low. All that burned in the electrically powered vehicles was upholstery, tires, and goods abandoned when the occupants bailed out in terror of the oncoming juggernaut.

The military trucks picked up speed behind the tanks. Citizens still ran alongside, screaming hatred if they had nothing to throw. Soldiers fired into the air. They were using live ammunition. Mark saw a flash and puff of dust from a building's roof coping.

"A lawsuit is a normal business risk, madame," Holperin explained. "Quite a different matter. We can't fight the Alliance, after all."

"There's the hotel," Daniels said with satisfaction. "The Safari House. I was afraid it was going to be involved in the trouble, but the troops seem to be turning the other way, toward the Protectorate offices."

The aircar dropped onto the parking area on the roof of a building with a textured plastic facade. It looked like a twenty-story grass hut.

"Typical Zenith taste," Mark said. He was frightened by what he'd just seen. *It's the same on Quelhagen . . .*

"We'll have our first court appearance tomorrow," Elector Daniels said. "That's all we have to worry about for now."

"If things like that riot are happening," said Amy, "then we've got other things to worry about too. Everybody does."

Mark squeezed her hand in full agreement.

14. Zenith Law

Mark and Amy arrived at the courtroom after a morning of sightseeing in New Paris. The city was ten times the size of any place Amy had ever visited before. She wasn't involved in the case, and Mark didn't feel a need to arrive before the scheduled start of the proceedings at noon.

Court was held in half of the third story of the Civil Affairs Building. The remainder of the floor was the Council Chamber, and the walls between the rooms and the central foyer could be removed for exceptionally large assemblies.

Since they were on Zenith, Mark wasn't a bit surprised to see that the whole third floor was decorated in Ancient Egyptian style. The fat pilasters had papyrus-bud capitals; the shafts were red or green, with stylized yellow leaves springing from the bases. The walls were white but decorated with stiffly posed figures in garish contrasting colors.

"Oh, it's gorgeous!" Amy said, gazing around the big room.

Mark blinked. It struck him for the first time that Quelhagen's muted notions of what was attractive weren't universal. In fact, they might well be the minority view.

That was hard to imagine. *Everybody on Quelhagen knows what good taste is, so how can so many other human beings be too stupid to feel the way we do?*

And Amy isn't stupid.

"This way!" hissed an usher whom the investors had hired to guide the defendants during the court proceedings. The man wore a pink-and-gray-striped costume. The color combination was attractive, but the fellow had ruffs at his throat, waist, wrists, and ankles. He looked like an oddly patterned poodle.

The usher stared at Amy, checked her face against his array of air-projected holographic portraits, and said, "Not you! Find a seat in the gallery or get out."

Mark thought of hitting him. Amy nodded and patted Mark's hand before vanishing up the staircase to the visitors' gallery.

"Come on!" the usher said. He tugged Mark's arm.

Mark gently tweaked the usher's nose. The man gasped and staggered backward. Mark followed him to the defendants' section, on the left front of the courtroom.

The plaintiffs' enclosure, on the right, was as gorgeous as a flock of tropical birds. Hostile birds, too. Though there were more than twenty folk within the low railings— plaintiffs, aides, and attorneys—only two of them stood out. They, a plump fiftyish man in blue and gold uniform and a taller, slightly younger fellow in blue and red, glared at one another.

Mark had watched his father in court many times. The

only times he'd seen equal anger and loathing between the parties was during contested divorces; this time he was viewing people on the same side.

Mark halted in the aisle. The usher glared and raised a hand to protect his nose.

"Who are they?" Mark demanded, nodding toward the Zeniths. "In uniforms."

The usher risked a look. He seemed still to be worried that Mark was going to sneak a hand under his guard. "Ah," the usher said. "Mayor Heinrich Biber wears the dress uniform of the New Paris Civic Watch. And Vice-Protector Berkeley Finch is commander of the Zenith Protective Association, a voluntary assembly of public-spirited citizens."

"The Zenith militia," Mark said bluntly. "And the two men are political rivals."

"I wouldn't be able to speak about politics, I'm sure, sir," the usher said. He started to give Mark a look of snooty superiority—then realized that the last thing he wanted to do was to call renewed attention to his snoot.

The usher cleared his throat. In a careful tone he went on, "I understand that the gentlemen may not be the best of friends, though, that's true. And as for a militia . . . Protector Giscard has declared any armed body of Zenith citizens to be illegal, so as I understand it the Protective Association cannot be a militia in the normal sense of the term."

Mark bowed in acknowledgment. "Thank you, sir," he said. That seemed to surprise the usher as much as having his nose pinched had. He minced down the aisle toward the defendants' enclosure, looking worried.

Theoretically all spectators were supposed to be in the mezzanine gallery, while seats on the lower level were reserved for those who had official connection with the court or case. The reality seemed to be that the hearing of this action was the social event of the season for Zenith's elite. Folk in gorgeous, garish clothing packed the benches, there to see and be seen.

The visitors' gallery was by contrast only sparsely occupied. Mark saw Amy looking primly by the front railing. To Zenith society, sitting in the gallery meant you weren't of any importance.

Amy didn't care—shouldn't care, anyway—what a bunch of overdressed clowns thought was important. She had a better view from where she was, besides. Mark thought of waving but contented himself with a nod before walking on.

He was becoming uncomfortably aware of his clothes. Mark wore one of the two pairs of coveralls he'd brought on his journey to the frontier. They were neat and clean but absolutely utilitarian, in no way the sort of formal garb he'd worn to court back home.

His idea had been that he didn't want to stand out from his Greenwood fellow-defendants, whom he'd expected would dress in leather and coarse fabrics as they did at home. Boy, had *that* been a miscalculation.

Yerby's sparkling green coat and a pair of fluorescent peppermint-striped trousers that he must have bought last night in New Paris—and OK, he'd been drunk then but he was presumably sober now and he was *wearing* them—weren't the most dazzlingly ugly garments among the defendants. The prize went to Dagmar Wately, in a fur ensemble that made her look like a road-kill Frankenstein, pieced together from a number of planets. None of the animals who'd given their all to clothe her were native to Greenwood.

The other five defendants were in lesser degrees of holiday finery. They weren't quite as striking as Yerby and Dagmar, but all told they made the Zeniths in the rest of the courtroom look staid. Mark wouldn't have believed that was possible.

Elector Daniels, acting as chief counsel for the defendants, was within the enclosure with a half-dozen junior legal personnel from both Quelhagen and Zenith. Daniels had dressed in the height of Quelhagen's severe fashion: charcoal gray coat, charcoal gray trousers with a single black stripe on either leg, and a gunmetal gray vest over a white shirt. The elector saw Mark and nodded in approval. A moment before Mark had been embarrassed to appear without formal garments, but Daniels seemed to be pleased that at least one of his clients didn't look like an explosion in a fireworks factory.

Mark entered the enclosure and squirmed to Yerby's side. Yerby clapped his shoulder with numbing cheerfulness. Seconds later, a stentorian bailiff roared, "Court of Common Pleas of the New Paris District is now in session! Judge Reesa Maglaglen presiding!"

Judge Maglaglen, a small woman in scarlet robes, entered from behind the bench and took the middle of the three seats. She'd be sitting alone during this preliminary hearing for the presentation of documentary evidence and motions.

Maglaglen's eyes swept the courtroom, pausing for a

moment on the defendants' enclosure. Mark had seen more pleasant expressions on a tangle of razor wire.

"I'll now accept documentary evidence relating to the case of Biber et alia against Wately et alia, an action in ejectment," Maglaglen said. "Counsel for the plaintiffs may come forward."

The procedure was a lot more abrupt than what Mark was used to on Quelhagen, but that didn't mean it was unfair. Or does it? he wondered.

Biber and Finch approached the bench with an usher. The two principals didn't look at one another. The usher between them handed a set of recording chips to the bailiff and said, "Your Honor, the plaintiffs wish to place in evidence true copies of grants made by Protectors LaCoque, Manering, and Giscard during their terms as Protectors of Zenith."

"Accepted for verification by the Public Record Office," Maglaglen said. "Counsel for the defense, if you have any documentary evidence to offer you may come forward."

Elector Daniels stepped forward. Finch smirked at him as the plaintiffs returned to their enclosure. "Your Honor," Daniels said, "the defendants wish to place in evidence true copies of grants validly issued by Protector Greenwood of Hestia."

Daniels held out a chip case. The bailiff ostentatiously refused to accept it.

Judge Maglaglen said, "As the world commonly termed Greenwood was never subject to the control of the Protectors of Hestia, such material has no bearing on the matter at issue. I therefore refuse to accept it. Do the defendants offer any other documentary evidence supporting their right to possession?"

"Your Honor, I protest!" Daniels said. He looked genuinely outraged. "The Protector of Hestia was acting under at least color of the authority of his office in—"

Instead of raising a gavel in the traditional style still followed on Quelhagen, the judge touched a button. A gong rang in the ceiling of the courtroom. When the metallic note had quavered to silence, Maglaglen said, "As defendants offer no evidence to support their claims, I find for plaintiffs."

Her bitter face swept the room. "Plaintiffs' counsel," she continued, "will provide an order for my execution as soon as the plaintiffs' grants have been verified by the relevant authorities."

She rang the gong again.

"What is this?" Yerby Bannock said. He stepped forward.

One of the junior counsel put a hand on his arm. Yerby brushed the man aside like a fly. "What the *hell* is this?"

"Defendant, you're out of order!" the judge said, her voice rising with each word as if she were reciting a musical scale. Bailiffs and ushers were converging from all points in the courtroom.

Yerby took another step. He missed the enclosure's opening and smashed the rail into shards of plastic with a quick jerk of his arm.

Elector Daniels and the bailiff before the bench stopped in the middle of their strides toward the frontiersman. Judge Maglaglen hunched down, ready to bolt like a fuzzy red bunny. Mark stumbled on the bottom of the barrier's framework as he followed Yerby.

He didn't think about what he was doing. He was *afraid* to think, and anyway, this didn't seem to be the time for it.

"Oh, don't get your bowels in an uproar!" Yerby said. "I'm not going to hurt any of you delicate flowers."

The frontiersman turned and looked slowly around the whole courtroom. He seemed surprised to see Mark jumping out of the way beside him, but he put his arm around the smaller man. "All right, you lot!" he said. "It may be that on Zenith the sun rises in the west and there's no human justice. But I tell you—"

He turned slowly to face the bench again. The bailiff leaped back so suddenly that he fell over. Daniels had already eased himself toward the aisle, trying not to come too close to Yerby. Even the other Greenwood defendants stood uneasily within the enclosure. Nobody but Mark was within ten feet of the big frontiersman.

"I *tell* you," Yerby repeated. "If any of you fine folk come to Greenwood, I think you'll learn that the sun there still rises in the usual place."

He spun and marched down the aisle.

"Hey, wait for me, Yerby!" black-bearded Holgar Emmreich cried, scrambling to follow. All the Greenwoods fell in with a haste just this side of panic. What they were probably afraid of was the whole unfamiliar situation, not what the bailiffs or municipal police were going to do because of the outburst. They followed their leader because that was a lot easier than thinking for themselves.

Mark paused where he stood. Thinking wasn't doing him a bit of good. Spectators in dazzling clothes swirled out of the Greenwoods' way, then swirled back, chirping and gabbling. It was like watching a windstorm in a parrot cage.

Amy no longer sat where she had been. Mark thought of searching for her, but the chances were she was coming down to join him. His best choice was to stay put. If they both wandered around in this brilliant chaos, they'd never find each other.

"Mark," said a familiar voice, "your counsel and I have never been formally introduced. Will you do the honors?"

Mark looked at the speaker, a slim, gray-haired man. He wore brown Quelhagen formalwear, so he'd been lost in the clouds of color.

"Hi, Dad," Mark said. He cleared his throat and added, "I didn't expect to see you here."

And boy! was that ever the truth.

15. Fallback Positions

"There aren't so many interplanetary attorneys that news of my son appearing as defendant on Zenith wasn't going to reach me, Mark," Lucius Maxwell said. "Now, will you introduce us? Because I have business to discuss with your counsel."

"Elector Daniels, allow me to present my father, Mr. Lucius Maxwell," Mark said. He bowed to each party as he spoke his name. "Dad is . . ."

"An attorney of note," Daniels said, voicing the words that Mark had smothered because he hadn't wanted to sound like he was bragging. "A pleasure to make your acquaintance, sir. Though there wasn't a great deal of law to be seen here today."

He glared balefully at the judge's bench, now empty.

"Zenith law," Lucius said with a cool smile. "Which one might compare to Zenith art—flashy, with very little at the core."

His tone changed as he went on. "What do you intend to do now? Appeal?"

Amy appeared through the crowd. She would have stayed apart from the three men if Mark hadn't motioned her closer.

Daniels nodded. "Yes, of course," he said, "though I don't know that we have much chance."

"If you mean to appeal to the Council of State under Zenith procedure," Lucius said, "you have no chance whatever. Vice-Protector Finch sits as president of the council, and half his fellow-councillors have shares in the Greenwood grants at issue."

Lucius spoke crisply, stating facts with no perceived possibility of argument. Mark had heard that cold tone often enough. He swayed closer to Amy.

"If you're empowered by your principals to associate additional counsel—" Lucius continued. He raised an eyebrow in question.

"Yes, of course," Daniels said. "Goodness, I hope you don't think these hicks have anything to do with planning the defense!"

Lucius exchanged glances with Mark. Daniels had the decency to look embarrassed and the sense not to try to unsay the words he'd already blurted.

"I don't know that the hicks, as you put it, could have been less effective in their own defense," Lucius said without heat. "Be that as it may, if you'll authorize me to act in the matter I'll carry it to Protector Giscard instead of to the Zenith council."

"Mr. Maxwell," Daniels said in puzzlement, "the grants by which we're being dispossessed were *issued* by the Protectors of Zenith. Some of them were issued by Giscard himself."

"Exactly what do you believe we have to lose, Elector Daniels?" Mark said. His tone was sharper than he'd intended, but at this stage in the proceedings he didn't much care.

Daniels stiffened. Lucius nodded to his son.

"Oh, all right," Daniels said. "What is your proposed fee, sir?"

Lucius smiled again. For some reason, the expression made Mark think of Yerby Bannock. "One Quelhagen franc," he said, "to bind the deal. Beyond that, reasonable expenses. The first of which . . ." He looked at Mark with a slight curling of his lip. ". . . will be to buy a set of proper clothes for my son, who will act as my aide when I approach the Protector. It'll be tomorrow before I can get a meeting anyway."

Everyone stared at Mark. He folded his hands over his belly to cover the slight tear in the coveralls there.

"We'll dress you as a gentleman of Quelhagen, boy, not as a painted whore from Zenith," Lucius said. "But you *will* be dressed appropriately."

16 Plotting with the Enemy

Pulsing light and a bugle call awakened Mark in the middle of the night. He shot bolt upright in a bed disguised as a tussock of grass,

It was pitch dark; the only sound was the vague traffic noise to which Mark had fallen asleep. Zeniths might have odd ideas of decoration, but the rooms here in the Safari House were at least soundproofed.

The eyes of the little lion statue on the nightstand strobed red and its belly trilled *Charge!* again. Mark grabbed the statue and wrenched its head off. That was the right move, because the lion turned out to be a telephone.

"Huh?" Mark said.

"Mark, is your father there?" asked Amy's voice.

"Huh," Mark repeated. He wasn't one of the people who were at their best when awakened from a sound sleep. "No, he's staying at the Quelhagen trade mission. He had a lot of things to do before tomorrow, he said."

He looked at the clock masquerading as a pair of assegais rotating across the face of an imitation-bullhide

shield, It was three in the morning of a twenty-six-hour
Zenith day. "Before today," Mark corrected himself.

"Well, you'll have to do," Amy said. "Will you come
over to our rooms right away? We're on the corner, the
Ishandlwana Suite."

Huh? thought Mark.

"Yerby went out with some of the plaintiffs," Amy
continued. "He isn't back yet and I'm worried. We have to
do something!"

"Ah," said Mark. "Ah. Sure, I'll be right over."

He put on his coveralls rather than his new suit. He had
no idea what Amy thought was appropriate garb. On
Quelhagen it was never appropriate for a gentleman to
visit a lady's room alone.

Except under circumstances that clearly weren't what
Amy had in mind.

At least Mark hoped that wasn't what Amy had in mind.
He'd played second fiddle to his father in a lot of ways, but
that would *really* hurt.

Amy snatched the door open at the first knock. "I don't
know what to do," she said by way of greeting. "If we were
on Kilbourn I'd go searching bars, but everything's so big
here! I'm afraid they're going to do something terrible to
him."

Mark didn't recall a time when he'd thought Yerby was
in more danger than everybody else around him was. He
said soothingly, "Well, the Zeniths won in court, so they
shouldn't be too angry . . ."

He looked about him. The central room of the
Ishandlwana Suite had furniture that looked as if it were
made from rocks, rifles, and spears. Slit curtains covered

the walls. When the fabric moved in the draft, Mark caught sight of fierce-eyed warriors painted behind the hangings. It was the sort of place that would have given him the creeps even if he'd had a good night's sleep.

"Can we go somewhere else?" he asked, meaning the hotel lobby. Amy wore Kilbourn-style street clothes. They'd stand out a little on Zenith because they were so staid, but Mark didn't suppose that mattered at three in the morning.

"Right, the kitchen," Amy said. "In case they come in while we're—"

Good as the hotel's soundproofing was, it wasn't up to Yerby Bannock singing "Fanny Bay" as the doors of the elevator down the hall opened. Other voices tried to hush him—loudly, because otherwise Yerby couldn't have heard them over his song.

Mark bolted for the kitchen between the suite's two bedrooms. He wasn't worried about whoever might be with Yerby, whether they were from Zenith or not. He was a lot worried about how the frontiersman would react if he found Mark alone with Amy at this hour in a hotel room. Even when they were sober, guys could get very upset about their sisters. There wasn't a high likelihood that Yerby was sober at the moment.

Amy had just closed the slatted door behind them when the hall door opened and Yerby called, "Welcome to my humble abode! Time for a drink, I'd say."

Mark squatted to peer between the slats. If he held his head at exactly the right angle, he could look out into the main room. Amy sat cross-legged beside him, doing the same thing at a lower level.

Yerby slid open the liquor cabinet against one sidewall. Six of the men—no women—Mark had seen in the plaintiffs' enclosure in court watched dubiously. The frontiersman lifted out a bottle in either hand.

"I don't think we need to drink more until we've got the terms worked out," said Heinrich Biber. He and Vice-Protector Finch now wore civilian clothes. Mark suspected, though he couldn't be sure, that the other Zeniths present were aides or servants rather than principals in the lawsuit.

Yerby snorted. "Don't worry about me being able to figure terms, laddie," he said. "But it's a fact that you haven't said what you want me to do. Not in so many words, anyhow."

Amy sucked in her breath with a sharp gasp. Mark didn't let himself move or make a sound. *Surely Yerby isn't going to let the plaintiffs buy him off?*

Yerby unstoppered a bottle with a flick of his horny thumb and drank. He waved the other bottle toward the Zeniths as an invitation. None of them took it.

"We're just trying to avoid trouble," Berkeley Finch said. His voice was melodious, but his arm's oratorical sweep accompanying the words was completely ridiculous in the present setting.

Yerby lowered the bottle. He belched. "Well, I guess you come to the wrong address, then," he said. "Stirring up trouble's about the most fun there is. Most fun I've found, anyhow."

"All right," Biber said. "You want plain words, I'll give you plain words. We know you've got influence with your neighbors on Greenwood. We'll pay you to use that influence to prevent them from acting violently against the agents we send to enforce our claim on the land."

"You'll be doing them a favor," Vice-Protector Finch interjected. This time he spread both arms wide. *Here's a guy who's on stage every waking moment.* "Obviously they can't withstand the enormous power of Zenith."

Yerby shrugged and drank again. A good half the quart bottle had gurgled down his throat in the minutes since Mark watched him enter the suite.

"We'll permit current settlers to reclaim their land under our grants," Biber said. "We'll offer them special rates. Say, only two-thirds of what we normally charge."

Yerby belched again. This time the lamps rattled. "Awright," he said. "I want five thousand Zenith dollars a month. A Greenwood month, that is."

"*Are you—*" Finch began in an angry voice. He shut up instantly when he saw Yerby's smile start to broaden.

"We're thinking more in terms of a thousand a month," Biber said carefully. "With a bonus for success, of course. A large bonus."

Amy clasped her hands tightly together as though she was praying. Mark didn't look directly at her, but from the corner of his eye he could see that her face was white. She'd never thought her brother was a saint, but this barefaced treachery amazed as well as horrified her.

"Five thousand a month," Yerby repeated nonchalantly. "The first six months now, in cash. Later payments paid quarterly into my account on Kilbourn."

"That's absurd!" the Vice-Protector said. "Mr. Bannock, that's absolutely absurd!"

Yerby chuckled, eyed the level in the liquor bottle,

and took another mouthful. "Is it, laddie?" he said after swallowing. "Well, I'll tell you what I think is absurd. That's you figuring that because you got a hellacious lot of people on this planet, that you can put enough of them on Greenwood to chase out the folks who're there already. If you really believe that, you're even dumber than you look."

Finch drew himself up stiffly. Biber glared at him, then said in a would-be reasonable tone, "There's a level of truth to what you say, of course, Mr. Bannock. That's why we're talking with you. The actual figures involved, however—"

"You heard the figures," Yerby said. He hadn't shown a sign of anger or anxiety during the whole discussion. "You can pay me and I'll do what I can to bring my neighbors to what I think's the right attitude. *Or* you can come to Greenwood yourselves and try to talk folk around. But I recommend if you do that—" He smiled like a crocodile. "—you not wear such fancy clothes as you got on now. Because chances are that people are going to give you a guided tour of cesspools and manure piles."

Vice-Protector Finch swore, softly and bitterly.

Mayor Biber's face was as black as a thundercloud for a moment. Finally he shrugged and said, "All right, we accept your terms. We'll have the money for you tomorrow, as soon as the banks open at ten."

Yerby laughed with the same thunderous abandon as he'd been singing in the hallway. "Ten o'clock?" he said. "Well then, laddies, why don't we go out and find what bars are still open, shall we? We got some celebrating to do!"

"Oh God," moaned one of the Zeniths. Those were the first words any of the aides had spoken since they entered the suite.

Yerby waved the Zeniths out ahead of him with a flourish and banged the door closed behind him. Mark stood up, feeling a little dizzy from the way the awkward posture had cramped his legs.

Amy got smoothly to her feet again. Her face was flushed. "Thank you for being willing to help," she said primly to Mark. "I think you'd better go now, though."

"Right," said Mark. He waited until the elevator closed on the strains of "Fanny Bay" before he went out into the hall.

"It was very foolish of me to worry about my brother being in physical danger," Amy said in a bitter voice. "And obviously it was far too late to worry about his morality— or the lack of it!"

"Good night, Amy," Mark murmured. He half believed that he'd dreamed the whole business. *It just couldn't be true . . .*

17. The High and the Mighty

The palace of Guillaume Giscard, Protector of Zenith, was on a mountaintop 270 miles from New Paris. Eastward through the glass walls of the anteroom to Giscard's office Mark could see a breathtaking sweep of bare ridges plunging thousands of feet toward the foothills.

To the immediate south, Alliance troops bundled in winter uniforms like so many gray snowmen were being drilled in a courtyard two stories below. The site was a barracks as well as a palace. Judging from the number of corrugated-plastic huts, there must be several thousand soldiers quartered here.

Very uncomfortable soldiers, too. It was only fall in this hemisphere, but the palace was high enough that snow already drifted around the shelters.

A servant so gloomy that he could have been a basset hound threw open the doors to the office. "His Excellency will see you now, Mr. Maxwell," he said, as if he were reading the burial service for a very sinful man. Mark entered behind his father.

There were seven people in the large room. Four, including both women, wore Alliance military dress uniforms. Protector Giscard was a tall, stooped man. He rose from behind a desk littered with papers, recording chips, and three different styles of hologram projector. The remaining civilians were an older man across the desk from the soldiers and a supercilious-looking youngster.

"Mr. Maxwell," Giscard said, extending his hand, "I'm seeing you out of respect for those who recommended you, but there's absolutely no way that I can interfere in the matter you raise. Or would want to."

Lucius shook hands politely; Mark bowed in Quelhagen style, feeling very tense. He didn't worry about the Alliance officials, but he didn't want to embarrass himself in front of his father.

"Well, I appreciate your position," Lucius said. "However, I thought—"

"I mean, my own Vice-Protector's involved in the matter, I understand," Giscard interrupted. He played nervously with the papers on his desk. "With all the trouble going on here, I'm certainly not going to get him and the rest of the local council stirred up."

"Stirred up, hell," said a heavyset officer with close-cropped, iron gray hair. "If you took my advice, Finch would be in jail right now."

"And if he resisted," added a woman of similar age and physique, "he'd be under the jail. He's a prancing little prick."

Giscard forced his face into a smile. "Paris thought if I

associated responsible local people in the government, things would . . . there'd be less trouble," he said to Lucius apologetically. "So I appointed Mr. Finch, but—"

He broke off and waved a hand, frustrated at his own dithering. "Anyway, I can't interfere. I'm sorry you had your trip for nothing, but I'm sure my secretary warned you you were wasting your time."

"Many times," said the young man. He couldn't have stuck his nose farther in the air if there'd been a turd on the carpet. "But Mr. Maxwell absolutely insisted."

"I thought it only fair that I give you a chance to cover yourself before the matter goes to Paris," Lucius said. His nonchalance made Mark shiver with its glacial perfection: polite but at the same time utterly superior and dismissive. It was the tone that Mark had expected the Protector to be using on *them*.

"Paris?" Giscard said. "You can't—"

"I'm afraid that in some quarters your decision to let planetary courts invalidate Alliance grants won't be very well received," Lucius said. This time he raised his voice enough to override the Protector's.

"Those Hestia grants *are* invalid!" said the elder civilian.

Lucius cocked an eyebrow. "That's certainly the position a Zenith court took," he said. "Very possibly a commission set up by the proper Alliance authorities might agree. But I very much doubt that officials in Paris will believe that a Zenith court had authority to make that decision on its own."

Giscard swallowed. He looked at the aide who'd just spoken. That fellow cleared his throat and said, "There are no grounds for appeal of a local decision to authorities in Paris." Mark could almost hear the question in his voice.

"Grounds?" said Lucius. "Oh, I think if the proper people in the Protectorate Office learn of what's happened here, they'll find grounds at least to recall His Excellency—"

Lucius bowed to Giscard.

"—to explain why he allowed local authorities to overrule the actions of an Alliance protector. But of course that's your decision, Your Excellency. Thank you for your time."

"Wait!" Giscard said.

Lucius raised an eyebrow. "Yes, Your Excellency?" he said, as if he were only vaguely interested in what the protector had to say.

"I can't invalidate my own grants," Giscard said, wringing his hands. "I just *can't.*"

One of the military officers sneered and ostentatiously turned her back.

"Why, of course not," Lucius said. "This is clearly a case that a commission from the Protectorate Office has to decide. It seems to me that a responsible official in your position would freeze all proceedings in local courts and refer the question of validity back to Paris for determination. That's what a *strong* and responsible Protector of Zenith would do."

"That could take years," said the civilian aide, apparently Giscard's legal advisor. "That could take a decade."

Lucius smiled more broadly than he had before during this discussion. "Yes, it could well defer the question of enforcement until long after Protector Giscard has been appointed to some distant post."

"Yes, that's right," Giscard said. "Yes!" He bobbed his head three times as if shaking the point down into his consciousness. He looked at his legal advisor and said, "Candace, see what you can do, will you? And quickly, this has gone on long enough."

"As a matter of fact, Mr. Candace," Lucius said, "I happen to have a draft right here that you might like to look at."

He took a recording chip from his breast pocket and offered it to the advisor. Lucius' smile had the same authority Mark had seen on the face of Yerby Bannock as he surveyed the unconscious thugs on Dittersdorf.

The limousine Lucius had borrowed from Daniels purred softly at a thousand feet. The land below showed few marks of human involvement: a road, scattered farms; a village of thirty or forty houses. Before he visited Greenwood, Mark would have thought of this as wild country.

Before Greenwood . . .

"Dad," Mark said. He forced himself to look at his father as he spoke. If one or the other of them had been driving, there'd have been an excuse to avoid eye contact.

Lucius waggled a finger toward the ground. "I suppose you find this a change from Earth," he said. "And Greenwood, on the other end of the scale."

"I was thinking about Greenwood," Mark explained. "It's—Dad, what do you think would happen if the plaintiffs offered Mr. Bannock a bribe to, to see things their way?"

Lucius laughed wholeheartedly. Since most of his

actions were muted by calculation, this loud amusement was like seeing the sun come out in the middle of a blizzard. "Oh, surely they wouldn't be that stupid, would they?" he said at last.

Mark felt an enormous sense of relief. "You think he'd turn them down even if he sounded tempted?" he said.

"No, no," his father said with a dismissive sweep of his hand. "That kind, the Yerby Bannocks—they'll never turn down a franc, a drink, or a woman. But he'll weasel-word his promise and then he'll go right ahead and do exactly what he intended to do from the first."

"Ah-h-h," Mark said as the light dawned. He thought for a moment and went on, "So Yerby's a type, then? I've never met . . ."

"Yerby Bannock's a type in the same sense that the Mars Diamond is a type," Lucius said. He studied Mark with an intensity Mark didn't understand. "There are many other diamonds, but the rest aren't flawless and don't weigh thirty-seven pounds."

Lucius looked at the ground out his side of the clear compartment. After a moment he turned back to Mark and said, "Ah . . . sometimes there might be a situation where soldiers were required to destroy an enemy automatic weapon."

Mark looked blank. He didn't have any idea of why his father had changed the subject. For the first time in Mark's memory, he thought he saw embarrassment beneath the normal cool expression.

"Generally, almost always, there's a better way to deal with the gun than charging straight at it," Lucius continued, holding eye contact. "But every once in a while there's a case where you really do have to go in head-on. Then it's useful to have a Yerby Bannock around."

"Ah!" said Mark. He was glad to have a context, though he knew there had to be more in the explanation than he was seeing at the moment.

"The odd thing is," Lucius continued, "the Bannocks survive that sort of activity more often than you'd imagine. But it's not a good idea to stand very close to them. Unless you have to,"

"I see," said Mark. And now he did.

18. Plotting Against the Enemy

The Ishandlwana Suite was slightly less hideous with daylight streaming through the west windows. Mark still didn't envy Dagmar Wately, seated in a chair around which a fake python coiled with its jaws open to engulf her head.

Yerby stumbled out of the bedroom, holding his temples. He was the last to join the gathering of defendants, investors, and attorneys, even though they were meeting in his suite as arranged.

"Jesus Christ, our Lord and Savior," he muttered, holding his head with both hands. "I think there was something wrong with the booze I got last night at . . ."

His voice trailed off. Mark figured the reason was that Yerby couldn't possibly remember the names of all the places he'd been drinking the past night and this morning.

"I believe we're all present," Lucius said. He stood with his legs spread slightly and his hands crossed behind his back. "Elector Daniels, would you care to proceed?"

"Go on, Maxwell," Daniels said. He'd been noticeably more deferential toward Mark's father since they returned with the Protector's order taking jurisdiction away from the Zenith courts. "You've brought us to this point, after all."

Lucius eyed the room. The Greenwoods looked either cowed or hungover, though nobody else appeared to have tied one on quite as tightly as Yerby had. Amy, seated primly in a corner, had been staring at her brother with smoldering anger. When Daniels spoke she raised her camera to record the meeting.

"Simply put, mesdames and gentlemen," Lucius said, "the question of your grants' validity has been referred to the Paris bureaucracy. I'll be traveling to Earth to put your side—our side—to the authorities there. I'm an attorney, not a fortuneteller, but I believe your claims will receive a fairer hearing there than here on Zenith."

Dagmar snorted. "You mean they'll give us blindfolds before they shoot us?" she said.

"Perhaps a little better than that," Lucius replied. His smile was like the sun reflecting from a glacier.

"This doesn't mean that you can let your guard down on Greenwood," Ms. Macey said. "Finch and the others know that their best chance of success would be to seize possession before the Alliance commission has time to act. The risk of an actual invasion is even greater than it was before."

"But that wouldn't be legal, would it?" Amy asked from behind her camera. She looked at Lucius. "If Protector Giscard's ruled in our favor?"

"He hasn't ruled in anyone's favor, Ms. Bannock,"

Lucius said. "And Ms. Macey is quite correct. Possession isn't nine points of the law, but it certainly tends to be nine-tenths of any political decision. Politics, not laws, are the matter at issue in the case from now on."

"Don't worry about us keeping up our end," Yerby said. He was still wearing his fancy jacket. Mark saw rusty stains on the right cuff and lapel. Blood, he thought, but not surprisingly it didn't seem to be Yerby's blood.

"I don't believe there's anything more to say," Lucius said. "I've booked passage to Paris for later in the week. As Ms. Macey suggested, it might be desirable for those of you who are defendants to return to your homes as soon as possible."

He smiled, nodded to Yerby, and added, "To make sure that they remain your homes. Despite the attractions of urban entertainments."

"If I never take another drink, it'll be too soon," muttered Buck Koslovsky. "There's some green stuff, absinthe, in the bar and I figure, one of these sweet liqueurs. I tell you, a bottle of that and I didn't know what hit me."

"What did you do last night, Yerby?" Amy asked in a cold, clear voice. "Was there anything interesting that you ought to share with the company?"

"Huh?" Yerby said. He looked surprised but not really furtive. "No, I wouldn't say that. Partied, you know. Did a bit of drinking."

He reached into the side pockets of his jacket. He brought out a room key in one hand and a lipstick-smeared bar napkin in the other.

"Nothing else, Yerby?" Amy said. "You're absolutely sure of that?"

The others in the room looked at her oddly. Mark wished he'd had an opportunity to tell Amy what Lucius had said about the chance of bribery succeeding.

"There was another thing," Yerby admitted. He peered, then fumbled into his breast pocket. "I found a poker game and didn't do so very bad."

This time his hand came out with a sheaf of currency. It looked impressive even before you realized that the top bill was a thousand Zenith dollars. He waved the cash to the room.

"Krishna saves!" Dagmar shouted, hopping up from the threatening chair. "How much is that?"

"Well, I don't really think of it as my money," Yerby said with a broad smirk. "Seeing's I won it here where we come for the case, you see. So I figured I'd use it to pay the boys, the Woodsrunners, for training. I don't worry about folks showing up when there's real trouble, but it's a pain in the ass to drop everything when you know it's just playacting. Sound good?"

"I think that's an extremely good idea, Mr. Bannock," Lucius said. He looked at Mark and winked.

Amy looked from Lucius to Yerby to Mark. She picked up the connection a good deal faster than Mark thought he'd have done if their roles were reversed.

Amy threw herself into her brother's arms and said, "Yerby, I can't *tell* you how good that sounds!"

Among a herd of elephants molded on the walls of the Safari House's lobby, Lucius turned to his son and said, "I could use an aide on Earth, you know. Would you care to come? I don't believe you've seen Paris yet, have you?"

"I wasn't much use to you here with the Protector," Mark said. He was buying time while he thought about his real answer.

"Don't you think so?" Lucius said. He sniffed. "I think you underestimate the disadvantage a lone man is at in a group of his opponents. In any case, your usefulness is a matter for me to determine. Your decision is whether or not to accept the offer."

"Dad," Mark said, forcing himself to meet his father's eyes. "I think I'd rather go back to Greenwood. I think . . ."

He wasn't sure if he was going to finish the thought. He wasn't even sure it was true. But it *was* what he believed.

"Dad," he said, "I think they need me there."

Lucius gave him a thin smile. It was very hard to tell what was behind the older man's eyes. "Yes, I was rather of that opinion too. Well, I'll take my leave now."

He nodded formally to Mark. Then, almost as an after-thought, he said, "We both want the same thing for you, Mark: that you become a man worthy of your upbringing. So far, so good, I believe."

Lucius turned and walked through the doors onto the street. Slim, erect; every inch a gentleman.

What I really want, Mark realized, *is to become a man my father can respect. And I guess that's what he just said.*

19. The Home Front

The starship landing system for the Spiker was housed in a rough stone-and-concrete hut between the tavern compound and the magnetic mass. Beside the hut was an internally braced antenna thrusting up a hundred feet like a silvery needle. The four modules in the hut included a flat-plate display, keyboard, and output/input ports under latched flaps. The designers had built a gooseneck light into the terminal module, though the screen alone could have provided enough illumination to work by.

Mark suspected he was the first person to call up the unit's embedded menu and take a look at what the equipment could really do. Default mode was fully-automated operation: a ship in orbit engaged the landing system, which brought the vessel down without anybody on the ground being involved or even aware of what was happening. That had been good enough for Greenwood up till now.

The situation had changed with the Zenith trouble, Mark figured. This equipment was the same as that installed in major ports where a human operator oversaw traffic movements. It cost less to build the full capabilities into every set than it did to degrade individual units to minimum local needs.

Mark wasn't an electronics technician, but the landing system was meant to be installed by construction workers with only the most rudimentary knowledge of anything more complex than a backhoe. For three years Mark had used teaching software of a much higher degree of sophistication. By now he'd enabled the identification and tracking functions. His next job was to set parameters so that he could switch the whole system whenever he wanted to remote-control from the standard VHF radio in Yerby's compound.

Yerby's bulk darkened the doorway. "Morning, lad," the big man said. "Blaney said you were out here."

Mark laughed. "I wouldn't call three in the afternoon morning," he said. "Did you and Amy just get back?"

"Ah, the trip to Bottomless Pool," Yerby said with a slight frown. "No, to tell the truth, I spent the night here, lad. Met a few of my friends last night and, you know, partied some."

Mark felt his expression harden. "Amy's been looking forward all week to seeing the fish in Bottomless Pool," he said. "I'm sorry to hear that you missed the appointment again, Yerby."

Dr. Jesilind had visited the site with Yerby. According to him, the Bottomless Pool was the vent of an ancient volcano that siphoned salt water from the ocean at least a hundred miles away. The crater lake was rich in brilliantly colored plant life and fish with no resemblance to shallow-water forms.

Mark didn't wholly accept the doctor's claim of a unique ecology, but the pool certainly sounded interesting. He'd have asked to go with the Bannocks except for the overhanging threat of Zenith invasion. It was more important to finish his work with the landing system.

Besides, Mark had the vague thought that maybe after Yerby showed his sister where the pool was, Mark and Amy would go by themselves.

"Oh, well, that's all right," Yerby said. He sounded a trifle uncomfortable. "The doc knows where the place is, so he offered to take Amy there. I know, she don't get along with Doc the way you'd like, but she wanted to go so bad and me, well, I just wasn't up to coming home last night for another dustup with Desiree."

"I see," said Mark. Actually, Amy got along with Jesilind exactly the way Mark liked, which was just barely. But as Yerby said, she'd really wanted to see the pool.

"To tell the truth, though," Yerby said, "I'd sorta thought they'd be back before now. They're off in the blimp, but the guidance beacon isn't working real good and, you know, I can't seem to raise them on radio."

"They're not back at the compound?" Mark asked, feeling suddenly cold.

Yerby scratched his ribs with a look of great concentration. "Desiree says not," he admitted, glaring at his fingers. "Says they went off at first light and that's the last anybody's seen of them. Desiree said some other things too."

He raised his eyes to Mark. "Might be she was right about some of those things," Yerby said. "Not that I really think there's a problem, but if you ain't seen her like I

hoped you had, maybe I'll take my flyer out to the Pool.
Want to come along?"

A series of possibilities clicked through Mark's mind.
His face remained frozen. Turning from Yerby, he called a
movement chart up on the landing system's screen. The
unit had to be able to track aircraft also in order to bring
ships down safely in busy environments.

"The Pool's south of here, isn't it?" he asked sharply.

"South-southwest of the Spiker, south from the house,"
Yerby said. "What's wrong, lad?"

"Nothing," Mark lied. He could almost hear his father's
voice saying, *"Generally, almost always, there's a better
way than charging straight in."*

"Yerby," he said, facing the big frontiersman again,
"I've got to pick up some tools at the compound right now.
It's important to get this system working so that we at least
know who's landing here before they arrive. I'm sure you
can take care of any little problem the blimp has by
yourself."

Yerby's head jerked back in surprise. "Sure, I see that, Mr.
Maxwell," he said. "Well, I'll leave you to your business,
then."

Yerby ducked out of the hut and jogged toward the
compound where he must have left his flyer the day
before. His arms pumped more vigorously than his pace
seemed to justify.

Mark got into his own flyer beside the hut. His guts felt
heavy and frozen by Yerby's shocked disapproval; but
Mark knew that if he'd told Yerby the truth, the result
would have been as violent and certain as pulling the
trigger of a gun.

Yerby's compound lay at the northern edge of the circle the system's plotting lidar swept. The dirigible's track from the compound at 6:47 in the morning was clearly marked, and as the vehicle rose to a thousand feet it stayed on the screen for another twenty miles.

Dr. Jesilind was headed northwest, not south toward the Bottomless Pool. There were a number of reasons Jesilind might have gone off with Amy in a direction nobody would think to search for them.

But all of them added up to Mark wanting very much to join the pair as fast as he could.

20. An Afternoon in the Country

Mark's holoviewer rested on his lap, projecting a holographic terrain map in the air before him. He kept the flyer a thousand feet high, so he didn't need to worry about what was directly in front of him unless a bird got very unlucky.

Or, come to think, unless he managed to collide with the dirigible itself. Mark assumed his quarry would be below him, probably on the ground; but he could imagine his first gymnastics coach shouting, "Always check the fastenings of equipment before you trust your weight to it! Assume makes an ass of U and me, boy!"

Dutifully, Mark raised himself in the saddle to peer over the top of the opaque hologram. The sky was as empty as a politician's promise.

He didn't know where Jesilind had gone, but the dirigible had flown straight from the point it lifted from Yerby's compound until the track vanished at the limit of the lidar's range. A one-hundred-foot cigar of royal blue fabric ought to show up pretty well. By keeping high and swiveling his eyes constantly, Mark figured he'd find the dirigible sooner or later.

It had better be sooner, though, or he was going to run out of daylight.

The flyer overflew another wooded ridge. *It might be the one where Yerby took me and Amy to picnic when we fast arrived on Greenwood.*

As the thought struck him, Mark saw the waterfall. It was richly golden in the low sunlight, so lovely that Mark flew for some moments further before he noticed the dirigible nestled near the cliff face at the bottom of the falls. He banked and brought the flyer down like a brick, a risk he'd never have taken if he'd been thinking about it.

Dr. Jesilind stood on the gondola's open deck. There was no sign of Amy. The howl of air past the flyer's frame tubes drew the doctor's attention.

Jesilind grabbed the door of the closed cabin, but it wouldn't open for him. He fumbled an object from his pocket, dropped it on the deck, and finally used both hands to pick it up again.

"Mark!" Amy screamed from a side window of the dirigible's cabin. "Stay back! He's got a gun!"

Jesilind leaned over to grab the window. Amy slid it shut, barely in time.

Mark's landing strained the flyer's framework but halted him within ten feet of his touchdown. His holoviewer flew onto the pebbly ground.

He remembered how he'd worried about the viewer when the thugs surrounded him in the caravansary. Not now. He wasn't worried about *anything*. That utterly amazed the part of Mark's mind that viewed the situation from a cool distance.

Mark clambered out of his flyer. Dr. Jesilind remained on the dirigible's deck, clamping the gate of the railing closed with one hand. He'd thrust the other into the pocket of his jacket again.

"Hello, Doctor," Mark said. He walked toward the dirigible.

Jesilind took his hand from his pocket with a gun. It had a wide, slightly flared muzzle. Mark supposed it was lethal.

"Stop where you are or I'll shoot!" Jesilind said. His voice was as high as if he'd gotten his balls caught in a car door.

Mark took another step forward. Close up he could see where Amy's fingernails had raked three long gouges down Jesilind's cheek.

"Well, Doctor," Mark said, "you've got two choices. You can shoot or you can give me the gun. If you give me the gun, I'll see to it that you get off Greenwood before Yerby learns what's happened here."

Mark stopped just out of arm's reach of Jesilind. He put his hands on his hips, unconsciously mimicking the stance Yerby used to face down opposition. He continued, "If you shoot, well, I don't give long odds that I'll survive. But I've got a lot better chance than you do."

Jesilind swallowed. His face was blotchy white except for the scratches. He sidled against the far railing and put the pistol in his pocket. Mark stepped onto the deck, walked to Jesilind, and took the weapon from the pocket. Jesilind didn't resist.

Amy opened the cabin door. "Stay clear, Amy!" Mark warned.

Instead of speaking, Amy went to the junction box on the outer bulkhead. She began to reconnect the power and control conduits, which Jesilind had unscrewed.

"This is all a mistake," Jesilind said. His voice quavered. He was sweating furiously.

"Yes, I rather think it was," Mark said. His whole body trembled with reaction. More hormones were racing in his bloodstream than even after the fight in the caravansary.

He cleared his throat. "Doctor," he said, "you'll take my flyer to Wanker's Doodle and board whichever ship there is going to take off soonest."

Mark looked up at the sky. "I doubt you'll be able to make it tonight," he continued, "but I strongly advise you to get as far as you can. I'll have your goods shipped after you if you're willing to leave a destination. I doubt Yerby will come searching for you when you've left Greenwood, but that's a decision you're going to have to make for yourself."

Amy walked to Mark's side. She stepped very carefully around the edge of the deck so that she wouldn't come between the two men.

"That gun doesn't really work," Jesilind said. He tried to wipe his face with a handkerchief. He dropped the square of cloth but didn't notice it. He mopped his forehead with his bare hand.

"Doesn't it?" Mark said. He looked at the weapon, wondering if Jesilind had threatened Amy with it also. "Well, that doesn't matter."

He turned and hurled the pistol as hard as he could into the waterfall's spray. It clinked on the rocks somewhere beyond.

"I fear that you've both misunderstood me," Jesilind said, desperately trying to smile.

"Well, that's a pity, Doctor," Mark said as he stepped forward. "But I really wouldn't want you to misunderstand me."

He punched Jesilind in the pit of the stomach. Jesilind doubled up. He must not have had anything to eat that day, because all that sprayed from his mouth was a little bile.

"Amy," whispered Mark. He sagged against the railing. "Would you mind dragging this fellow onto the ground so that we can get out of here? I don't feel strong enough just now."

Mark sat in a corner of the cabin shivering while Amy flew the dirigible through the darkening sky. They must be getting near the Bannock compound. Mark didn't look out the cabin windows to be sure.

"What happened an hour ago," he said wonderingly. "It's as if somebody else did it."

"You did it, Mark," Amy said. "I don't think . . . I never thought I'd meet anybody who could do what I watched you do."

"Yerby would," Mark said. "He wouldn't have stopped where I did, either."

"Being willing to stop is as important as being brave enough to start," Amy said. She kept her eyes resolutely on the terrain ahead.

"Wonder what my dad would think to see me brawling that way?" Mark said with a sneer for his own behavior. "I guess the only thing I've learned since I left Quelhagen is what your brother taught me: Never hit a man in the jaw with your bare hand."

He shook his head and added bitterly, "Of course, Yerby'd be ashamed of me for hitting him with my bare hand at all."

"Yerby wouldn't be ashamed of you, Mark," Amy said softly. Pumps whined, compressing hydrogen in the ballonets so that the dirigible would sink. They must be just about to land. "And I've met your father. I don't think that he'd be ashamed of you either."

Mark managed to stand. He felt better than he thought he would; just weak, really. The dirigible was descending into the Bannock compound. The lights in all the buildings were on. People were coming outside to wave and cheer.

Amy looked over from the controls. "Mark," she said, "not everything my brother has to teach you is wrong. It's just that sometimes he doesn't use the best judgment about where to display what he knows."

They landed lightly. A dozen of the folk in the courtyard grabbed dangling lines and held the dirigible down against any chance gust that might hit before the pumps had squeezed most of the lift back into the high-pressure tanks between the ballonets.

Mark reached for the door latch. Before he touched it, Yerby burst into the cabin bellowing, "In the name of all that's holy, girl, where have you been?"

The frontiersman paused, looked around him, and added, "And where in thunder is Doc Jesilind?"

"The doctor was called off-planet abruptly. He said it was a once-in-a-lifetime opportunity, Yerby," Amy said in a clear voice. "We'd gotten confused on direction, but Mark very kindly guided me home."

"Direction?" Yerby said, his brows knitting as he tried to understand.

Amy put one arm through Mark's and led him out of the cabin, clearing a path with an imperious wave of her free hand. "Because we got lost," she said, "I didn't get to see the Bottomless Pool after all. Since human guides are so unreliable, I think the best choice is for Mark to navigate me there using the map in his holoviewer."

Amy looked at Mark. "If he's willing," she added.

Mark blushed and cleared his throat. "I'm willing," he said in a squeak.

21. Company Coming

Nothing unusual had happened in the month since Mark enabled the full range of the landing system at the Spiker, so he'd pretty well forgotten about it. Now when the alarm he'd rigged in the Bannock compound rang loudly, it took him a moment to recall what it meant. He dropped the extrusion nozzle he'd been cleaning in a shed and ran for the main house.

The commo room was on one end of the ground floor, across the central hall from the parlor. The kitchen, the large dining room, and an office/workroom completed the floor plan. The second story was broken into spartan bedrooms for guests—Mark had one of them, while the top was for the Bannocks themselves. During the time Mark had been on Greenwood, Yerby had slept in the guest room beside Mark's rather than on the third floor with Desiree.

Yerby had been asleep when the alarm rang. He crashed into the commo room just behind Mark, still wearing the clothes Mark had seen him in the night before.

"There's an anomaly in the data the ship's captain radioed down," Mark explained. "He says they're the three-hundred-ton *Judy* from Hestia, but the ship's own core memory says they're the *Aten,* a twenty-eight-hundred-ton liner in the Zenith-Earth trade."

Amy and three of the men who worked for the Bannocks arrived in the hallway outside the commo room. Tomse, the cook, wiped his floury hands on his apron.

Desiree managed the plastics plant, but she must have been up at the compound when the alarm sounded, because she appeared only a heartbeat later. She gestured the employees out of the way so that she could stand stone-faced beside Amy in the doorway.

"If they bothered to fake their landing announcement," Mark continued, "then this is the invasion we've been expecting. You've got to call out the militia at once. A ship that big could hold five hundred troops!"

"Now, don't have kittens, lad," Yerby said. He sat at the console, brushing Mark aside without noticing the contact. His big hands rested on the keyboard. "You've took over the whole system here, that's right? They can't land by themselves so long as this—" He rapped the terminal feeding through the compound's radio. "—is hooked to the box at the Spiker?"

"That's right," said Mark. He hadn't thought Yerby was following the description of the changes Mark had made in the automatic landing system. Yerby's "simple frontiers-man" act covered a mind just as surprising as his physical strength. "They'll wait awhile for a control signal, because there might be another ship on the magnetic mass. But before long, they'll just decide to land at Wanker's Doodle."

Yerby chuckled. He changed screens and began to type information into the keyboard. He used two fingers, but he didn't need to hunt for the keys he hammered.

"They'll get their control signal, never fear," Yerby said as he worked. "For most nearly a year me and our daddy—"

He flicked a smile toward Amy. "D'ye remember that, girl? Or was you too young?"

"I remember," Amy said. She was tense with concern.

"Anyhow, we brought ships down on Kilbourn when the module packed up and we couldn't get a replacement in. Guess I haven't forgotten how to do it."

"Yerby," Amy said. Her voice trembled with suppressed emotion. "If you crash the ship, you'll kill hundreds of people. Many hundreds. Even though they're enemies—"

"Now, hold your tater!" Yerby snapped. "First thing, I don't guess a bunch of softies from Zenith are going to pack themselves near as tight as Mark says. Besides, they're going to have a lot of big equipment—aircars and such. That's right, ain't it, lad?"

He rotated his head to look at Mark. "I guess so," Mark said.

They are enemies. Maybe the only way to deal with them is to smash the Aten *on hard rocks that can't hold enough of a magnetic field to slow the ship for a landing. But—*

Mark's mind couldn't imagine a future in which he let something so horrible happen. And he couldn't imagine how he could prevent it *from* happening.

"Yerby, you can't kill all those people!" Amy cried.

Desiree looked from Amy to her husband. Her face

had no more expression than a billet of wood, but Mark knew by now not to confuse stolidity with stupidity. Yerby's wife was anything but stupid.

"Now, who said a single flaming word about killing?" Yerby said loudly. He slapped the Execute key to transmit the landing codes he'd just entered.

He stood and faced the others. "I don't guess I'm risking anybody's life. Leastways, nobody's life more than I am my own, because I'll be going to fetch them myself. They'll have a soft landing, I guarantee."

Yerby smirked at his audience. He was enormously pleased with himself.

"Yerby, what have you done?" Amy asked.

"I brought them down on the big island in The Goo," Yerby said. "The wet ground'll build enough field that they won't smash to bits, but I don't guess they'll be invading any time soon."

Thomse chuckled; even Desiree's face seemed to soften somewhat. Mark and Amy looked blankly at one another.

"The Goo's a swamp just in from the coast," Yerby explained cheerfully. "It's a bowl twenty miles across and it drains out through cracks in the rock, not by a proper river. I reckon they'll have time enough to get out of the ship, the folks will. The cargo hatches are going to be under a couple yards of muck as soon as they hit, though."

He stretched and grinned. "By the time I show up, I don't guess there'll much to see of the ship but another hummock in the swamp. Even the island's not as solid as all that, you know."

"I see," Mark said. Yerby's beaming face had just melted away the field of smashed bodies he'd been imagining.

Amy switched the radio to normal operation instead of data link to the landing system. "This is Woodsrunners command to all Woodsrunners," she said into the microphone. "Pass this message on."

"Tell 'em to gather at the north end of The Goo," Yerby ordered in a stage whisper. "That's where I'll take our visitors out."

Amy nodded. Mark and Yerby stepped into the hallway, where they could speak without interfering with Amy. She was switching bands after each set of radioed instructions.

"Are you planning to fly in alone?" Mark asked.

"I'm going to *walk* in," the frontiersman said. "I figure our visitors are going to keep their personal guns, most of them. I don't want them to capture a flyer. There's enough Zenith settlers on Greenwood that somebody'd likely mount a rescue try if he heard about it. Nobody's going to walk out of The Goo, though, without I lead him and he's *real* polite."

"I didn't know there was any way into The Goo, Yerby," said Tindouf, a hired logger whose cracked ribs had kept him hanging around the compound for the past few days. "Except you fly."

"There's a way," Yerby insisted. "But nothing some Zenith is likely to find by himself. I'll bring 'em all out and it won't cost them a centime they haven't paid already."

He frowned regretfully and said, "I'd sure like the aircars and other fancy stuff they brought, but I'm not going to try and dig down through a swamp neither. Guess we'll get some guns out of the business, though."

Mark started to speak, then closed his mouth in embarrassment at what he'd been about to ask. Yerby grinned at him and said, "Say kid? How'd you like to come along with me? It'll be muddy, mind."

Amy paused, half turned, then hunched closer to the microphone. She continued to reel off instructions to the militia.

"If you'll have me," Mark said, "I'd be honored."

He'd been afraid of putting himself forward into a situation where he clearly didn't belong; a form of boasting, and therefore unworthy of a gentleman.

"Yeah, I would," Yerby said. He scowled with embarrassment and continued, "Now, don't take this wrong, lad . . . but I want to make sure the path's safe for somebody who hasn't, you know, spent as many years outdoors as I have. OK?"

Mark grinned. "I'm your guinea pig," he said. "Let's get started!"

22. Greenwood Justice

The mud was gray, sulphurous and stuck like glue. Mostly it was covered by vegetation. Shrubs on firm ground grew as much as ten feet in the air and spread their leaves widely, and dazzling little splotches lifted themselves six inches from the nearly liquid surface.

Every once in a while, a tall stem that cantilevered itself out from a hummock decoyed Mark into placing a foot a little beyond where Yerby'd stepped. As a result, Mark had as good a view of the mud as anybody could wish: it coated his coveralls to the throat. That was a much closer acquaintance than Mark desired, certainly.

Yerby prodded the surface ahead of him with a long piece of tubing. Mark had tried to carry a similar staff, but he'd quickly decided that he was better off with his hands free to clutch shrubs or his companion in the frequent crises. "How you doing, lad?" the frontiersman asked over his shoulder.

"I'm all right," Mark lied. He didn't think he'd ever been as exhausted in his life. The mud was warm as well as being sticky. Trying not to gasp, he added, "I guess this basin must be volcanic."

"Yeah, I reckon," Yerby agreed as he hopped nonchalantly to what Mark would have guessed was a sinkhole. The footing easily held the big man's weight. "It's the prettiest thing you ever saw in winter if the mist blows away, all green and cheerful in the middle of the snow."

Mark jumped. His muddy legs weighed him down. Yerby grabbed Mark's hand and snatched him from disaster. The ground felt like rock beneath a slime of mud.

"Don't worry, lad," Yerby said. "We're just about there. If them Zeniths do half so good as you, we'll get them clear no problem."

Mark took another step by rote. He was too tired to do anything except previous actions. Yerby caught him and steered him to the right, through a copse of virid shrubs. To Mark the ground looked exactly the same.

"Right there," Yerby explained with a nod, "there's a pit that don't stop till you're on the other side of the planet."

He walked Mark through a screen of diaphanous tendrils. About a hundred frightened-looking men and women milled or squatted fifty feet away. The *Aten*'s splashdown had disturbed the expanse of mud between them and Mark. Alternate bands of tumbled plants and glutinous mud marked the arcs of compression.

The starship was a low gray dome behind the Zeniths. Yerby'd been right when he guessed that the ship would have sunk almost out of sight by the time he reached it.

Zenith soldiers—to Mark's surprise they were wearing light blue uniforms—lurched to their feet. A squat man in particularly brilliant garb pointed at Yerby and Mark.

"Hold it right there!" he shouted. "I warn you, we're armed!"

"Ah, but you won't be when you leave here," Yerby said without concern. He eyed the pattern of ripples, shock waves frozen or at least numbed into the ground. Despite his weight, Yerby hopped from one point to the next without his boots ever sinking above the instep. Mark followed, his heart in his throat. For a wonder he managed to join the frontiersman and the Zenith troops without another minor disaster.

"Hello, Mayor Biber," Mark said to the Zenith commander, panting only slightly. Success at crossing the open space made him feel so good that he didn't notice the pressure of the dozen or more guns pointed at his head and chest. "I didn't expect to find you here."

Biber glared at Mark, trying to place him. The Mayor of New Paris was all mud to the hips. The same misstep had sucked off one of his knee boots.

"You're under arrest!" Biber said. "Captain van den Brook, take these men into custody!"

These weren't soldiers, they were police—the New Paris Civic Watch, according to the garish yellow-and-orange patches on their left shoulders. Their weapons were a mélange of a dozen different sorts—mostly nonlethal, at least by design. Mark remembered Yerby's warning about the dangers of a badly made nerve scrambler.

"I think you've misplaced your jail, Mayor," Yerby said. He hooked a thumb in the direction of the starship. The vessel gave a sad groan; the ground shivered. "Matter of fact, you've misplaced just about every durn thing, ain't you? Including food."

"All right, Bannock," Biber ordered curtly. He drew a long-barreled, chrome-plated pistol from a holster and pointed it in Yerby's face. "You're going to lead us out of here. Now!"

"And so I am," Yerby agreed. "That's what I come here for. But first you're going to lay all your pretty hardware down. Understood?"

"We can force you to tell us the path!" said Captain van den Brook, a woman whose face could give Desiree points for grim.

Mark started to laugh. Only a shade of his chortling peals was hysteria. "Oh, Captain!" he said. "Oh, *Captain!*"

When he managed to control himself—*boy! had he needed a laugh*—Mark pointed at his muddy coveralls. "Look," he said, "this is the best I could do following Yerby step by step."

The Zeniths already appeared cowed and puzzled. Mark grinned and continued, "If you think you can torture directions out of him, you'd better think again. He's got to lead, and he's got to be free when he does. I couldn't find my way back across the patch right there, and I just came over it."

He swept his hand in a broad circle at the rippled muck behind him.

"I can't let you keep your guns, you see," Yerby said in a tone of calm reasonableness. "But they wouldn't do nothing save drag you under if I did. You'll have work enough getting back to dry ground as it is."

Biber scowled. Instead of answering immediately, he walked a few steps in the direction from which Mark and Yerby had arrived. Maybe he was looking for footprints.

"Watch," Yerby said to Captain van den Brook. He put the tip of his thin rod on the ground beside him and thrust it several feet down at an angle.

Biber turned to see what the frontiersman was doing. A huge bubble, nauseating with sulfur and rotting vegetation, burped from the gooey soil at Biber's feet and swallowed him.

"Eee!" the Mayor screamed as he sank.

Yerby stepped over, grabbed, and dragged Biber up by the collar just as the return wave was about to flow over the mayor's mouth and nose. Yerby smiled at the man he held. "D'ye take my point, son?" he asked gently.

"Stack arms!" Captain van den Brook ordered. Biber nodded, but he was still too terrified to speak.

"Not there, boy!" Mark shouted at a Zenith policeman probably twice his age. "Bring your foot another six inches left or you'll sink to the other side of the planet. And I'm *hanged* if I bother to fish another of you losers out!"

Triumph had brought out a facet of Mark's personality he was pretty sure he was going to be ashamed of in the morning. Furthermore, the feeling of power didn't bring any real strength back into his muscles. His arms seemed to weigh tons, not just from the coating of mud he'd gotten pulling Zeniths to safety, and his legs were numb.

But oh! the triumph! Yerby led the column. He'd left Mark at the first really tricky spot, a dogleg where the bush that looked like a perfect handhold was actually covered by hair-fine poisonous thorns. When Mark had chivvied the last of the prisoners past that point, he'd tramped his way to the front of the line again.

Yerby had used him three more times as a human signpost. That made Mark as proud as the praise Dr. Kelsing had given his seminar paper, "The Evolution of Civil Law on Quelhagen."

After the first hundred yards of The Goo, a couple dirigibles had moved close to the line of march. By then, any weapons the Zeniths might have concealed in their clothes were too gummy to be used to hijack a vehicle. Ropes dangling from the dirigibles pulled a number of floundering Zeniths from the muck, but none of them were allowed to ride. Yerby was making sure that the invaders were punished and humiliated as well as being defeated.

In one sense that meant a lot of unnecessary effort for him and Mark, but Mark knew that it was at least as important to prevent the Zeniths from repeating their invasion as it was to stop them dead this time. He didn't think any members of this police unit would be back to Greenwood during their present lifetimes.

"Come on!" Mark snarled to the back of the last Zenith, who was swaying on the trunk of a sapling to gather strength. The hands of the folk ahead in the column had worn away the tree's soft bark. "You'll have plenty of time to rest when you head back to Zenith in a freighter's hold. Move it!"

Mark's civilized part was amazed at the way he was acting toward the prisoners. You'd have thought he was a frontiersman as barbaric as Yerby himself. The Zeniths probably did think that. . . .

A dirigible dropped close. Amy wasn't in this one, but she'd followed most of the line of march with her camera.

A dozen dirigibles bobbed through the foliage in the near distance. The lip of the basin had to be close.

Mark's boots scraped the first firm ground in what felt like a lifetime. The vegetation changed abruptly from fleshy shrubs to Greenwood's equivalent of grass. He was out of The Goo.

"There you are, lad!" Yerby boomed. He offered a hand-blown bottle. "Say, I'll tell the world that you're a man! Come have a sip of something to cut the mud, why don't you?"

Well over a hundred Greenwood settlers, armed to the teeth, guarded the Zeniths on the downslope beyond The Goo. Many of the Greenwoods carried weapons that the police themselves had left behind at the *Aten*.

Groups of ten or a dozen prisoners at a time were herded into cargo nets slung from dirigible gondolas. Amy had her camera out. The Zeniths would squeeze together like fruit in a mesh bag when the dirigibles rose, but Mark didn't suppose anybody'd be seriously injured in the short flight to the Spiker.

He managed to stay upright for the few steps it took to reach Yerby and the bottle. Other Woodsrunners stood nearby, nodding to Mark with obvious respect. Yerby sounded as vibrant as he ever had, but Mark noticed that the big man was leaning on his staff. He'd dragged Zeniths from the clinging muck dozens of times during the trek; exertion like that took a toll even on Yerby.

Mark lifted the bottle, knowing that everybody was watching him, and drank deep. He gagged, coughed, and spewed the liquor out through his nostrils. It burned like molten lead on the delicate mucous membranes.

"Atta boy!" Yerby said, pounding Mark's back. "Clean the goo out, and by all that's holy, that's just what he did!"

The frontiersman expertly retrieved the bottle from Mark's numb fingers and went on, "Now, let's get off to the Spiker and finish this game, shall we?"

"Sounds good to me," Mark wheezed.

Yerby had to walk him onto the deck of the Bannock dirigible. It was nearly a minute before Mark's eyes stopped watering enough that he could see again. If what was in the bottle was whiskey, then Mark would ask for varnish remover the next time.

Desiree was at the controls. They were the last of the line of dirigibles, none of them more than twenty feet off the ground because of the overload of prisoners dangling below in the nets. Zeniths cursed with all the strength the trek had left them, which wasn't very much.

Flyers circled overhead like insects dancing. Mark had noticed that settlers hadn't taken them over The Goo, though. If bad luck or bad judgment landed a flyer in the slime, it and the pilot would sink out of sight before help could arrive.

The crusted mud was starting to flake off. Mark now itched as well as felt filthy.

"I can't believe I did that," he whispered. The phrase was starting to be a habit. He wondered how many more times he'd say it on Greenwood.

He wondered how much longer he'd *survive* on Greenwood. Assuming that he'd really survived this time. He was so tired . . .

Yerby took another pull from the bottle and hugged Mark with one arm. "You did fine!" he said. "Amy, child?

Did you get a ship at the Spiker to take these fools off-planet soonest?"

"Yes and no," Amy said. Mark had expected at least a minor explosion to follow "Amy, child," but she looked affectionately at both men. "Captain Krause of the *Brother Jacques* is willing to take them to Dittersdorf, but he wants you to pay him before they board. Since most of them will have to make the flight awake, he's doubtful that they'll be in any mood to pay when they arrive."

Yerby chuckled. "I'll see he gets paid," he said. He nodded toward the cabin and said in a lower voice, "Surprised Desiree didn't tell him to load them or she'd stick him for a bow ornament on his ship."

Amy's smile became wintry. "She said something like that," she said. "I said that wasn't acceptable in a civilized society."

She cleared her throat and glared. "Which Greenwood is."

Yerby started to throw the empty bottle over the side of the gondola. Mark raised a hand in reminder. "Oh, right," the frontiersman said. He stuck the empty inside his shirt. "Hard to remember this stuff, though."

The *Brother Jacques* was already winching itself onto the magnetic mass. Captain Krause was easy to identify because of his white coat with six inches of gold braid on the wrists. He stood just outside the Spiker in a group of Woodsrunners, spectators, and the prisoners brought by the leading dirigibles.

Desiree landed more forcefully than usual, giving the Zeniths a solid thump before she was done with them. Captain Krause strode toward the dirigible, waving his hat and shouting, "Yerby, you know I'm always willing to do you a favor, but this, this is a whole cargo! You must pay me!"

Yerby stepped briskly to the ground. Mark stumbled as he followed; he wondered if he should have tried another swig of that liquor, since it seemed to have worked wonders for Yerby. Amy steadied him, smiling again even though touching Mark muddied her hand.

"Where's Biber?" Yerby shouted cheerfully as if he were calling a dog. "Here, Mayor-Mayor-Mayor! Ah, there you are."

Mayor Biber was covered, head to toe, with half-dried muck. He'd managed to blow his nostrils and mouth open; his eyes glared furiously out from deep mud caves.

"I demand you provide us with showers and clean clothes this instant, you *pirate!*" he cried, showering chunks of dirt. The other Zeniths edged away from him.

"Oh, I don't figure we'll do that," Yerby said mildly. "You folk were so determined to take our land that it'd be right unneighborly to let you go home without some of it. But that's not what we need to talk about."

"I demand!" Biber screamed.

Settlers began to laugh. Mark noticed from the corner of his eye that Amy was recording the scene.

"The question," Yerby said, as if the Mayor hadn't spoken, "is whether you pay your folks' passage back to Dittersdorf or I do."

"There's no way you can make me pay anything, you bandit!" the mayor said. "Any payment will be extorted by force! My bank will refuse any such demand if it's presented."

"Not a bit of it," Yerby said. "Amy, dear, you're getting all this?"

She nodded from behind the camera.

"What I'm saying is that I *will* pay the passage for every single one of your people to Dittersdorf myself," Yerby said. "Because I'm a friend to the distressed. It's just yours I won't pay. And you won't be held a prisoner if you don't want to pay, neither. I'll return you to your own ship this instant."

Biber's mouth opened, closed, and stayed closed for a moment.

"That's a damned good idea," a woman said. She was one of the prisoners. "A *damned* good idea!" There was a general rumble of agreement among the Zeniths close enough to hear.

"I'll pay," Biber squeaked.

"One more thing, Yerby," Mark said. "Our guests should be stripped and hosed off right here before they board."

Yerby planted his fists on his hipbones. "I like 'em the way they are," he said truculently.

Mark grinned and shook his head. "One at a time," he explained. "While Amy records the process. For history."

Yerby guffawed and hugged Mark. "See how smart the little fellow is?" he called to the laughing crowd.

"And while that's going on," Mark added, "*I'm* going to the tavern and taking a proper shower!"

23. More Company

The Zeniths would get clean enough in the jet from the firehose, but hot water in the Spiker's shower room sucked the fatigue from Mark's muscles as well as sluicing the mud away. He was stretching, wondering what could be a greater luxury, when a draft from the door opening made the mist swirl. Mark peered from the spray.

"Mr. Maxwell?" Blaney called. "There's a fellow here wants to see you when you're free. A gentleman, I shouldn't be surprised."

Mark shut off the taps. "What's he want?" he asked, taking the borrowed towel from a sheltered niche. Under the towel were the canvas work clothes he'd borrowed also. He wasn't sure he'd ever believe the coveralls that went through The Goo were clean enough to wear again.

"Wouldn't say, sir," Blaney said, helping Mark on with the pull-over shirt. "Got in this morning from Dittersdorf. When he saw you come in, he said he'd wait till you cleaned up. He figured you'd want that."

"He was right," Mark muttered. It couldn't be some-body from Zenith intending to kidnap him, could it? Surely not here at the Spiker!

The local boots were soft and almost shapeless. Mark cinched them to his legs with the external straps and strode with Blaney into the barracks-style bunkroom to see who was waiting for him.

His father was waiting for him.

Lucius put a finger to his lips and said "No names just now!" before Mark could blurt a greeting. "Let's take a walk, shall we?"

He gave Blaney a nod of bland approval. Down the hallway somebody overset a tray with a crash. A man and a woman began to shout recriminations at one another. Blaney shook his head regretfully and scurried off to take charge.

"Yeah, I guess we ought to," Mark agreed. He followed his father toward the back door. Lucius wore loose-fitting battle dress that had been used hard in the past. It gave Mark the general impression of being gray, but in the sunlight he could see that it was really a mix of many tiny dots of color from violet to deep red.

As well as being practical, the garment was a perfect disguise. No casually met Greenwood settler would connect this figure with Attorney Maxwell of Quelhagen. It was typical of Lucius to wear something absolutely appropriate. Mark only wondered where his father had found it.

"I wasn't expecting you," he said. Boy, he was repeating *everything* since he came to Greenwood.

Lucius shrugged. "I had a question that only you could

answer," he said. "It wasn't one I thought I could entrust to anybody else to carry, so I—" He smiled, a tight expression to cover embarrassment with humor. "—took the excuse to visit you in your new environment."

They were at the back of the tavern, overlooking the river. From here the view was beautiful. If you got closer to the edge of the bluff, you could see the moraine of garbage and slaughterhouse waste. The recycling plant hadn't been delivered yet, and Mark hadn't figured quite how to deal with the accumulation from previous years either.

"I believe," Lucius said, fixing Mark with his eyes, "that the Alliance Protectorate Office is going to suggest a compromise: that all Hestia grants held by actual settlers be confirmed, but that Hestia grants in the hands of nonresident investors become void. I suspect that the Zenith syndicate will be smart enough to accept the offer." He grinned coldly. "Certainly I would advise them to accept it if they were my clients. I need to know what your feelings about the offer are, Mark."

Mark's face remained blank. The question didn't matter. What worried him was why his father had asked *him*. He couldn't imagine a reason.

"Ah," Mark said. There were two dirigibles and dozens of flyers in the sky, more than you'd usually see airborne at one time. Settlers were pouring toward the Spiker from distant tracts, either too late to join the defense or just interested in the spectacle of victory.

Mark met his father's gaze again. "Dad," he said, "I can't speak for Greenwood. I don't have any idea what the people want. There's probably as many notions as there are settlers. It's that sort of place."

He cleared his throat and added diffidently, "Besides, it's the investors who're really paying your costs, isn't it? Surely they wouldn't agree to that."

"If I wanted to know what the whole citizenry of Greenwood wished," Lucius said, each syllable snapping out like a trap shutting, "I suppose I'd hold a referendum. I cannot imagine bothering to do so, since they've put Yerby Bannock in charge. If they're wise, they'll do whatever he says and like it."

Mark stiffened to attention. "Father—" he said.

"As for the investors who may ethically be considered my clients, Mark," Lucius continued with the same cold passion, "I assure you that if it becomes impossible for me to meet both my personal and my professional obligations, I will resign the latter without a qualm. I was a man before I became a lawyer. Now—" His tone softened minutely. "—will you please answer the original question?"

"Yes, sir," Mark said. "Sir, I stand with Greenwood. With the planet, I mean. I hope with the people too, but I can't say about that."

He coughed and wiped his lips with the back of his hand. His skin smelled of the harsh soap with which he'd scrubbed off The Goo.

"Dad," Mark went on, "if the Zeniths win—and that's winning—they'll bring in preformed cities, hundreds of thousands of people. Settlers like that aren't really immigrants, they're people Earth governments have exiled to get them off the welfare rolls. They'll swamp the planet and turn it into a garbage dump. I don't want that."

Lucius' grin had a cruel edge. "Do you think Elector Daniels heads a syndicate of altruists, then?" he asked.

"No," said Mark. "No, they're the same sort of people as the Zeniths, I know that. But Biber and Finch own the Zenith government."

He slapped the wall of the Spiker. "The Greenwood Assembly's going to meet right here in ten days' time," he said. "That's everybody on the planet who wants to come. They're going to pass a minimum requirement of owning two thousand square miles for anybody who stays on the planet for more than thirty days!"

"Clever," Lucius said. "Did you come up with the idea?"

Mark grinned. "Yeah, I sort of did," he admitted. "Daniels' lot can't say a word about it."

Lucius nodded. "So far as the Alliance is concerned, Greenwood remains under Zenith administration," he said. "But you know that."

He chuckled. "And we can let the evil of the day be sufficient unto it," he added. "Well, Elector Daniels will be pleased, and I'm rather pleased to be able to continue taking his money in good conscience. That's all the business I had to transact here."

"Ah, Dad?" Mark said. "I guess you'll be here a few days."

Lucius nodded.

"Let me introduce you to some people, then," Mark said. "Even the ones you've met are a lot different here than when you saw them on Zenith."

"Except," Lucius said, "for Yerby Bannock, I suspect. Yes, I'd like that."

He linked his arm with Mark's. They walked through the tavern to the celebration on the other side.

24. Local Political Differences

The giant ribbonfish was at least a quarter of a mile long. It glittered beneath the slow billows like a bracelet made of millions of tiny jewels, each a separate living organism. Amy had been careful to keep the dirigible to the east of the creature so that their shadow wouldn't spook it. One of the high clouds moved across the afternoon sun. The whole huge assemblage dived slowly, following the microorganisms that were its food.

"I'm so glad we got to see that, Lucius," Amy said. "I hope it made the last day of your stay memorable."

Mark straightened; he'd been leaning over the deck railing. "You bring good luck, Dad," he said. "I hadn't seen a ribbonfish myself. Yerby'd mentioned them, is all."

"The luck was the sharp eyes of our hostess, I'd say," Lucius remarked. "Amy, I'm much obliged to you. Greenwood is indeed a lovely planet, and I couldn't have had a better pair of guides to it."

The men went into the cabin to join Amy at the controls.

They'd followed the giant ribbonfish for nearly an hour, entranced by the shifting patterns of its structure, so it was probably time they headed home anyway. The Bannock compound was a good eighty miles away, so they wouldn't be reaching it till pretty close to nightfall.

"There's a village down there," Amy said, nodding to the right as she turned the rudder and four engine nacelles to full lock. The dirigible was the safest vehicle Mark could imagine for a planet as sparsely inhabited as Greenwood, but it was glacially slow to execute any change. "Where are we, Mark?"

Mark brought up a map display on his viewer. Lucius watched over his shoulder, hunching slightly to be able to see the air-formed holograms.

"I think . . ." he said. "OK, it must be Blind Cove. About ten houses?"

He peered out the side window. The community was several miles away, but its size seemed several times the figure in the atlas. The Spiker's database was out of date.

Several flyers were lifting from the houses. The sky was mostly sunny with sharply defined clouds. The locals would have no difficulty joining the dirigible in a few minutes.

"Blind Cove sounds familiar," Amy said. The slight breeze was still enough to make the dirigible handle like a barge in a millrace. As the bow came around, the whole vessel drifted downwind at better than a walking pace.

"A magistrate in Blind Cove issued the summonses in the ejectment suit," Lucius said. "Mark, are there any weapons aboard?"

Mark didn't know. He began to bang open the doors of

the deck-level cabinets around the cabin. There were ropes and quite a lot of obvious trash, but nothing useful. The black patch on the royal blue fabric made the Bannock dirigible identifiable as far as anybody could see it.

Lucius checked the toolbox on the back of the cabin. "Some wrenches and screwdrivers," he announced. "Useful in a pinch, but I think we'll be better off not displaying them until we're quite sure of the others' intentions."

He not only sounded calm, he sounded as if this were the sort of thing that happened to him every day.

Mark walked out on the open deck. There were four flyers. They moved sluggishly, indicating they were heavily loaded even though each had only one man aboard. Amy was gaining altitude as quickly as she could without emergency measures. No matter what she did, the flyers could still outclimb the clumsy dirigible in ten or fifteen minutes, so there was no point in dumping ballast.

The dirigible wallowed, losing a noticeable amount of height and power. They'd entered the shadow of a cloud. The engines picked up again as the batteries came online, boosting the output of the solar cells on the top of the envelope. The Blind Cove flyers were of off-world manufacture and had working battery packs, though they had to keep beyond the shadow to climb.

"Amy," Lucius said. He stepped to her side. "Give me the controls, please." As he spoke, he put his hands on the helm without waiting for the woman to reply.

"Dad?" Mark said in amazement.

Amy backed away from the controls. Blank calm replaced her initial look of consternation. She didn't know what Lucius planned to do, but she was willing to trust his judgment in a case where she saw no way out.

Mark watched the flyers. When Amy joined him on the open deck he said, "I suppose they think we're Yerby."

"I suppose," Amy agreed in a flat voice.

Lucius had dropped the dirigible to twenty feet above the shadowed forest by the time the flyers from Blind Cove reached them. Three flyers mounted high while the last circled close to the gondola. The pilot was a bearded man whose face was red with drink and anger.

"Where d'ye think you're going, Bannock?" the man shouted. "We're not going to let you get away so easy, you know!"

He hurled a bottle one-handed at Mark. It didn't come within twenty feet of the dirigible. Several more empty bottles plunged past the vessel, warbling as the air streamed past their mouths. A clank and a shower of broken glass indicated that one of the flyer pilots above had found the range.

Amy took out her camera. A flyer dived past the gasbag, then zoomed up again as the pilot shouted curses in a hoarse voice.

Mark pressed his lips together and said nothing. Lucius had headed basically downwind. With a following breeze, the dirigible was about as fast as a flyer, but this course was going to take them out over the ocean again very shortly.

More missiles dropped. Several hit; the locals were improving their technique with practice. Even though they weren't using lethal weapons, the impacts would damage the solar cells. Sooner or later they'd start tearing holes in the ballonets. Mark didn't want to be over salt water if the dirigible was forced down.

When the dirigible was forced down.

"Dad?" he called. "If you get some altitude, we can maybe get a radio signal through to Yerby or the Spiker."

"In good time," his father said. He didn't raise his voice, but there was steel in his tone.

The dirigible crossed the sandy beach, still only twenty feet above the surface. A jagged piece of metal screamed past them and splashed in the surf. What sounded like a wooden crate of bottles smashed on the upper surface and rained shards of glass down on all sides.

The flyers were holding course directly above the dirigible, so now they hit more often than not. Mark put an arm around Amy without looking at her. She leaned forward, recording the pattern of fragments splashing in the water.

The dirigible was traveling at nearly forty-five miles an hour. Immediately ahead of them the sea brightened to sunlit splendor; they were about to leave the shadow of the cloud in which they'd been proceeding since before Lucius took the helm.

"Hold tight!" Lucius shouted. The dirigible entered sunlight. Lucius pulled the lever that dumped the entire water ballast from the bottom of the gondola. The sea roiled like a storm surge as the dirigible shot upward faster than Mark had dreamed it could.

Somebody screamed in fear from above them. The flyers flicked past to either side. Three were under marginal control; the wing of the last was cocked up at a 45° angle with a bent spar. It spiraled wildly down toward the sea as the bearded man who'd thrown the first bottle fought his controls in vain.

The dirigible gained five hundred feet in a few seconds and continued to rise. "Amy?" Lucius called from the helm. "Would you care to take the controls again? I'm not sure I could find the compound."

"Dad, what did you do?" Mark asked as Amy took the helm. They'd passed a thousand feet. At this rate, the flyers wouldn't be able to reach the dirigible again in less than an hour, even if the Blind Cove settlers had the stomach to try.

"The gas cools in the cloud's shadow," Lucius said. He rubbed the back of his hand across his eyes. "When we came into the sunlight, it expanded very quickly and gave us a great deal more lift. In combination with dumping the ballast, I thought we could rise fast enough to . . . at least disconcert the others."

"There's only a few hundred settlers on Zenith grants on the planet," Mark said quietly. "I suppose they've been treated pretty roughly the past month or two."

"No doubt," his father said. Lucius turned to Amy and went on, "Ms. Bannock? I'm very sorry about the ballast, but I thought it was necessary. I'm afraid it will make landing difficult."

"I'll manage, Lucius," she replied. "And I'm still Amy, remember."

Mark lifted the radio handset and said, "This is the Bannock blimp to all Woodsrunners. We're headed home from just west of Blind Cove, and I'd *really* like some company!"

25. A Pause for Reflection

The fireworks for Lucius' send-off celebration were homemade. The first bomb *choonk*ed into the night sky from the tube by the Spiker's front entrance and exploded in a green flash five hundred feet over the starport. The second followed twenty seconds later and burst brilliantly white.

The third blew the launcher up in a great scarlet eruption. Fragments of metal pinged off the courtyard wall. The pyrotechnics crew, four brothers jointly settling a tract well to the east, capered and beat at places where sparks had ignited their clothing and hair. The crowd—those who hadn't been close enough to have their own mini-fires to deal with—cheered wildly and continued drinking.

There were several hundred people at the gathering, far too many for the tavern itself to put up. Lights and fires dotted the slope down to the landing field. Folk were camping in tents or just bedrolls, and many were heating their dinners besides.

The freighter *Ice Queen*, bound for Quelhagen after a

quick turnaround on Greenwood, had been winched onto the magnetic mass. The starship's underside was brightly lit as the crew gave a last-minute check to an induction module.

When the brothers started to light the fireworks, Lucius had backed himself and Mark into the nook beside the gateposts—out of direct sight of the nearby launchers. Now father and son eased forward again.

"Good thing we were covered," Mark said, patting the gatepost with the heel of his hand. "Good thing you thought of it."

Lucius looked at the cheerful settlers. They were a scattering of silhouettes and shadows; firelight picked out an occasional bearded face or the glint of a bottle. He knew only a handful of them, and many didn't know him. They were present for a party, and because Yerby Bannock had called them to honor an ally.

"What are you thinking, Dad?" Mark asked. His father's smile was oddly wistful.

Lucius looked at him. "That for people on the edge of disaster, risking their lives every day, living in enormous discomfort and often squalor," he said, "they're oddly happy, aren't they? But perhaps it's not so odd. Just something one becomes too sophisticated to appreciate."

"We're trying to do something about the squalor, at least," Mark said defensively. "The *Ice Queen* brought the recycling plant for the Spiker. You've seen the unit Yerby's installing, right?"

His father laughed wholeheartedly, a sound as unlikely and disconcerting as sight of Lucius in battle dress on his arrival had been. He'd returned to being a proper

Quelhagen gentleman for his departure. "I'm sure you will, Mark," he said. "One of the problems with frontiers is that they attract folk whose only concern is where their next meal is going to come from. Of course those are the people most likely to survive on a frontier, as well."

Lucius cleared his throat. "We don't talk very much, you and I. About personal matters."

"No, sir," Mark said, feeling his body stiffen. They both stared in the direction of the waiting starship rather than meet one another's eyes.

Lucius chuckled. "Well, don't worry," he said. "We're not going to start now." He rested his fingers lightly on Mark's shoulder. "There are a few things that I should say, however."

Mark turned. He grinned, but his muscles were still tense. He wondered what Yerby's relationship with his own father had been like.

"I won't ask if you'll be all right," Lucius said, "because none of us know the answer to that. And I won't ask you to be careful, because I know you're young."

He smiled tightly. Mark nodded without returning the smile.

"I will tell you, though," Lucius continued, "that in the long run it's even more important to know which battles to fight than it is to win the battles you do fight."

He cleared his throat. "Well," he said, "I think I'll get down to the ship. I'd appreciate it if you'd stay here and make my excuses. If I take formal leave of everyone I've met, they'll each ask me to take a drink with them. I don't care to be churlish, but neither do I want to be poured into my capsule on the *Ice Queen*."

He smiled again at the bit of deliberate humor.

"I understand," Mark said. He understood perfectly: neither he nor his father knew how to say goodbye for what might be the last time. "I'll explain to people."

He nodded to Lucius, one Quelhagen gentleman taking leave of another.

"Mark," Lucius said, "know that while you're doing your duty, whatever that may be, your father is doing the same in his own way."

He turned abruptly on his heel and strode toward the starship. He moved with ease through the crowd of reveling settlers.

"Say, that's Lucius!" Yerby Bannock said as he walked toward Mark from the group in the vicinity of the late fireworks launcher. "Is he coming back, then?"

Yerby's broad-brimmed hat was still smoldering. An odor of burned leather clung to him. Amy followed her brother, looking diffident and concerned. Mark was glad to see she'd avoided the gout of sparks.

"Ah, not this trip," Mark said. "He asked that I thank everyone for their hospitality. Goodbyes embarrass him." Lucius would have winced to hear that truth, but he wouldn't have disagreed.

"Well, he'll be back," Yerby said, still watching the elder Maxwell walk briskly toward the starship. He took off his hat and fanned himself with it, blurring together the tendrils of smoke.

"You know," the frontiersman added, "your old man ain't a big package, but I sure *hell* wouldn't choose him for an enemy. Not so long as I've got to sleep sometimes, anyhow."

"I'm glad we could show your father some of Greenwood, Mark," Amy said quietly.

Mark swallowed and nodded. "Like Yerby says, he'll be back," he said. "We'll have the recycling plant here at the Spiker working by then, too."

"Next thing to do," Yerby said, still looking in the direction of the *Ice Queen,* "is to take care of Blind Cove. Tomorrow night, I figure. That's the other reason I called this get-together."

26. More Local Politics

Mark leaned on the dirigible's railing to peer forward past the cabin. He could see Blind Cove's forty-odd dwellings clearly, because Greenwood's third moon was at mid-sky, but the only artificial light in the community was the lamp hanging above Magistrate Saunderson's two-story house.

Twenty dirigibles were packed with nearly three hundred Woodsrunners. Two more airships approached the community from the sea, carrying only a few marksmen each.

Blind Cove was a fishing village. There was a chance that the locals would try to escape in the boats hauled up on the shore. Yerby didn't intend to allow anybody to get away.

The Woodsrunners weren't using flyers, since the attack was timed to arrive at Blind Cove at midnight. To Mark's slight surprise, the armada had managed to keep together and wasn't running more than ten minutes late.

Most of the dirigibles landed beyond the outer buildings of the community. As planned, Desiree brought the

Bannock vessel down in the small park fronting Saunderson's house. "Come on!" Yerby called, vaulting over the rail with his flashgun in his free hand.

The overload of militiamen followed as suddenly as a dump of ballast. Nobody was waiting to grab the mooring lines, so the airship bounced skyward again.

By the time Mark reached the gate—he wasn't about to go over the railing when he was burdened with a heavy-duty nerve scrambler—the deck was ten feet in the air. He jumped anyway. The shock of landing drove the breath from his lungs, but at least he didn't lose his footing and fall flat.

The last man off the deck cannoned into Mark and *knocked* him flat. The shoulder-stocked nerve scrambler flew out of Mark's arms like a javelin to spear the ground at Yerby's feet.

If Yerby even noticed he'd almost been crippled by the sharp muzzle, he didn't seem to care. "All right!" he ordered. "Let's wake them up!"

Militiamen pulled the igniters of light spikes, thermite/paraffin candles that gave five minutes of brilliant illumination even in a thunderstorm. The spikes' rippling glare turned the sleepy village into a suburb of Hell.

The Wily brothers were in one of the dirigibles that had landed on the beach. They tossed the bombs they'd prepared into the fishing boats whose empty holds would magnify the blasts.

The bombs flashed white in quick stuttering succession. It seemed to Mark that they'd have been plenty noisy without the cavernous echoes. Three of the eight went off almost simultaneously. The villagers would have been justified in expecting the next sound to be that of buildings falling into a huge crack in the earth.

The pole supporting one boat's net-stretching boom shot skyward, nearly skewering an airship on the way up. It plunged back down through the thick plastic roof of Saunderson's house.

"*Yee-ha!*" Yerby cried. "Come on out, you Zenith land-robbers! The law's just caught up with you!"

Lights went on in most of the houses, though Mark noticed some of the locals had realized that there was nothing good to be gained by illuminating themselves. It wasn't going to matter in the long run. Eight or ten Woodsrunners were breaking into every dwelling. Yerby had brought such overwhelming numbers that none of the villagers would even think of resisting.

Mark wiped at the muzzle of his nerve scrambler as he ran with Yerby to Saunderson's door. He'd gotten the discharge needle dirty and he was afraid he'd bent it besides.

It might not matter. Mark wasn't sure he was willing to shoot somebody even with a weapon that wasn't supposed to be lethal.

Yerby kicked the lockplate. He bounced back as the panel boomed. In Blind Cove the settlers built their houses of stone or concrete; whatever the magistrate used for his front door was a lot sturdier than wood. Yerby hobbled away on one foot, swearing a blue streak as he tried to squeeze life back into the numbed heel of the other.

"Let me get it, Yerby!" Troll Larsen bellowed. Troll was barely five feet tall, but he weighed as much as Yerby and was reputed to be equally strong. The other thing everybody knew about Troll was that he was the ugliest man on Greenwood.

He ran toward the door, adding his forward speed to the velocity of the twenty-pound sledgehammer he was swinging with the strength of both enormous arms. "I've got—"

The door opened from the inside. "What's the meaning of this?" demanded an erect, middle-aged man wearing a nightgown.

Troll spun through the open doorway, dragged by the inertia of the heavy hammer. Saunderson stepped back. "*Yeeeeeeee!*" Troll screamed. He hit something out of Mark's sight with a crash like another noise bomb.

The woman standing on the stairs behind Saunderson screamed also. That was a pretty common reaction for women meeting Troll for the first time, but this one had more reason than most.

"Mr. Ardis Saunderson?" Yerby boomed. "I hereby arrest you as a traitor to the citizens of Greenwood! George, hold him while we ferret out other miscreants."

Amy had waited for Desiree to set the airship down properly before she followed the armed Woodsrunners, but she was now on the ground recording events. At the moment the way Yerby stood like a stork on one leg rather spoiled what would otherwise have been an impressive scene.

"You have no authority whatever, you villain!" Saunderson cried.

George, one of Yerby's loggers, snatched the magistrate out of the way enthusiastically. Yerby skipped by them, using the toe only of his right foot. Mark, Amy, and half a dozen Woodsrunners jogged along behind.

The house's interior partitions weren't as sturdy as its outside walls. Troll lay in the wreckage of an imported sideboard and the dishes it had held. He still gripped the handle of his sledge. The twenty-pound head had knocked a huge hole into the kitchen. The dent beneath the hole was from Troll's head, judging from the paint sticking to his bare scalp.

The woman threw herself at Yerby, screaming and clawing. He grabbed her wrists and tossed her to another of the men, saying, "Take her outside, Elmont, and mind she don't blood you!"

"Mama!" cried a three-year-old child who appeared at the stairhead. He put his hands over his eyes, though he was still peering through the gaps between his fingers.

Child and mother wailed together. "I'll get him!" Mark said, glad of the excuse to drop the gun that made him feel so uncomfortable. "He's all right!"

He swept the boy into his arms and stood aside so that three Woodsrunners—man, wife, and a boy who couldn't be more than twelve—could thunder past. In the room below, Yerby plucked a Zenith flag from the wall and tossed it through the front door to be collected. There were two holoviews of New Paris, the Civil Affairs Building and the statue of the first Protector in the central park. They followed the flag.

Mark walked outside, carrying the child. Elmont held Saunderson's wife while a woman bound her.

"No," said Mark. "Not her." He gave the child to Mrs.

Saunderson. Mother and son wrapped their arms around one another. They continued to cry, but not quite so noisily.

The first light spikes were burning low; drops of blazing wax dribbled down the support rods. Woodsrunners lit replacements. The airships carried enough spikes to illuminate the park until dawn if necessary.

Mark found he was standing beside Amy. He hadn't consciously worked through the crowd to find her; or maybe he had. She recorded the scene in twenty-second takes, focusing on a face or an incident that gave meaning to what was chaos if you tried to view the whole thing at once. Her expression was set, withdrawn.

The villagers had been dragged from their beds and tied. Most were half naked. The night wasn't dangerously cold, but they were at a terrible psychological disadvantage compared to their captors.

Torchlit Woodsrunners walked in and out of the houses, emptying them of weapons and anything associated with Zenith. A father and son staggered from a house on the square, almost hidden behind the pile of clothing they carried.

"Hey!" Yerby cried from the Saundersons' doorway. Most people turned to look at him, but the pair with the garments continued to sidle toward an airship.

"Cooch Jezreal?" Yerby said. "You'll stop now or you'll wish you had! What's that you're carrying?"

The men halted. The father peeked from behind a mound of lace and velvet. "Aw, Yerby," he said. "You know my wife—"

"I know how to deal with a damned thief when I find

one, Jezreal!" Yerby said. "We're the instruments of justice, not a gang of brigands."

The Jezreals obviously had a notion of how Yerby would deal with a thief. They hunched back to the house they'd come from, moving rather faster than before.

Yerby walked into the park. Zenith paraphernalia was heaped in one corner. The cowed villagers stood beside it, more threatened than guarded by the crowd of militiamen.

Yerby held a sealed and embossed document in his left hand. He waved it under the magistrate's nose and said, "Ardis Saunderson, you're charged with being the agent of a foreign power, the Protector of Zenith. This very paper convicts you! How do you plead?"

Saunderson stood as straight as he could with his arms tied behind his back. "I am a magistrate appointed by the Protector of Zenith," he said in a clear voice. "You have my commission there, yes. The only thing I'll plead with you, Yerby Bannock, is that you spare my family and neighbors. They have no part in any actions I've taken in discharge of my duties."

Light from the illuminating spikes pulsed across Saunderson's face. He blinked. "It's the smoke!" he cried. "It's only the smoke!" There were tears on his cheeks.

The child was whimpering in his mother's arms. Mrs. Saunderson watched Yerby in silent terror, looking like a rabbit in the headlights.

Yerby wrenched a half-burned spike out of the ground, ignoring the occasional flaming droplet. He tossed it onto the pile of everything the villagers had brought with the name or a view of Zenith on it. Thick smoke rose as fire twisted down through frames and fabrics. Even metal burned at the touch of the spike's thermite core, throwing flickers of ghostly color over the conflagration.

Yerby hurled the magistrate's commission onto the fire. "Citizens of Greenwood!" he roared. "Do you find this man guilty of treason?"

"*Guilty!*" shouted the flame-shot night. Deep in the chorus were other shouts: "Hang 'em!" and "Burn them all alive!"

Mark shivered. His eyes stared straight ahead. His hand gripped Amy's. "They attacked us," he whispered. "They might have killed us all."

"That was them," Amy said. She'd stopped recording, but now she raised the camera again. "This is *us.*"

"Ardis Saunderson!" Yerby said. He took an unlit spike from Dagmar Wately. "You stand convicted before the court of your fellow-citizens. I sentence you to have your house burned and all your possessions with it!"

Yerby turned and jerked down the igniter tape. As the illuminating spike sputtered to life, he spun it twice above his head and flung it onto Saunderson's roof. The device rolled halfway down the moderate slope before heat softened the dense plastic roof plates. Tendrils of the molten surface gummed the spike to a halt. Sparks and the paraffin's yellow softness began to raise the plastic into low, smoky flames. They were the color of drying blood.

The other villagers had moved as far from Saunderson as the Woodsrunners let them. Most of the dozen children were crying. A man sobbed in abject terror. Another man, perhaps his brother from their similarity of features, watched him with mingled distaste and concern.

Saunderson's wife knelt, crooning to the child with her

head bowed so that she didn't have to look at the house. The magistrate moved closer to them. He stood with his feet planted firmly, watching the red flames creep across his roof like gangrene on an injured limb.

Yerby looked from Saunderson to his wife and son. "Ah, Christ almighty and His holy saints!" he said. He gestured to Mark and Amy. "You two—come cast me loose, fool that I am!"

Yerby shouldered his way through the crowd. By staying close, Mark and Amy were able to follow. Mark didn't have the slightest idea of what the frontiersman intended.

Woodsrunners passed around bottles, some of which resembled those the Blind Cove flyers had cascaded onto the dirigible the day before. Mark had the feeling that Yerby and the rest of the settlers considered liquor as much a necessity of life as air, so prohibitions on looting didn't apply.

". . . ought to burn a few more of them out!" somebody said louder than he needed to speak to a neighbor. "And you know—"

"Holophernes Maynard?" Yerby shouted over the sound of the crowd. "I know that if you do light off another house against my orders, I'll use your fat ass to smother the flames!"

He swung himself onto the deck of the Bannock dirigible. Mark started to follow. "No!" Yerby ordered from the control cabin. "Cast off the lines fore and aft!"

The airship was tied to a pair of trees the settlers had planted in the park. They weren't species native to Greenwood; Mark thought he'd seen similar ones, much larger, around the Civil Affairs Building in New Paris.

It took him a moment in the flickering light to decide which end of the clove hitch to feed back through the loop to release the tension. By the time Mark found it, Yerby was already bleeding hydrogen from the storage tanks into the ballonets where it could expand. The dirigible lurched upward, snatching the line from Mark's hands.

"Yerby?" a Woodsrunner called. "What the *hell* are you up to, Yerby?"

The dirigible lifted only forty feet in the air. The props were spinning at coarse pitch as Yerby cranked the big vessel sharply to starboard. Because it had no forward motion, the airship turned with surprising nimbleness.

"I don't know what he's doing," Amy said close to Mark's ear. "Do you?"

"I've no idea at all," Mark said, his eyes on the dirigible. The nose continued to swing. The updraft from Saunderson's burning roof shook it.

Mark's chest tightened. He cupped his hands into a megaphone and shouted, "Yerby! You're drifting over the fire! Watch the fire!"

Hydrogen had much greater lifting ability than any other gas, and because it was cheap an airship's tanks could be vented whenever water vapor started to weigh the ballonets down. The only thing that kept hydrogen from being perfect rather than simply the best choice was that it oozed through any container and burned with a hot blue flame if ignited. Normally that wasn't a problem, since leaking hydrogen rose . . . but so did sparks popping from bubbles of roof sheathing.

The dirigible slid forward, over the fire.

Half the roof was now covered in flames no higher than

moss growing from rocks in a slow stream. The plastic didn't burn easily, but the thermite torch had raised it to ignition temperature. The blaze would continue until the trusses collapsed and poured a gout of red fire through the building's interior.

Yerby dumped his ballast. The dirigible shot skyward in a booming mushroom of steam. Mist and hot water sprayed over the crowd. Frontiersmen screamed and cursed—

And started laughing, most of them, as they usually did after a surprise. And resumed drinking, as they always did. Woodsrunners started to untie villagers.

It took Yerby ten minutes to recompress enough of his hydrogen to bring the dirigible back to the open square. Forty or fifty people grabbed the drag ropes to haul the vessel the last of the way down. By that time, the bottles were passing to villagers as well.

Yerby stepped from the gondola and walked to Saunderson. The bonfire gave off a smudgy light. The magistrate had been holding his wife and child since Desiree untied him. He moved away from his family to face Yerby.

"Saunderson," Yerby said, "I'm going to give you a chance to stay here. I warn you, though—from now on act like a good citizen of Greenwood, Do you understand? If this is where you live, then this better be where you're loyal to."

He waved toward Saunderson's house. The thick roof sheathing hadn't burned through at any point, but the plastic sagged inches-deep between trusses at the center of the blackened, bubbled patch.

"Go on," Yerby ordered. "Clean it up. Go back to your houses, all of you. And pray neither you nor your neighbors bring me back here, for you'll regret that if it comes!"

Villagers edged, then trotted from the square, as eager to get away from the Woodsrunners as they were to return to their homes. Militiamen clapped their former captives on the back; friendly enough to look at, but also a warning of where the power continued to lie.

"I'm glad you did that, Yerby," Mark said in a low voice. "But it was very dangerous."

"Don't guess I'll do it again sober, leastways," Yerby said. He watched the Saundersons reenter their house. The roof still smoldered, and they'd have a job getting the boat's mast out of the hole it had punched in the other side.

"But you know?" Yerby continued so softly that Mark had to lean close to hear. "There ain't so many brave men that I want to chase one off Greenwood unless I have to."

27. Bedroom Games

Noises in the corridor woke Mark from a sound sleep. It was probably just Yerby staggering drunk to the room he used next to Mark's, but . . . hadn't he come in earlier?

Mark glanced out his window, but he couldn't see even the outbuildings. Tertia had waned to a sliver in the Earth month since the raid on Blind Cove, and neither of the other moons gave more light than a star.

Mark got out of bed. His door opened. There were a number of people in the lightless hallway. "Yerby?" he said.

A dazzling light blinded Mark. Something heavy slapped him in the chest, knocking him a step backward. The missile burst on impact, enveloping him in a cold fog. *Gas gun!*

"We're attacked!" Mark said. He meant to shout but his voice was a croak. He couldn't see. He grabbed his bedside chair by memory and lifted it for a weapon. Though he held his breath, the gas was obviously being absorbed through his skin. His chest was numb and he was already losing feeling in his legs.

"Attacked!" Mark gasped as he lunged forward. He started to fall. Another gas shell hit him. Mark thought somebody slugged him on top of the head besides, but that might have been the floor as blackness absorbed him completely.

Everything was suddenly in focus, but it wasn't all in the *same* focus. He felt the cords binding his wrists and ankles, he saw the figures carrying him and another bundle through the gate out of the Bannock compound, and he heard that other bundle snarl a curse in Yerby's voice.

A stranger was talking. "I dumped the gas from the blimp. They'll be a day refilling it. Did Woolsey get the radio?"

All those sensory inputs were clear, but it was a moment before they integrated with the consciousness that knew it was Mark Maxwell of Quelhagen. It was sort of like shaking a box of cornflakes and seeing them settle into half the original space.

Most of all, Mark tasted the aftereffects of the gas. His mouth felt as if it were full of powdered copper, an unspeakably foul sensation. The paralysis was already starting to wear off, and he'd be immune to a reapplication of the gas for the next several days; but if this taste lasted, Mark would almost rather be unconscious.

"Somebody help me!" snarled the man holding Yerby's legs. "I swear he weighs a ton!"

"Shut up, you fool!" said Berkeley Finch. Mark hadn't recognized the man's figure, but his voice was unmistakable even when tension raised its pitch. "Until we get—"

"Hey you!" somebody bellowed from the courtyard. A

light shone across the kidnappers. All but one wore tan uniforms with Zenith Protective Association patches on the shoulders. The exception was Dr. Gabriel Jesilind, who hid his face in his hands as the light caught him.

"Come *on!*" Finch shouted. He fired a burst from his repeller. Either Finch was a lousy shot or he was more squeamish about murder than he was about kidnapping. His pellets shattered sparkling dust from the wall twenty feet to the left of the light. The cloud of ionized aluminum from the pellets' driving skirts hung in the air, glowing faintly.

An aircar started its motors fifty yards downslope. The Zeniths carrying Yerby and Mark broke into a run. Others turned and fired their gas guns toward the compound. A Zenith with a repeller shot straight in the air, and another sent a flare streaking its red arc toward the main building.

People were shouting within the compound's walls. The light vanished when Finch shot.

If somebody fires a flashgun at the kidnappers, they've got as good a chance of hitting me or Yerby as they do anybody else . . . The thought should have scared Mark. Instead it just made him wonder. Maybe he was still feeling the effects of the gas.

The aircar started forward, flattening the vegetation to all sides. Jesilind threw himself into the front seat beside the driver. The big vehicle had been lightened by removal of its roof, but it still wouldn't be able to fly normally with all the Zeniths and their captives aboard.

"Shoot!" Finch said to the woman beside him. She was loading her gas gun with another clip of fist-sized cartridges. Finch fired his repeller, this time skyward.

Three men and a woman struggled with Yerby's dead weight. Another man had to join them before they were able to dump him on the floor between the rear-facing middle bench seat and the front-facing seat in back. The pair who'd carried Mark had no difficulty in tossing him on top of the big frontiersman.

The kidnappers climbed in with nervous haste. The car's underside tilted against the dirt, bounced up, and grounded firmly when the last two Zeniths boarded. The driver cursed in despair and fed full power to his motors. The car wallowed a few inches into the air in a gout of dust and pebbles.

"We're too heavy!" the driver cried. "Colonel, you've got to leave them here!"

"Get going!" Berkeley Finch said. "If anybody's left here, it'll be you!"

The car got under way after scraping the undercarriage twice, the first time so hard that Mark thought he heard metal tear. The downslope helped. The overloaded vehicle accelerated to thirty miles an hour with the help of gravity and was able to climb, though very sluggishly, when the terrain started to rise again.

They needed surface effect to proceed. Instead of flying, the car lurched along on the blanket of air squeezed between their skid plate and the ground. The beam of the car's broad bar headlight wriggled down aisles of trees so massive that their branches had shaded out the undergrowth.

The last view Mark had of the Bannock compound was a blaze of light through the trees. He wondered which of the residents were still able to move. It seemed likely that everybody who slept on the second floor had been knocked out by gas.

"I don't generally complain about a guest, lad," Yerby rumbled, "but I'd sure appreciate you taking your toe out of my eye-socket."

"Sorry," Mark said. He had normal feeling back in his limbs; enough at least that he felt the sting of the tight cords binding him. He didn't have proper muscle control yet, but he and Yerby managed to squirm so that they were side by side rather than stacked.

Yerby tried to sit up. A Zenith hit him with the butt of her repeller. "Keep your head down or I'll blow it off!" she snarled.

"Now, now," Yerby said in apparent unconcern. "I just want to chat with my good friend Dr. Jesilind. Doc, it's been a while. And to tell the truth, I didn't expect to find you in the present company."

Yerby leaned back so that his shoulders rested on the boots of the Zeniths on the backseat. His eyes remained below the level of the car's sides.

For a moment, Mark didn't think Jesilind was going to reply. Finally the doctor twisted to look over the front seat and said, "Mr. Bannock, I'm very sorry to have to take this action, but I'm doing it in the best interests of Greenwood and for mankind in the larger sense."

"How much are they paying you, Jesilind?" Mark said. He was so angry that his voice warbled. "Since it's not a normal kidnapping, you won't just take a share of the ransom, I suppose."

"It's not a kidnapping at all, Maxwell," Berkeley Finch said. He was squeezed onto the rear seat, from which he'd been looking back the way they'd come. "We're a legally constituted posse, carrying those we've arrested back to a court of competent jurisdiction to stand trial. It's that simple."

"Yerby," Dr. Jesilind said, "I realize that you were acting with no more malice than a willful child has, but your presence on Greenwood was a disruptive influence. I couldn't let the progress of civilization be interrupted for reasons of personal friendship. I hope that some day you'll understand."

"Oh, I guess we understand each other, Doc," Yerby said. Mark wondered if Jesilind was smart enough to know that the mild words ought to terrify him.

The car was making better speed than before, mainly because the driver had learned how to handle the vehicle under the present conditions. A dirigible might barely be able to keep up with them, but the kidnappers' repellers would rip the ballonets to shreds in a burst or two. At the speed the pellets traveled, the sparks of one hitting a frame tube would ignite the escaping hydrogen into a pale blue inferno.

A Zenith had claimed he'd "dumped the gas from the blimp." Mark hoped that was true. He particularly hoped Amy wasn't pursuing in the Bannock dirigible.

From the car's heading, the Zeniths had landed at Wanker's Doodle. Their ship was probably waiting for them on the magnetic mass.

The Zenith militia were nervous. They kicked him every time they turned or tried to make a little more room than the car had. That was fair. Mark figured he deserved to be kicked. He'd really *meant* to set a remote link to the

Doodle's landing system the way he had at the Spiker, but he'd been busy . . .

"Mr. Finch!" Mark said. "Or is it 'Colonel' that you're calling yourself now? May I ask what charges have been brought against me?"

Finch had been looking behind again. He turned. There was almost no light in the vehicle, but his face was a pale blob in greater shadows.

"An informant has identified you as one of the ringleaders of the criminal conspiracy, Maxwell," he said. "We wouldn't have gone after you alone, but we hoped to find you."

Mark began to laugh. "Well, I'm glad to hear Dr. Jesilind has been earning his pay so well," he said. "Or does he get thirty pieces of silver for each of us?"

He wouldn't have recognized that harsh, cruel voice as his own if he hadn't felt it trumpeting from his throat. They'd tied his body, but Mark Maxwell of Quelhagen was still a better man than these thugs from Zenith and the traitor who guided them!

"You see," Mark went on, "I thought perhaps my crime was preventing Dr. Jesilind from committing rape. Having seen what passes for the law on Zenith, that seemed very likely."

"Rape?" said Finch.

Yerby shifted his huge shoulders so that he could look at Mark. "Is this something you've forgot to tell me, Maxwell?" he said with no emotion at all.

"It was a matter that didn't concern you, Yerby," Mark said. "I took care of it, at your sister's request."

Yerby laughed. "Feisty little pup, ain't you, lad?" he said. "Well, I'm right glad you took care of it so good."

"I don't know anything about rape," Berkeley Finch said. He looked uneasily from Mark to the front seat.

"Your guide does, Colonel," Mark said. "Why don't you tell him about it, *Doctor?*"

"Attempts to blacken my name with falsehoods are of no use to you now, my man," Jesilind said in a haughty voice. "You face the justice of a civilized community."

"Oh, Doc," said Yerby Bannock mildly. "If it's your name you're worried about now, you've missed the point about as bad as you can."

"Colonel?" said a Zenith looking over the back of the vehicle. "There's somebody after us. I think it's an aircar."

"That's impossible!" Jesilind blurted. "The aircar at Bannock's doesn't work!"

Finch turned. His face was a mask of white rage in light reflected from a passing treetrunk. "What aircar?" he shouted. "You didn't say anything about an aircar!"

"It can't be Bannock's," Jesilind said. "I swear, that one doesn't work!"

The Zenith vehicle lurched into a broad lowland too boggy to support the dryland giants of the higher ground. The car bottomed once in a geyser of watery mud, but the driver didn't lose forward motion.

The going was actually a little easier for the overburdened vehicle, though they wallowed like a slowing roller coaster. The soft-leaved plants covering the ground here flattened beneath the car into a surface smoother than the forest floor. The vegetation was phosphorescent. The vehicle trembled forward in a faint green glow, as if it were being driven through the screen of a light-enhancing device.

The trees growing in the marsh had knobby surface roots that spread as much as twenty yards from their trunks. They didn't pose a real obstacle, because they were so sparsely scattered, but the car on surface effect needed to go around them.

The pursuing vehicle came into sight. It *was* an aircar, if you didn't care what you said. It staggered from among the treetops, apparently unable to climb over them, and quickly dropped to within a few feet of the ground. Its bow cocked up at fifteen degrees and kinked about the same amount to the direction of flight. It didn't have any headlight or running lights, but one of the motor nacelles glowed dull red.

"By the Lord God Almighty!" Yerby said in amused approval. "That's Desiree or I'm a—" He looked at one, then the other, seatful of his nervous captors. "—gentleman from Zenith! No way Elmont'd risk his neck like that, and George, heck, he don't know how to drive nothing!"

Mark levered himself into a sitting position. All the Zeniths but the driver were looking over the back of their vehicle. They were too worried to care what their prisoners did at the moment. The other aircar was a hundred yards away and closing the gap very slowly. A bearing or a rubbing drive fan screamed a note of utter high-pitched fury.

"I didn't think that car flew either, Yerby," Mark said. It just about didn't. Whatever metal screamed *had* to fly apart soon. At the speed the parts of an aircar's drive train spun, failure was likely to look like a grenade going off.

"I tell you, lad," Yerby said, "last time I flew her, she flipped and tried to squish me like a bug. If the courtyard wall hadn't caught the bow and held it up, that's just what she'd have done. But I guess maybe Desiree don't weigh so much or something."

The woman beside Finch leaned over the side of the car to give herself more room and fired her gas gun. The heavy projectile sailed through the air at least twenty feet above its target and twenty yards behind.

The recoil overbalanced the shooter; she pitched over the side. Yerby threw his full weight against her legs, pinning them within the vehicle. The Zenith dropped the gas gun, flailed for a moment, and finally managed to grasp the side of the car and pull herself in.

"Careful there, missie," Yerby said with a chuckle. "Wouldn't want to lose a sweet child like you."

"You sanctimonious prick!" the woman screamed in Finch's face. "You were going to lighten the car, weren't you? You *wanted* me to go overboard!"

Finch grimaced. "Go on," he ordered. "We'll have to shoot it down. Try not to kill the driver."

He fired his repeller. The stream of pellets didn't come within a country mile of the target, partly because Finch kept a worried eye on the angry woman beside him. Maybe he thought she was going to sling him out of the car. Maybe she thought the same thing.

Zeniths crammed beside Finch in the back started shooting with a repeller and a gas gun. A woman in the middle seat stood to launch a rocket flare. She stumbled sideways when the vehicle swayed, jostling the man seated beside her. His gas shell missed Finch's cheek by less than the colonel's razor had that morning.

Finch squealed and hunched down. His second burst chewed the back fender of his own car.

"Oh, you people!" Yerby said in obvious amusement. "You don't know Desiree the way I do. Why don't you just pack it in now? I promise I'll keep her off you."

"Shut up, you fool!" Finch snarled. As he raised his repeller to fire, he glanced nervously over his shoulder at the Zeniths behind him. He ducked down without actually pulling the trigger.

Mark looked at Yerby. He wondered how much of the frontiersman's nonchalance was an act. It also struck Mark that the relationship between Yerby and Desiree was a good deal more complex than the loud hostility he'd initially thought it was limited to.

The other car had pulled within fifty feet and was slightly to the right of the Zenith machine. One of the kidnappers with a repeller started hitting despite the vehicles' doubled motion. Pellets danced across the bow of the target, exploding in friction-heated violence. They had no effect on the car.

The Bannock aircar had at least the virtue of being sturdy. Its body shell was heavy plastic that cratered but didn't disintegrate at the high-velocity impacts. Occasionally a second or third pellet might hit the same point. The passenger compartment was of double-box construction for stiffness, so even those lucky coincidences didn't endanger the driver.

The two cars separated to round a tree that dangled aerial roots from its branch tips. The vehicles closed the wide circuit at increasing velocity. A gas shell burst on the target's bow and spread its cold fog across the plastic. The driver was the only target on which the Zeniths' weapons could have an effect, and she was protected by the skewed angle of flight of a vehicle with only two and a half of its four motors working.

The Zenith driver was focused on his compass course and the terrain ahead. As they rounded the tree, he steered toward rather than away from the oncoming vehicle. The Bannock car raced toward the Zeniths with its leading edge three feet above the ground.

"Turn!" Finch screamed. "Turn, you idiot!"

The Zenith with the flare gun fired it into the backseat of her own car. It zipped between the legs of a man desperately trying to reload his repeller in the crowded, jouncing vehicle. He screamed and threw himself forward as if the gout of red fire were rocket exhaust.

Desiree peered over the bow of her aircar, visible for the first time. She eased her leading edge over the Zenith vehicle's right rear inlet duct. The fan choked off for lack of air. The other three fans, operating at maximum output, flipped the car like a tiddlywink.

Mark had a view of the ground, then a sky full of flailing figures and weapons all on separate courses; then the ground again.

The aircar managed the last half turn the instant before it hit.

That was the difference between Mark's survival and him being driven into the ground like a tent peg.

The prisoners hadn't been flung out with the others because they were on the floor at the axis of the car's revolution. The ground was marshy. When the car hit, its undercarriage cut deep to form an air cushion with a perfect seal. Thin mud exploded in a brown curtain. An instant later the drive fans sucked in the mixture and ripped off impellers that were set too coarse for any medium but air.

"By all that's holy!" said Yerby Bannock. "Lad, if we could sell tickets to a ride like that, we'd make our fortunes!"

Mark managed to sit upright. The world had stopped spinning, but his head hadn't figured that out yet. The Bannock aircar was nearby, sticking out of the ground at a forty-five-degree angle. The two forward fan nacelles were clearly visible. The impellers were winding down; the damaged unit still glowed and gave off a faint moan.

Desiree Bannock climbed slowly out of the backseat of her vehicle. Her face had no particular expression. Since anger was the only emotion Mark had seen her express, he supposed that was just as well.

"Honey love, you're surely a sight for sore eyes!" Yerby called. "Come cut my hands loose before they fall off, the beggars tied me so tight!"

The Zeniths were picking themselves up from the bog. Mark couldn't be sure, but it looked like they'd all survived the crash also. Berkeley Finch stood knee deep in a particularly wet patch. He pointed a dripping repeller at Desiree and shouted, "Halt! You're under arrest for interfering with officers of the law!"

Desiree continued to stump toward the Zenith aircar. "You put that thing down," she snarled, "or I'll feed it to you! You hear me?"

Yerby cackled. "You better listen to her, Colonel!" he said. "You peeve my Desiree and you'll be lucky if it's your teeth that get first look at what you're stuffed with."

Desiree reached the car. "There's forty of our neighbors on the way here," she said. "By daybreak there'll be two hundred. The blimp's empty, so I took that bitch of a car up to three thousand feet and put a call out before I come chasing you."

She snipped the cords from her husband's ankles with a pair of wire cutters, then freed his wrists. "Yerby," she added, "I told you you were the biggest fool in all space to buy that piece of junk. Do you know the sucker flipped twice on me before I got her back down?"

"I'm sorry, honey love," Yerby said contritely. He stood and flexed his arms to work life back into them. "I'll get you a proper car next time I'm on Zenith, see if I don't."

The Zeniths had gathered in a tight bunch like sheep in a blizzard. Dr. Jesilind was trying to worm his way into the center of the group. Boots and elbows drove him back with universal determination.

"If you're thinking you got help coming from the Doodle," Desiree called to them as she cut Mark free, "you can forget it right now. There's folks there by now ready to blow the nose off anybody who peeks out of the ship you lot come in."

Some of the kidnappers had kept or found their weapons. The chances that anything would shoot without a thorough cleaning was nothing to bet your life on, though. The battered Zeniths didn't look as though they were up to a fight in any case.

Mark stood. His feet felt as if somebody were hammering needles into them. Still, they held him.

A dirigible approached from the northeast. It crawled along low to the ground so that the crew could jump to safety if Zeniths shot the gasbag to bits. More dirigibles bobbed closer from all points of the horizon.

Yerby rose in the passenger compartment of the Zenith aircar as if he were on a dais addressing a rally. "Now, I tell you what I'm going to do, Finch my boy," he said. "I'm going to let you and your band of heroes stick all your guns here with me where they can be collected. Then I'm going to tell my friends to take it easy. We'll haul you lot to the Doodle and you can go back where you came from."

"After they've paid for the damage they caused on Greenwood," Mark interjected. "That includes a working— a demonstrably working—aircar destroyed."

Yerby chuckled. "Yep, he's a feisty one, my attorney here," he said. In a tone with more hard edges than a file he went on, "Now, I hope you take the deal offered, Finchie. If you don't, the best thing that's going to happen is that you walk around a while, and that won't be longer than sunrise. I don't much mind what happens to you, but there's me and mine here too . . . and a bullet don't have eyes."

Colonel Finch wiped his forehead. "Stack arms in the car," he ordered hoarsely.

The community of Wanker's Doodle was at the south end of Centipede Lake, a multibranched thickening of the glacial White River. The lake was three hundred miles long, and its shoreline was ten or twenty times as great. Heavy loads of the sort that had to be ferried to the Spiker by dirigible could be rafted to the Doodle from any point on the lake's circumference.

Despite that, Wanker's Doodle wasn't as busy a port as the Spiker. The Doodle itself was a finger of basalt, the core of an ancient volcano, that thrust up through soil deposited by the floods every spring. The hard rock spreading from the base of the Doodle could hold only three starships at a time—four if they were smaller than average—and other ground nearby was too soft for the concentrated weight.

There were two typical freighters on the basalt at the moment. The third, larger vessel waiting on the magnetic mass was much shinier than what usually landed at Greenwood. Frontiersmen with guns and bottles sat in the big ship's open hatches while crewmen in spiffy white uniforms watched them glumly.

Yerby was leaning over the rail of Bat Lunaan's dirigible to view the approaching community. "Pretty as a picture, that ship, ain't it? Bet the captain's having conniptions because the boys are tracking mud on his clean floors."

Because the prisoners in the netting below weighed so much, Lunaan had only Yerby and Mark with him in the gondola. Even so, his airship was slower than the others. The flat ground near the Doodle was brilliant with the coverings of thirty or more dirigibles and the wings of flyers that had started arriving soon after the sun came up.

"There's Amy," Mark said, pointing. She stood near the starship's hatch holding a gas gun.

Somebody must have picked her up on the way to the Doodle. It would be another day at least before enough water had been electrolyzed into hydrogen—the oxygen was vented—to refill the tanks of the Bannock dirigible.

Yerby stepped back from the railing. "What do you figure our friends from Zenith are going to try next, lad?" he asked quietly. "Oh, not this lot," he added, gesturing toward the deck and the captives who dangled beneath it.

"The syndicate of folks that wants to steal our land, I mean."

"I think . . ." Mark said. "I think there'll be a peace conference. Protector Giscard'll call it, or maybe even a delegation from Earth. You've made the Zenith authorities look very foolish. They'll make a compromise offer to avoid worse."

The dirigible settled in the cleared space near the starship's hatch. Pumps whined to suck hydrogen from the ballonets now that the prisoners' weight rested on the ground.

"I thought maybe something like that," Yerby said as if he were making idle conversation. "Myself, I've never been much for compromise, though."

Yerby jumped from the gondola while the deck was still six feet above the ground. Mark sighed and followed. He didn't fall over when he hit, so he figured the paralysis must have worn off completely by now.

Mark's mouth still tasted worse than he could imagine. The swig of what Lunaan claimed was whiskey had added its own ghastly flavors without in the least cutting the miasma of the gas.

The cargo net collapsed about the Zeniths when Lunaan dropped it and moved the dirigible off the starport. Desiree took charge of freeing them. Yerby nodded approval, then sauntered to the starship's captain standing beside the boarding ramp. Mark smiled to Amy as they both followed her brother without speaking.

"Well, Captain . . ." Yerby said, peering at the nametag. "Captain Drumm. I'll bet you're not very pleased about how things went this voyage, are you?"

"My ship's been looted!" Drumm said. He was a dapper man with, at the moment, the red face of someone on the verge of a stroke. "Are you responsible for this, sir? My liquor cabinet's been emptied and my passengers' private lockers have been broken into as well!"

Yerby nodded sympathetically. "Looting's a terrible thing, yes sir. But—did you lose anything besides booze, Captain?"

"My pistol," Drumm said. Apprehension was replacing anger as he realized how very powerful Yerby was. "I don't know that there was anything else. Except the liquor."

"Peaceful visitors don't need guns on Greenwood," Yerby said with the smile of a cat for the mouse between its paws. "Reckon we can forget that."

"It isn't important, no," Drumm agreed. "And the liquor—"

"And the liquor's the sort of hospitality a smart fellow'd offer people when he came waltzing into their house without a by-your-leave," Yerby continued, overriding the captain's nervous mumble. "Which is the thing I wanted to take up with you, Captain. The next time you want to land on Greenwood, why don't you hold in orbit until I've radioed you a personal invitation? Because if you land without my permission again, you'll never take off."

Drumm licked his lips. His face was as sallow as it had been red a moment before. "I understand," he said.

Yerby smiled and patted Drumm on the shoulder. "I thought you would," Yerby said. Whistling "Men of Harlech" between his teeth, he turned to watch the prisoners being marched in line toward the ramp.

Dr. Jesilind felt the weight of Yerby's stare. He eased to

the side to put Colonel Finch between him and the frontiersman. A Woodsrunner thrust Jesilind back into place. Yerby walked toward him, still whistling.

Berkeley Finch swallowed and deliberately faced Yerby. "One moment, please, sir," he said in a voice that got higher with every syllable. "My troops and I surrendered our weapons upon your promise of safe conduct until we were off-planet."

"And that's just what you'll have if you step out of my way," Yerby said in a tone Mark had never heard him use before. It was like listening to millstones speak. "There's a personal matter between me and the doc, though I guess you can have part of it if you're fool enough to want it."

He brushed the Zenith aside with an arm as hard as the threat he'd just implied.

If it hadn't been for Finch's terrified courage, Mark wouldn't have been able to step in front of Yerby himself. "Yerby," he said. He was so tense that he wasn't sure whether his voice squeaked as he feared it did. "If it's a personal matter, it's the one I've already taken care of. *Please*. It's on my honor if I let you kill him."

"You don't let me do any blame thing I choose, *boy!*" Yerby shouted. He tried to step around Mark.

Mark grabbed Yerby's right wrist with both hands. It was like trying to hold a spinning driveshaft. Yerby bent Mark's arms back and took a handful of his shirt. He lifted Mark completely off the ground with one hand.

"Yerby!" Amy cried. She pressed the fat muzzle of her gas gun against her brother's chest. "Stop this right now! Put him down!"

"I don't need a woman to fight for me!" Mark wheezed.

He wasn't exactly being strangled, but he sure wasn't getting the amount of air his lungs thought they needed.

"And I don't need a man to fight for me!" Amy replied. "Yerby, put him down this instant."

Yerby looked at her. He lowered Mark gently to the ground. "Sorry, lad," he muttered. His big hands tried to straighten Mark's shirt. "Got a bit above myself there."

Amy let out her breath in a vast sigh. She flung her gun down.

Nobody else had moved during the confrontation. Now Finch got cautiously to his feet and the other spectators relaxed sightly.

"Doctor," Yerby said to the trembling Jesilind, "I think you and I better not meet again. I don't figure I'll ever go to Marques . . . but if I see you anywhere else, anywhere at all but your home planet—"

He didn't finish the sentence. He just smiled.

Jesilind said in a tiny voice, "I'm leaving immediately, Mr. Bannock."

"How right you are," Yerby said. Before anyone could react, he'd grabbed Jesilind by collar and waistband. Yerby took a step forward, swinging the doctor back; then took a second step and launched Jesilind toward the open hatch.

It was a beautiful throw. Jesilind didn't touch anything but air for the twenty feet before he crashed into the starship's hold.

28. Democracy in Action

Major Ustinov was one of the military aides Mark had seen in Protector Giscard's office. The Alliance emissary wore a gray field uniform in place of the sky-blue jacket and silver trousers of the previous occasion, but he still looked remarkably neat and clean to eyes that had gotten used to Greenwood settlers over the past four months.

Yerby hammered the table that had been brought into the Spiker's bunkroom for the meeting. All six legs jounced off the floor. "And just how do you figure to keep me from going, Dagmar Wately?" he shouted. Ustinov winced even though the anger wasn't directed at him.

"By knocking you cold as a trout with a gas gun," Zeb Randifer replied, leaning over the table from the other side. "If you're that big a durned fool, that is. And I mean it!"

This had started as a Woodsrunner muster called because a Zenith ship wanted to land. When the passengers turned out to be from Protector Giscard instead of more thugs sent by the investment syndicate, what might have been a battle turned into a meeting almost equally heated. The three dim lamps shone on angry, puzzled faces.

"You put me in charge!" Yerby said. "That means I go!"

The rain that hammered the tavern's uninsulated roof would probably be sleet by nightfall. By clearing out all the bedframes, most of the hundred or so Woodsrunners at the Spiker could squeeze into the barracks-style sleeping room. The rest were in the hallway—or the taproom below, drinking instead of worrying about Protector Giscard's offer of truce negotiations.

The meeting was very likely going to decide the fate of Greenwood. It bothered Mark that the people present were a small fraction of the settlers and had been called for a purpose completely different from the one they were involved with now. On the other hand—

You could make a case that folks who came out in dangerous weather to defend their planet had as much right to decide for that planet as any group could possibly have.

"Yeah, you're in charge, Bannock," Dagmar said. "And that's exactly why you're not going back to Zenith. They'd snatch you sure, and much as I'd like to be shut of you for a neighbor, we can't afford that now."

The concrete wall was directly behind Yerby with Major Ustinov to his right. Mark was to the left, and Amy stood on a low stool in the corner behind Mark, recording the proceedings for posterity. Mark wondered if Blaney had deliberately arranged things so that the table was a barrier in case Yerby really lost his temper.

Probably not. In a rage, Yerby was strong enough to use the massive table for a weapon.

"All envoys will be under the protection of the Atlantic Alliance!" Ustinov said huffily. "You need have no fears on that score."

Desiree stared at the Alliance envoy. She stood directly opposite Yerby, as fitting a place as there was for her. "You can stuff *that* up your ear," she snorted.

"Look, Bannock," Dagmar said. "I'm not trying to say you're not boss."

She gestured to Ustinov. "I'm not even saying that this guy's a lying prick in a fancy uniform. I'm saying that after the way you did Biber and Finch in the eye, there's no chance they won't grab you, I don't care what anybody promises. Not if they went to jail for it, which they wouldn't."

"If you don't want to deal, Yerby," Randifer said, "we don't deal. But it ain't going to be you on that ship to Zenith. That's free passage all right. Free passage to a cell you won't leave till you're old and gray!"

"And we need you," Dagmar repeated. "Little though I care to admit it."

"Aw, you worry like a bunch of old women," Yerby muttered; but his grimace and mild tone showed that he'd accepted the argument against him.

"Seems to me Zeb put his finger on it the first time," said Buck Koslovsky, one of the defendants in the ejectment action. "What does any of us want to be going to Zenith again for? You name me one thing we got out of going the first time!"

The rumble of the settlers' response was varied, but it was mostly agreement. The chorus of "Yeah!" and "Damn right!" far outweighed the one peevish, "Well, Zeb can stick his finger right back where it was!"

"There's a problem with that course," Mark said. He shouted to be sure of being heard, but he hoped he didn't sound like he wanted to start a fight.

Yerby banged his fist on the table again. "All you shut up and listen what my legal advisor's got to say!" he bellowed. "Or I'll start knocking heads till you do shut up!"

Mark smiled faintly. Nobody had to worry about sounding belligerent so long as Yerby Bannock was present to do it for him.

"Fellow . . ." He'd started to say, "Fellow-citizens," as if he were addressing a meeting on Quelhagen. "Friends and neighbors!" he said instead. "It's not the Zenith investors or even the Zenith government who's proposed this meeting."

"It is so the Zenith government!" Koslovsky said. "I just heard that fellow Ustinov say it was!"

"We're being summoned by the Alliance!" Mark said, wishing he had Yerby's presence and leather lungs, "speaking through its representative, who happens to be the Protector of Zenith. If we reject out of hand Protector Giscard's attempt to mediate, it will leave the Alliance very few options as to how to proceed."

He looked over the table at a sea of blank stares.

"What the lad's saying and you lot are too dumb to understand," Yerby said, "is that if we don't send somebody to this meeting, Giscard's going to send his soldiers to drag us there by the neck. That's right, ain't it, Mark?"

"The citizens of Greenwood would never fail to obey the Protector's request," Mark said. He turned toward Ustinov so that he could be sure the major heard him. "We are all loyal citizens of the Atlantic Alliance."

Ustinov sniffed, but he looked more disdainful than hostile. So long as he didn't report to his superiors that Greenwood was in a state of rebellion against the Alliance . . .

"All right, Bannock," Randifer said. "But you still don't go."

"I'll go!" said Emmreich enthusiastically. He'd been too cheerfully drunk to walk to his capsule for the trip home from Zenith after the hearing.

"You will not go!" Yerby said. His voice alone shook the heavy table.

The room quieted. In a somewhat diminished tone, Yerby continued, "I'm still in charge, right? I grant you that I don't go, but I still decide who does."

The room buzzed like a hive of bees the size of grizzly bears. Dagmar Wately's voice cut through the background noise with, "Why don't you tell us who you pick, Bannock, and we'll tell you whether we go along with it?"

"All right!" Yerby said. "We need a settler whose been on Greenwood long enough to know pretty much all the players. I figure you'll do for that, Dagmar."

People nodded, clapped, or stamped their feet. From the faces Mark saw, all the different versions meant *yes*.

"*And!*" Yerby bellowed. "Shut up, now, you all! *And* we need somebody along who's got the sense God gave a goose. As Dagmar does not, and I know she don't from the way she carried on about transit rights across my property!"

"Want me to feed you them transit rights, Bannock?" Dagmar shouted back over the laughter.

"So I figured the right person to go along with Dagmar was Mark Maxwell," Yerby continued. "For those of you who don't know him, he's smart as all the rest of you lot together."

Yerby put an arm around Mark's shoulders. "And I'll tell you something else about the lad!" Yerby said. "You couldn't ask to have a better man at your back than him in a fight!"

Mark felt himself blush with pride. He didn't feel particularly honored to be called smart in this company, because to Yerby and the other settlers the word meant "formally educated." But even though he knew that the other half of the compliment *wasn't* true, he'd never been praised in a fashion that meant more to him.

29. Preparing the Trap

A tank with its Klaxon groaning slid past the front of the Safari House. The monster terribly dwarfed the elephants molded into the lobby walls. Behind the tank were three trucks with mounted gas projectors. The soldiers in the sandbagged truck beds carried repellers and rocket launchers.

A platoon of Alliance troops wearing body armor and armed with lethal weapons guarded the front of the hotel against the mob in the square. A brick had shattered one of the broad front windows. Members of the hotel staff were trying to cover the hole with stiff plastic sheeting.

Ms. Macey came in through a side door, looking agitated. She didn't see Mark until one of her aides coughed and pointed to him.

"There's a ban on aircars, Maxwell!" she said. "I had to come through the streets from the trade mission!"

Gas guns thumped in the square. Mark thought he heard the snarl of nerve scramblers as well, a more painful way of paralyzing the motor nerves of a person within a hundred feet or so. The scramblers' field generated conflicting chemical messages that knotted the target's muscles with violent cramps.

The mob howled over the Klaxon's moan.

"I'm very sorry, madame," Mark said, "but my only transportation was the car and driver which Protector Giscard provided. I didn't care to alert him that I was meeting you, since you investors aren't permitted at the negotiations."

"Yes, yes," Macey said. The broken window kept drawing her eyes, though she shuddered every time saw it. Viewing the riot was for her like touching the stump of an amputated limb. "Why is it so important that I see you in person, then?"

Repellers cracked. Each hypersonic pellet bounced shock waves from the building facades. The echoes were individually tiny, but the total of them sounded like sleet on tin.

There were no other guests in the lobby. The clerk cowered behind his counter looking blank-eyed. The party of waiters covering the window focused on their task so that they didn't have to think about what was happening outside now, and what might happen to them in the next instant or the next day.

"I have a hologram master," Mark said, taking the video chip from his breast pocket. He was wearing casual Zenith-style clothing he'd bought at a kiosk in the starport. For most of his stay he wanted garb less conspicuous than the Quelhagen formalwear he'd put on for the conference the next day.

Macey took the chip but looked at it with only vague

interest. Her eyes kept drifting back to the scene beyond the windows.

"I want you to have this copied onto thirty-second projection cubes—as many as you can, thousands if possible," Mark said in a louder voice. "Distribute them—give them away—all over New Paris, especially right downtown here. They have to be on the street by the end of the truce meeting tomorrow afternoon. Can you arrange that?"

Macey shuddered and returned her attention to Mark. "Yes, I suppose," she said. "The mission has a duplicating lab for commercial presentations. What is this, anyway?"

"Necessary for your syndicate's purposes," Mark said without answering. "Look, I don't want anybody else to know where it came from. None of the other Greenwoods, do you understand?"

Macey raised an eyebrow.

"No, I'm not selling them out!" Mark said harshly. "Some of them might think I was, though, if they knew what I was doing. I'm doing what I think's right for Greenwood. Maybe I'm wrong, but I'm not a traitor."

A sickly green flash lit the square momentarily. A tank had fired the huge Cassegrain laser it carried as main armament. The pulse must have been aimed skyward. The only sound was the sharp *hissCRACK!* of cold air slapping the heated track closed, instead of the roaring collapse of a building.

"I don't suppose my father's on Zenith now, is he?" Mark said softly.

"What?" said the investor. "No, no. This meeting wasn't announced, you know. The only reason I'm here is that my associates and I thought it was best to leave one of us here in case the Zeniths tried something of the sort."

Macey looked at the chip again. "I'll take care of this," she said, but she showed no signs of wanting to leave the doubtful security of the hotel while the riot continued. Her aides—two of the three were clearly bodyguards—paced restively nearby.

"I'd planned to have the material duplicated at a local shop," Mark said. He wasn't sure whether he ought to stay with the investor or go back to his room and hope that she'd return to the Quelhagen trade mission building more quickly. "I wasn't expecting a—"

He nodded toward the windows. The hotel staffers were outside now, considering ways to attach more sheeting to protect the still-undamaged panes.

"A riot like this," Mark continued. "Is this common?"

"There's trouble every day," Macey said, staring toward the square, "but I've never heard of it being this bad. I don't know where it's going to go from here. And there's trouble on Quelhagen too."

"Madame?" Mark said. "I want to be very clear about my position in all this. I'm not on your side, I'm on Greenwood's. There happens to be a convergence of interests at the moment, that's all."

Macey turned sharply. "What are you talking about?" she demanded. "There *isn't* any Greenwood except dirt and dirty people. And the investment potential. Are you telling me that you want to be paid? Is that it?"

There was no more cutting insult that one Quelhagen aristocrat could fling at another. Mark felt his lips instead spread into a smile. As if he could be worried about money with what was happening outside the hotel right now!

But Macey was. To her, money was always the first principle. Concern about losing money had brought her out tonight, even though that meant risking her life.

"No, ma'am," said Mark. He realized for the first time how much he'd changed in the past months. "Nothing like that. I just felt honor-bound to let you know where my basic loyalties lie. Honor is important, even to a dirty Greenwood settler like me."

"Bah!" Macey said. She held the video chip out to one of her aides. "Langley, don't lose this," she ordered. "We've got to get back to the mission and hope the riot hasn't spread in that direction."

She swept Mark again with her eyes. "I couldn't understand how you and Bannock got along, Maxwell," she said coolly. Her fear of the riot seemed to have passed, or at least been controlled. "Now I do. I've never seen intelligent men as determined to go off in crazy directions as the pair of you. You're human pinballs!"

She turned and strode toward the door by which she'd entered the lobby. Her aides fell into step with her.

At the door Macey looked back over her shoulder. "Also," she added across the empty room, "I suspect you're both too dangerous to live!"

30. Watching the Fireworks

The windows of the seventh-floor conference room looked down on the street in front of the Civil Affairs Building and the central park. Vehicles and pedestrians were moving normally, though Mark thought there was less traffic than he'd seen on his previous visit to New Paris.

Several cars, crushed and burned out, had been pushed through hedges to get them out of the travel lanes. Clothes, repeller magazines, and gas canisters littered the view. One of the streetscape's trees was now a shattered stump three feet across. A maintenance crew wearing orange dickeys was sawing up the wooden corpse for disposal.

Candace, Protector Giscard's legal advisor, closed the door behind him as he returned to the conference room with a sour expression. Everyone in the room—Mark and Dagmar Wately, Biber and Finch representing the Zenith claimants, and Colonel Wordsworth of the Alliance military forces—stared at Candace silently.

"I believe we can get started now," the counselor said

briskly as he pulled out a chair at the circular table. "Protector Giscard has just informed me that I'm to deputize for him at this meeting. The events of last night require his urgent attention at headquarters."

Colonel Wordsworth snorted. Her iron gray hair was cut short to fit under a helmet. "What he should turn his attention to is finding a pair of balls to replace the ones he lost before he was appointed protector here," she said, glaring at Candace.

"If Giscard's afraid to come to New Paris," Dagmar asked, "why isn't he holding the meeting at his palace?"

"Because to guard against spying and sabotage in the present state of unrest," Wordsworth said gratingly, "no Zenith citizens are being permitted into the headquarters area. That particularly includes—" She rotated her grim expression toward the pair of Zenith investors. "—our esteemed vice-protector there. Eh, Finch?"

"Colonel," Candace said coldly, "if you choose to discuss local politics, I strongly recommend you find another venue for it. Your words in this company might well be considered treason against the Atlantic Alliance if they were reported by an enemy of yours."

Wordsworth grimaced. "Giscard knows what I think about all this pussyfooting around," she muttered, but she didn't meet the legal advisor's eyes.

"Very well," Candace said. He waited until everyone was seated, then continued, "For the purpose of this meeting, Mr. Finch is acting as a private party rather than as a representative of the Alliance. I wish to be very clear on that point."

Finch flushed. "We're here to negotiate, Candace," he

said. "If instead you plan to play tin god, then I have better ways to spend my time."

"Finch has no more rights here than anybody else," Mayor Biber said. "And you bet we're here to end this nonsense once and for all."

Both men were in flashy civilian clothes in place of the uniforms they'd worn for their court appearance. Nevertheless, Wordsworth glowered at them like a cat eyeing caged birds.

It struck Mark that he and Dagmar were the only two people in the room who didn't heartily dislike all the others. Zenith's internal muddle was worse in some ways than what was happening on Greenwood, and all the players were looking for other people to blame.

Of course, nobody was threatening to plant a city of fifty thousand in Mayor Biber's front yard.

"We accept that Protector Giscard is acting on behalf of the Alliance, not for parochial interests," Mark said. "This meeting isn't an attempt by a corrupt official to circumvent the plans of his superiors on Earth."

Candace gave Mark a smile of respect if not liking. He'd understood Mark's threat to go over Giscard's head if matters didn't develop to Greenwood's liking.

"I'm glad positions are clear," Candace said. "Now, first." He looked at the investors. "While Protector Greenwood of Hestia clearly had no authority to make settlement grants for the planet that now bears his name, it appears that a number of Alliance citizens have in good faith transported themselves and their chattels to Greenwood on the basis of such grants. It would be inequitable to displace those innocent parties."

Heinrich Biber started to rise. "If you think," he said, "that I'm going to let Giscard take the money I paid into his *pocket* for those grants go with a 'Sorry, guess I made a mistake,' then you haven't seen the *start* of trouble on this planet!"

Dagmar opened her mouth to speak. Mark quickly put his hand across hers to silence her. It wouldn't help if she blurted the threat he knew was on the tip of her tongue.

"Do you plan to negotiate this matter from a cell in the Protector's palace, Biber?" Finch said with a sneer. "Counselor Candace, continue with your appraisal. We'll refrain from comment until you're done." He glanced at the Mayor and added, "Further comment."

Biber's face was angry, but there was a touch of unease in his expression also. He knew that his outburst had indeed been grounds for arrest under the emergency regulations, though Protector Giscard wasn't confrontational enough (or probably brave enough) to jail a prominent citizen.

Candace focused his attention on the settlers' representatives. "A right to remain on Greenwood doesn't mean a right to ignore legal obligations, however," he said. "Administrative control of the planet is in the hands of the Protector of Zenith. Unless you settlers are willing to accept that, you're in rebellion against the Atlantic Alliance."

Dagmar looked worriedly at Mark. He touched her hand again. "We're loyal citizens of the Alliance, sir," he said to Candace. "Of course we accept her laws and administrative structures."

Mark wasn't sure how true that was, even for himself. He *was* sure it was the proper thing to say.

"As a corollary to that," Candace continued, "illegal

armed groupings on Greenwood will have to disband immediately or face suppression by the armed forces of the Alliance. The Alliance will guarantee the rights of individual settlers, but harassment of officials properly appointed by authorities on Zenith has to stop immediately."

He glared at Mark. Mark, who'd faced a furious Yerby Bannock, tried to avoid smiling. He nodded solemnly and said, "Our only desire is for justice, sir."

The counselor seemed to have taken Mark's statements as gospel truth, because he relaxed noticeably at the mild replies. One of the problems faced by people who deal with words—and laws are only words—is that those folk tend to mistake the image for reality.

"Very well," Candace continued. "You realize, I'm sure, that the above discussion applies only to settlers in good faith. Speculators who bought up large tracts on grants which they knew to be invalid have no rights under any agreement we reach here."

"What's he mean?" Dagmar said to Mark. "I'm no speculator!"

"Ms. Wately's tract is of twenty-five hundred square miles," Mark said to Candace instead of answering Dagmar directly. "That's a typical holding for Greenwood."

"That's absurd," said Finch. He looked from Mark to the counselor. "That's absolutely absurd! You can't call a tract that large a homestead."

"Are we to understand that you'll disallow Ms. Wately's holdings, then?" Mark said. He fully intended to blow off any possible deal, but he couldn't afford to have it look that way. "In effect, to disallow all the present holdings, despite lip service to the contrary?"

"Large homesteads are normal on undeveloped worlds," Candace said coolly. "Mr. Finch, we're discussing a planet, not a tract in the middle of New Paris. I think we can allow holdings of up to the stated figure—" His face rotated to Mark. "—so long as they're undivided tracts held by resident individuals. Yes?"

"Please continue," Mark said. He was acting the part of a cautious negotiator who wasn't willing to commit to anything until he was sure the whole deal was on the table.

Candace nodded in grudging approval. "And there will be an indemnity from criminal and civil prosecution for actions taken by parties on both sides during the past, shall we say, six months," he said. "I think that covers the relevant points. Do you require further clarification, Mr. Maxwell?"

"If we were to agree to the offered arrangement," Mark said, "we'd be signing on behalf of the Greenwood Council, an elective body."

"Nothing of the sort," Candace said, flatly but without anger. The counselor had obviously expected this ploy and would have been disappointed if Mark hadn't tried it. "You'll be signing as representatives chosen ad hoc by Greenwood settlers to negotiate the planet's return to peaceful authority. For this matter *only.*"

He smiled coldly at Mark. "No permanent citizens' body is legal without the express agreement of the relevant Alliance authorities. Without attempting to predict the future, I would judge it very doubtful that Protector Giscard or his vicar will form such a body on Greenwood, given the problems that have arisen—" Candace looked at Vice-Protector Finch. "—on Zenith and elsewhere, when local councils attempt to usurp power properly wielded by the Alliance alone."

Finch's eyes narrowed; Biber's expression hardened. Candace meant powers like the allocation of taxes raised from the citizens of the "protected" planet, Mark knew. Finch and Biber were both Zenith patriots . . . but as with Ms. Macey the night before, the most important question for them at the moment was their chance for a profit. They held their tongues.

"We can accept that," Biber said. "It seems to me that crimes are crimes and shouldn't be papered over in a land deal, but I can live with it."

He looked at Finch. Finch nodded curtly, unwilling to give his rival the courtesy of verbal agreement.

"Look," Dagmar said to Mark. "What's he saying about *my* land? And Bannock's, and the rest of us—what we bought?"

"You'll still own that land," Mark said. "You'll even be able to buy more if you're ready to pay these gentlemen's price."

He nodded across the table toward Biber and Finch, feeling the corners of his mouth spread in a slight grin. "But there'll be no way you can prevent them from putting a modular city down on any tract they own, even if that's right next to your property."

Candace nodded cool agreement. His bony fingers were crossed in front of him on the table. The Zenith investors were trying not to stare, but their faces showed a focused intensity. Colonel Wordsworth merely glowered at the whole gathering.

"But it won't be *on* my tract?" Dagmar said. "That's what you're saying, right?"

"Yes," said Mark. "That's what I'm saying."

"Well," said Dagmar, "I got no problem with that. I never asked to run somebody else's business. I just want them to keep their nose out of mine. That's pretty much how everybody feels. That's why we took up land on a place like Greenwood, I guess."

She looked from the investors to Candace. "So?" she said. "There's something we sign or what?"

The people who settled a new world—the survivors, at least—were folk who thought in terms of the immediate future. They didn't have time to worry about crowding and pollution that would come ten years down the road unless they took preventative measures now. Getting through the next winter was too pressing a problem.

"I think," said Mark, "that we'll sleep on the matter overnight, madame and gentlemen."

The investors' expressions hardened, but Candace allowed himself a bare smile. The counselor would have been horrified had the Greenwood contingent accepted the offer so quickly, even though that was the result he and Protector Giscard wanted.

Dagmar Wately looked in question at Mark but didn't speak. Mark continued, "If the parties are of the same mind tomorrow, then perhaps we can meet again to discuss the wording of the agreement."

What right had Mark Maxwell to put his judgment over that of folks like Dagmar Wately? He and Amy and maybe Yerby might be the only people on Greenwood who wouldn't welcome this compromise. Most of the settlers would willingly trade their planet's future for what they had now in their hands.

Maybe Mark had no right at all. But the Woodsrunners had sent him to this negotiation because they trusted his judgment in an affair they didn't understand themselves. So be it. They would get Mark Maxwell's best judgment.

Candace nodded approval. "Shall we say the same time and place, then?" he asked with a lifted eyebrow.

Mark got up from his chair and looked out the window. Crowds were gathering at many points in the park and streets below, but they didn't have the edgy violence of the mob the night before.

Colonel Wordsworth walked to the window beside him. "What in the name of *heaven* is going on?" she snarled. She turned and moved for the door at a pace just short of running. "This utterly and totally *damned* planet!"

"I'm going with her," Mark muttered to Dagmar.

In fact they all followed Wordsworth as fast as they could, Candace included. Under the present conditions on Zenith, any unusual event could be the fuse that ignited real trouble.

The colonel was still in the lead when the group reached the bronze-and-glass street doors. She barged through and skidded to a surprised halt outside.

A platoon of Alliance troops manned a sandbagged checkpoint in front of the Civil Affairs Building. Instead of tensely holding their guns and gas bombs, the soldiers were chortling in small groups. Holographic images quivered in the air before them.

"Let me see that!" Wordsworth said to the nearest group. The sergeant in the middle snapped to attention, startled by the colonel's sudden arrival. He handed over a thimble-sized cube. When its sides were squeezed, it projected a moving hologram for thirty seconds.

"Here," called a woman wearing the silver-winged uniform of a New Paris delivery service. She tossed a handful of the projection cubes over the sandbag barricade to Wordsworth and the negotiators.

Mark picked up a cube with the rest of them, mostly to check the resolution. *It was clever of Ms. Macey to hire a local service to distribute them. . . .*

He squeezed the cube. Heinrich Biber, stark naked except for a coating of mud, twitched miserably in the jet of the firehose washing him clean. His face was readily identifiable to anyone who'd seen the Mayor before. So, Mark suspected, were the Mayor's other attributes.

"You know," a female soldier said to her fellows, "I've seen Pekingese *dogs* that were hung better than he is!"

Gales of laughter came from the street and park. Mayor Biber had wealth and power, but he wasn't the sort of man his fellow-citizens weren't willing to laugh at. Chances were that out-of-work Zeniths disliked the local moneymen about as much as they did the Alliance troops.

"Who did this?" Biber screamed. He flung a projection cube to the ground and jumped on where it would have been if it hadn't bounced away. "Who?"

"Why, Heinrich," Berkeley Finch said through the faint curtain of the hologram he was projecting over and over. "I now see an aspect of you I'd never imagined!"

Biber tried to throttle him. Finch backed away, still laughing. A pair of soldiers caught the Mayor's arms.

"It doesn't really matter," Mark said. His soul trembled but he was glad to note that his voice stayed steady. "You've already agreed that Yerby and me and all the Woodsrunners will keep our possessions on Greenwood, Mayor Biber."

Biber shook himself loose. *"You,"* he said in a venomous voice, pointing at Mark.

"In fact," Mark said, "you've made us incredibly rich because of the way land prices will shoot up when you begin bringing in settlers by the tens of thousands."

"You think I'm going to make you rich after what you and your other swine did to me in that swamp?" Biber screamed. He turned to Candace. "There's no deal!" he said. "There's no deal but that every one of the bastards on Greenwood now gets scooped up in their *underwear* and dumped on an asteroid!"

"Biber, you don't speak for the syndicate," Berkeley Finch said in a worried voice. He'd suddenly realized the wider ramifications of what had just happened.

"And the syndicate doesn't speak for me if it plans to compromise with these grubby lice!" the mayor replied.

Candace tried to step between the men. Biber pushed the counselor back out of the way. "I'm telling you, Finch, I'm going to clear the tracts *I* own of all trespassers, and if—" He turned to Candace again. "—Protector Kiss-My-Ass Giscard has a problem with that, it's *really* too bad!"

Biber stumped out of the checkpoint, slapping at the projection cubes in the hands of the people he passed. Colonel Wordsworth watched him go with a speculative look.

"Well, Dagmar," Mark said to his fellow delegate. "I don't think we need stay on Zenith any longer. It appears that an agreement won't be possible after all."

He nodded to Counselor Candace, who seemed to be in shock.

31. Off the Deep End

Zenith's rich, red-orange dawn looked like the mouth of hell backlighting the new barricade on the spaceport approach road. As the taxi carrying Mark and Dagmar pulled up, soldiers backed a dump truck loaded with sand to the other side of the swinging crossbar and shut off the engine.

"What's going on?" the taxi driver called through his open window, sounding worried as well as angry at the delay.

The barricade was a hasty improvisation of sand-filled fuel drums and concrete blocks. It closed three of the four travel lanes; the dump truck now filled the other. Flashing emergency lights had made the structure look like a construction site as the taxi approached.

Mark stuck his head out to be sure. The folk at the barricade wore the tan uniforms of the Zenith Protective Association. A number of the troops looking worriedly over the line of drums carried repellers and other projectile weapons. The gun on the back of a pickup behind the

barricade fired two-inch-rockets through a charger-fed
launching tube.

The dump truck began to settle with a loud hiss. The
vehicle had a central inflation pump. The militiamen were
using it to vent all the air from the tires so it was impossible
to roll the truck out of the way.

"Hey!" cried the taxi driver. "What're you doing?"

"Ms. Wately," said Mark, formal because he was frightened. "I think we'd better get out. We may have to leave
our gear."

An officer with red shoulder boards on her tunic
ducked under the crossbar and walked to the taxi. More
traffic was backing up. Horns blew in a variety of timbres.

"I can buy more clothes," Dagmar said as she and Mark
got out of opposite sides of the vehicle with their hand
luggage. "So long as I don't get my head blown off first."

"There's no more traffic into the port!" the militia officer
snarled. She was young, petite, and obviously as scared as
Mark was. "Go on, get away from here! There's an Alliance
column on the way and we're going to stop them!"

During the night everything on Zenith had changed
as suddenly as a trap shuts. Mark didn't know whether
there'd been a precipitating incident or if the general
tension had suddenly coalesced into war the way rain
forms from water vapor. When heavy gunfire began to
shake the city, he and Dagmar headed for the starport.

They stepped toward the barricade. Mark had paid the
driver when they got in, the only way the man would agree
to drive through New Paris and the chance of trouble at
any instant.

"Stop!" the officer cried to Mark. "I've got my orders!"

She wore a handgun of some sort in a covered holster on her wide belt. Her hands groped for the weapon, but she couldn't seem to get the flap open.

"Don't get your knickers in a twist, sister," Dagmar snapped. She was either a great actress or a lot more relaxed than Mark was. "We're Greenwood citizens going home. This fight is nothing to do with us."

"Madame Captain," Mark said, "your orders are to stop vehicles. We're going to Greenwood to bring help back here to you."

It was the best lie he could think of at the spur of the moment. Whatever happened, it didn't look like Greenwood need worry about another Zenith invasion any time soon.

A fast-moving aircar, low but nonetheless airborne and therefore in breach of the emergency regulations, came from the direction of New Paris. It looked as though the driver planned to cross at the normal entranceway instead of rising to hop over the high earthen berm surrounding the port proper.

The crew of the gun on the pickup fired three rockets in quick succession. Instead of a roar, the rounds blasted from the launching tube with a *crack!/crack!/crack!* that made Mark grab his ears as he hunched over.

If the militia meant the shots as a warning, they cut it closer than Mark would have recommended. One of the sizzling green balls snapped within arm's length of the vehicle's canopy. The car skidded in the air as the driver not only backed his fan nacelles but banked to use the vehicle's whole underside as a brake. The aircar settled to the shoulder of the road beside the taxi.

Heinrich Biber popped out of the back like the cuckoo from a clock, shrieking, "What are you doing? I could have been killed!"

Biber was in a police service uniform like the one he'd worn on Greenwood. The man and woman who got out of the vehicle with him, and the driver who stayed at the controls, were members of the New Paris Watch also.

"Colonel Finch says there's no entry to the port," the militia officer said. "There's a column of Alliance troops coming to seize control."

"I know there's an Alliance column coming, you idiot!" Biber said. "They've got tanks and you can't possibly stop them! I couldn't get through to Finch any other way, so I've come to warn him in person!"

Mark saw metal gleaming rosy orange a mile and a half away where the spaceport approach road left the main highway. By concentrating, he could feel the low-frequency drumming of hundred-ton tanks that pounded the highway with the cushion of pressurized air that supported them.

"I think," he said, "that it's too late even for that, Mayor. Dagmar, come on—run! And the rest of you run too, if you're smart, because those tanks will slide right over you even if they don't bother to shoot!"

Mark dodged around the dump truck, looking over his shoulder to make sure Dagmar was following. She was. They ran for the terminal building a quarter mile away. Mark could already hear the tank intakes shrieking like a flock of approaching harpies.

Two huge crawlers were moving the *James and John*, the ship that would carry Mark on the first leg of the journey back to Greenwood, toward a magnetic mass near the terminal. The *James and John* wasn't scheduled to launch until local midnight, but Captain Cobey obviously planned to leave Zenith as quickly as he could get the starship in order.

Mark felt the same way, so he didn't figure he could blame Cobey. He still felt a flash of anger to realize the captain would have abandoned his passengers if they hadn't headed for the port before dawn.

Folk moving with the aimless busyness of ants from a disturbed hill swarmed about the doors to the terminal building. Spaceport staff, passengers and crew from ships in the port, and dozens of men and women in uniform or partial uniforms watched, shouted to one another, and wandered in or out. Two city buses, a dozen trucks, and scores of lighter vehicles including aircars were parked around the building in defiance of normal regulations.

Dagmar nodded at the chaos. "To blazes with that!" she said. "There's the *James and John*. Let's get aboard now. Nobody's going to be checking exit documents today."

Mark eyed the starship. The crawlers wouldn't have it on the mass for another twenty minutes, and even abbreviated liftoff preparations would take ten or fifteen minutes more. To advise Yerby and the Greenwood Council, Mark needed to know as much as possible about what was happening on Zenith.

Besides, he was curious.

"Dagmar," he said, "you go to the ship. Don't let them take off without me. I'll see what's happening in there and be with you in a few minutes."

Or not at all. Well, there was a risk in entering the

terminal building, but the only certainty in life was that it ended sometime.

Mark trotted toward the entrance. *Before Dagmar can object,* he thought, but that was a remnant of his Quelhagen attitudes. Dagmar was a frontier settler who didn't figure it was her business if her neighbors risked their lives.

The rumble of the approaching tanks shook the starport as badly as the high frequency hum of starships landing. Mark didn't hear any shots. He couldn't imagine anybody firing small arms at the impenetrable bulk of the Union vehicles, but everything happening today was beyond Mark's previous experience.

It was beyond the previous experience of everybody in the spaceport and probably most of the soldiers in the Alliance column as well. That made it as dangerous as playing catch with live grenades.

Mark squeezed through the doorway crowded with people uncertain whether to go in or out. "Let me through!" shouted the man behind him as they shoved together into the wailing room. Bits of clothing and equipment lost or broken in the nervous confusion littered the terrazzo floor. "Where's Finch? I need to speak with Colonel Finch!"

Mark looked at the man who'd spoken. He was Mayor Biber, who'd left or lost his aides somewhere between the barricade and here.

"He's in the control room," a woman with a nerve scrambler said. She wore a tan Zenith Protective Association jacket, but her orange cap said CARGO and had the spaceport's arrow-in-circle logo. She was staring in puzzlement at her weapon as if trying to remember where it had come from.

At least two sirens wailed within the port area. The tanks' intake whine was already louder, though it came from the other side of the berm.

The pair of guards at the door to the control room carried repellers. One man looked blank. The other, a teenager, was gleefully bright-eyed and had his finger on the trigger.

The past several months had given Mark an experience with weapons he'd never expected to need. He immediately noticed that the boy hadn't thrown the cocking switch that would drop the first pellet into the repeller's chamber.

Mark didn't plan to tell the fellow. That mistake was very likely the only reason he hadn't accidentally blown holes in the ceiling and probably the twenty nearest people as well.

"Let me by," Biber said curtly. "I'm the Mayor and I need to talk to Finch immediately."

The older guard blinked. The boy's finger tightened unconsciously on the trigger.

"It's all right," Mark said, patting the youth on the shoulder. "We're bringing reinforcements and need to know where to place them."

Biber looked up in recognition. Until then Mark had been only a shape on the fringes of Biber's awareness. He nodded and led Mark in.

Holographic displays covered three walls of the control room. A dozen people were present, four of them space-port staff. Berkeley Finch stood in front of a real-time image of the port's barricaded entranceway, speaking into a radiophone with earnest desperation.

The display was fed by cameras at the upper corners of the berm, twenty feet above ground level. Two tanks led a score of buses and trucks filled with Union soldiers.

One of the tanks halted crossways so that its armor screened the soft-skinned vehicles from any shots that might be fired from the barricade. The other tank slid forward to clear the obstacles. Civilian vehicles, halted when the militia blocked the entrance, crunched and burst into flames beneath the tank's massive bow.

Mark couldn't see any Zenith militiamen at the barricade. The truck with the rocket gun had been driven away. A lone officer crouched in the shadow of the thick berm, speaking into a phone—perhaps to Finch in the control room.

"Finch, I've just come from downtown!" Biber said. "They've taken the Civil Affairs Building, your Association headquarters, and they're moving into Watch substations one by one. We can't stop them!"

The two men had been enemies and would never be friends, but for now they had to be allies. Both appreciated Ben Franklin's advice in similar circumstances: "We must all hang together, or assuredly we shall all hang separately."

The tank pushed a wad of smoldering cars into the line of blocks and barrels. The driver pivoted his vehicle, ramming the mass out of the travel lanes and up the sixty-degree slope to the left of the roadway. Sand from crumpled barrels swirled in the whirlwind blasting beneath the tank's skirts. Some of the concrete slabs facing the end of the berm broke as the vehicle's bow brushed them.

The mass of debris sagged down as the tank swung away, but there was still room for truckloads of soldiers to drive through the gap. The tanker was proceeding to clear the rest of the entranceway nonetheless. The militia officer had run away.

"There aren't ten thousand Earth troops on Zenith!" Finch said. He squeezed the phone in his hand as if he wanted to crush it. "There's three million of us!"

"Yes," said Biber. "And all those millions can't stop Giscard from sending his soldiers wherever he pleases so long as they have tanks and we don't have anything that'll more than scratch their paint. Get your people out of here, Finch!"

Finch wiped his face with his free hand. He looked from Biber to the display, but there couldn't have been much solace there. The Alliance tank was using its bluff bow to bulldoze the remainder of the obstacles to the other side of the entranceway. The dump truck's ten tons of chassis and load skidded inexorably toward the end of the berm, pushed by a tank whose power plant could accelerate ten times that weight to fifty miles an hour. Parts tore off the truck's underside in a torrent of sparks.

"We can't escape now," Finch said miserably. "As soon as they're through the entrance, they'll control the whole port from the inside. Those lasers can sweep us off the top of the wall if we try to climb out in some other direction."

"Then we have to surrender," Biber said bluntly. "Hang yourself in your cell if you insist on committing suicide. If you try to fight, Giscard'll destroy the port instead of just taking it over. Zenith can't afford that, and New Paris certainly can't!"

The *James and John* showed on the room's left-hand display, almost in position over the magnetic mass. *The Earth troops aren't likely to blast a ship that's taking off. Things aren't quite that bad yet.*

"Gentlemen," Mark said, "I know where the tanks and artillery you need are, and I know how to get them for you. It'll cost you—"

"Get them where?" Finch snapped.

"On Dittersdorf," Mark said. "You won't be able to get enough troops off planet to do it, but we Woodsrunners can do it for you. You've got to pay the costs, and you'll have to agree—for Zenith! Agree on behalf of the whole planet—that Greenwood is free and self-governing from now on."

"We can't free you from Earth," Mayor Biber said. "We can't free ourselves, you young fool!"

He gestured toward the entrance display. The tank's bow had pushed the wreckage of the barricade halfway up the slope. The dump truck suddenly tilted downward onto its side, spilling tons of loose sand over the top of the armored vehicle. Rivers of sand flowed through the intakes on the whirlwinds the drive fans sucked down.

The abrupt silicon hammer blows sheared half the blades from the forward impellers before burning out the motors in gouts of nacelle-devouring blue fire. The machinery screamed like a hundred-ton child being spanked.

The tank bucked to a halt as the driver cut the rear fans before the inflowing sand could destroy them as well. The armored bulk rested squarely across the port entrance, blocking access as completely as the twenty-foot earthen wall to either side.

"There's your chance to escape, gentlemen!" Mark said. "Now, if you accept the deal, I want one of you to come to Greenwood with me on the *James and John*. We'll need somebody who can speak for Zenith and your syndicate. Do you agree?"

Mark couldn't believe what he was hearing himself say. It was as though his father or Yerby Bannock stood at his side, snarling the uncompromising demands. But it was Mark Maxwell alone—

And he'd won. Finch and Biber exchanged glances. They were both decisive men or they wouldn't have been able to create the positions they had despite Alliance attempts to stifle all colonials to docility.

"I'll go," said Biber. "You get your troops out, Finch. We'll need them again when we have tanks of our own."

Finch nodded and raised his radiophone to send his militia over the berm to safety. Mark ran for the door. Mayor Biber, panting but determined, was at his heels.

32. Some Are More Equal Than Others

"So if you'll help us by providing the arms we need to free ourselves from Alliance tyranny," Mayor Biber said, as Amy recorded him, "Zenith will see to it that Greenwood also becomes independent. Vice-Protector Berkeley Finch has authorized me to make this pledge on behalf of the Zenith Assembly." Biber bowed deeply to the assembled settlers and stepped back from the microphone.

Before Yerby could resume speaking to the crowd, a burly man whose fur coat and fur hat nearly doubled his bulk took one of the mikes in the crowd below. "I'm Magnus Newsome," the fellow boomed. "I got a double section on Big Bay north of the Doodle . . . and what I want to know is, is why anybody with the sense God gave a goose would trust a Zenith? If that fat bastard said the *sun* was shining, I'd look up to be sure!"

He waved skyward. Hundreds of the Greenwoods present thundered agreement.

The sun was indeed shining, though it wasn't a day that Mark would have been outside for long if he'd been back on Quelhagen. There was no wind, but the brilliance of sunlight on snow didn't change the fact that the air temperature was well below freezing.

The starship that had landed ten minutes before steamed sullenly. A pool of meltwater had refrozen in the dimple that hundreds of ships had hammered into hard ground. Friction and magnetic eddies had heated the hull enough during descent to vaporize the ice again now.

A man had disembarked almost immediately. He walked toward the Spiker with the stolid determination of somebody virtually blinded by ghost images from sleep travel.

The crowd had trampled the slope west of the tavern into muddy slush. Mark certainly wasn't going to show weakness, and nobody else seemed to mind the conditions. There wasn't any choice but to meet outdoors. No building on Greenwood could hold the five hundred people present, and the assembly was far to important to exclude anybody who wanted to attend.

This might decide the future not only of Greenwood, but of every individual settler on the planet. The problem was, nobody could be certain *what* effect any particular decision would have.

"May I speak to that?" the PA system boomed in a familiar, unexpected voice. Mark was so startled that he might have fallen forward off the wall if Amy hadn't clutched him.

"Aye, you may," Yerby said. "And you can come up here on the platform to do it, because there's nobody on Greenwood who can advise us better. People, this is Lucius Maxwell!"

The man from the newly landed ship was Mark's father.

Yerby squatted and lifted Lucius to the eight-foot-high platform as virtually a dead weight. Mark knew that his father was doing well just to walk a quarter mile this soon after coming out of his transit capsule.

Lucius swayed. Mark half rose, ready to hop up on the platform to help his father, but Yerby had already provided an arm.

"Mr. Newsome's right," Lucius said. Dizziness made him look as white as a vampire's victim, but his voice was strong and vibrant. "You can't trust Zenith—not the Zenith Assembly or any members of it."

He paused for effect, looking down at the settlers' worried faces. "But I'm advising you, I'm begging you, to do what Mayor Biber asks anyway. Because while you can't trust Zenith to help, you can trust the Atlantic Alliance to crush Greenwood and all of you individually unless it's stopped now!"

The last words were in a ringing shout that brought a collective gasp from the assembly. Lucius let the exclamation die away, then raised his spread hands to silence the buzz of conversation that followed.

"There's open rebellion against the Alliance on a score of worlds," Lucius continued. "I'm a delegate from Quelhagen to the parliament of free planets forming on Hestia. The Quelhagen Committee of Governance sent me here first, though, because you on Greenwood know me. Join us and other free peoples and help throw the Alliance out of our lives!"

"Maybe you lot want to get your heads shot off!" shouted a woman Mark didn't know. "I don't see how that makes it our fight here!"

"That's the question you all should be wondering," Lucius agreed, using the PA system to override the arguments that immediately broke out below. "And the answer is, if Earth crushes Quelhagen and the rest of the worlds that are protesting the closure of ports and factories to aid Earth manufactures, then the Alliance will try to prevent a recurrence by shipping millions of Earth citizens onto every settled world."

He pointed to the front of the crowd. "You all remember the city they would have built on Dagmar Wately's land! There'll be a dozen cities here and hundreds on planets like Quelhagen, swamping the present citizens. The Alliance government knows the forced exiles won't get along with real settlers—and they'll make sure they don't by sequestering the best land on each planet for these modular cities. The new arrivals will have to support the Alliance or lose everything a second time to the real owners of the land!"

Lucius gained strength with every word. Yerby had moved aside and stood arms akimbo, smiling and nodding at each point.

"Look," Magnus Newsome said, "I'm not calling you a liar like I do the fellow from Zenith—you I don't know, Maxwell. But it don't make sense to me that Earth's going to send soldiers and what-all here if we don't get their backs up to start with. Sounds like they've got plenty on their plates already."

"Mr. Maxwell," Dagmar Wately added through another of the microphones in the crowd, "you're a smart man and you've helped us a lot, I don't deny. If Earth sends soldiers here to fight us the way they sent soldiers to Zenith—well, they can look for a fight with me. Everybody who knows me knows that I'll hold up my end."

The stocky woman turned to face the crowd as if daring anyone to doubt her word. In the pause, Yerby leaned to the mike on the platform and said, "All right, Dagmar, we all know you chew steel plates and spit out nails. Make your point!"

"I'll make my point, Yerby Bannock!" Dagmar retorted. "I don't go *looking* for fights. I don't go gallivanting off to some mudhole to steal guns that somebody else needs for a fight that's none of mine. And I'm not going to change!"

At least quarter the crowd sounded agreement, though there were a number of people trying to shout the sentiments down as well. Mark's father stepped back so that Yerby could take the microphone unhindered.

When the initial reaction had bled away, the frontiersman said, "What a lot of pussies! And what a lot of fools with their heads in the sand!"

The response was a near riot. Yerby raised his hands and bent his head to look at his boot toes rather than the crowd. Despite the PA system, it was almost two minutes before he could be heard again. "All right, all right," he resumed in apparent concession. "I don't figure I'd ever be willing to live with an Alliance soldier's boot on my neck, but I guess there's some of you that would. That's your business, I reckon."

He cocked his head back and grinned in challenge at the assembly. "*My* business is simple. I figure to go to Dittersdorf and pick up hardware for some friends of mine. And I'll bet there's a hundred or two fellows on Greenwood who've got the guts to go with me! Is that true?"

The shout of agreement wasn't general, but it was certainly the hundreds Yerby had asked for. Burly men and not a few women started to push forward to join him.

"Yerby Bannock, you got no right to commit the whole blame planet!" Magnus Newsome said, his amplified voice barely audible over the crowd noise. "I—"

Mark wasn't sure what Newsome meant to say next. Desiree Bannock stepped to the man's side and decked him with one punch as Amy recorded the scene.

Democracy in action, Mark supposed. He was shivering with adrenaline, but he wasn't sure whether fear or excitement was the cause.

Sometimes a man squatted by himself in the night with only his bedroll and a bottle. More often ten or a dozen folk sat in a circle around a lamp or a fire, passing a bottle. At a number of campsites, a couple shared their bottle in front of a small tent.

It bothered Mark that booze was the only social constant he'd found on Greenwood. He knew that life was hard here and that liquor was as much a painkiller as it was recreation, but he knew also that being drunk worsened the problems while it masked them.

But that was none of Mark Maxwell's business. Like Yerby's relationship with Desiree, Mark had both his opinions and the sense to keep them to himself.

"Hey, Yerby!" said one of six men around a fire of oil burning in a tub of sand. "Have a sip of this!"

"Don't mind if I do, Jace," Yerby said as he took the bottle. "Wanted to introduce my friends the Maxwells,

Lucius and Mark. We'd be in a right pickle now without the two of them helping us mind our step. And that's my sister Amy with the camera."

The firelight made the settlers' faces even ruddier than the liquor had. To Mark they looked sweaty and cheerful, though mud was spilling from all four sides of the ground-sheet on which they sat.

Mud seemed to be the universal fact of Greenwood. When Mark flew over the forest in the daytime, it was a green carpet, and even tonight Tertia's light turned the ground at a distance into a plate of beaten silver, but close up there was always mud.

"Honored, sirs," Jace said. "This is my Uncle Jerry Burns, my cousin Chris, and Bob, Ben and Obed, my brothers."

"Have a drink!" Jerry said brightly, holding out a bottle of his own. "Tell me if this ain't better stuff than the eyewash Jace brews!"

Lucius took the bottle and lifted it to his lips without first wiping the glass with his palm. "Whoo-ee!" he said, handing the liquor to Mark. "Guess I'll let you know what I think about the flavor after I get some feeling back in my mouth. You know how to run your batch strong, friend!"

Mark tilted the bottle upward, blocking the opening with his tongue. This was the twentieth campsite they'd paused at as Yerby led them through the gathering. Even Yerby wasn't taking more than a mouthful from each bottle that came by

"Be sure to stick around tomorrow," Yerby said to the men around the fire. "We'll be choosing delegates to send to Hestia. If there's going to be a federation of free planets, we can't afford for Greenwood to be left out. Lucius here'll explain it all tomorrow."

"You want some of this, miss?" Jace said, offering Amy the bottle Yerby had returned. "It's a mite strong for a girl like you, I guess."

"Don't mind if I do!" Amy said sharply. She lifted the bottle and, to Mark's horror, really took a swig. He saw the bubble rise through the fire-reddened liquor.

"Heck, Yerby," another of the seated men said. "You pick who you want. That's good enough for me!"

"Hey, but look," Jace said, patting the ground beside him. "You know Chink Ericsson, don't you? Set for a minute and let me tell you about the problem we're having with him. Can you do that?"

Yerby glanced back. Lucius nodded minusculely. Yerby squatted in the circle of settlers, listening intently as they talked. Lucius, Mark, and Amy moved a few steps back into shadow.

"It feels as if I washed my mouth out with full-strength lye," Amy said in a tiny voice.

"My tongue's numb," Lucius said. "I hope you didn't think I was really drinking, Amy. Nor Mark either, since he's still standing and he wouldn't be if he'd been swallowing what he pretended to be."

"Dad?" Mark said. He spoke quickly, before he lost the courage to say what he needed to. "Do you really think the Alliance would move troops and settlements here if Greenwood kept out of the fight? It wasn't Earth, it was people from Zenith who were going to plant the city on Dagmar's land."

Amy raised her camera. Mark shook his head quickly, harshly. "Not this," he said. "This is just between us."

"I don't know, Mark," Lucius said, meeting his son's eyes. "I think it's not unlikely."

This was their first chance to talk since the assembly had closed at dusk. Lucius had suggested to Yerby that they shake some hands to make sure the assembly wouldn't balk the next day at the notion of sending delegates to the parliament on Hestia. Yerby didn't need much urging to socialize and drink with his fellows.

"But not a certainty like you told people today," Mark said. He didn't know whether he was angry or just confused; and, though he hadn't really been drinking, by lifting so many bottles to his lips he'd probably absorbed enough alcohol to affect him.

"It's a certainty for Quelhagen," Lucius said quietly. "I'm here representing Quelhagen, son."

Mark grimaced. "I hate to lie, even by shading the truth," he said. "Greenwood has more in common even with Zenith than it does with Earth, I know that! If we didn't break away now, we'd have to do it later and it might be worse then. But to lie to people who trust me . . ."

"I haven't heard you lie, Mark," Amy said. "Or your father either. You have an opinion about what's going to happen. Maybe you're right, and maybe you haven't shared it with—" She nodded toward the group around the nearby fire. "—Jace Burns and his kin. But you just heard Obed say that whoever my brother wanted to send to Hestia was fine with them. There's a lot here who feel that way—and the ones who don't, you know they'll have a chance to speak tomorrow too."

Somebody near the wall of the tavern fired a flashgun at Tertia. Some of the concentrated light might actually reach the moon in a few seconds. The nasty *crack* of the discharge had scarcely died away before a dozen other folk also shot into the sky.

Mark shivered. "I'm afraid to be responsible for everything that could go wrong," he whispered.

"You're right to be afraid," Lucius said. "But very generally the worst decision possible is to refuse to make a decision at all and just let events occur by themselves."

He smiled wanly. "I don't think that's likely to happen in an environment that includes Yerby Bannock, though," he went on. "I'm trying to guide him, and the two of you are also. But don't ever imagine that we're pushing Yerby in a direction he wouldn't have gone without us. Don't ever be that arrogant."

"It was terrible on Zenith," Mark said, almost to himself.

"It's terrible on Quelhagen," Lucius agreed. "It'll be even more terrible when we have weapons to fight back with, but at least then there's the possibility that it'll become better in the future. Until there's revolutionary change, conditions on every 'protected' planet will continue getting bit by bit worse."

"Mark would be a good choice for delegate to Hestia," Amy said.

"No," said Mark. He didn't realize how strongly he felt about it until he'd spoken. "No! I'll be going with Yerby to Dittersdorf."

"There's more to a revolution than fighting, boy,"

Lucius said. His tone was suddenly as coldly angry as Mark had ever heard it.

"I know that," Mark said, straightening to attention, "but there's fighting too. Sir —Dad. I don't want to explain when I'm your age why I let other people fight for me. I know what you've said about only butchers and fools being fit to be soldiers."

Lucius nodded grimly. "That's right," he said. "But did I ever explain why that was? Because if other kinds of people become soldiers, they find themselves doing things they'll regret for the rest of their lives!"

"You're not going to change my mind!" Mark said. He stared at a campfire three hundred yards beyond the tip of his father's left ear.

Lucius laughed with something close to humor. All the cold passion had vanished from his voice. "I'm not even trying, son," he said. "But when you were complaining a moment ago about the way we weren't telling—" He gestured. "—your neighbors everything we thought we knew . . . do you like it better now that I *have* tried to tell you all the things I think I know about this subject?"

Mark chuckled and put his arms around his father, giving him a brief squeeze. Nobody on Quelhagen would have been that demonstrative, but they weren't on Quelhagen now.

"Mark?" Lucius said. "If you like, I'll arrange for you to become a lieutenant in the Quelhagen Defense Forces. The force will certainly grow rapidly, and opportunities for promotion will be considerable." He grinned without humor. "For those officers who survive."

"All right, I'll talk to him," Yerby said in a loud voice.

He lurched to his feet, looking around for his companions. "Let's go find Chink Ericsson, Lucius. You can help me bring him around. If we start having wars of our own on Greenwood, we'll never get shut of the Alliance!"

"We're coming," Mark said. In a softer voice he added, "Thanks, Dad, but my business is on Greenwood. And I guess Dittersdorf."

33. A Nice Day to Visit

The sun was shining. It was pale because there was a high overcast, but it was shining.

Mark stood in the hatchway of the *Chevy Chase* and tried to count. This was the . . . The fifth? The sixth? Anyway, he'd been on Dittersdorf a number of times, and never before could he have sworn that the sun *ever* shone over the spaceport.

He'd have taken it for a good omen, except that his vision was as fuzzy as it usually was when he come out of a transit capsule. This time trying to focus his eyes gave him a headache as if trucks were driving over his skull, crushing it against a concrete roadway.

The *Bloemfontein* must have landed some hours earlier, because the Woodsrunners in the group walking toward the *Chevy Chase* showed no signs of disorientation from their voyage. The third ship of the little fleet, the *Santaria*, wasn't here yet. She might not arrive for days if the glitch with her oxygen system took longer to fix than her captain hoped.

Three ships and fifty-three personnel, all that the commandeered vessels had transit capsules for. There was no point in trying to carry more people without capsules. They wouldn't be sane enough to speak coherently until they'd had a month on the ground to recover.

That wasn't much of an army for a raid on which a multi-planet rebellion depended, but it was what there was available.

"Mark, can you help me guide Yerby?" Amy asked in a faint whisper. Her brother walked like a long-legged zombie, veering from one side of the corridor to the other with each step. Amy's grip wouldn't have been enough to keep him from going right out the edge of the hatch.

"I drank a bottle of Chink Ericsson's brew before we lifted," Yerby said in a dead voice. His eyes were closed. "Sloe gin, he called it. Slow death is more like. I'll tell the world, I'm sick as a dog!"

"Let's wait here, Yerby," Mark said, touching the big man's arms. "Dagmar and some other of the people from the *Bloemfontein* are coming over."

Yerby's eyes opened. They looked alert, if bloodshot. "Right," he said. "Dagmar! Did you capture the control room?"

"What's there to capture?" Dagmar said with a snort. "But here's the controller, if that's what you mean."

Half the two dozen men with Dagmar—and one other woman—weren't from Greenwood. The several strangers in rainsuits were locals, but the others looked and dressed with the variety of folk who happened to have been in the port when the Woodsrunners arrived.

"Look, we don't handle any military traffic here,

buddy," said the controller, a young man and ill at ease. "They've got their own port over on Minor. But I can tell you, there was a ship landed there last week, not the usual supply run, and everybody here figures it must've been full of reinforcements."

A man in the colorful one-piece rainsuit that marked those who had to live on this rain-sodden world nodded solemnly. "Stands to reason Earth's going to build up the fort on Minor when hell's a-popping right across settled space," he said. "Not much that happens anywhere that we don't hear about it on Dittersdorf!"

Mark opened his mouth to sneer, *"Dittersdorf, hub of the universe."* He held his tongue because he realized that all he'd be doing was trying to hurt the locals in revenge for the way they'd hurt him—by saying something that they thought was the truth, and that he didn't want to hear.

"We got all the transport we could find, Yerby," Dagmar volunteered. "That ain't much—two aircars and a surface-effect truck the guy says'll still run, but I dunno. They don't have flyers nor blimps here, it's mostly wheels on the ground. Which don't help us a lot getting across the water to this fort."

"Let's go inside," Mark said. "I want to check something in the dead storage room."

"Say, you know they got showers here?" a Woodsrunner said. He probably lived in a tent or lean-to on Greenwood and the luxury awed him. "And they run all the time!"

"Water goes at a discount on Dittersdorf," Amy muttered grimly. "But we're not going to be here long. One way or the other."

The party strode toward the caravansary entrance. "Now, I guess we can go scout out this fort, Yerby," Zeb Randifer said, "but that's likely to warn them, don't you think? Besides, I figure they'll just shoot first and ask questions later. From what these boys been telling us—"

His thumb hooked to the locals and the off-planet travelers with them. They nodded gloomy agreement. Mark was quite sure that nobody in the whole port except him and Yerby had ever visited Minor, but there's never a shortage of people to swear to a rumor of disaster.

Though if an unscheduled starship had landed at the port, then the rumor really did have some substance.

"Don't worry yourself," Yerby said as they entered the caravansary. The building felt wet, though the humidity inside couldn't possibly have been higher than that of the open air. "I been in the place before and I'll go again. You can't tell what's happening in a place like that from the outside."

He stretched mightily and added, "So long as I'm around, Zeb, I don't guess anybody'll need you to go stick your nose where somebody might nip it off."

"Hey, you've got no call to say that!" Randifer protested. "I volunteered for this just the same as you did!"

"We're going to take a look through the abandoned property," Mark said to the watchman. The storage room's door was closed, but the padlock wasn't in place.

The watchman shrugged. He wasn't a man Mark remembered from previous trips though Dittersdorf. Sight of Amy had made his eyes widen, though he'd probably seen his share of women like Dagmar Wately here on the men's side. Mark didn't know Dagmar well, but he was quite certain that she didn't worry about sexual harassment any more than Yerby did.

"What sort of communication with the fort do you have, sir?" Amy asked the controller. Her voice sounded strong, though her face was still pinched.

Mark found that having to think cleared his mind faster than he otherwise recovered from transit. Maybe that was true for Amy as well.

"No communication at all, miss," the controller said. "We don't need to talk to them, and they don't want to talk to us."

Mark began lifting boxes of ragged clothing out of the storage room and setting them carefully on the floor of the common area. *It isn't there.* He wanted to hurl the trash out of the way, but he was irrationally convinced that if he let Fate know he was desperate, Fate would punish him.

"Look, I'm not going to tell you fellows what to do," another local said, "but what I say is, you're going to get yourselves killed if you so much as fly over Minor the way things are."

"Well, I'm glad you're not trying to tell me what to do," Yerby said, "because I *am* going to head over to Minor myself and see what's going on in the fort."

Something rattled in the box Mark lifted. He reached into a jumble of boots—individuals, not pairs—and came out with the hologram reader he'd noticed on his first visit to the caravansary. He switched the sealed unit on. The seed catalog's opening images appeared, a profusion of flowers and succulent vegetables.

"Bingo!" Mark called. He turned, holding up the reader. Everybody was staring at him.

"You're not going to go, Yerby," he said. "You'd be recognized even by somebody as dotty as Captain Easton. But I won't have any trouble passing for a seed salesman like the poor guy who brought this here however many years ago!"

"And I," said Amy calmly, "will go along to make *sure* they won't connect Mark with their visitors six months past."

Dagmar Wately looked from Amy to Mark. "You know," she said, "it might work. If they don't just blow you to vapor the first time they see a speck on their sensor screens."

"Well, if they do that," Zeb Randifer said judiciously, "then we know what we're up against."

34. Back to the Funny Farm

Amy circled the fortress slowly, a hundred feet in the air. She was carefully avoiding the appearance of being sneaky or threatening. "I didn't really think they'd just shoot us out of the air without warning," she said in a small voice.

"Me neither," Mark agreed heartily. Of course, the car's radio might not work, leaving the fort with no way to warn intruders that they were about to shoot.

"Though I wasn't sure they could warn us," she added. "I don't trust the radio." *Great minds running in the same direction*, Mark thought. *Nervous minds, at any rate.*

Amy was driving to provide an excuse for her presence. It might have strained the credulity of even Captain Easton to believe that a Terran seed company had sent a pair of salespeople over so many light-years. This car was a twin-fan design, inherently unstable despite stub wings that worked only in forward flight. It was in better shape than the vehicle Yerby'd rented six months before, though, and Amy was a better driver. Less ham-fisted, at any rate.

"There he is," Mark said, pointing to the figure hoeing energetically in the garden to the west of the fort's outer wall. "It must be Easton, I mean."

Amy brought them in fast. Hovering in a two-fan aircar was like riding a bicycle along a tightrope—and just as likely to be fatal if you screwed up.

"Don't crush his plants!" Mark warned. He remembered the kids' nickname for Easton and added, "Especially his cabbages."

Amy sniffed. She turned the car ninety degrees just before touching down, aligning the undercarriage perfectly with the outer furrow and a foot beyond it. Easton looked up with a puzzled expression.

"Good evening, Captain!" Mark called as he hopped out of the vehicle. "I'm with Sunrise Seeds of Vermont, and you're clearly just the sort of discerning customer we're looking for. Have we got a deal for you!"

"Seeds?" repeated Easton on a note of rising hope. "No, let me come to you, young man. You might . . ."

Easton hopped spryly to Mark's side, the tools in his belt jingling. His red waterproof boots didn't so much as brush a leaf of his carefully tended plants.

Mark held his catalog reader so the captain could view the projected images. He ran his thumb over the index button and said, "Have you ever seen more gorgeous examples of—"

Problem. Mark didn't have the slightest idea of what the projected flowers might be.

"Heliotrope!" Captain Easton gasped. "Hellebore! Ageratum!"

Not a problem after all. As for "gorgeous," Mark had never seen a catalog image that wasn't at least as pretty as any example of the object that existed in the sidereal universe.

"Perhaps we could go inside, sir?" Mark prompted. "I'm sure you'll want to take some time with these, these *riches*."

"By heaven I will!" Easton said. He started for the armored access port in the wall nearby.

"Perhaps the gentleman would like to fly into the courtyard, sir," Amy suggested with sugary deference. "It seemed to me, humble driver though I am, that there are wonderful expanses for sheltered planting within these walls."

Easton paused with his foot raised for another step. He turned his head. "In the courtyard?" he repeated.

"Our prices are very reasonable," Mark said. "I'm confident that Sunrise Seeds can undercut the prices you're now paying by . . ."

He raised his eyebrow. "Am I correct in supposing that all your supplies come by special order from Earth?" he asked.

"Except for some of the bulb stock that provides me with its natural increase," Easton agreed. "I have a long-term plan to border the external wall of the fort in paper-white narcissus. Though of course that's very long-term."

Mark waved his hand airily. "Sunrise Seeds has built a warehouse on Dittersdorf Major to supply this entire arm of the galaxy, sir," he said. "For no more than the cost of what you have in the ground here—"

He nodded toward the garden, about an acre and a half of varied plantings. The growth was lush. The plot must have good soil, and Mark was sure there was a sufficiency of rain everywhere on Dittersdorf.

"For no more than your present cost," he continued, "you can have enough narcissus to plant a border three feet wide. And our narcissi are of particularly *white* paper, I might add."

Amy winced. "Paper?" said Easton. His puzzlement turned to a frown. "Ah, you're joking. Well, have your joke, young man, but I trust that by the time you're my age, you'll have learned that plants are no fit subject for humor!"

"I beg your pardon, sir," Mark said contritely. Apparently paper-white narcissi weren't paper after all. "I assure you that our prices are no joke, though. Ah—do you have the labor on hand to carry out a beautification project of such magnificence?"

"Come on inside," Easton said brusquely. "Never mind the courtyard for now. We'll deal with that later. We've got to see Hounslow at once. He'll supply the labor!"

Easton popped through the access door like a rabbit diving for its burrow an inch ahead of snapping jaws. "You know," his voice drifted back as Mark followed Amy down the ladder, "I could do a two-level border with narcissi against the wall and a row of erythronium on the outside. Or even three-level . . ."

Mark and Amy had to skip from a walk to a run to keep up with Captain Easton's course along the half-lit corridors. The tunnels of the fort were an environment as changeless as the depths of the sea. The lights never went out—unless they failed, in which case they never came on again. There was no more maintenance than the depths of the sea had, either.

Children's voices echoed, but there weren't any specifically martial sounds. The civilian port controller on Major hadn't any idea how big the ship that arrived last week had been. Each of the vessels Mark had seen when he first landed on Zenith had several hundred soldiers on board, and they'd also been carrying heavy equipment of the sort that was already stockpiled in enormous quantities on Dittersdorf.

The troops lounging in the corridor looked pretty much the same as those Mark had seen when he was here the first time. He couldn't swear they were the same people, but they looked equally scruffy and there weren't any more of them visible.

"Hey, sir, how you doing?" a man called to Easton's obvious agitation. "Don't have cabbage blight, do you?"

The laughter was general but good-natured. Easton's troops didn't hate him. That would be like hating a teddy bear.

"Now, vegetables," the captain said as he trotted along. He was too lost in dreams of expanded plantings to notice his troops or hear what they might be saying. "What sort of a selection of edible plants can you supply?"

"Anything your heart desires, Captain," Mark said soothingly. "Anything you can dream of can be in your hands in seventy-two hours."

In so big a fort, an influx of troops could be concealed far beyond the corridors connecting the garden and the Command Center. There wasn't any reason for such deception, though. Nothing Mark saw appeared to have changed from the previous visit.

And Captain Easton was the same man. It was hard to imagine circumstances in which the Alliance would reinforce this base but leave Easton in command of it.

Mark knew to hold his breath as they strode past the pump room converted to an open latrine. Amy didn't, and the smell shoved her against the far wall in midstride.

"Wonderful natural fertilizer!" Easton muttered. "Most of it well rotted into the best nitrate enrichment you could imagine! And then my troops flatly refuse to remove and spread it for me. Mutiny! If I weren't a forgiving man, I'd . . ."

"It's certainly well rotted," Amy agreed in a faint voice.

"The door's supposed to be closed, though," Easton added, pulling the panel shut. That was the first evidence Mark had seen that any aspect of the normal world could penetrate the tangle of vegetation choking Easton's mind.

When Mark stepped close to Amy in case the brown miasma had stunned her into falling, he noticed that her small belt purse whirred. Her camera was scanning through a hole in the front of the purse. Though she wasn't able to spread the triple lenses to get a direct three-dimensional image, the camera's microprocessor would be able to build complete holograms from changes in perspective the lens got jouncing down the corridor.

Always assuming that nobody noticed the camera and had Amy shot as a spy. He hadn't guessed she was going to take such a risk.

The door with the hand-printed COMMAND CENTER sign was ajar. It couldn't be fully closed, since the latch and jamb Yerby had smashed six months ago still hadn't been replaced. Instead of dithering outside as he had before, Captain Easton barged straight in.

Lieutenant Hounslow was arguing with a forty-year-old woman wearing sergeant's chevrons on the collar of her fresh-looking uniform. Both of them turned when the door opened. Hounslow seemed surprised, but the sergeant's expression remained one of angry frustration.

"Hounslow!" Easton snapped. "How many troops do you have?"

"Well, with the addition of Sergeant Papashvili's squad, sir, fifty-one effectives," Hounslow said. "I'm sorry to say that the sergeant here is questioning my task assignments, however."

He glared at Papashvili. Hounslow had been filling out another multicolored duty chart before the sergeant had come into the office. Now another thought struck him; he whisked the sheet of graph paper off his desk to hold behind his back. He seemed to be afraid Captain Easton had gone nuts and would start tearing up the items of greatest value to Hounslow.

Well, nuts in a different way from usual.

"I need them all," Easton said. "Immediately! We don't have much time—"

"Oh, heaven be praised, Captain!" Sergeant Papashvili cried. "I knew you *both* couldn't be completely bughouse!"

"—before the narcissus planting season here is over," Easton continued, ignoring the sergeant. "We'll need a border spaded around the outer circuit of the walls, three feet wide and I think six inches deep."

He pursed his lips and added, "Though we may have to settle for a shallower bed, given the time available. Well, see to it, Hounslow."

The lieutenant and sergeant both stared at Easton, transfixed. They regained control of their tongues and blurted simultaneously, "Are you *crazy?*"

Easton drew himself up stiffly. "Stand to attention when you address your commanding officer!" he ordered.

Hounslow and Papashvili clicked their heels as they obeyed. They looked like a couple being savaged by their pet goldfish.

"Sir, my duty rosters are made out for—" Hounslow began.

Easton brushed the protest aside incomplete. "Well, you'll have to change them, then," he said crisply. "This is a time-dependent project. It's going to be close, getting so many bulbs ino the ground before first frost anyway."

"*Captain,*" Sergeant Papashvili said in a despairing moan. She looked like a sturdy, no-nonsense woman, but the week she'd spent on Dittersdorf had obviously shaken her. "For heaven's sake, sir, there's a permanent garrison of five hundred troops arriving next month and I've got the job of refurbishing living quarters for them. Not to mention temporary accommodations for up to four thousand more who might stage through here. One month!"

"Why, I'd forgotten that!" the captain said in sudden cheerfulness. "Five *hundred* troops! Wonderful! Why, I'll be able to develop the courtyard after all!"

"Change my charts," Hounslow repeated sepulchrally. He stared at the half-completed roster in his hand as if it were his death sentence. "I don't believe this."

I believe it, Mark thought. *You've known Easton a lot longer than I have, so it shouldn't be a surprise to you either that he's around the bend.*

"I wonder if we might look at the courtyard?" Mark said aloud. "To get a notion of how best to convert it into a garden."

As they flew in, he'd noticed pieces of tarpaulin-covered equipment which hadn't been there when Yerby and Mark visited earlier. If they were fighting vehicles, the raiders had to know about it.

"A Garden of Eden," Amy added, "with a man of your genius guiding the project."

"Yes, of course," Easton said absently. "Papashvili, take them up, will you? You and your engineers will be a great help on this, sergeant. A *great* help!"

"Oh God," the sergeant murmured. "Our help in ages past . . ."

"Ah, young man?" Easton asked in sudden concern. "Would it be possible for me to keep your catalog until you return with the initial order for narcissi? In three days, you said?"

"That's right, Captain," Mark said. "And sure, you're welcome to hold on to the catalog. I hope it'll make your days a little brighter."

"Oh, it will!" Easton said, snatching the reader from Mark's hands. "Now, let's see. At six inches between bulbs, that will be . . ."

Mark and Amy followed Papashvili out into the corridor. The sergeant walked like an unusually gloomy zombie. Behind them, Captain Easton was calculating aloud the number of bulbs he'd need.

Mark felt a twinge of guilt. This was certainly better than shooting people, but Mark really did feel as though he were being mean to a teddy bear.

35. The Better-Laid Plans

Yerby Bannock's left index finger followed the green holographic route Mark's reader projected in the caravansary's common court. He swigged from the bottle in his left hand, careful not to lift the container high enough to block his view.

"Seems to me, lad," he said, "we're best off to land right here, slap in the middle." His finger tapped air in the courtyard. The longer path from the hatch by Captain Easton's garden was blue.

Amy's camera could project miniature images for editing, but they'd decided to transfer the chip to Mark's reader for the sake of the larger display. The whole force, now swelled to eighty men and women by transients recruited in the port, was trying to watch. It wasn't necessary that everybody be able to see, but if anybody thought he or she was being ignored there'd be hell to pay.

The raiders weren't an army: they were a gathering of extreme individualists. They'd *follow* Yerby, but there wasn't a soul among them who thought their leader was in any sense better than they were. Everybody had to be treated alike, at least on the face of it.

"Won't work," Dagmar explained. "The truck we got is surface-effect. It skims the ground, but it won't fly over a wall,"

"I'm not so flaming sure it'll skim any ground, neither," said Holgar Emmreich. "We're working on it, though."

"The other problem is that Sergeant Papashvili and her squad of construction engineers have built a shelter for themselves in the courtyard," Mark said. Amy adjusted the reader to show the workmanlike construction of plastic sheet-stock, nestled into one of the fort's six points. "They're likely to be alert."

"Ain't there rooms in the fort?" Yerby asked with a frown.

"None fit for human habitation, she believes," Mark said. "And she's right. According to the rosters there's supposed to be guards inside the fort, but the sergeant and her people aren't as . . ."

"Rotten," Amy said. "Captain Easton's company has been stationed on Dittersdorf too long. They've just mildewed away."

"But all these corridor junctions have emergency doors," Mayor Biber noted. "If one of them is shut, what are you going to do? You don't have any way to blast or burn through them."

A splendid though sodden figure entered the common room from outside. He wore red trousers, a dark blue tunic, and enough medals to anchor a small boat. He was Berkeley Finch, wearing the dress uniform of a Zenith Protective Association colonel.

Finch threw back his shoulders. "Thank goodness I've arrived in time!" he declaimed as if he were addressing a political rally.

"Finch!" said Mayor Biber in the tone of a man who's just found his dog on the dinner table eating the roast. "What in blazes do you think you're doing here?"

"I've just arrived from Hestia," Finch said, striding to the center of the gathering where Yerby stood with Amy and Mark. "The Assembly of Self-Governing Worlds has granted me a colonel's commission in its own armed forces and appointed me to command of the Dittersdorf expedition."

"The devil you say!" Biber blurted. "The devil!"

Finch's boots squelched. He took a recording chip from his pocket case and offered it to Amy. "Here's the commission," he said. "Really, Biber—you didn't imagine that the Assembly would overlook someone of my long experience with military affairs, did you?"

Amy didn't take the chip.

"Ah . . ." Finch said. "There wasn't time to have a new uniform made, so I'm wearing my Zenith kit still. But the Assembly commission is fully valid."

"Finch, I'm not having this!" Biber said. His voice rang from the caravansary's high dome. "You think being a war hero's going to make you president of Zenith when we've got free elections. Well, you're *not* hijacking this expedition! I've paid all the costs out of my own pocket. I have to stay here to guarantee return of the truck, and you're staying too!"

"Tsk!" Finch replied with a sneer of disdain. The effect would have been greater if rain weren't still dripping from his nose. "Zenith's only been a member of the Assembly of Self-Governing Worlds for ten days, and already traitors are appearing."

He looked at Yerby and added, "You understand the situation, don't you, my good man? At any rate, I'm sure your legal advisor—" A nod toward Mark. "—does."

"I understand that Greenwood hasn't joined your assembly on Hestia," Mark said. *By now we probably have, but Finch can't be sure of that. He must have left Hestia before Dad and the Greenwood envoys arrived.*

"Dittersdorf has sent envoys, however, Mr. Maxwell," Finch said, his expression hardening. "An operation on Assembly territory must be conducted under Assembly auspices if it's not to be judged piracy punishable by hanging rather than an act of war."

Mark wondered if the colonel was bluffing about Dittersdorf's position. Would the stockbreeders here have emerged from their blanket of rain clouds to send a delegation to Hestia? Finch was a lawyer and clever enough to try a double bluff. Mark wasn't sure the Zenith aristocrat fully understood the terms on which this power struggle might be fought by a frontiersman like Yerby Bannock, though.

"Now, lad," Yerby said with a chuckle. He stepped toward Finch, forcing the colonel to sideways or be literally overshadowed by the frontiersman's greater bulk. "We don't stand on ceremony on Greenwood. What's a little formality like that between friends?"

Finch looked surprised. Mark *was* surprised. He'd thought Yerby's most likely response would be to toss Finch back through the outside door. The other possibilities ranged from more violent to very violent indeed, including tossing Finch through the outside door with his torso separate from his head and limbs.

"Well, fellows," Yerby continued to the raiders, most of whom looked as dumbfounded as Mark, "you've heard Mr. Finch. He's come here with some words from a bunch of people none of us ever heard of and a pretty uniform. A *real* pretty uniform if it was dry, I reckon."

"I have battle dress in my luggage!" Finch said sharply. "I have six complete *sets* of battle dress in my luggage."

"And I reckon they're pretty too, Colonel," Yerby said as if he were praising a child's drawing. "Besides which, Mr. Finch is a military genius. A lot of you remember how he showed us that a few months ago on Greenwood."

Laughter chorused through the common room. Woodsrunners bent to explain the joke to recruits from other planets. The story didn't lose anything in the telling, and the merriment continued for some time.

"So I guess it's clear to all of you," Yerby resumed with a grin as broad as a jack-o'-lantern's. "You've got to follow Mr. Finch here." He patted Finch on the head as a final insult.

"Like hell," Dagmar Wately said. "We didn't come here with some pretty boy from Zenith."

"Yeah," Zeb Randifer agreed. "Look, if the choice is go home or go on with that dipstick leading us, I'm going home. And the ship's right outside, too!"

The chorus of agreement was loudest from the non-Greenwood recruits. They were determined to show they were part of the same team as the original Woodsrunners.

Berkeley Finch went white, then red. It was hard to tell whether his primary emotion was anger or embarrassment.

Yerby smiled gently at him and said, "Well, Colonel, it seems like it's this way. You can join the expedition I'm leading. Or you can go dig up an expedition of your own, which I wish you the best of luck for doing. Now, what'll it be?"

Finch swallowed. Amy's camera was on him, its lenses the triple eyes of fate. Finch had only one option unless he wanted to go on record as being the man who'd scuttled the independence movement because it conflicted with his personal ambition.

"Colonel Bannock," he said formally, "I would be honored if you'd let me join your expedition."

"Glad to have you, Finch," Yerby said. "And glad to have your pretty uniforms, too. Now, getting back to just what we're going to do tomorrow night . . ."

As the meeting broke up for dinner and serious drinking, Berkeley Finch bent close to Amy's ear and said, "Ms. Bannock? Might I have a word with you in private?"

"No," said Mark, "you can't. I've had experience of what it means to be caught alone by you, Finch."

Mark was jealous. He knew that, but he could legitimately claim there was a chance that Finch hoped to use Amy as a hostage to control her brother.

Finch grimaced. "Nothing like that," he muttered.

Amy nodded coolly. "I think this is as private as we need to be, Vice-Protector," she said, using the Alliance title to keep Finch ill at ease. "Nobody's listening to the three of us."

That was true. The court echoed with people calling to one another. Most of the raiders were donning rain gear to splash outside in search of food and drink more interesting than the rations they'd brought from Greenwood.

"Of course," said Finch. "I've noticed that you're very scrupulously recording events as they occur?"

Amy nodded. "Yes I am," she said. "And I have no intention of wiping any image at the request of someone who doesn't care for the way it makes him look."

"Not that," Finch said. "Not at all. But what I would like, and what I'd be willing to pay very well for, would be copies of recordings of my actions during the raid to come. Particularly images that might show me involved in—"

He looked around to see where his rival, Mayor Biber, was. Biber was talking to Yerby and the husky local who owned the truck that three of the expedition's better mechanics were trying to put in running order.

"— the sort of heroic actions that would interest voters in a political campaign on Zenith," Finch went on in a still lower voice. "In return, besides paying you, I would be *very* supportive of your planet's independence from Zenith. One hand washes the other, as the saying goes."

He winked.

"I'll see what can be arranged, Vice-Protector," Amy said. "No promises, but—we'll see."

It wasn't an offer a Greenwood patriot could afford to reject, Mark knew; but he hadn't trusted Finch before and now he *really* didn't trust the man. Listening to the Vice-Protector planning to turn a dangerous, maybe bloody, raid into political capital made Mark want to wash all over, not just his hands . . .

36. Once More into the Breach

The land ahead loomed out of the sea's soft phosphorescence. "See?" Yerby crowed. "Didn't I tell you we'd be OK? I don't need a compass, I got a natural compass in my head!"

"It was monstrously irresponsible to leave before navigational aids were installed in this vehicle!" Berkeley Finch said. "I didn't dream that you were considering such a thing!"

"You were welcome to stay at the spaceport, Colonel," Amy said.

"Naw, Finchie," Yerby said. "I knew I could find Minor. It'd have been a lot riskier to wait around the port, looking for a radiocompass that maybe we wouldn't find anyhow."

"And have the Alliance reinforcements arrive early while we were cooling our heels," Mark put in. "On the frontier, we learn to make do."

He was talking as if he'd been raised in a log cabin instead of conditions of luxury as civilized as those of the

Vice-Protector himself. The past months had changed
Mark, though. He hadn't blinked when Yerby announced
that he'd need to eyeball their overwater course because
the compass didn't work.

A few of the recruits from more ordered planets had
indeed backed out when they heard about the compass.
The frontiersmen from Greenwood and other planets had
taken the matter in stride. Yerby said he could get them to
the fort on Minor; and if he didn't, well, they'd make do.

Finch had come anyway. His hopes for a political
future were greater than his fear of drowning.

"Now hang on, everybody!" Yerby roared over his
shoulder. "This may get a mite rough."

The surface-effect truck looked like a conventional aircraft with wings and a pair of turbine engines at the roots
of the vertical tail. The wings were too stubby to support
the fat fuselage in normal flight. Their steep camber
trapped a cushion of air between them and the surface of
the ground or sea so long as the vehicle flew forward.

The truck could sail ten feet in the air at 220 miles an
hour with a modest expenditure of energy, perfect for
carrying heavy loads over water or flat ground. It couldn't
hover, though, and crags or a wall would rip the vehicle
apart.

If the engines failed you'd better like the immediate
terrain, because you were either going to land there or
crash.

Mark tensed as the shoreline approached beyond a
frill of seafoam. He hadn't paid any attention to the coast
on his previous trips to Minor, and he doubted Yerby had
either. If the margin rose too abruptly, rocks were going

to take the truck's bottom off as sure as a grater scrapes cheese.

"Amy," he said. "Lift your feet."

"Why—" said Berkeley Finch.

The truck dipped, then lifted as if the shelving beach were a trampoline. Vegetation whickered beneath their keel like the brushes of an automatic car wash. Occasionally something more solid would thump the vehicle, but for the most part even the tree trunks were soft and sappy. Nothing came ripping through the bottom plates, at any rate.

"This is a much bigger vehicle than the ones you used to scout the fort earlier," Finch muttered. "It may well be above a detection threshold that the cars escaped."

"Naw, nothing much works down there," Yerby said unconcernedly. "You ain't seen the place, Finchie."

"Don't call me that," Finch said, but he spoke in an undertone that carried no conviction. Yerby chuckled and tousled Finch's hair.

"There's a signal!" Mark said. "There's a light flashing ahead of us!"

"That's the warning light on the fort's antenna tower, lad," Yerby said. "It flashes in the daytime too, when we was there before, but I guess you didn't pick it out."

He throttled back the turbines and rotated the big horizontal steering wheel hand over hand. You couldn't bank the truck without spilling the supporting cushion of air, so the rudder had to supply all the turning force. The vehicle wallowed and sideslipped as it curved around the nighted bulk of the fort.

They coasted down on a three-hundred-foot strip on

the north side of the fort, where the walls' shade stunted the vegetation. The ground sloped but not badly. The double-bogie wheels on the truck's hull jounced brutally, but the vehicle tracked straight enough that the small wing outriggers could handle the sideways jolts.

The turbines roaringly reversed thrust, and the wings pivoted further down into airbrakes instead of lifting devices. The truck stopped with a final whiplash.

"Next time we do this, Bannock," said Axel Kockler as he picked himself from the tangle of other raiders who'd lost their hold on the bulkhead straps, "we bring blimps, you hear me? This is no way for human beings to travel!"

"Who decided you was human, Kockler?" a neighbor called. Sliding hatches in the cargo compartment rumbled open.

Yerby opened the door on his side of the cab. "Well, anyhow," he said across the general laughter, "it's fast."

"If I wanted fast," Kockler muttered, checking the flashgun he'd dropped when he fell, "I wouldn't drink whiskey. I'd just club myself on the head and get straight to the hangover."

Vines curtained the outer wall of the fortress. The stems were leafless until they reached the top and exploded in a profusion of foliage. Some of the more active raiders were already climbing, carrying rope ladders for the others to follow by.

"All right, Colonel," Yerby said to Finch. "I want you and your people to be special careful when you pick up the families. Chances are, most folks won't want trouble because they got their kids around; but there'll be a few who get panicky for the same reason. I'll tell you right now, anybody who hurts a kid because of an itchy trigger finger had better shoot me too before I hear about it. Right?"

"Nobody's going to get hurt, Yerby," Zeb Randifer said. "It's going to be like Blind Cove, no trouble at all."

"I'd like to accompany the body that captures the Command Center, Bannock," Finch said formally—for at least the fourth time since Yerby decided in the caravansary who'd go where on the raid.

"I'd like you to get on with the job I give you, Finch," Yerby said. There was enough granite for a landslide in his tone. "Or if you like, you can guard the truck here in place of Rinaldi."

"As you please," Finch said with pinched nostrils. He turned to the nearest ladder and climbed, the repeller on his back swinging with the violence of his motions. Mark braced the rope with one hand till Finch reached the top, then followed him.

Yerby backed a few steps and took a run at the wall. His boot got enough purchase on the vines that the frontiersman was able to catch the lip and swing himself onto the broad battlement. Amy shook her head at her brother's showing off, but she was recording him nonetheless.

Dittersdorf had no moon. The raiders' only light came from the warning flasher on the antenna. Somebody missed his footing on the inner ladder. He fell with a clatter of equipment and curses, his own and those of the people he bounced into. Mark expected an alarm, but the only answering sound was that of the nightbirds. Papashvili's engineers were all the way across the starport, and there was probably nobody else in the garrison above ground.

One of the raiders started to wander off toward the stairwell that led directly down to quarters for the soldiers living in family groups. The underground corridor between those rooms and the barracks-style arrangements for the remaining troops was open, but none of the ceiling lights worked.

Married quarters were Finch's responsibility. "Hey you!" he called to the man. "Where do you think you're going?"

The frontiersman turned. "I'm going down the stairs, like I'm supposed to," he said. "But if you want, pretty boy, I'll clean your clock before I do that."

"Now, you just hold where you are, Casey Tafell," Yerby said in a mild but carrying tone. "Nobody goes anywhere till we're all ready."

Tafell grimaced. "Who died and made you God?" he asked, but he spoke in a lowered voice which Yerby was willing to ignore.

"The little prick sure gets up a fellow's nose," Yerby said to Mark in a generally audible aside. "But we can't have folks haring off on their own."

Finch was welcome to think Yerby was talking about Casey Tafell if he liked. Anyway, all the raiders stayed at the base of the wall until the last person—Dagmar, making sure that nobody was still screwing around in the truck—was over the wall.

"That's it," she said. "My lot, come on, we'll collect them engineers before somebody gets up to take a leak and sees us."

She headed across the vast paved courtyard, cradling a repeller captured in one or the other of the Zenith invasions. Ten frontiersmen followed her. They weren't moving fast, but neither does the surf as it sweeps up the shore; and like the surf, they'd keep going until they were darned good and ready to stop.

"Finch, good luck to you," Yerby said. "And remember, watch out for kids."

Yerby sauntered to the entrance by which he'd entered the fort the first time. He didn't give orders to the raiders who were supposed to go with him. Mark wasn't sure if Yerby knew everybody would follow or if he just didn't care.

Mark didn't look over his shoulder either. He couldn't imagine that the people who'd come this far wouldn't go the rest of the way. Besides, Amy was a half step behind her brother; Mark was going in even if it was nobody but the three of them.

Boots shuffling on the slotted metal stair treads set up echoes in the shaft. By the time Mark was three-quarters of the way down to the first level, it sounded as though an army or an extremely large centipede was coming down the stairs behind him.

"Yerby?" he said. "We'd better stop before you open the door to the corridor. The racket'll wake the guards up even if they've all been dead for three days."

Yerby got to the first landing and reached for the door latch. He hadn't heard Mark's warning over the clatter of feet.

"Yer—" Mark shouted.

The door opened inward to the hallway before Yerby

touched it. An Alliance soldier, half turned to say something to his companion in the corridor, jerked his head around. He faced Yerby Bannock in the dim light of the stairwell.

Amy peered around her brother's shoulder with the three lenses of her camera spread like the eyes of a monstrous insect. Mark was on the first step behind the Bannocks, trying to aim his gas gun. In back of him the stairs were full of hairy, ragged frontiersmen, armed to the teeth.

"*Mother!*" the Alliance soldier screamed. He flung his repeller down the corridor in one direction and fled in the other.

His companion raised and pointed her own weapon. Her face was pallid in the light in the ceiling above her.

"The door!" Mark cried. He couldn't level the gas gun because the sling swivel in the butt was tangled in the belt of the man behind him.

The door was made of quarter-inch armor plates that sandwiched an insulating honeycomb. The hypervelocity pellets would disintegrate on the panel's first layer without penetrating. If Yerby could pull the door closed—

Yerby jumped straight toward the gun and clouted the soldier with a sweep of his left arm. He held his flashgun to the side in the other hand, out of the way.

The Alliance soldier bounced like a rubber ball off the far wall of the corridor. Her repeller sparked and skidded along the concrete flooring. Mark grabbed it, trying to glance in both directions to see if there were more soldiers coming.

Mark couldn't tell anything except that there was nobody in the two pools of light in the distance to the right. The other way there was no light at all, though an occasional clatter suggested the fleeing soldier was caroming from one side to the other at a dead run.

The rest of the raiders crowded into the corridor, jostling Mark aside. "Hey, now," Yerby said. "Don't step on the poor child I whacked on, here. She's had enough trouble tonight."

Mark slung his gas gun and peered at the repeller. Yerby cradled the dazed sentry in the crook of his arm like a mother with her infant.

"Yerby," Mark said, "that was a crazy thing to do. She'd have blown your head off if her gun was in better shape!"

He'd thought the repeller might be on safe. It wasn't. The receiver was so corroded that the trigger hadn't made contact when the sentry tried to shoot.

"Well, lad," Yerby said judiciously. "There's a lot of things that can happen in a fight, that's true. But I generally find the best rule is go right at the other fellow and not stop till he's down."

The thirty Woodsrunners in this group were milling in the corridor. The single overhead fixture lighted them grotesquely. Yerby bent toward his captive and said, "Well, little lady. To tell the truth, I wasn't expecting to find you awake. How many of you lot are on guard?"

"Nothing to report, Lieutenant Hounslow, sir," the soldier mumbled. Her eyes didn't focus, but at least the pupils were the same size. "Just like every other bloody night in this bloody place."

Yerby propped the soldier in a sitting position against the wall. "Somebody set here with her," he said. "I wouldn't want the poor thing to wander off before she comes around proper like and hurt herself."

He straightened. "Let's finish this, fellows," he said, starting toward the barracks and command post. Mark took long strides to keep up, but Amy had to jog to stay on her brother's other side.

Glowstrips lighted the corridor alongside the enlisted barracks; there weren't any soldiers standing in the hallway as they had been the previous times Mark visited the fort. Although the garrison seemed to spend no more time in the upper world than a cave fish does, they kept a day and night schedule religiously. Mark didn't understand that, but as he saw more of life he was beginning to realize that *nobody* understood why other people lived the way they did.

Three of the barracks doors were closed; the last was only ajar. Yerby gestured four raiders to each door. At the end, he pointed four more to watch down the corridor in the direction of the Command Center and officers' quarters. With Mark, Amy, and old Pops Hazlitt poised behind him, Yerby pushed the panel fully open. Mark ducked past and turned the bank of light switches to the left of the door on.

There were loud crashes from down the hall. The other raiders were smashing their doors open, though Mark didn't imagine that any of them were locked.

Roused sleepers groaned and shouted in irritation. Something between a dozen and twenty of the bunks were occupied.

"Oh, who's the joker?" a soldier cried as she sat up in bed. "Carstairs, if that's you I'll break your—"

Her eyes focused on the shaggy faces glaring over the muzzles of their guns. She fell completely silent.

"Now you all sit tight," Yerby said with cheerful nonchalance. The flashgun's short, fat barrel enclosed a nest of mirrors which multiplied the laser beam's lens path. He waggled the big weapon toward the captives as if it were his index finger. "The fellows here are going to tie you up for a little bit, but nobody's going to get hurt. Everybody hear me?"

The flashgun nodded from one awakened soldier to another, sweeping the room. The weapon was a single-shot. After firing, it couldn't be recharged until daylight. It still looked horrifying, and Mark knew that the real effect of the gun's momentary pulse was even more shocking than the threat.

Some of the captives nodded agreement; others held themselves as stiff as statues chipped from rock salt. None of them looked as if they were even *thinking* of resistance.

"You lot tie them up," Yerby said, sweeping his left hand to indicate all the raiders who'd entered by the other three doors. He crooked his arm to rest the barrel of his flashgun on his right shoulder as he walked out of the barracks. Whistling an old tune, "The Irish Washerwoman," Yerby sauntered down the corridor with his usual lack of concern about whether anybody was coming with him.

The door to the latrine was slightly ajar. Amy pulled it closed with a click; Mark assumed she felt a perfectly understandable queasiness at the odor oozing through the previous opening.

Yerby paused in the hallway outside the door marked COMMANDANT. He motioned the others to stand clear and pointed his flashgun at the panel. Mark turned his head aside; so did Amy, though her camera continued to whir as it recorded the scene.

"Come out, you damned old rat, or I'll smoke you out!" Yerby bellowed with all the strength in his lungs. He fired.

The flashgun's spike of coherent light was saffron verging on chartreuse. Its millisecond brilliance was swallowed in a deep red fireball as the plastic door panel disintegrated. The shock wave slammed Mark into the far wall and knocked several Woodsrunners down. Yerby remained as solid as a crag in the surf.

The room beyond the blasted door was being used for storage. Racks of gardening implements, drawers containing bulbs, and bags of lime, fertilizer, and potting soil filled all but a narrow path to the bed.

The bed was empty except for two more bags of potting soil.

Lieutenant Hounslow burst from the adjacent room. "What's going on!" he cried. He was wearing a uniform shirt, a conical cloth nightcap with a tassel, and a pair of polka-dotted boxer shorts. "What's—"

Yerby poked the flashgun, discharged and as harmless as a club of the same size, in Hounslow's face. "Surrender, you son of a Paris whore!" he thundered.

"Oh, my goodness," Hounslow said. A raider opened the door marked COMMAND CENTER. The room was empty. "Oh, don't do that!" Hounslow protested. "You'll scatter my charts!"

Mark started to speak. He shut his mouth, then changed the subject by saying, "Where's Captain Easton, Hounslow?"

The lieutenant pulled the command center door closed. "What?" he said. "How would I know? Out in his garden, I suppose."

"I'll get him," Mark said. "I know where he is and, well, I wouldn't want him to get hurt by accident."

"I'll come along," said Amy.

The hand-lettered sign was tacked to the wooden door of the Command Center. She tugged it loose and added wryly, "I'll get the real pictures, but then we'll stage something for public release. Yerby, you've got no sense of history."

"Huh?" said her brother.

"I suspect," Mark said as he started down the corridor toward the ladder to Easton's garden, "that most of the people making history are too busy to have a sense of it."

It was late in the year, but some of Captain Easton's flowers gave off a rich, spicy perfume.

"Night-blooming cereus," Amy murmured. "It's a cactus, really."

The flowers of the cereus were huge and white with tendrils all around the bloom. They showed up even in the starglow between pulses of the antenna light.

There was what Mark had taken to be a toolshed at the near edge of tilled area. He heard soft snores coming from it. Amy raised her camera. She was using image intensification instead of the built-in light. The images would be grainy, but flooding the scene with a harsh glare would have been *wrong*. As wrong as Yerby Bannock in Quelhagen formal dress.

"Captain Easton?" Mark said. He tapped on the side of

the shed, then opened the door. "I'm afraid you'll have to come with us, sir."

"What?" said Easton. He was sleeping on a cot with only a pillow and a rough blanket for comfort. The Sunrise Seeds catalog reader hung from the cot's frame so that it didn't risk damage on the damp ground.

"Is it . . ." Easton said. "Why it is! Have my bulbs come, young man?"

"Sir," said Mark, "I'm very sorry, but that's not what I'm here about at all. We've captured the fort and taken you prisoner with the rest of your troops."

"Oh, dear," Easton said. "Oh."

He got up, shuffling his feet to find his slippers. He was wearing a flannel nightshirt long enough to cover his ankles. His patched uniform and tool belt hung from pegs on the wall of the shed.

"We'll want you to come into the fort and surrender formally," Amy said. "You do have a dress uniform of some kind, don't you?"

"I suppose I still do," Easton said morosely. "I haven't been into that closet in . . ."

He paused and shook his head. "This isn't going to look very good on my record, is it?" he said. "Well, I don't suppose I was really cut out for the military anyway. That's why they sent me here."

"When we're at the Command Center," Amy continued, "my brother will ask you to surrender. You'll say, 'In whose name do you call me to surrender?' And he'll say, 'In the name of almighty God and the Assembly of Self-Governing Worlds.' And you'll surrender. Have you got that?"

"I'll do my best," Captain Easton said. He shook his head again.

"We can try it a few times until you've got it right," Mark said soothingly. "And Captain? You can take the seed catalog if you like. You're welcome to keep it forever."

Easton's face brightened as though a moon had appeared. "Really?" he said. "Why, you are a very generous young man."

He snatched up the reader. "Now," he said firmly, "I suppose we'd better get this business taken care of."

37. One Hand Hoses the Other

The raiders' portable lights made the corridor in front of the enlisted quarters brighter than it had been in a decade. A pair of recruits from Hestia had started to line the Union soldiers up against the wall, but the Greenwoods didn't see any point in that. Now some of the prisoners huddled for mutual support, watching glumly as raiders went through the room's contents, but others chatted with their captors. A few card games had started.

Mark came out of Hounslow's office. The fort's real Command Center was sixty feet down in the bedrock, but the office terminal worked—to Mark's surprise—and was linked to the main unit.

"Yerby," Mark said, "it looks like at least half the defensive guns are still operable. I'm the closest thing to an expert and I'm not very close, but I think we can get one turret turning. That'll keep off any Alliance ships that arrive before whoever the Assembly sends to take over from us. Or capture them if they do land."

"Good work, lad," Yerby said cheerfully. "It was a bright

day for Greenwood when you showed up. Ain't that the truth, Amy girl?"

"Yes it is," Amy said. She grinned at her brother, then gave Mark a smile that was warm enough to make him blush with pleasure.

Lights were coming down the corridor from the direction of the garrison's married quarters. Crying children and the voices of angry adults, mostly women, echoed ahead of them. A man was singing, ". . . *violate me in the violet time, in the vilest way you know!*"

Mark thought he recognized the singer as Casey Tafell. Colonel Finch wasn't straitlaced, but he had a civilized sense of propriety. The bawdy song would bother him a great deal. Tafell's sense of humor was more subtle than Mark would have guessed.

The married prisoners with their spouses and offspring arrived as a wailing horde. Half a dozen of the women and a couple men weren't soldiers. Mark wondered whether they'd drifted over from Minor or if some of the garrison's members had managed to bring in companions on the supply vessels.

Finch marched at the head of the mob. He straightened when he noticed that Amy was recording them, but his momentary grimace showed that he knew just how absurd he looked.

Finch had probably tried to impose discipline on the others, but the raiders were even less likely to obey a silly order like that than the prisoners were. The rest of the entourage walked, shambled, or—in the case of some of the younger prisoners—skipped while calling shrilly to their friends.

"Colonel Bannock," Finch said. He saluted. "My troops and I have accomplished our mission without casualties."

"Glad to hear it, Finchie," Yerby said. His eyes narrowed slightly. "I hope that nothing happened to the other folks neither?"

"No," said Finch. He shook his head. "No, there were no incidents."

He scanned the mob of raiders and captives until he found Captain Easton sitting by himself, wearing a blue uniform with tarnished gold braid. "Colonel Bannock?" Finch said. "There'd be no difficulty, I trust, if Ms. Bannock here recorded me, ah, seeming to take the fort's surrender from the commandant?"

"We can do much better than that, Mr. Finch," Amy said crisply.

"We can?" Yerby and Mark blurted at the same time.

"We can show you blasting your way into the Alliance Command Center," Amy said. "Not the real Command Center, of course. You might damage the terminal that we need. But you can shoot your way through this door to the living quarters. No one on Zenith will be able to tell the difference."

She held the hand-lettered COMMAND CENTER sign up to the door by which she stood. "Yerby," she went on. "Please drive the nail in."

Yerby turned slightly and drove the tack home with a quick, perfectly aimed stroke with his flashgun. The laser's buttplate clunked, seating the head flush with the door panel. Yerby's face was expressionless.

"But—" an Alliance soldier said.

Mark, behind Finch's back, pointed one index finger at

the soldier and drew the other across his own throat. Pops
Hazlitt pulled a big skinning knife from his belt and raised
an eyebrow to Mark for instructions.

The soldier gulped into silence. Mark nodded with a
slight smile.

"This is very handsome of you," Finch said in amazement.
"I assure you that from the position of responsibility I
expect to reach on Zenith, I'll do everything I can to help
you folk on Greenwood."

"I'm sure you will," said Amy. "After all, you're already
committed to insuring that Zenith drops any claim to rule
Greenwood, aren't you? As well as voiding your syndicate's private claims."

"Of course, of course," Finch agreed. "There can't be
any doubt about that!"

Raiders looked at one another in puzzlement. They
obviously couldn't believe that Amy would take the
Zenith's word for even the time of day. Finch himself was
probably just as surprised as the Greenwoods were, but he
was a politician and therefore used to hiding the truth.

Finch looked around. "It would help, I think, if a few of
your militia were in the frame appearing to follow me.
Those six should be enough," he added, pointing to Dagmar
Wately and the Greenwoods standing closest to her.

Maybe Finch chose that group because they looked
particularly rugged and hard-bitten. So far as Mark could
see, there wasn't a soul in the raiding party who wouldn't
have sent citizens scurrying for cover on any street in
Quelhagen.

Dagmar glared and said, "I think it'd help if you'd kiss
my—"

"Now, now," boomed Yerby. "We're going to do just like Finchie here says. I wonder, Colonel . . . would you like me to trot along behind you myself? Following your example, I mean. I won't hog your spotlight on this one."

"Why yes, Bannock," Finch said. "And I won't forget your help, either."

"Don't reckon you will," Yerby agreed in a neutral tone.

"I don't see why we got to help this fellow do any blessed thing!" Zeb Randifer complained. "You *know* he's just going to cheat us once he don't need us no more!"

Yeah!/Too right!/Damn straight! were specific variations Mark heard of the agreement almost every raider expressed.

"No, Yerby's right," Mark said. "This thing we're about to do guarantees that Colonel Finch will make sure Zenith gives up its claim to Greenwood, whatever that costs him personally."

"And anyhow," Yerby added, turning his head so that his gaze swept every member of the raiding party, "I'm giving the orders. Right?"

"Now, Colonel," Mark said. "Aim your repeller directly at the lock plate. Blow it off, then hit the door with your shoulder at full speed so that you burst into the room. And remember, get it right the first time because you won't have another chance."

"I think I'm capable of handling this without your help, my man," Finch said with a sniff.

He pulled back his repeller's cocking handle, charging the weapon. The pellets were no bigger than unpopped popcorn grains, but when the repeller's electromagnetic coils accelerated them to many times the speed of sound their impact was as devastating as so many lightning bolts.

"Make sure you just shoot the door, Colonel," Yerby said. "The beads won't ricochet, they'll just blow up and do no harm. But if you hit the concrete—" He patted the corridor wall. "—a piece might fly out big enough to hurt somebody. Understood?"

"Yes, all right," Finch said. "May we get on with it?"

"I want everyone but the actors back twenty feet behind me," Amy said briskly. "Colonel Finch, run to within a few feet of the door, pause, and look over your shoulder so that I get a clear view of your face. You can shout something to your men. *Then* shoot the lock off and batter the door down to show exactly how much of a hero you are."

Finch scowled. He didn't like being lectured, especially by a young woman, but he didn't object aloud. He was smart enough to realize both that Amy was right and that he was dependent on her to record his actions.

"Are we ready?" he said in a less demanding tone.

"You bet we are, Colonel!" Yerby said, clapping Finch on the back. Mark unslung his gas gun and joined the group of bemused Greenwoods.

"Action!" said Amy.

"Come on, men!" Finch shouted. He ran down the corridor with the raiders stumping along behind him. Arm's length from the door, Finch turned to face the camera. Mark hunched so that he wouldn't block Amy's view, *"Zenith and freedom!"*

Finch pointed his repeller and held the trigger down for almost five seconds, emptying the thousand-round magazine. The *crack* of each multisonic pellet merged with the *whack! of* the shot when it hit the door. The racket was as echoingly loud as a saw cutting the whole fortress in halves.

The latch vanished in bright roaring sparks like a high-amperage electrical short. The stream of pellets ate a black hole in the plastic panel as if it was still hungry for a solid surface after the lock was gone.

"Follow me!" Finch cried as his shoulder hit the door and he lurched into the room beyond. His momentum carried him into the board that served as the latrine's seat. He broke it and plunged into the eight-foot hole in the floor.

"Holy sh—" Finch screamed.

There was a loud plop. A brown geyser spouted above the floor and sank back.

The Greenwoods crowding forward behind Finch stopped dead as though the horrible stench were a brick wall. Mark had known what to expect, so he'd held his breath, but his eyes started to water.

Yerby stepped into the converted pump room. "I don't guess I've ever been taken for a coward," he said, "but I'll tell the *world* I never done a braver thing in my life than this."

He bent over the hole. When he straightened again, he held Colonel Berkeley Finch dangling by the collar. Yerby walked into the hall, keeping the dripping, sputtering Zenith out at arm's length.

Almost everyone in the corridor, raiders and prisoners alike, dissolved in helpless laughter. Amy moved to the other side of the scene so that she could record Finch together with the spectators laughing at him.

"But you know," Captain Easton said sadly, "with proper preparation, it makes a really wonderful fertilizer."

"Don't worry, Colonel Finch," Amy called from behind her camera. "You'll get the only copy of this recording just as soon as the government of Zenith declares Greenwood to be a free and independent world."

Mark hugged the Alliance commandant. "Captain," he said, "believe me, your fertilizer has done more good for the whole planet of Greenwood than it could possibly have done for your plants!"

38. Next

Lucius Maxwell was the first man to disembark from the freighter *Stellar Conveyor* when it arrived at the military port on Dittersdorf Minor from Hestia. Four more starships waited in orbit for landing instructions.

Amy hadn't completely catalogued the heavy weapons warehouse in the bowels of the fort, but she'd guessed it would fill at least twenty vessels the size of the *Stellar Conveyor*, or over a hundred tramps like the ones trading to Greenwood. The Atlantic Alliance had saved money and effort by storing equipment on the frontier instead of shipping it home at the end of the Proxy Wars.

Now, twenty years later, the Alliance had to pay for that savings. The price would be their whole interstellar empire.

Mark waited at the bottom of the boarding ramp. There wasn't an official delegation to greet the reinforcements, but about half the raiders were standing around out of curiosity. Amy recorded events; Yerby's smile was one of real warmth.

Colonel Finch was present also, wearing his dress uniform. Nobody made a pointed comment, but he blushed whenever a Greenwood looked hard at him.

"I guess I should've expected you'd turn up, Dad," Mark said. He hugged his father. "I'm glad to see you."

"I'll be glad to see you, as soon as my eyes focus again," Lucius said. "On a matter of this significance the Assembly had to send an envoy, and I seemed the obvious one to go."

He chuckled and added, "For one thing, because I was willing. Dittersdorf isn't viewed as the garden spot of the universe, though I've always found Minor more attractive than the civilian port."

Lucius was in formal clothes. The four men and two women who followed him down the ramp wore battle dress of six individual styles. A squat, fifties-ish man noticed the turret from which a laser with a five-inch objective lens pointed toward the *Stellar Conveyor.* "Hey!" he said. "Does that thing work or is it just for show?"

"I guess it works," Mark said sharply. He was reacting to the challenge that he might not have recognized six months before. "I burned an acre of woods clear to test it, and last week we warmed an Alliance transport in orbit hot enough they decided to go back where they came from. Zeb's supposed to redirect it now that we're sure who you are, though."

As he spoke, the laser tube pivoted vertically again. Tags of vine, cut but not completely cleared from the turret, fluttered like deliberate camouflage.

The man who'd spoken raised an eyebrow. "Not bad,

kid," he said. "I'm General Carswell. Come see me in a day or two and we'll talk about a job."

"I need to see an inventory soonest," said one of the women. "Can we . . ." She shrugged.

"I'll take them to the Command Center," Amy said, folding the lenses of her camera. She grinned wryly. "We can't be so busy recording history that we forget to make it, after all."

"I'll accompany you, if I may," Finch said. "General, I'm Colonel Berkeley Finch. I have an Assembly commission."

"Glad to meet you, Finch," Carswell said, but he didn't bother to shake the hand the Zenith offered.

Amy took off across the paved courtyard with the uniformed personnel in tow. The new arrivals walked like drunks, upright only because their determination overbore their disorientation.

A second starship glinted in the high sky at the start of its landing approach. The militia who'd come for the show walked away also, correctly deciding there was nothing more to see here.

"Yerby," Lucius said, "we've scraped up three hundred troops to take over from you here. With your permission, of course."

Yerby nodded. "Wasn't a place I figured to spend any more time than I had to," he remarked, glancing at the drab concrete and drabber vegetation surrounding them.

"The Assembly has voted you a colonelcy and a lifetime pension," Lucius continued. He smiled slightly. "How much the pension is worth depends on whether the Assembled Planets gain their freedom from the Alliance, of course."

Yerby's laughter was briefer than Mark expected. "I never turned down money, Lucius," he said. "If it don't do nothing else, at least it looks pretty, most of it. But being colonel, that you can keep."

"The decision's yours, of course," Lucius said. He looked down as if he were examining his fingernails.

"It's not like I don't see the honor," Yerby said uncomfortably. "It's just—Lucius, I don't like the idea of killing other folks. I know, there's a lot of things a guy's got to do in life and I've done most of them, good and bad, one time or the other. But that's one I druther leave for other folks if I can."

"It's good to meet a man with principles," Lucius said. He bowed to Yerby, then turned to his own son. "Mark," he continued, "you've been elected in your absence to the Greenwood Committee of Governance. One of three members, your delegates to the assembly on Hestia tell me. Congratulations."

"Me?" said Mark. "But I can't serve. I'm with the Woodsrunners. The army, I suppose we are now."

Yerby snorted. "If you mean you think the boys is going off to Zenith to fight just because we put our oar in here, you couldn't be more wrong, lad. I don't guess there'll be ten fellows leave with Lucius, and half them's going to come back to Greenwood in a week."

"If they leave with General Carswell," Lucius said grimly, "they'll stay till the general releases them. His men called him Iron Sam when he was a captain, and I don't believe the past twenty years have changed his ideas of discipline."

He returned his attention to his son. "Mark," he said,

"you've proved you can be a soldier. I hope by now you realize how easy that is anyway. Go back to Greenwood."

Yerby squeezed Mark's shoulder as gently as if he was pinching a raw egg. "We need you, lad," he said. "More than we know, I shouldn't doubt, but even the folks we left on Greenwood *do* know it or they wouldn't have picked you like they done."

Mark scowled. The two older men were the stones of a mill, trying to grind away his determination.

"It's time to prove you can be a statesman, son," Lucius said. "That's a great deal harder, I assure you."

"Deputy Maxwell?" a uniformed officer shouted from the hatch down to the Command Center. "There's a question about the initial division of the captured equipment. General Carswell would like your input."

"In a moment!" Lucius replied in a voice that showered echoes from the multiple interior angles of the fort. Mildly he added to Mark and Yerby, "Everyone in the delegation is from a different planet. We'll have to bring our ships in at minor ports on the worlds where the Alliance is trying to enforce their embargo. That's going to be difficult enough, and one might wish that general success would be the first priority of each member. I'm afraid that lies beyond the realm of real-world politics. I'd best go."

"I'll come down in a little bit, Dad," Mark said. "I'd like to think."

"Do," Lucius said. He nodded and strode away.

"Did I ever tell you I met your old man twenty-odd years ago?" Yerby said, his eyes on the elder Maxwell. "Saw him, I mean. I was just a little nipper."

Mark stared at the frontiersman. "No," he said, "you didn't."

"He was a major, then," Yerby said. "Had a battalion of Quelhagen commandos in the Proxy War. I heard they'd been the ones who took Dittersdorf Base from the Easterns the first time, but I didn't see that with my own eyes."

"That can't be true!" Mark said. He realized he'd shouted. More quietly he went on, "Dad's always said soldiering was no fit life except for fools and butchers, Yerby."

Yerby nodded, then turned to look Mark in the eyes. "Did you ever ask him why he was so sure of that, lad?" he said.

"My God," Mark said softly.

"Guess I'll check things inside myself," Yerby said. The corona discharge of the incoming starship was beginning to blanket the ground beneath with its crackle. Raising his voice slightly, Yerby went on, "You know, it won't take more than maybe a year to get a real government working on Greenwood. Earth's a big place. This rebellion's going to last plenty long enough for you to have a chance to go soldiering no matter what you do right now."

The big frontiersman sauntered across the courtyard, his thumbs hooked in his belt. He was whistling "Lillibullero." Amy had come up from the command center and was walking toward Mark.

"Well, I'll be," Mark said.

He started thinking about the challenge of governing a society of individuals as cantankerous as the settlers of Greenwood.

The Following is an excerpt from:

THE
TULORIAD

By

JOHN RINGO
& TOM KRATMAN

Available from Baen Books
October 2009
hardcover

Chapter One

Tell of the star-crossed kessentai, O spirits,
Who wandered long after being driven
from the blood-drenched citadel of Aradeen.
—The Tuloriad, Na'agastenalooren

Anno Domini 2009
North Carolina

The screech and thunder of human artillery, flying through the air and impacting on the ground nearby, drowned out the shuffling of Posleen feet, the confused and frightened grunts of the cosslain, and the despair-filled sobbing of their remaining hundred or so human captives.

None of those captives knew why, but that number had not changed in some days. If they'd asked, if they'd been able to ask, the chief of the alien group probably could not have explained why they'd been spared. It was possible that he, himself, didn't know.

At the point of the ragged column, head drooped in defeat, walked that Posleen chief: Tulo, lord of the clan of

Sten and war leader of the vast hosts gathered to fight the humans on this part of the planet Aradeen, known locally as "Earth." Those hosts had within the last few days been very nearly annihilated in that fighting.

Tulo'stenaloor, once lord of the greatest Posleen war host ever assembled and now just a ragged fugitive, stopped suddenly, his head rising and his crest—reminiscent of a Lakota headdress—erecting itself automatically. There was a small being, one of the bat-faced, green-fuzzed, pacifist Indowy blocking what passed for a trail.

"Who are you?" the Posleen God-king, Tulo'stenaloor, asked, suspiciously. He had reason for suspicion. His armies crushed, his people nearly exterminated . . . and here he found himself standing before one of the "harmless" green ones who provided the never-sufficiently-to-be-damned humans with their fighting machines. The green being was in turn surrounded by more armed humans, closer, than the Posleen war chief had ever hoped to see again in this life. The fuzzy being seemed to be studying the pitiful remnants of the Posleen horde that shambled along behind Tulo'stenaloor.

We're dead, Tulo thought. *And perhaps just as well. I don't know why I bothered trying to run, anyway.*

The ragged remnant of his horde that stretched out behind Tulo was composed of several hundred crocodilian centaurs, with scaly skin and yellow eyes. About a third of the beings had crests, not dissimilar to the feathered bonnets favored by some of the Plains Indians in the old American west. These they could erect at will, in a display of dominance or of urge to battle. The crests would also erect themselves, automatically, when faced with a threat.

It was not insignificant that, of the over one hundred crested individuals in the pack, not one, except for Tulo and his bodyguard, had their crests erected. Rather, they hung along the creatures' necks, as if in shame and despair.

Tulo's guard, Brasingala, a large and stout young kessentai who had over the years demonstrated both aptitude and dedication amounting to paranoid obsession in guarding his chief, immediately began to draw his boma blade to hack the little being into steaks, along with as many of his human escorts as could be managed.

"Hold," Tulo whispered, putting one skilled claw in front of Brasingala. The young guard immediately froze in place.

"I am the Indowy, Aelool," answered the little one, with a broad and toothy, and very feral, smile. If the Indowy was afraid of Brasingala, or even of the remnants of Tulo's host, the fear was tolerably hard to perceive. "And I would like to make you an offer you can't refuse."

"A quick death?" the god-king asked, curiously enough without any hostility. After all he been through, Aelool didn't wonder that the Posleen might prefer death to life. "That would be generous."

"No," the Indowy said. "A long life. Perhaps even a fruitful and happy one."

At that the kessentai laughed, bitterly. "I don't believe in fairy tales, Indowy."

The Indowy's fingers reached up to stroke a bat-like, furry chin. "Neither do I," he agreed. "There is a ship behind me, hidden under ground" Aelool said. His fingers wriggled as his arm swept in the surrounding humans, both those guards close by and others glimpsed as dimly seen shadows as they moved into position around the remnant of the host. "That is no fairy tale. I could have had you destroyed just now—you will agree that the humans are remarkably good at destruction, yes?—yet I did not. That is no fairy tale. There are other humans coming and those I don't control. That's no fairy tale, either. Your people are tired, demoralized, weak, hungry, and as very nearly out of ammunition as they are of hope. Do I speak a fairy tale?"

The Posleen sighed. "It is cruel to remind me of my failure," he said. "I thought you people had some scruples."

"Scruples enough," Aelool said. "Scruples enough to save this remnant, Tulo, Lord of the Clan Sten."

"To what end?" Tulo asked.

"Not so much to an end," the Indowy corrected, with an odd twist of his ears, "as to avoid an end. The galaxy would be a poorer place without your people in it. You are, in your way, nearly as admirable as these feral humans. You could, in your way, become as or even more valuable."

"We're as valuable as hunks of thresh hung up for curing," the god-king said, adding, "for those who care for the perversion of cured thresh. There is no possibility of getting a ship out through the human blockade of the planet."

"There is no possibility of getting one of your ships out, Tulo. There are other kinds of ships."

The Indowy pointed up into the trees. Tulo's eyes followed and searched. Something . . . something . . . *but, no, I can't see it. It's as if my eyes were trying to tell my mind something that my mind refused to accept.*

"Show yourself, Himmit Argzal," the Indowy called.

The Posleen nodded as the purple outline of an alien being, symmetrical but with a head at each end, began to form among the trees. It had been there all the time, so he assumed, but the Himmit were *good* at camouflage.

The Posleen couldn't hide a sneer. "We're to be saved by the galaxy's cowards? How truly sad."

"There may be more to the Himmit than you realize, Tulo'stenaloor," Aelool answered. "More than we do, either," he muttered, *sotto voce*. The little being's feral smile changing briefly to a puzzled frown. The frown disappeared as Aelool continued, "Be that as it may. They have a ship— life for the remnants of your people. Will you take ship?"

I don't want to live, Tulo thought. *Live for what? Live for shame? Live for disgrace? Live for the knowledge I failed my people?*

Aelool could hardly know what Tulo was thinking, in perfect detail. Even so, it was hard not to know what was in the god-king's mind, in principle.

"Live to expiate shame," the Indowy said. "Live to recover from disgrace. Live to rebuild the People of the Ships."

"I could live for revenge," the god-king said.

"That you shall not have," Aelool answered. "Nor do you deserve it. Nor, in time, will you come even to want it."

Again, the kessentai laughed. "Those first two may well be true, Indowy. That last is inconceivable."

Overhead, a flight of artillery passed, its freight train racket for the moment drowning out speech. In the distance the forest rumbled as earth was plowed and trees cropped by the humans' high explosive. After the sound had passed, and before the next could come, Aelool said, "Believe what you want, Tulo'stenaloor. Conceive of what you will. But believe this, too: If you and your people do not get aboard the Himmit's ship, that artillery will soon find you. Will you come?"

"Can you fit all my people?" he asked.

"Most, certainly," Aelool answered. "There is space for the kessentai, the kessenalt, most—maybe all—of the cosslain. The normals will not fit, or not many of them anyway. And of course your human captives must be released without harm."

"My immediate oolt has no normals. The captives we can let go; they're hardly enough to feed us for long anyway." *Even were I of a mind to eat them.*

"Then you will come? The ship I have brought can feed you."

"Yes, dammit. Come where?"

"Follow me," Aelool said, turning. As he turned, the Himmit disappeared once again among the trees.

Argzal was waiting when the procession arrived at the tunnel, Posleen surrounded by humans led by an Indowy. *This I simply must relate to the story gatherers*, the Himmit thought, wryly.

Seeing the Posleen come to a shuddering stop at the opening of the tunnel, the Himmit said, "Fear not, lordlings, the tunnel leads to the ship of life."

"The ship tunnels for cover," Aelool explained to Tulo'stenaloor. "The displaced material is turned into . . . well, call it neutronium, for lack of a better term . . . the better to aid in camouflage."

"We really don't like tunnels much," Tulo said. "Even leaving aside the legends, we've had a lot of bad experiences underground since we met the humans."

"Not as bad as you will have if you don't go into the tunnel," Aelool observed.

"Essthree!" Tulo called, turning his great head toward the mass of the column. This was a title, one Tulo had borrowed from the humans in his efforts to create a mightier host than any that had gone before. The Essthree was concerned with planning and operations, as the Essone was with personnel management, the Esstwo with intelligence, and the Essfour with logistics.

"Here, Lord," answered an ancient kessentai with the gleam of fierce intelligence in his one remaining yellow eye. Despite that gleam, the Essthree had the look of weariness about him, a fatigue no ordinary rest could touch.

"Take Essfour with you. Go forward and organize boarding. I will . . ."

A series of screeches, followed by organ shaking bangs, was heard perhaps a thousand of the humans' meters away.

"I will stay above with Brasingala and push the others in," Tulo finished.

"As you say, Lord." With a hand signal to the Essfour, the Essthree warily entered the tunnel.

"Essone?"

"Here, Tulo'stenaloor," said a youngish looking god-king. This one's eyes were no less intelligent than Essthree's, yet he looked much younger and considerably the better for wear.

"How many are we?"

The god-king didn't need to consult any notes, nor could he consult the defunct artificial sentience, or AS, he normally wore on a golden chain about his neck. The humans' last, horde-crushing anti-matter strike had generated an electro-magnetic pulse sufficient to destroy even the EMP-hardened artificial sentiences of the Posleen. Most of the kessentai had tossed theirs as redundant, useless weight. And if Essone had not tossed his, it was only a matter of time. Of all the kessentai and kessenalt in Tulo'stenaloor's oolt, only Binastarion intended to keep his. And that device had been more friend and confidant than servant.

"We are three-hundred and eighty-seven left, Tulo. Two-hundred and twenty-six cosslain, one hundred and thirty-seven kessentai, twenty-four kessenalt. Plus the thresh, of course."

"We'll be leaving the thresh behind." Tulo turned his great crested head to Aelool. "Can we fit so many?"

"The ship will suffice for that," Aelool agreed. "Yet it will be tight, Tulo'stenaloor, and your seniors must control the lesser ones among you."

"That will be no problem, Indowy. My personal oolt is not much given to panic. Though some are given to excessive mourning."

At that Aelool noticed one among the Posleen kessentai, clutching a gold-colored metal disc to its chest while keening piteously. Nearby an old looking Posleen, followed by a cosslain bearing a gilded chest upon its broad back, attempted to console the weeping kessentai. The Indowy twitched an ear in puzzlement.

"That's Binastarion," Tulo explained. "He was very close to his artificial sentience. The humans' anti-matter weapon that broke us also generated enough of an electro-magnetic pulse to scrub all of our artificial sentiences. Binastarion mourns for a dead friend."

Aelool nodded his understanding.

Tulo pointed at a group. "Into the tunnel," he said to them. Aelool was pleased but unsurprised to see that the Posleen followed their orders without question. Tulo'stenaloor was, after all, not just any god-king.

The Indowy thought, *We might just get away after all.*

Tulo noticed one particular god-king, Goloswin the Tinkerer, hanging back as the rest shuffled forward uncertainly into the dark, dank tunnel.

No, that's not quite right, Tulo thought, looking more carefully at the expression on Goloswin's face. *He's not hanging back; he's* studying. *Well, Golo always* studies.

That he was a little shorter and thinner than the kessentai norm was only the beginning of Goloswin's personal oddities. Among the kessentai most were, Tulo would frankly admit, idiots who should have been excised from the gene pool. (Ruefully, too, the chief kessentai would have noted, the humans had done just that.)

His own oolt wasn't like that, of course. Of kessentai he had nothing but what the humans called, "five percenters," those one in twenty kessentai who were demonstrably, and fearfully, not idiots. Of those, Tulo had chosen only the best for the oolt. But even among those who were one in one hundred of that one in twenty, Goloswin stood out. For he was the Michelangelo, the Leonardo Da Vinci, the Gauss and the Newton and the Einstein, the Ford and the Edison of the Posleen race.

Goloswin, as he himself would have cheerfully told anyone who asked, was fucking *smart.*

"What holds you, Golo?" Tulo asked. "We can afford to

lose many . . . any, really . . . of the people. But we cannot afford to lose you."

"I am operating on a guess, Tulo," Golo said. "The first and the last loaded have a chance to be the foremost inside that hidden ship. I may be able to discern something of its principles by being closer to the control room."

Tulo's answer was interrupted by one of the humans' artillery shells, this one much closer than the last. It was an adjusting round. In an earlier day, before the Posleen had obliterated the Global Positioning System, there probably would have been no adjustment required and the first warning of an incoming shell would have been dismemberment by that shell . . . and the couple of hundred siblings that would have accompanied it.

"There is a team of them watching us," Aelool surmised. "They're almost as disorganized by victory as you are by defeat . . . else that last shell would have been here, and it would have been followed by hundreds." To his human escorts, he said, "Find the observers. Silence them. Do not harm them."

Wordlessly, one of the human escorts used his fingers to indicate to a brace of his men that they were to follow him. In perfect silence those three took off into the woods and disappeared from view.

"They are very good," Tulo told Aelool, as the three humans disappeared.

"They are," the Indowy agreed. "I'm told they're Swiss . . . mmm . . . Swiss . . . 'Guards.' Or a special subset of that group, anyway. They're on loan to my organization."

The Posleen shrugged. The details didn't matter much when the humans had, as a race, proven so deadly.

Another shell landed, this one closer still. Tulo thought he saw treetops rising majestically, only to sink again, slowly, in the not very far distance. The trees fell as if with regret. He looked around. Only he and Golo, Brasingala, and the Indowy remained above the surface; those, plus the human captives and what some among the humans might have called the "mess sergeant." Tulo had shortened that to "mesergen."

"You have made a great mistake," the mesergen said to Tulo. "I am not enough, on my own, to butcher these properly. Nor is there time for me to do so."

"We're not butchering any of them."

"What? That's nonsense! I didn't curry these along merely to—"

"Brasingala!"

So fast was the guard's blade that the messergen's lips were still moving as his head hit the forest floor.

"I am not in the mood to be argued with," Tulo'stenaloor whispered to the corpse, after it had finished settling to the ground.

Mesergen forgotten as quickly as he had been killed, Tulo turned his attention back to the tunnel ahead. He could just see the twitching rumps of the last of the remainder, losing themselves in the dark.

"Maybe you're right, Golo," Tulo'stenaloor said. "Let us enter this place and see."

"What of your humans?"

Aelool answered, "Some of my escorts will take charge of those you have freed and lead them to their own people. The rest of my escorts will disperse as soon as we are boarded. I think that, even with your former captives, no observer will see them."

Tulo shrugged that off. Let himself and his people escape and what matter what the human's saw on their own world? He, his guard, Goloswin, and Aelool entered the tunnel and walked forward. Clawed Posleen feet, and sandalled Indowy ones, made an odd sound on the surface of the base of the tunnel. What should have been dirt was, instead, turned to some other substance, something that felt almost like gold.

The tunnel continued on, deep into the earth. It twisted only once, near the end. Just past that hard right twist a large portal stood open, with a ramp in front of it, leading from ship to "soil." The ramp appeared to be of a much different shape from the portal, yet Goloswin sensed it was intended to fold into it. A bluish-greenish glow came from the opening, turning ramp and tunnel much the same color.

Once inside, they saw that the disconcerting blue-green seemed to come from no place in particular, but simply to be everywhere at once. The cabin in which the refugees found themselves was small, perhaps twenty-five of the humans' meters by thirty. With nearly four hundred of the massive creatures stuffed into that space, there was hardly room, and an excellent chance of being inadvertently injured, for one tiny Indowy. Standing near to Goloswin, with the Indowy on his feet in between the two, Tulo'stenaloor suggested, "Maybe you should climb on my back, Aelool. Here, let me give you a hand up." The God-king reached down with claws that, under ordinary circumstances, would have sent a normal Indowy gibbering.

Aelool was not a normal Indowy, however. With the god-king's help, he scrambled onto its broad, muscled back, sitting there side saddle as his legs were too short to take a comfortable riding position.

"Something really bothers me, here, Tulo" Goloswin said, leaning over to whisper to Tulo.

"I hate this fucking blue-green light, too."

Golo twisted his head in negation. "The light? No, no, I hadn't even noticed the light. Though now that you mention it, it is a little unsettling. No, I was thinking about the size of this thing. Even if it recycles the waste at one hundred percent efficiency, it would have to do so instantaneously or we'll spend half the time hungry. And we cannot make a long journey crowded in like this, muzzle to asshole. I wonder if . . ."

A voice came from everywhere and nowhere. "Attention. Attention Posleen lord and lordlings and servants. This is Argzal, captain of the scout smuggler, *Surreptitious Stalker*, Himmit Sixth Fleet—"

"Sixth Fleet?" Golo questioned. "Himmits have fleets?"

"Shhh! Listen. Besides, we don't know if they mean by 'fleet' what we or the humans would mean by 'fleets.'"

"—going to be passing through the humans' interdiction forces now gathered around the planet. Unlike most of the humans' weapons and sensors, those ships can potentially sense us and could possibly harm us. Do not worry; I am very good at my job. I intend to bluff."

"'Don't worry,' he says. 'I intend to bluff,' he says."

"Shhh."

"—placing an inertial dampening field around your compartment. This will retard your movements, slightly and temporarily. The inertial dampening field, while not dangerous, is also not what is normally used for livestock."

"Livestock!"

"Dammit, be quiet, Golo!"

"—should not fear this; it is necessary. In the interim, to keep you entertained, look to the nearest bulkhead. You can see our progress there. I will also adjust your light to something more comfortable."

The compartment, not exactly raucous to begin with, went deathly silent as most of the walls were seemingly replaced with totally black holographic rectangles. The ambient light likewise shifted to a red-orange more suitable to Posleen visual rods and temperament. Between the two changes, the pitiful remnants of the great host of Tulo'stenaloor calmed down completely.

"I wish I had my AS," Tulo whispered. Sadly, every AS in the oolt had been wiped by the electro-magnetic pulse of the humans' ultimate anti-matter weapon. Off in the distance, Binastarion could still be heard weeping over his own.

To Brasingala, the chief said, "Migrate through the oolt as best you can. Find our Chief Rememberer. Tell him it would please me if he would lead our people in a prayer of thanks to the ancestors for our deliverance."

"We're not delivered yet, Tulo," Goloswin said.

"Yes we are. We just don't know whether we're delivered from death or from shameful life. Either is cause for thanks."

Beneath and around the Posleen and Aelool the Himmit ship began to hum as it prepared to break free of the Earth and the war which had nearly consumed it.